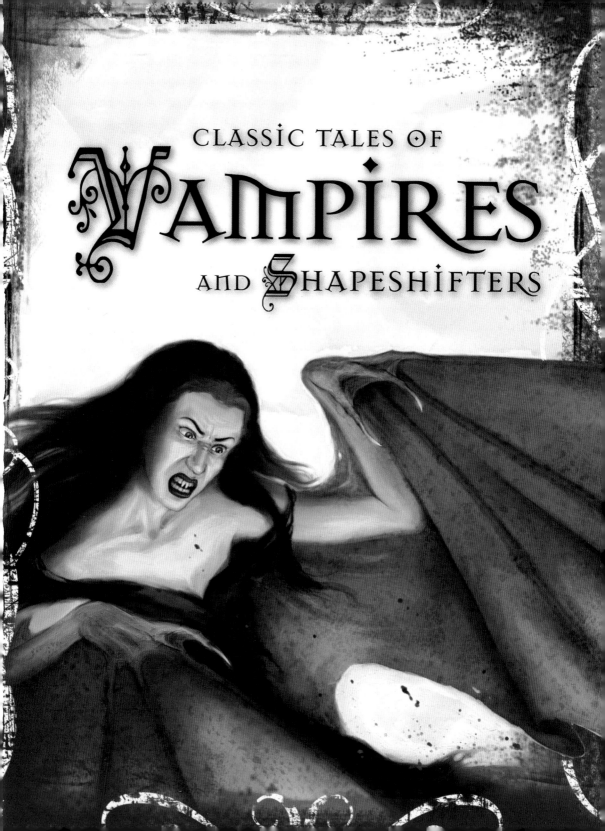

CLASSIC TALES OF

Vampires

AND Shapeshifters

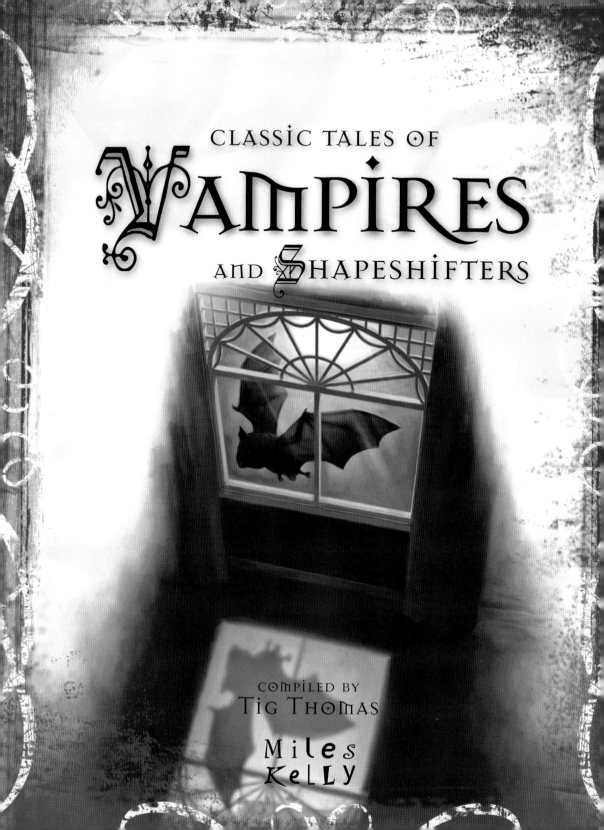

CLASSIC TALES OF

Vampires

AND Shapeshifters

COMPILED BY
Tig Thomas

Miles
Kelly

First published in 2011 by Miles Kelly Publishing Ltd
Harding's Barn, Bardfield End Green, Thaxted, Essex, CM6 3PX, UK

2 4 6 8 10 9 7 5 3 1

Publishing Director Belinda Gallagher
Creative Director Jo Cowan
Editorial Assistant Lauren White
Designer Kayleigh Allen
Production Manager Elizabeth Collins
Reprographics Stephan Davis

ISBN 978-1-84810-541-6

Printed in China

British Library Cataloguing-in-Publication Data
A catalogue record for this book is available from the British Library

ACKNOWLEDGEMENTS
The publishers would like to thank the following artists
who have contributed to this book:
Advocate Art: Jason Juta
The Bright Agency: Malcom Davis, Fabio Leone, Patricia Moffett, Dave Shephard

Cover photograph: Ivan Bliznetsov/iStockphoto.com

Made with paper from a sustainable forest

www.mileskelly.net
info@mileskelly.net

www.factsforprojects.com

Self-publish your
children's book

buddingpress.co.uk

CONTENTS

In the Dark of the Night

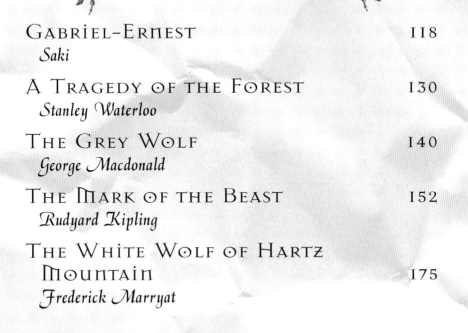

The Beast Within

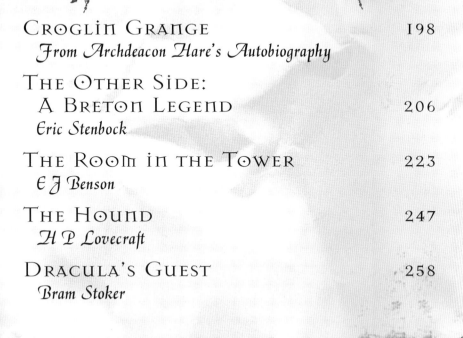

Nameless Horror

Fatal Women

THE CAPTURED SOUL

FOREWORD

Tig Thomas

THE THEME OF these stories is blood – blood and death, and life after death. Fear of the night and the unknown has always created terror in humankind and out of that terror come the themes in this book – tales of dark beings seeking to satisfy a thirst, who can have an almost irresistible allure to their victims. Tales of transformation, bat to man, man to wolf, innocent young girl to fatal seductress. This chilling collection invites you to enter the sinister world of these shapeshifters as they invade their victims' dreams and – if their plans succeed – entrap their very souls. You will discover some of the most terrifying, spine-tingling stories ever written, tales of wild beasts bounding over moors, and malevolent figures bent on feeding their thirst for blood. In the world of the shapeshifter, you can never be sure anyone is what they seem. You will encounter wolves and vampires in many forms – living, dead, undead, young, old, male and female. As you will discover from these stories, no one can tell where the forces of darkness will strike.

Included are stories about Count Dracula, the most infamous of vampires, the beautiful but deadly female blood-drinkers, Clarimonde and Carmilla, snarling werewolves, and the unseen horrors of the Horla, a formless shape seeking a host body to possess. Against these forces of evil are ranged the people who seek to defeat them – who succeed at times… but fail at others.

In the Dark of the Night

Count Magnus

M R James

Y WHAT MEANS the papers out of which I have made a connected story came into my hands is the last point which the reader will learn from these pages. But it is necessary to prefix to my extracts from them a statement of the form in which I possess them.

They consist, then, partly of a series of collections for a book of travels, such a volume as was a common product of the forties and fifties. These books usually dealt with some unknown district on the Continent. They gave details of hotel accommodation and of means of communication, such as we now expect to find in any well-regulated guide book, and they dealt largely in reported conversations with intelligent foreigners, racy innkeepers and garrulous peasants. In a word, they were chatty.

The writer was a Mr Wraxall. For my knowledge of him I have to depend entirely on the evidence his writings afford, and from these I deduce that he was a man past middle age, possessed of some private means, and very much alone in the world. He had, it seems, no settled abode in England. As to his character, it is not difficult to form some superficial opinion. He must have been an intelligent and cultivated man. His besetting fault was pretty clearly that of over-inquisitiveness, possibly a good fault in a traveller, certainly a fault for which this traveller paid dearly enough in the end.

On what proved to be his last expedition, he was plotting another book. Scandinavia, a region not widely known to Englishmen forty years ago, had struck him as an interesting field. He set out in the early summer of 1863.

Of his travels in the North there is no need to speak, nor of his residence of some weeks in Stockholm. I need only mention that some resident there put him on the track of an important collection of family papers belonging to the proprietors of an ancient manor house in Vestergothland, and obtained for him permission to examine them.

The manor house, or *herrgard*, in question is to be called *Råbäck* (pronounced something like Roebeck), though that is not its name. It is one of the best buildings of its kind in all the country. It was built soon after 1600, and is very much like an English house of that period in respect of material – red brick with stone facings – and style. The man who built it was of the house of De la Gardie, and his descendants possess it still. They received Mr Wraxall with great kindness and courtesy, and pressed him to stay in the house as long as his research lasted. But, preferring to be independent, and mistrusting his powers of conversing in Swedish, he settled himself at the village inn, which turned out quite sufficiently comfortable, at any rate during the summer months. This arrangement would entail a short walk daily to and from the manor house of under a mile.

The house itself stood in a park, and was protected with large old timber. Near it you found the walled garden, and then entered a close wood fringing one of the small lakes with which the whole country is pitted. Then came the wall, and you climbed a steep knoll – a knob of rock lightly covered with soil – and on the top of this stood the church, fenced in with tall dark trees. It was a curious building to English eyes. The nave and aisles were low, and filled with pews and galleries. In the western gallery stood the handsome old organ, gaily painted, and with silver pipes. The ceiling was flat, and had been adorned by a seventeenth-century artist with a strange and hideous 'Last Judgment', full of lurid flames, falling cities, burning ships, crying souls and brown and smiling demons. The pulpit was like a doll's house covered with little painted wooden cherubs and saints; a stand with three hourglasses was hinged to the preacher's desk. Such sights as these may be seen in many a church in Sweden now, but what distinguished this one was an addition to the original building. At the eastern end of the north aisle the builder of the manor house had erected a mausoleum for himself and his family. The roof was of copper externally, and was painted black, while the walls, in common with those of the church, were staringly white. To this mausoleum there was no access from the church. It had a portal and steps of its own on the northern side.

Past the churchyard is the path to the village, and not more than three or four minutes brings you to the inn door.

On the first day of his stay at *Råbäck*, Mr Wraxall found the church door open, and made these notes of the interior. However, he could not make his way into the mausoleum. He could, by looking through the keyhole, just see that there were fine marble effigies and sarcophagi of copper, which made him very anxious to spend some time in investigation.

The papers he had come to examine at the manor house proved to be of just the kind he wanted for his book. There were family correspondence, journals and account books of the earliest owners of the estate, very carefully kept and clearly written, full of amusing and picturesque detail. The first De la Gardie appeared in them as a strong and capable

man. Shortly after the building
of the mansion there had been
a period of distress in the
district, and the peasants had
risen and attacked several
châteaux and done some
damage. The owner of
Råbäck took a leading part
in suppressing trouble, and
there was reference to
executions of ringleaders
and severe punishments
inflicted with no
sparing hand.

   The portrait of this
Magnus de la Gardie was one of the best in
the house, and Mr Wraxall studied it with no little interest
after his day's work. He gives no detailed description of it,
but I gather that the face impressed him rather by its power
than by its beauty or goodness. In fact, he writes that Count
Magnus was an almost phenomenally ugly man.

   On this day Mr Wraxall took his supper with the family,
and walked back in the late but still bright evening.

   'I must remember,' he writes, 'to ask the sexton if he can

let me into the mausoleum at the church. He evidently has access to it himself, for I saw him tonight standing on the steps, and, as I thought, locking or unlocking the door.'

I find that early the following day Mr Wraxall had some conversation with his landlord. His setting it down at such length as he does surprised me at first; but I soon realized that the papers I was reading were, at least in their beginning, the materials for the book he was meditating.

His object, he says, was to find out whether any traditions of Count Magnus de la Gardie lingered on in the scenes of that gentleman's activity, and whether the popular estimate of him was favourable or not. He found that the Count was decidedly not a favourite. If his tenants came late to their work on the days which they owed to him as Lord of the Manor, they were flogged and branded in the manor house yard. One or two cases were of men who had occupied lands that encroached on the lord's domain, and whose houses had been mysteriously burnt on a winter's night, with the whole family inside. But what seemed to dwell on the innkeeper's mind most – for he returned to the subject more than once – was that the Count had been on the Black Pilgrimage, and had brought something or someone back with him.

You will naturally inquire, as Mr Wraxall did, what the

Black Pilgrimage may have been. But your curiosity on the point must remain unsatisfied for the time being, just as his did. The landlord was evidently unwilling to give a full answer, or indeed any answer, on the point.

So Mr Wraxall had to go unsatisfied to his day's work at the manor house. The papers on which he was engaged soon put his thoughts into another channel, for he had to occupy himself with glancing over the correspondence between Sophia Albertina in Stockholm and her married cousin Ulrica Leonora at *Råbäck* in the years 1705–10. In the afternoon he had done with these, and after returning the boxes in which they were kept to their places on the shelf, he proceeded, very naturally, to take down some of the volumes nearest to them, in order to determine which of them had best be his principal subject of investigation next day. The shelf he had hit upon was occupied mostly by a collection of account books in the writing of the first Count Magnus. But one among them was not an account book, but a book of alchemical and other tracts in another sixteenth-century hand. Not being very familiar with alchemical literature, Mr Wraxall spends much space that he might have spared in setting out the names and beginnings of the various treatises: *The Book of the Phoenix*, *Book of the Thirty Words*, *Book of the Toad*, *Book of Miriam*, and so forth; and then he announces his delight at finding, on a leaf originally left blank near the middle of the book, some writing of Count Magnus himself headed *Liber nigrae peregrinationis* (*Book of the Black Pilgrimage*). It is true that only a few lines were written, but there was quite enough to show that the landlord had that morning been referring to a belief at least as old as the time of Count Magnus, and probably shared by him. This is the English of what was written:

'If any man desires to obtain a long life, if he would obtain a faithful messenger and see the blood of his enemies, it is necessary that he should first go into the city of Chorazin, and there salute the prince...'

Here there was an erasure of one word, not very thoroughly done, so that Mr Wraxall felt pretty sure that he was right in reading it as *aeris* (of the air). But there was no more of the text copied, only a line in Latin: *Quaere reliqua ujus materiei inter secretiora* (see the rest of this matter among the more private things).

It could not be denied that this threw a rather lurid light upon the tastes and beliefs of the Count. After a prolonged contemplation of his picture in the hall, Mr Wraxall set out for home, his mind full of thought of Count Magnus. He had no eyes for his surroundings, no perception of the evening scents of the woods or the evening light on the lake. All of a sudden he pulled up short, astonished to find himself already at the gate of the churchyard, and within a few minutes of his dinner. His eyes fell on the mausoleum.

"Ah," he said, "Count Magnus, there you are. I should dearly like to see you."

'Like many solitary men,' he writes, 'I have a habit of talking to myself aloud, and I do not expect an answer. Only the woman who, I suppose, was cleaning up the church, dropped some metallic object on the floor, whose clang startled me. Count Magnus, I think, sleeps sound enough.'

That same evening the landlord of the inn, who had heard Mr Wraxall say that he wished to see the clerk or deacon (as he would be called in Sweden) of the parish, introduced him to that official in the inn parlour. A visit to the De la Gardie tomb house was soon arranged for the next day, and a little general conversation ensued.

"Can you tell me," Mr Wraxall said, "anything about Chorazin?"

"I have heard some of our old priests say that the Antichrist is to be born there, and there are tales —"

"Ah! What tales are those?" Mr Wraxall put in.

"Tales, I was going to say, which I have forgotten," said the deacon and soon after that he said good night.

The landlord was now alone and at Mr Wraxall's mercy, and that inquirer was not inclined to spare him.

"Herr Nielsen," he said, "I have found out something about the Black Pilgrimage. You may as well tell me what you know. What did the Count bring back with him?"

Mr Wraxall notes that the landlord spent at least one minute in looking at him before he said anything at all. Then he came close up to his guest, and with a good deal of effort he spoke.

"Mr Wraxall, I can tell you this one little tale, and no more — not any more. You must not ask anything when I have done. In my grandfather's time — that is, ninety-two years ago — there were two men who said: 'The Count is dead, we do not care for him. We will go tonight and have a free hunt in his wood' — the long wood on the hill that you have seen behind *Råbäck*. Well, those that heard them say this, they said: 'No, do not go, we are sure you will meet with persons walking who should not be walking. They should be resting, not walking.' These men laughed. There were no forestmen to keep the wood, because no one wished to live there. The family were not here at the house. These men could do what they wished.

"Very well, they go to the wood that night. My grandfather was sitting here in this room. It was the summer, and a light night. With the window open, he could see out to the wood, and hear.

"So he sat there, and two or three men with him, and they listened. At first they hear nothing at all, then they hear someone – you know how far away it is – they hear someone scream, just as if the most inside part of his soul was twisted out of him. All of them in the room caught hold of each other, and they sat so for three-quarters of an hour. Then they hear someone else, much nearer this time. They hear him laugh out loud. It was not one of the two men that laughed, and, indeed, they have all of them said that it was not any man at all. After that they hear a great door shut.

"Then, when it was just light, they all went to the priest. They said to him: 'Father, put on your gown and your ruff, and come to bury these men, Anders Bjornsen and Hans Thorbjorn.'

"You understand that they were sure these men were dead. So they went to the wood – my grandfather never forgot this. He said they were all like dead men themselves.

The priest, too, he was white with fear.

"So they went to the wood, and they found these men on the edge of the wood. Hans Thorbjorn was standing with his back against a tree, and all the time he was pushing with his hands – pushing something away from him that was not there. So he was not dead. And they led him away, and took

him to the house at Nykjoping, and he died before the winter, but he went on pushing with his hands. Also Anders Bjornsen was there, but he was dead. And I tell you this about Anders Bjornsen, that he was once a beautiful man, but now his face was not there, because the flesh was sucked away off the bones. You understand that? My grandfather did not forget that. And they laid him on the bier which they brought, and they put a cloth over his head, and the priest walked before, and they began to sing the psalm for the dead as well as they could. So, as they were singing the end of the first verse, one man fell down, who was carrying the head of the bier, and the others looked back, and they saw that the cloth had fallen off and the eyes of Anders Bjornsen were looking up because there was nothing to close over them. And this they could not bear. Therefore the priest laid the cloth upon him and sent for a spade, and they buried him in that place."

The next day Mr Wraxall records that the deacon called for him soon after his breakfast and took him to the church and mausoleum. He noticed that the key of the latter was hung on a nail just by the pulpit, and it occurred to him that, as the church door seemed to be left unlocked as a rule, it would not be difficult for him to pay a second and more private visit to the monuments if there proved to be

more of interest among them than could be digested at first.
The building, when he entered it, he found not unimposing.
The central space of the domed room was occupied by three
copper sarcophagi, covered with finely engraved ornament.
Two of them had, as is commonly the case in Denmark and
Sweden, a large metal crucifix on the lid. The third, that of
Count Magnus had instead, a full-length effigy engraved
upon it, and round the edge were several bands of similar
ornament representing various scenes. One was a battle
with cannon belching out smoke, and walled towns and
troops of pikemen. Another showed an execution. In a third,
among trees, was a man running at full speed, with flying
hair and outstretched hands. After him followed a strange
form; it would be hard to say whether the artist had
intended it for a man, or whether it was intentionally made
as monstrous as it looked. In view of the skill with which the
rest of the drawing was done, Mr Wraxall felt inclined to
adopt the latter idea. The figure was unduly short, and was
for the most part muffled in a hooded garment which swept
the ground. Mr Wraxall noted the finely worked and
massive steel padlocks – three in number – which secured
the sarcophagus. One of them, he saw, was detached, and lay
on the pavement. And then, unwilling to delay the deacon
longer or to waste his own time, he made his way onward to

the manor house.

'It is curious,' he notes, 'how, on retracing a familiar path, one's thoughts engross one to the total exclusion of surrounding objects. Tonight, again, I had failed to notice where I was going (I had planned a private visit to the tomb house to copy the epitaphs), when I suddenly, as it were, awoke to consciousness and found myself (as before) turning in at the churchyard gate, and, I believe, singing or chanting some such words as, 'Are you awake, Count Magnus? Are you asleep, Count Magnus?' and then something more which I have failed to recollect. It seemed to me that I must have been behaving in this nonsensical way for some time.'

He found the key of the mausoleum where he had expected to find it, and copied the greater part of what he wanted; in fact he stayed until the light began to fail him.

'I must have been wrong,' he writes, 'in saying that one of the padlocks of my Count's sarcophagus was unfastened; I see tonight that two are loose. I picked both up and laid them carefully on the window ledge, after trying unsuccessfully to close them. The remaining one is still firm, and, though I take it to be a spring lock, I cannot guess how it is opened. Had I succeeded in undoing it, I am almost afraid I should have taken the liberty of opening the sarcophagus. It is strange, the interest I feel in the personality of this ferocious and grim old noble.'

The day following was the last of Mr Wraxall's stay at *Råbäck*. He received letters connected with certain investments, which made it desirable that he returned to England – his work among the papers was practically done and travelling was slow. He decided to make his farewells, finish his notes and be off.

These finishing touches and farewells took more time than he had expected. The hospitable family insisted he dine with them – they dined at three – and it was verging on half past six before he was outside the iron gates of *Råbäck*.

When he reached the summit of the churchyard knoll, he lingered for many minutes, gazing at the limitless prospect of woods near and distant, all dark beneath a sky of liquid green. When at last he turned to go, the thought struck him that he must bid farewell to Count Magnus as well as the rest of the De la Gardies. The church was but twenty yards away and he knew where the key of the mausoleum hung. It was not long before he was standing over the great copper coffin, and, as usual, talking to himself aloud: 'You may have been a bit of a rascal in your time, Magnus,' he was saying, 'but for all that I should like to see you, or, rather –'

'Just at that instant,' he says, 'I felt a blow on my foot. Hastily I drew it back and something fell on the pavement with a clash. It was the last of the three padlocks that had fastened the sarcophagus. I stooped to pick it up, and – Heaven is my witness that I am writing only the bare truth – before I had raised myself there was a sound of metal hinges creaking and I distinctly saw the lid shifting upwards. I may have behaved like a coward, but I could not stay for one moment. I was outside that dreadful building in less time than I can write – almost as quickly as I could have said – the words, and what frightens me more, I could not turn the key in the lock. As I sit here in my room noting these facts,

I ask myself whether that noise of creaking metal continued, and I cannot tell whether it did or not. I only know that there was something more than I have written that alarmed me, but whether it was sound or sight I cannot remember. What is this that I have done?'

⁓◈⁓

POOR MR WRAXALL! He set out for England the next day and arrived safely, but as I gather from his inconsequent jottings, a broken man. One of the notebooks that have come to me gives an inkling of his experiences. Much of his journey was made by boat, and I find not less than six attempts to enumerate and describe his fellow passengers. The entries are of this kind: *24. Pastor of village in Skane. Usual black coat and black hat. 25. Commercial traveller from Stockholm going to Trollhättan. Black cloak, brown hat. 26. Man in black cloak, broadleafed hat, old-fashioned.*

This entry is crossed out and a note added: *Perhaps identical with No. 13. Have not yet seen his face.* On referring to No. 13, I find that he is a Roman priest in a cassock.

The result is always the same. Twenty-eight people are counted, one being always a man in a long black cloak and broad hat, and another a *short figure in dark cloak and hood*. It is noted that only twenty-six people appear at meals, and that the man in the cloak is perhaps absent, and the short figure is certainly absent.

On reaching England, Mr Wraxall landed at Harwich, and resolved to put himself out of the reach of some person or persons whom he never specifies, but whom he had come to regard as his pursuers. He took a vehicle and drove to the village of Belchamp St Paul. It was about nine o'clock at night when he neared the place. Suddenly he came to a crossroad. At the corner, two stood two figures. Both were in cloaks, the taller one wore a hat, the shorter a hood. He did not see their faces, nor did they make any motion. Yet the horse shied and broke into a gallop. Mr Wraxall sank into his seat in desperation. He had seen them before.

At Belchamp St Paul he found a decent lodging, and for the next day he lived, comparatively speaking, in peace. His last notes were written on this day. He is expecting a visit from his pursuers – how or when he knows not – and his cry is 'what has he done?' and 'is there no hope'? Doctors would call him mad, policemen would laugh. The parson is away. What can he do but lock his door and cry to God?

People still remember last year at Belchamp St Paul how a strange gentleman came one evening in August years back, and how the next morning but one he was found dead, and there was an inquest. Seven of the jury who viewed the body fainted, and none would speak of what they saw, and the verdict was a visitation of God. The people who owned the house moved away. But they do not, I think, know that any glimmer of light has ever been thrown on the mystery. It so happened that last year the house came into my hands as part of a legacy. It had stood empty since 1863 and there seemed no prospect of letting it. So I had it pulled down, and the papers of which I have given you an extract were found in a cupboard under the window in the best bedroom.

VARNEY THE VAMPYRE

James Malcolm Rymer

One of the earliest vampire stories, published in a series of pamphlets from 1845, this extract is taken from the beginning of what became an epic novel of over half a million words.

THE SOLEMN TONES of an old cathedral clock have announced midnight. The air is thick and heavy. A strange, death-like stillness pervades all nature. All is still, still as the very grave. Not a sound breaks the magic of repose. What is that, a strange pattering noise, like a million fairy feet? It is hail, yes, a hailstorm has burst over the city. Leaves are dashed from the trees, mingled with small branches, and windows that lie most opposed to the direct fury of the pelting ice are broken. Oh, how the storm raged! Hail – rain – wind. It was, in truth, an awful night.

There is an antique chamber in an ancient house. The ceiling is low and a large bay window, from roof to floor, looks to the west. The window is latticed, and filled with curiously painted glass and rich stained pieces, which send in a strange, yet beautiful light, when the sun or moon shines into the apartment. There is but one portrait in that room, although the walls seem panelled for the express purpose of containing a series of pictures. That portrait is of a young man with a pale face, a stately brow, and a strange expression, which no one cared to look on twice.

There is a stately bed in that chamber, of carved walnut-wood made rich in design and elaborate in execution. It is hung with heavy silken and damask furnishing. The floor is of polished oak.

The bed in that old chamber is occupied. A creature formed in all fashions of loveliness lies half asleep upon that ancient couch – a girl as young and beautiful as a spring morning. Her long hair has escaped from its confinement and streams over the blackened coverings of the bedstead – she has been restless in her sleep, for the clothing of the bed is in much confusion. One arm is over her head, the other hangs nearly off the side of the bed near to which she lies. She moaned slightly in her sleep, and once or twice her lips moved as if in prayer.

She has endured much fatigue, and the storm does not awaken her, but although it does not destroy her slumbers entirely, it does disturb them. The turmoil of the elements awake her senses, but cannot entirely break the repose they have lapsed into.

The hail continues. The wind continues. The uproar of the elements seems at its height. Now that beautiful girl on the antique bed awakens. She opens those eyes of celestial blue and a faint cry of alarm bursts from her lips. It is a cry, which amid the noise and turmoil, sounds but faint and weak. She sits upon the bed and presses her hands upon her eyes. Heavens! what a wild torrent of wind, and rain, and hail! Another flash – a wild, blue, bewildering flash of lightning streams across that bay window, for an instant bringing out every colour in it with terrible distinctness. A shriek bursts from the lips of the young girl and with her eyes fixed upon that window, which, in another moment, is all darkness, and with such an expression of terror upon her face as it had never before known, she trembled, and the perspiration of intense fear stood upon her brow.

"What – what was it?" she gasped. "Real, or a delusion? Oh, God, what was it? A figure tall and gaunt, trying from outside to unclasp the window. I saw it. A flash of lightning revealed it to me. It stood the length of the window."

There was a lull in the wind. The hail was not falling so thickly. What was left of it now fell straight, and yet a strange clattering sound came upon the glass of that long window. It could not be a delusion – she is awake and she hears it. What is it? Another flash of lightning – another shriek – there could be now no delusion.

A tall figure is standing on the ledge immediately outside the long window. Intense fear paralyses the limbs of the beautiful girl. That one shriek is all she can utter – with hands clasped, a face of marble, a heart beating so wildly in her bosom, that each moment it seems as if it would break its confines, eyes distended and fixed upon the window, she waits, frozen with horror. She fancies she can trace the darker form of that figure against the window, and she can see the long arms moving to and fro, feeling for some mode of entrance. What strange light is that gradually creeping up into the air? Red and terrible – brighter and brighter it grows. The lightning has set fire to a mill, and the reflection of the rapidly consuming building falls upon that long window. There can be no mistake. The figure is there, still feeling for an entrance, and clattering against the glass with its long nails. She tries to scream again, but a choking sensation comes over her and she cannot. It is too dreadful – she tries to move – each limb seems weighed down by tons of lead – she can but in a hoarse faint whisper cry, "Help – help – help – help!"

She repeats that word like a person in a dream. The red glare of the fire continues. It throws up the tall, gaunt figure in hideous relief against the long window. It shows, too, upon the one portrait that is in the chamber, and that portrait appears to fix its eyes upon the attempting intruder, while the flickering light from the fire makes it look fearfully lifelike. A small pane of glass is broken, and the form introduces a long gaunt hand, which seems devoid of flesh. The fastening is removed, and half of the window, which opens like folding doors, is swung open on its hinges.

And yet now she could not scream – she could not move. "Help!" was all she could say. But that look of terror that sat upon her face was dreadful – a look to haunt the memory for a lifetime.

The figure turns half round and the light falls upon the face. It is perfectly white – perfectly bloodless. The eyes look like polished tin, the lips are drawn back, and the principal feature next to those dreadful eyes is the teeth – the fearful-looking teeth – projecting like those of some wild animal, hideously, glaringly white, and fang-like. It approaches the bed with a strange, gliding movement. No sound comes from its lips. Is she going mad – that young and beautiful girl exposed to so much terror? She has drawn up all her limbs – she cannot even now cry for help. The power of articulation is gone, but the power of movement has returned to her. She draws herself slowly along to the other side of the bed to which the hideous appearance is approaching.

What was it? What did it want there? What made it look so hideous – so unlike an inhabitant of the earth?

Now she has got to the verge of the bed and the figure pauses. It seemed as if when it paused she lost the power to proceed. The clothing of the bed was now clutched in her hands with unconscious power. She drew her breath short and thick. Her bosom heaves and her limbs tremble, yet she cannot withdraw her eyes from that marble-looking face. The storm has ceased – all is still. The winds are hushed and the church clock proclaims the hour of one. A hissing sound comes from the throat of the hideous being and he raises his long, gaunt arms – the lips move. He advances. The girl places one small foot from the bed on the floor. The door of the room is in that direction – can she reach it? Has she power to walk? Can she withdraw her eyes from the face of the intruder, and so break the hideous charm? The figure has paused again, and half on the bed and half out of it, the young girl lies trembling. Her long hair streams across the entire width of the bed. As she has slowly moved along she has left it streaming across the pillows. The pause lasted about a minute – oh, what an age of agony. That minute was, indeed, enough for madness to do its full work.

With a sudden rush that could not be foreseen – with a strange howling cry that was enough to awaken terror in every breast, the figure seized the long tresses of her hair, and twining them round his bony hands he held her to the bed. Then she screamed – Heaven granted her the power to scream. Shriek followed shriek in rapid succession. The bedclothes fell in a heap by the side of the bed – she was dragged by her hair completely onto it again. He drags her head to the bed's edge. He forces it back by the hair still entwined in his grasp. With a plunge he seizes her neck in his fang-like teeth – a gush of blood and a hideous sucking noise follows. The vampyre is at his hideous repast!

Lights flashed about the building and various doors opened – voices called one to the other. There was a stir and commotion among the inhabitants.

"Did you hear a scream?" asked a young man, half-dressed, as he walked into the chamber of another about his own age.

"I did – where was it?"

"God knows. I dressed myself directly."

"All is still now."

"Yes, but unless I was dreaming there was a scream."

"We could not both dream there was. Where did you think it came from?"

"It burst so suddenly upon my ears that I cannot say."

There was a tap now at the door of the room where these

young men were, and a female voice said, "For God's sake, get up!"

"We are up," said both the young men, appearing.

"Did you hear anything?"

"Yes, a scream."

"Oh, search the house – search the house. Where did it come from – can you tell?"

"Indeed we cannot, mother."

Another person now joined the party. He was a man of middle age and as he came up to them, he said, "Good God! What is the matter?"

Scarcely had the words passed his lips, than such a rapid succession of shrieks came upon their ears, that they felt absolutely stunned by them. The elderly lady, whom one of the young men had called mother, fainted, and would have fallen to the floor of the corridor had she not been promptly supported, as those piercing cries came upon the night air. He, however, was the first to recover, for the other young men seemed paralyzed.

"Henry," he cried, "for God's sake support your mother. Can you doubt that these cries come from Flora's room?"

The young man mechanically supported his mother, and then the man who had just spoken darted back to his own bedroom and returned in a moment with a pair of pistols, shouting, "Follow me, who can!" he bounded across the corridor in the direction of the antique apartment, from whence the cries proceeded, but which were now hushed.

That house was built for strength, and the doors were all of oak and of considerable thickness. Unhappily, they had fastenings within, so that when the man reached the girl's chamber, he was helpless, for the door was fast.

"Flora! Flora!" he cried. "Flora, speak!"

All was still.

"Good God!" he added, "we must force the door."

"I hear a strange noise within," said the young man, who trembled violently.

"And so do I. What does it sound like?"

"I scarcely know, but it nearest resembles some animal eating, or sucking some liquid."

"What on earth can it be? Have you no weapon that will force the door? I shall go mad if I am kept here."

"I have," said the young man. "Wait here a moment."

He ran down the staircase and returned with a small, but powerful, iron crowbar.

"This will do," he said.

"It will, it will. Give it to me."

"Has she not spoken?"

"Not a word. My mind tells me that something very

dreadful must have happened to her."

"And that odd noise!"

"Still goes on. Somehow it curdles the very blood in my veins to hear it."

The man took the crowbar, and with some difficulty succeeded in introducing it between the door and the side of the wall. It required great strength to move it, but it did move, with a harsh, crackling sound.

"Push it!" cried he who was using the bar, "push the door at the same time."

"It opens – it opens," cried the young man.

"Another moment," said the stranger, as he still plied the crowbar "another moment, and we shall be inside the chamber. Be patient."

This stranger's name was Marchdale, and even as he spoke he succeeded in throwing the massive door wide open, clearing a passage to the chamber.

The young man, Henry, rushed in with a light in his hand.

"Flora – Flora!" he cried.

Then with a sudden bound something dashed from the bed. The concussion against him was so sudden and so utterly unexpected, as well as so tremendously violent, that he was thrown down and the light was extinguished.

All was in darkness, save a dull, reddish kind of light that now and then came into the room from the nearly consumed mill in the immediate vicinity. But by that light, dim, uncertain and flickering as it was, someone was seen to make for the window.

Henry, although stunned by his fall, saw a figure, gigantic in height, which nearly reached from the floor to the ceiling. The other young man, George, saw it, and Mr Marchdale likewise saw it, as did the lady who had spoken to the two young men in the corridor when first the screams of the young girl awakened everyone.

The figure was about to pass out at the window, which led to a kind of balcony, from where there was an easy descent to the garden.

Before it left they each caught a glance of the face, and they saw that the lower part of it and the lips were dabbled in blood. They also saw, the fearful-looking, shining, metallic eyes, which presented so terrible an appearance of unearthly ferocity.

No wonder that for a moment a panic seized them all and paralyzed any exertions they might otherwise have made to detain that hideous form.

But Mr Marchdale was a man of mature years and had seen much of life, both in this and in foreign lands. Although astonished to the extent of being severely frightened, he was much more likely to recover sooner than his younger less experienced companions, which, indeed he did and acted promptly and calmly.

"Don't rise, Henry," he said. "Lie still."

Almost at the moment he uttered these words, he took aim and fired at the horrifying figure, which by then occupied the window as if it were a gigantic figure set in a picture frame.

"If that has missed its aim," said Mr Marchdale, "I'll never pull a trigger again."

As he spoke he dashed forward and tried to clutch at the figure he felt convinced he had shot.

The tall figure turned upon him and that face was one never to be forgotten. It was hideously flushed with colour – the colour of fresh blood. The eyes had a terrible savage and remarkable lustre. Before, they had looked like polished tin, but were now ten times brighter and flashes of light seemed to dart from them. The awful mouth was wide open, as if, from the natural formation of the face, the lips receded much from the large canine-looking teeth.

A terrifying howling noise came from the throat of this monstrous figure and it seemed upon the point of rushing to attack Mr Marchdale.

Suddenly, as if some strange impulse had seized upon it, it uttered a wild and terrible shrieking kind of cackling laugh. Turning, it dashed through the window, and in one instant disappeared from before the eyes of those who felt nearly annihilated by its fearful presence.

"God help us!" cried Henry.

Mr Marchdale drew a long breath, and then, giving a stamp on the floor, as if to recover himself from the state of agitation into which even he was thrown, he cried, "Be it what or who it may, I'll follow it."

As he spoke, he took the road it took and dashed through the window onto the balcony.

"And we, too, George," exclaimed Henry, "we will follow Mr Marchdale. This dreadful affair concerns us more nearly than it does him."

They hesitated no longer, but at once rushed onto the balcony and dropped into the garden.

The mother approached the bedside of the unconscious, perhaps murdered, girl and saw her weltering in blood. Overcome by her emotions, she fainted.

When the two young men reached the garden, they heard the voice of Mr Marchdale, as he cried, "There – there – towards the wall. God! How it bounds along."

The young men hastily dashed through a thicket in the direction of his voice. They found him looking wild and terrified with something in his hand, which looked like a portion of clothing.

"Which way, which way?" they both cried in a breath.

He leant heavily on the arm of George as he pointed along a vista of trees. In a low voice he said, "God help us all. It is not human. Look there – look there – do you not see it?"

They looked in the direction he indicated. At the end of this vista was the wall of the garden a full twelve feet in height. As they looked, they saw the hideous, monstrous form they had traced from the chamber of their sister, making frantic efforts to clear the obstacle.

Then they saw it bound from the ground to the top of the wall, which it very nearly reached, but each time it fell back again into the garden with such a dull, heavy sound, that the earth seemed to shake again with the concussion. They trembled – well indeed they might, and for some minutes they watched the figure making its fruitless efforts to leave the place.

"What – what is it?" whispered Henry. "God, what can it possibly be?"

"I do not know," replied Mr Marchdale. "I did seize it. It

was cold and clammy like a corpse. It cannot be human."

"It will be gone," exclaimed Henry, as at this moment, after many repeated attempts and fearful falls, the figure reached the top of the wall. It hung by its long arms a moment or two, previous to dragging itself completely up.

The idea of it escaping, seemed to give courage to Mr Marchdale, and he, as well as the two young men, ran towards the wall. They got so close to the figure before it sprang down on the outer side of the wall, that to miss shooting it was a matter of utter impossibility, unless wilfully.

Henry had the weapon and he pointed it full at the tall form with a steady aim. He pulled the trigger – the explosion followed and the figure gave a howling shriek as it fell headlong from the wall on the outside.

"I have shot him," cried Henry, "I have shot him."

The Horror from the Mound

Robert E Howard

STEVE BRILL did not believe in ghosts or demons. Juan Lopez did. But neither the caution of the one, nor the sturdy scepticism of the other, was shield against the horror that fell upon them – a horror forgotten by men for more than three hundred years – a screaming fear monstrously resurrected from the black lost ages.

Yet as Steve Brill sat on his porch that last evening, his thoughts were as far from uncanny menaces as the thoughts of man can be. His ruminations were bitter but materialistic. He surveyed his farmland and he swore. Brill was tall, rangy and tough as boot leather – true son of the iron-bodied pioneers who wrenched West Texas from the wilderness. He was browned by the sun and strong as a longhorned steer. His lean legs and the boots on them showed his cowboy instincts, and now he cursed himself that he had ever turned to farming.

Yet his failure had not all been his fault. Plentiful rain in the winter – so rare in West Texas – had given promise of good crops. But as usual, things had happened. A late blizzard had destroyed all the budding fruit. The grain, which had looked so promising, was ripped to shreds and battered into the ground by terrific hailstorms just as it was turning yellow. A period of intense dryness, followed by another hailstorm, finished the corn.

Now as Brill sat glumly, he was aware of the approaching form of his nearest neighbour, Juan Lopez, an untalkative, old Mexican who lived in a hut just out of sight over the hill across the creek, and grubbed for a living. At present he was clearing a strip of land on an adjoining farm and in returning to his hut he crossed a corner of Brill's pasture.

Brill idly watched him climb through the barbed wire fence and trudge along the path he had worn in the short, dry grass. Brill knew that he always followed the same path home. And watching, Brill noted him swerving far aside, seemingly to avoid a low rounded hillock, which jutted above the level of the pasture. Lopez went far around this mound and Brill remembered that the old Mexican always circled it at a distance. And another thing came into Brill's idle mind — Lopez always increased his gait when he was passing the hill, and he always managed to get by it before sundown. Brill's curiosity was aroused.

He rose, and sauntering down the slight slope on the crown of which his shack sat, hailed the plodding Mexican.

"Hey, Lopez, wait a minute."

Lopez halted, looked about, and remained motionless but unenthusiastic as the man approached.

"Lopez," said Brill lazily, "it ain't none of my business, but I just wanted to ask you — how come you always go so far around that old Indian mound?"

"No," grunted Lopez shortly.

"You're a liar," responded Brill genially. "You savvy all right — you speak English as good as me. What's the matter — you think that mound's haunted or somethin'!"

Brill could speak Spanish himself and read it, too, but like most Anglo-Saxons he much preferred to speak his own language.

Lopez shrugged his shoulders.

"It is not a good place, *no bueno*," he muttered, avoiding Brill's eyes. "Let hidden things rest."

"I reckon you're scared of ghosts," Brill bantered. "Shucks, if that is an Indian mound, them Indians been dead so long their ghosts 'ud be plumb wore out by now."

Brill knew that the Mexicans looked with superstitious aversion on the mounds that are found here and there through the Southwest relics of a past and forgotten age, containing the bones of chiefs and warriors of a lost race.

"Best not to disturb what is hidden in the earth," grunted Lopez.

"Bosh," said Brill. "Me and some boys busted into one of them mounds over in the Palo Pinto country and dug up pieces of a skeleton with some beads and flint arrowheads and the like. I kept some of the teeth a long time till I lost 'em, and I ain't never been haunted."

"Indians?" snorted Lopez unexpectedly. "Who spoke of Indians? I have heard the tales of my people, handed down from generation to generation. And my people were here long before yours, *Senor* Brill."

"Yeah, you're right," admitted Steve. "First white men in this country was Spaniards, of course. Coronado passed along not very far from here and Hernando de Estrada's expedition came through here, away back yonder, I dunno how long ago."

"In 1545," said Lopez. "They pitched camp yonder where your corral stands now."

Brill turned to glance at his rail-fenced corral, inhabited now by his saddlehorse, a pair of workhorses and a scrawny cow.

"How come you know so much about it?" he asked.

"One of my ancestors marched with de Estrada," answered Lopez. "A soldier, Porfirio Lopez, told his son of that expedition, and he told his son, and so down the family line to me, who have no son to whom I can tell the tale."

"I didn't know you were so well connected," said Brill. "Maybe you know somethin' about the gold de Estrada was supposed to have hid around here, somewhere."

"There was no gold," growled Lopez. "De Estrada's soldiers bore only their arms, and they fought their way through hostile country – many left their bones along the trail. Many years later, a mule train from Santa Fe was attacked not many miles from here by Comanches and they hid their gold and escaped, so the legends got mixed up. But even their gold is not there now, because Gringo buffalo-hunters found it and dug it up."

Brill nodded abstractedly. Of all the continent of North America there is no section so haunted by tales of lost or hidden treasure as is the Southwest. Uncounted wealth passed back and forth over the hills and plains of Texas and New Mexico in the old days when Spain owned the gold and silver mines of the New World and controlled the rich fur trade of the West, and echoes of that wealth linger on in tales of golden caches. Some such vagrant dream, born of failure and pressing poverty, rose in Brill's mind.

"Well, anyway, I got nothin' else to do and I believe I'll dig into that old mound and see what I can find."

The effect of that simple statement on Lopez was nothing short of shocking. He recoiled and his swarthy brown face went ashy. His black eyes flared and he threw up his arms in a gesture of intense protest.

"*Dios*, no!" he cried. "Don't do that, *Senor* Brill! There is a curse – my grandfather told me – "

"Told you what?" asked Brill.

Lopez lapsed into sullen silence.

"I cannot speak," he muttered. "I am sworn to silence. Only to an eldest son could I open my heart. But believe me when I say better had you cut your throat than to break into that accursed mound."

"Well," said Brill, "if it's so bad why don't you tell me about it"

"I cannot speak!" cried the Mexican desperately. "I know, but I swore to silence on the Holy Crucifix, just as every man of my family has sworn! It is a thing so dark, it is to risk damnation even to speak of it! Were I to tell you, I would blast the soul from your body. But I have sworn, and I have no son, so my lips are sealed forever."

"Aw, well," said Brill sarcastically, "why don't you write it out?"

Lopez started, stared, and to Steve's surprise, caught at the suggestion.

"I will! *Dios* be thanked the good priest taught me to write when I was a child. My oath said nothing of writing. I only swore not to speak. I will write out the whole thing for you, if you will swear not to speak of it afterward, and to destroy the paper as soon as you have read it.

"Sure," said Brill, to humour him, and the old Mexican seemed much relieved.

"*Bueno*! I will go at once and write. Tomorrow as I go to work I will bring you the paper and you will understand why no one must open that accursed mound!"

And Lopez hurried along his homeward path, his stooped shoulders swaying with the effort of his haste. Brill gazed after the receding figure of the old Mexican. A shallow valley, cut by a half-dry creek, bordered with trees and underbrush, lay between Brill's pasture and the low sloping hill beyond which lay Lopez's shack. Among the trees along the creek bank the old Mexican was disappearing. And Brill came to a sudden decision.

Hurrying up the slight slope, he took a pick and a shovel from the tool shed built onto the back of his shack. The sun had not yet set and Brill believed he could open the mound deep enough to determine its nature before dark. If not, he could work by lantern light. The thought of treasure came again to his mind.

What if that grassy heap of brown earth hid riches – virgin ore from forgotten mines, or the minted coinage of old Spain? Was it not possible that the musketeers of de Estrada had themselves reared that pile above a treasure they could not bear away, moulding it in the likeness of an Indian mound to fool seekers? Did old Lopez know that? It would not be strange if, knowing of treasure there, the old Mexican refrained from disturbing it. Ridden with superstitious fears, he might well live out a life of barren toil rather than risk the wrath of lurking ghosts or devils –

for the Mexicans say that hidden gold is always accursed.

Steve set to work with savage energy. The task was no light one. The soil, baked by the fierce sun, was iron-hard, and mixed with rocks and pebbles. Brill sweated profusely and grunted with his efforts, but the fire of the treasure-hunter was on him. He shook the sweat out of his eyes and drove in the pick with mighty strokes that ripped and crumbled the close-packed dirt.

The sun went down, and in the long dreamy summer twilight he worked on, almost oblivious of time or space. He began to be convinced that the mound was a genuine Indian tomb, as he found traces of charcoal in the soil. The ancient people who reared these chambers had kept fires burning upon them for days, at some point in the building. All the mounds Steve had ever opened had contained a solid stratum of charcoal a short distance below the surface. But the charcoal traces he found now were scattered about through the soil.

Then Steve yelped in exultation as his pick rang on a bit of metal. He snatched it up and held it close to his eyes, straining in the waning light. It was caked and corroded with rust, worn almost paper-thin, but he knew it for what it was – a spur-rowel. It was unmistakably Spanish with its long cruel points and he halted, completely bewildered. No

Spaniard ever reared this mound, with its undeniable marks of aboriginal workmanship. Yet how came that relic of Spanish caballeros to be hidden deep in the packed soil?

Brill shook his head and set to work again. He knew that in the centre of the mound, if it were indeed an aboriginal tomb, he would find a narrow chamber built of heavy stones, containing the bones of the chief for whom the mound had been reared and the victims sacrificed above it. And in the gathering darkness he felt his pick strike heavily against something granite-like and unyielding. Examination, by sense of feel as well as by sight, proved it to be a solid block of stone, roughly cut. Doubtless it formed one of the ends of the deathchamber. Useless to try to shatter it. Brill chipped and pecked about it, scrapping the dirt

and pebbles away from the corners until he felt that
wrenching it out would be but a matter of sinking the pick-
point underneath and levering it out.

But now he was suddenly aware that darkness had come.
In the young moon objects were dim and shadowy. A
whippoorwill called eerily from the dark shadows of the
narrow winding creek. Brill straightened reluctantly. Better
get a lantern and continue his explorations by its light.

He felt in his pocket with some idea of wrenching out
the stone and exploring the cavity by the aid of matches.
Then he stiffened. Was it imagination that he heard a faint
sinister rustling, which seemed to come from behind the
blocking stone? Snakes! Doubtless they had holes
somewhere about the base of the mound. There might be a
dozen big diamond-backed rattlers coiled up in that cave-
like interior waiting for him to put his hand among them.
He shivered slightly at the thought and backed away out of
the excavation he had made.

It wouldn't do to go poking about blindly into holes. And
for the past few minutes, he realized, he had been aware of a
faint foul odour exuding from small gaps about the blocking
stone – though he admitted that the smell suggested reptiles
no more than it did any other menacing scent.

Steve laid down his pick and returned to the house,

impatient of the necessary delay. Entering the dark building, he struck a match and located his kerosene lantern hanging on its nail on the wall. Shaking it, he satisfied himself that it was nearly full of coal oil, and lighted it. Then he fared forth again, for his eagerness would not allow him to pause long enough for a bite of food. The mere opening of the mound intrigued him, as it must always intrigue a man of imagination, and the discovery of the Spanish spur had whetted his curiosity.

He hurried from his shack, the swinging lantern casting long distorted shadows ahead and behind him. A good thing he opened it that evening, Brill reflected – Lopez might have tried to prevent him meddling with it, had he known.

In the dreamy hush of the summer night, Brill reached the mound and lifted his lantern, swearing bewilderedly and revealing his excavations. His tools were lying carelessly where he had dropped them and there was a black gaping hole! The great blocking stone lay in the bottom of the excavation he had made, as if thrust carelessly aside. Warily he thrust the lantern forward and peered into the small cave-like chamber, not knowing what to expect. Nothing met his eyes except the rocky sides of a long narrow cell, big enough to hold a man's body, which had been built of roughly cut stones, cunningly and strongly joined together.

"Lopez!" exclaimed Steve furiously. "The dirty coyote! He's been watchin' me work – and when I went after the lantern, he snuck up and pried the rock out and grabbed whatever was in there, I reckon. Blast his hide, I'll fix him!"

Savagely he extinguished the lantern and glared across the shallow, brush-grown valley. And as he looked he stiffened. Over the corner of the hill, on the other side of which the shack of Lopez stood, a shadow moved. The slender moon was setting, the light dim and the play of the shadows baffling. But Steve's eyes were sharpened by the sun and winds of the wastelands, and he knew that it was some two-legged creature that was disappearing over the low shoulder of the mesquite-grown hill.

"Beatin' it to his shack," snarled Brill. "He's sure got somethin' or he wouldn't be travellin' at that speed."

He swallowed, wondering why a peculiar trembling had taken hold of him. He tried to drown the feeling that there was something peculiar about the gait of the dim shadow, which had seemed to move at a sort of slinking lope.

"Whatever he found is as much mine as his," swore Brill, trying to get his mind off the abnormal aspect of the figure's flight. "I got this land leased and I done all the work diggin'. A curse, heck! No wonder he told me that stuff. Wanted me to leave it alone so he could get it hisself. It's a wonder he ain't dug it up long before this."

Brill, as he meditated thus, was striding down the gentle slope of the pasture, which led down to the creek bed. He passed into the shadows of the trees and dense underbrush and walked across the dry creek bed, noting absently that neither whippoorwill nor hoot-owl called in the darkness. There was a waiting, listening tenseness in the night that he did not like. The shadows in the creek bed seemed too thick, too breathless. He wished he had not blown out the lantern, which he still carried, and was glad he had brought the pick, gripped like a battle-axe in his right hand. He walked up the slope and onto the hill, and looked down on the mesquite flat wherein stood Lopez's squalid hut. A light showed at the one window.

"Packin' his things for a getaway, I reckon," grunted Steve. "Oh, what the –"

He staggered as from a physical impact as a frightful scream knifed the stillness. He wanted to clap his hands over his ears to shut out the horror of that cry, which rose unbearably and then broke in an abhorrent gurgle.

"Good God!" Steve felt the cold sweat spring out upon him. "Lopez – or somebody – "

Even as he gasped the words he was running down the hill as fast as his long legs could carry him. Some unspeakable horror was taking place in that lonely hut, but he was going to investigate if it meant facing the Devil himself. He tightened his grip on his pick-handle as he ran. Wandering prowlers, murdering old Lopez for the loot he had taken from the mound, Steve thought, and forgot his wrath. He would go hard for anyone he found molesting the old scoundrel, thief though he might be.

He hit the flat, running hard. Then the light in the hut went out and Steve staggered in full flight, bringing up against a mesquite tree with an impact that jolted a grunt out of him and tore his hands on the thorns. Rebounding with a sobbed curse, he rushed for the shack, nerving himself for what he might see – his hair still standing on end at what he had already seen.

Brill tried the one door of the hut and found it bolted. He shouted to Lopez and received no answer. Yet utter silence did not reign. From within came a curious muffled worrying sound that ceased as Brill swung his pick crashing against the door. The flimsy portal splintered and Brill leaped into the dark hut, eyes blazing, pick swung high for a desperate onslaught. But no sound ruffled the grisly silence, and in the darkness nothing stirred, though Brill's chaotic imagination peopled the shadowed corners of the hut with shapes of horror.

With a hand damp with perspiration he found a match and struck it. Besides himself only Lopez occupied the hut, stark dead on the dirt floor, arms spread wide like a crucifix, mouth sagging open in a semblance of idiocy, eyes wide and staring with a horror Brill found intolerable. The one window gaped open, showing the method of the slayer's exit – possibly his entrance as well. Brill went to that window and gazed out warily. He saw only the sloping hillside on one hand and the mesquite flat on the other. He turned back, as the match burned down to his fingers. He lit the old coal-oil lamp on the table, cursing as he burned his hand. The globe of the lamp was very hot, as if it had been burning for hours.

Reluctantly he turned to the corpse on the floor. Whatever sort of death had come to Lopez, it had been horrible, but Brill, gingerly examining the dead man, found no wound – no mark of knife or bludgeon on him. Wait. There was a thin smear of blood on Brill's hand. Searching, he found the source – three or four tiny punctures in Lopez's throat, from which blood had oozed sluggishly. At first he thought they had been inflicted with a stiletto – a thin round edgeless dagger – then he shook his head. He had seen stiletto wounds – he had the scar of one on his own body. These wounds more resembled the bite of some animal – they looked like the marks of pointed fangs.

Then Steve noticed something else. Scrawled about on the floor lay a number of dingy leaves of paper, scrawled in the old Mexican's crude hand – he would write of the curse of the mound, he had said. There were the sheets on which he had written, there was the stump of a pencil on the floor, there was the hot lamp globe, all mute witnesses that the old Mexican had been seated at the table writing for hours. Then it was not he who opened the mound chamber and stole the contents – but who was it then, in God's name? And who or what was it that Brill had glimpsed loping over the shoulder of the hill?

Well, there was but one thing to do – saddle his mustang and ride the ten miles to Coyote Wells, the nearest town, and inform the sheriff of the murder.

Cursing himself to keep up his courage, he lighted his lantern, blew out the lamp on the rough table, and resolutely set forth, grasping his pick like a weapon. After all, why should certain seemingly abnormal aspects about a sordid murder upset him? Such crimes were abhorrent, but common enough.

Then as he stepped into the silent starflecked night he brought up short. From across the creek sounded the sudden soul-shaking scream of a horse in deadly terror – then a mad drumming of hoofs that receded in the distance. And Brill swore in rage and dismay. Was it a panther lurking in the hills – had a monster cat slain old Lopez? Then why was not the victim marked with the scars of fierce hooked talons? And who extinguished the light in the hut?

As he wondered, Brill was running swiftly toward the dark creek. As he passed into the darkness of the brush along the dry creek, Brill found his tongue strangely dry. He kept swallowing, and he held the lantern high. It made but a faint impression in the gloom, but seemed to accentuate the blackness of the crowding shadows. For some strange reason, the thought entered Brill's chaotic mind that though the land was new to the Anglo-Saxon, it was in reality very old. That broken and desecrated tomb was mute evidence that the land was ancient to man, and suddenly the night and the hills and the shadows bore on Brill with a sense of hideous antiquity. Here had generations of men lived and died before Brill's ancestors ever heard of the land. In the night, in the shadows of this very creek, men had no doubt given up their ghosts in grisly ways. With these reflections Brill hurried through the shadows of the thick trees.

He breathed deeply with relief when he emerged from the trees on his own side. Hurrying up the gentle slope to the railed corral, he held up his lantern, investigating. The corral was empty – not even the placid cow was in sight, and the bars were down. That pointed to human activity, and the affair took on a newly sinister aspect. Someone did not intend that Brill should ride to Coyote Wells that night. Steve headed back towards the house. He did not enter boldly. He crept clear around the shack, peering shudderingly into the dark windows, listening with painful intensity for some sound to betray the presence of the lurking killer. At last he ventured to open the door and step in. He threw the door back against the wall to find if anyone were hiding behind it, lifted the lantern high and stepped in. His heart pounding, he gripped his pick fiercely, his feelings a mixture of fear and red rage. With a sigh of relief Brill locked the doors, made fast the windows and lighted his old coal-oil lamp. The thought of old Lopez lying, a glassy-eyed corpse in the hut across the creek, made him shiver, but he did not intend to start for town on foot in the night.

He drew from its hiding-place his reliable old Colt ·45, spun the blue-steel cylinder, and grinned mirthlessly. Maybe the killer did not intend to leave any witnesses to his crime alive. Well, let him come! He – or they – would find a young cowpuncher with a six-shooter less easy prey than an old unarmed Mexican. And that reminded Brill of the papers he had brought from the hut. Taking care that he was not in line with a window through which a sudden bullet might come, he read, with one ear alert for stealthy sounds.

And as he read the crude laborious script, a slow cold horror grew in his soul. It was a tale of fear that the old Mexican had scrawled a tale handed down from past generations — a tale of ancient times.

And Brill read of the wanderings of the caballero Hernando de Estrada and his armoured pikemen, who dared the deserts of the Southwest when all was strange and unknown. There were some forty-odd soldiers, servants, and masters at the beginning of the manuscript. There was the captain, de Estrada, and the priest, and young Juan Zavilla, and Don Santiago de Valdez — a mysterious nobleman who had been taken off a helplessly floating ship in the Caribbean Sea — all the others of the crew and passengers had died of plague and he had cast their bodies overboard. So de Estrada had taken him aboard the ship that was bearing the expedition from Spain, and de Valdez joined them in their explorations.

Brill read something of their wanderings, told in the crude style of old Lopez, as the old Mexican's ancestors had handed down the tale for over three hundred years. The bare written words dimly reflected the terrific hardships the explorers had encountered — drought, thirst, floods, the desert sandstorms, the spears of hostile Indians. But it was of another peril that old Lopez told — a grisly lurking horror that fell upon the lonely caravan wandering through the immensity of the wild. Man by man they fell and no man knew the slayer. Fear and black suspicion ate at the heart of the expedition like a canker, and their leader knew not where to turn. This they all knew — among them was a fiend in human form.

Men began to draw apart from each other and this mutual suspicion, that sought security in solitude, made it easier for the fiend. The expedition staggered through the wilderness, lost, dazed and helpless, and still the unseen horror hung on their flanks, dragging down the stragglers, preying on drowsing sentries and sleeping men. And on the throat of each was found the wounds of pointed fangs that bled the victim white, so that the living knew with what manner of evil they had to deal. Men reeled through the wild, calling on the saints, or blaspheming in their terror, fighting frenziedly against sleep, until they fell with exhaustion and sleep stole on them with horror and death.

Suspicion centered on a great black man, a slave from Calabar. And they put him in chains. But young Juan Zavilla went the way of the rest, and then the priest was taken. But the priest fought off his fiendish assailant and lived long enough to gasp the demon's name to de Estrada. And Brill, shuddering and wide-eyed, read:

'. . . And now it was evident to de Estrada that the good priest had spoken the truth, and the slayer was Don Santiago de Valdez, who was a vampire, an undead fiend, subsisting on the blood of the living. And de Estrada called to mind a certain foul nobleman who had lurked, in the mountains of Castile since the days of the Moors, feeding off the blood of helpless victims, which lent him a ghastly immortality. This nobleman had been driven forth. None knew where he had fled, but it was evident that he and Don Santiago were the same man. He had fled Spain by ship, and de Estrada knew that the people of that ship had died, not by plague as the fiend had represented, but by the fangs of the vampire.'

'De Estrada, the black man and the few soldiers who still lived went searching for him and found him stretched in bestial sleep fully gorged with human blood from his last victim. Now it is well-known that a vampire, like a great serpent, when well gorged, falls into a deep sleep and may be taken without peril. But de Estrada was at a loss as to how to dispose of the monster, for how may the dead be slain? For a vampire is a man who has died long ago, yet is quick with a certain foul unlife.'

'The men urged that the Caballero drive a stake through the fiend's heart and cut off his head, uttering the holy words that would crumble the long-dead body into dust, but the priest was dead and de Estrada feared that in the act the monster might waken.'

'So – they took Don Santiago, lifting him softly, and bore

him to an old Indian mound near by. This they opened, taking forth the bones they found there, and they placed the vampire within and sealed up the mound. Him grant until Judgment Day.'

'It is a place accursed, and I wish I had starved elsewhere before I came into this part of the country seeking work. So you see, *Senor* Brill, why you must not open the mound and wake the fiend –'

There the manuscript ended with an erratic scratch of the pencil that tore the crumpled leaf.

Brill rose, his heart pounding wildly, his face bloodless. He gagged and found words.

"That's why the spur was in the mound – one of them Spaniards dropped it while they was diggin' – and I mighta knowed it's been dug into before, the way the charcoal was scattered out – but, good God – "

Aghast he shrank from the black visions – an undead monster stirring in the gloom of his tomb, thrusting from within to push aside the stone loosened by the pick of ignorance – a shadowy shape loping over the hill towards a light that suggested a human prey – a frightful long arm that crossed a dim-lighted window…

"It's madness!" he gasped. "Lopez was crazy! They ain't no such things as vampires! If they is, why didn't he get me first, instead of Lopez. Aw, hell! It's all a pipe dream – "

The words froze in his throat. At the window two eyes glared and pierced his very soul. A shriek burst from his throat and that ghastly visage vanished. But the very air was permeated by the foul scent that had hung about the ancient mound. And now the door creaked – bent slowly inwards. Brill backed up against the wall, his gun shaking in his hand. It did not occur to him to fire through the door. In his chaotic brain he had but one thought — only that thin portal of wood separated him from some horror born out of the womb of night and gloom and the black past. His eyes were distended as he saw the door give, as he heard the staples of the bolt groan.

The door burst inwards. Brill did not scream. His tongue was frozen to the roof of his mouth. His fear-glazed eyes took in the tall, vulture-like form — the red eyes, the long black fingernails — the mouldering garb, hideously ancient — the long spurred boot — the slouch hat with its crumbling feather — the flowing cloak that was falling to slow shreds. A savage cold radiated from the figure — the scent of mouldering clay and charnel-house refuse. And then the undead came at the living like a swooping vulture.

Brill fired point-blank and saw a shred of rotten cloth fly from the Thing's breast. The vampire reeled beneath the impact, then righted himself and came on with frightful speed. Brill reeled back against the wall with a choking cry, the gun falling from his nerveless hand. The black legends were true then. Human weapons were powerless, for may a man kill one already dead for long centuries, as mortals die?

Then the claw-like hands at his throat roused Brill to a frenzy of madness. As his pioneer ancestors fought hand to hand against all the odds, Brill fought the cold dead crawling thing that sought his life and soul.

Of that ghastly battle Brill never remembered much. It was a blind chaos in which he screamed like a beast, tore, slugged and hammered, where long black nails like the talons of a panther tore at him, and pointed teeth snapped at his throat. Rolling and tumbling about the room, both half enveloped by the musty folds of that ancient rotting cloak, they smote and tore at each other among the ruins of the shattered furniture. The fury of the vampire was not more terrible than the fear-crazed desperation of his victim.

They crashed headlong, into the table, knocking it down upon its side, and the coal oil lamp splintered on the floor, spraying the walls with sudden flames. Brill felt the bite of the burning oil that spattered him, but in the red frenzy of the fight he gave no heed. Like a man battling a nightmare he screamed and smote, while all about them the fire leaped up and caught at the walls and roof. Through darting jets and licking tongues of flames they reeled and rolled like a demon and a mortal warring on the firelanced floors of hell: And in the growing tumult of the flames, Brill gathered himself for one last volcanic burst of frenzied strength. Breaking away and staggering up, gasping and bloody, he lunged blindly at the foul shape and caught it in a grip not even the vampire

could break. He dashed him down across the uptilted edge
of the fallen table as a man might break a stick of wood
across his knee. Something cracked like a snapping branch
and the vampire fell from Brill's grasp to writhe in a strange
broken posture on the burning floor. Yet it was not dead, for
its flaming eyes still burned on Brill with a ghastly hunger,
and it strove to crawl towards him with its broken spine, as a
dying snake crawls.

Brill, reeling and gasping, shook the blood from his eyes,
and staggered blindly through the broken door. And as a man
runs from the portals of hell, he ran stumblingly through,
the mesquite and chaparral until he fell from utter
exhaustion. Looking back he saw the flames of the burning
house and thanked God that it would burn until the very
bones of Don Santiago de Valdez were utterly consumed and
destroyed from the knowledge of men.

THE DEATH OF LUCY

Bram Stoker

Lucy Westenra has attracted the attention of Count Dracula. Three young men are also in love with her: Arthur Holmwood, whose proposal she has accepted, Dr John Seward, and Quincy Morris, an American. The three men have remained friends. Worried about Lucy's illness, John Seward has called in the help of Van Helsing, a doctor and expert in matters supernatural. Van Helsing is reluctant to speak of what he fears is afflicting Lucy, but he has urged her to sleep with garlic flowers around her neck and has also allowed Arthur and John to give her their blood in a transfusion, as something seems to have been draining blood from her body...

LUCY WESTENRA'S DIARY: 12 September. How good they all are to me. I quite love that dear Dr. Van Helsing. I wonder why he was so anxious about these flowers. He positively frightened me, he was so fierce. And yet he must have been right, for I feel comfort from them already. I do not dread being alone tonight and can go to sleep without fear. I shall not mind any flapping outside the window. Oh, the struggle that I have had against sleep so often of late, the pain of sleeplessness, or the pain of the fear of sleep. How blessed are some people, whose lives have no fears, no dreads, to whom sleep is a blessing that comes nightly, and brings nothing but sweet dreams. I never liked garlic before, but tonight it is delightful! There is peace in its smell. I feel sleep coming. Goodnight, everybody.

DR SEWARD'S DIARY: 13 September. Called at the Berkeley and found Van Helsing, as usual, on time. The carriage ordered from the hotel was waiting. The Professor took his bag, which he always brings with him now.

⁎⁂⁎

VAN HELSING and I arrived at Hillingham at eight o'clock. It was a lovely morning with bright sunshine and all the fresh feeling of early autumn. When we entered we met Mrs Westenra. She greeted us warmly and said,

"You will be glad to know that Lucy is better.

The dear child is still asleep. I looked into her room and saw her, but did not go in and disturb her." The Professor smiled and looked quite jubilant. He rubbed his hands together and said, "Aha! I thought I had diagnosed the case. My treatment is working."

To which she replied, "You must not take all the credit, doctor. Lucy's state this morning is due in part to me."

"How do you mean, ma'am?" asked the Professor.

"Well, I was anxious about the dear child in the night, and went into her room. She was sleeping soundly, but the room was awfully stuffy. There were a lot of those horrible, strong smelling flowers about everywhere, and she even had a bunch of them round her neck. I feared that the heavy odour would be too much for the dear child in her weak state, so I took them all away and opened the window slightly. You will be pleased with her, I am sure."

She moved off into her boudoir, where she usually breakfasted early. As she had spoken, I watched the Professor's face, and saw it turn ashen gray. He had been able to retain his self-command whilst the poor lady was present, for he knew her state and how mischievous a shock would be. But the instant she had disappeared he pulled me, suddenly and forcibly, into the dining room and closed the door.

Then, for the first time in my life, I saw Van Helsing break down. He raised his hands over his head in a sort of mute despair, and then beat his palms together in a helpless way. Finally he sat down on a chair, and putting his hands before his face, began to sob, with loud, dry sobs that seemed to come from the very racking of his heart.

Then he raised his arms again, as though appealing to the whole universe. "God!

God! God!" he said. "What have we done, what has this poor thing done, that we are so sore beset? Is there fate amongst us still, sent down from the pagan world of old, that such things must be, and in such way? This poor mother, all unknowing, and doing what she thinks is best, does such a thing as lose her daughter body and soul. We must not tell her, we must not even warn her, or she dies, then both die. Oh, how we are beset! How are all the powers of the devils against us!"

Suddenly he jumped to his feet. "Come," he said. "Come, we must see and act. Devils or no devils, or all the devils at once, it matters not. We must fight him all the same." He went to the hall door for his bag and together we went up to Lucy's room.

Once again I drew up the blind, whilst Van Helsing went towards the bed. This time he did not start as he looked on the poor face with the same awful, waxen pallor as before. He wore a look of stern sadness and infinite pity.

"As I expected," he murmured, with that hissing inspiration of his which meant so much. Without a word he went and locked the door, and then began to set out on the little table the instruments for yet another operation of transfusion of blood. I had long ago recognized the necessity, and begun to take off my coat, but he stopped me with a warning hand. "No!" he said. "Today you must operate. I shall provide. You are weakened already." As he spoke he took off his coat and rolled up his shirt sleeve.

Again the operation. Again the narcotic. Again some return of colour to the ashy cheeks and the regular breathing of healthy sleep. This time I watched whilst Van Helsing recruited himself and rested.

Presently he took an opportunity of telling Mrs Westenra that she must not remove anything from Lucy's room without consulting him. That the flowers were of medicinal value, and that the breathing of their odour was a part of the system of cure. Then he took over the care of the case himself, saying that he would watch this night and the next, and would send me word when to come.

After another hour Lucy waked from her sleep, fresh and bright and seemingly not much the worse for her ordeal.

What does it all mean? I am beginning to wonder if my long habit of life amongst the insane is beginning to tell upon my own brain.

LUCY WESTENRA'S DIARY: 17 September. Four days and nights of peace. I am getting so strong again that I hardly know myself. It is as if I had passed through some long nightmare, and had just awakened to see the beautiful

sunshine and feel the fresh air of the morning around me.
I have a dim half remembrance of long, anxious times of
waiting and fearing, darkness in which there was not even
the pain of hope to make present distress more poignant.
And then long spells of oblivion, and the rising back to life
as a diver coming up through a great press of water.
However, since Dr Van Helsing has been with me, all this
bad dreaming seems to have passed away. The noises that
used to frighten me out of my wits, the flapping against the
windows, the distant voices which seemed so close to me,
the harsh sounds that came from I know not where and
commanded me to do I know not what, have all ceased. I go
to bed now without any fear of sleep. I do not even try to
keep awake. I have grown quite fond of the garlic, and a
boxful arrives for me every day. Tonight Dr Van Helsing is
going away, as he has to be for a day in Amsterdam. But I
need not be watched. I am well enough to be left alone.

Thank God for Mother's sake, and dear Arthur's, and for
all our friends who have been so kind! I shall not even feel
the change, for last night Dr Van Helsing slept in his chair a
lot of the time. I found him asleep twice when I awoke. But
I did not fear to go to sleep again, despite the bats flapping
almost angrily against the window panes.

TELEGRAM, VAN HELSING, ANTWERP, TO SEWARD, CARFAX: (Sent to Carfax, Sussex, as no county given, delivered late by twenty-two hours.) 17 September. Do not fail to be at Hilllingham tonight. If not watching all the time, frequently visit and see that flowers are placed, very important, do not fail. Shall be with you as soon as possible.

DR SEWARD'S DIARY:18 September. Just off train to London. The arrival of Van Helsing's telegram filled me with dismay. A whole night lost, and I know by bitter experience what may happen in a night. Of course it is possible that all may be well, but what may have happened? Surely there is some horrible doom hanging over us that every possible accident should thwart us in all we try to do.

MEMORANDUM LEFT BY LUCY WESTENRA: 17 September, Night. I write this and leave it to be seen, so that no one may by any chance get into trouble through me. This is an exact record of what took place tonight. I feel I am dying of weakness, and have barely strength to write, but it must be done if I die in the doing.

I went to bed as usual, taking care that the flowers were placed as Dr Van Helsing directed, and soon fell asleep.

I was awoken by the flapping at the window, which now

I know so well. I was not afraid, but wished that Dr Seward was in the next room, as Dr Van Helsing said he would be, so that I might have called him. I tried to sleep, but I could not. Then there came to me the old fear of sleep, and I determined to keep awake. Perversely sleep would try to come then when I did not want it. So, as I feared to be alone, I opened my door and called out. "Is there anybody there?" There was no answer. I was afraid to wake mother, so closed my door again. Then outside in the shrubbery I heard a sort of howl like a dog's, but more fierce and deeper. I went to the window and looked out, but could see nothing, except a big bat, which had evidently been buffeting its wings against the window. So I went back to bed again, but determined not to go to sleep. Presently the door opened, and mother looked in. Seeing by my moving that I was not asleep, she came in and sat by me. She said to me even more sweetly and softly than usual, "I was uneasy about you, darling, and came to see that you were all right."

I feared she might catch cold sitting there, and asked her to come in and sleep with me, so she came into bed and lay down beside me. She did not take off her dressing gown, for she said she would only stay a while and then go back to her own bed. As she lay there in my arms, and I in hers the flapping and buffeting came to the window again. She was

startled and a little frightened, and cried out, "What is that?"

I tried to pacify her, and at last succeeded, and she lay quiet. But I could hear her poor, dear heart still beating terribly. After a while there was the howl again from the shrubbery, and shortly after there was a crash at the window, and a lot of broken glass was hurled on the floor. The window blind blew back with the wind that rushed in, and in the aperture of the broken panes there was the head of a great, gaunt gray wolf.

Mother cried out in a fright, and struggled up into a sitting posture clutching wildly at anything that would help her. Amongst other things, she clutched the wreath of flowers that Dr Van Helsing insisted on my wearing round my neck, and tore it away from me. For a second or two she sat up, pointing at the wolf, and there was a strange and horrible gurgling in her throat. Then she fell, as if struck by lightning, and her head hit mine and made me dizzy for a moment.

The room seemed to spin round. I kept my eyes fixed on the window, but the wolf drew his head back, and a whole myriad of little specks seemed to come blowing in through the broken window, and wheeling and circling round like the pillar of dust that travellers describe. I tried to stir, but there was some spell upon me, and dear Mother's poor body, which seemed to grow cold already, for her dear heart had ceased to beat, weighed me down, and I remembered no more for a while.

The time did not seem long, but very, very awful, till I recovered consciousness again. Somewhere near, a passing bell was tolling. The dogs all round the neighbourhood were howling, and in our shrubbery, seemingly just outside, a nightingale was singing. I was dazed and stupid with pain, terror and weakness, but the sound of the nightingale seemed like the voice of my dead mother comforting me. The sounds seemed to have awakened the maids, too, for I could hear their bare feet pattering outside my door. I called to them, and they came in, and when they saw what had happened, and what it was that lay over me on the bed, they screamed out.

The wind rushed in through the broken window and the door slammed. They lifted off the body of my dear mother, and laid her on the bed after I had got up. They were all so frightened and nervous that I directed them to go to the dining room and each have a glass of wine. The door flew open for an instant and closed again. The maids shrieked, and then went in a body to the dining room, and I laid what flowers I had on my dear mother's breast. When they were there I remembered what Dr Van Helsing had told me, but I didn't like to remove them, and besides, I would have some of the servants to sit with me now. I was surprised that the maids did not come back. I called them, but got no answer, so I went to the dining room to look for them.

My heart sank when I saw what had happened. All four lay helpless on the floor, breathing heavily. The decanter of sherry was on the table half full, but there was a queer, acrid smell about. I was suspicious, and examined the decanter. It smelt of laudanum, and looking on the sideboard, I found that the bottle Mother's doctor uses for her – oh! did use – was empty. What am I to do? What am I to do? I am back in the room with Mother. I cannot leave her, and I am alone, save for the sleeping servants, whom some one has drugged. Alone with the dead! I dare not go out, for I can hear the low howl of the wolf through the broken window.

The air seems full of specks, floating and circling in the draught from the window, and the lights burn blue and dim. What am I to do? God shield me from harm this night! I shall hide this paper in my breast, where they shall find it when they come to lay me out. My dear mother gone! It is time that I go too. Goodbye, dear Arthur, if I should not survive this night. God keep you, dear, and God help me!

DR SEWARD'S DIARY: 18 September. I drove at once to Hillingham and arrived early. Keeping my cab at the gate, I went up the avenue alone. I knocked and rang as quietly as possible, for I feared to disturb Lucy or her mother, and hoped to only bring a servant to the door. After a while, finding no response, I knocked and rang again – still no answer. I know that minutes, even seconds of delay, might mean hours of danger to Lucy, if she had another of those frightful relapses, and I went round the house to try and find an entrance. Every window and door was fastened and locked, and I returned baffled to the porch. As I did so, I heard the rapid pit-pat of a swiftly driven horse's feet. They stopped at the gate and a few seconds later I met Van Helsing running up the avenue. When he saw me, he gasped out, "Then it was you, and just arrived. How is she? Are we too late? Did you not get my telegram?"

I answered as quickly and coherently as I could that I had only got his telegram early in the morning, and had not a minute in coming here, and that I could not make any one in the house hear me. He paused and raised his hat as he said solemnly, "Then I fear we are too late. God's will be done!"

With his usual energy, he said, "Come. If there be no way open to get in, we must make one. Time is all to us now."

We went round to the back of the house, where there was a kitchen window. The Professor took a small surgical saw from his case, and handing it to me, pointed to the iron bars guarding the window. I attacked them at once and had very soon cut through three of them. Then with a long, thin knife we pushed back the fastening of the sashes and opened the window. I helped the Professor in and followed him. There was no one in the kitchen or in the servants' rooms, which were close at hand. We tried all the rooms as we went along, and in the dining room, dimly lit by rays of light through the shutters, found four servant women lying on the floor. There was no need to think them dead, for their laboured breathing and the acrid smell of laudanum in the room left no doubt as to their condition.

Van Helsing and I looked at each other, and as we moved away he said, "We can attend to them later." Then we ascended to Lucy's room. For an instant or two we paused at the door to listen, but there was no sound that we could hear. With white faces and trembling hands, we opened the door gently, and entered the room.

How shall I describe what we saw? On the bed lay two women, Lucy and her mother. The latter lay farthest in. The

edge the white sheet that had been covering her had been blown back by the draught through the broken window, showing the drawn, white face, with a look of terror fixed upon it. By her side lay Lucy, also with a white face, and still more drawn. The flowers, which had been round her neck, we found upon her mother's bosom and her throat was bare, showing the two little wounds, which we had noticed before, but looking horribly white and mangled. Without a word the Professor bent over the bed, his head almost touching poor Lucy's breast. Then he gave a quick turn of his head, as of one who listens, and leaping to his feet, he cried out to me, "It is not yet too late! Quick! Quick! Bring the brandy!"

I flew downstairs and returned with it, taking care to smell and taste it, lest it, too, were drugged like the decanter of sherry which I found on the table. The maids were still breathing, but more restlessly, and I fancied that the narcotic was wearing off. I did not stay to make sure, but returned to Van Helsing. He rubbed the brandy, on her lips and gums and on her wrists and the palms of her hands. He said to me, "I can do this, all that can be at the present. You go wake those maids. Make them get heat and fire and a warm bath. This poor soul is nearly as cold as that beside her. She will need be warm before we can do much more."

I went at once, and found little difficulty in waking three of the women. The fourth was only a young girl, and the drug had evidently affected her more strongly so I lifted her on the sofa and let her sleep.

The others were dazed at first, but as remembrance came back to them they cried and sobbed in a hysterical manner. I told them that one life was bad enough to lose and if they delayed they would sacrifice Miss Lucy. So, sobbing and crying they went about their way, and prepared fire and water. We got a bath and carried Lucy out as she was and placed her in it. Whilst we were busy chafing her limbs there was a knock at the hall door. One of the maids ran off, hurried on some more clothes, and opened it. Then she returned and whispered to us that there was a gentleman who had come with a message from Mr Holmwood. I bade her simply tell him that he must wait, for we could see no one now. She went away with the message, and, engrossed with our work, I clean forgot all about him.

I never saw in all my experience the Professor work in such deadly earnest. I knew, as he knew, that it was a stand-up fight with death, and in a pause told him so. He answered me in a way that I did not understand, but with the sternest look that his face could wear.

"If that were all, I would stop here where we are now, and let her fade away into peace, for I see no light in life over her horizon." He went on with his work with, if possible, renewed and more frenzied vigour.

Presently we both began to be conscious that the heat was beginning to be of some effect. Lucy's heart beat a trifle more audibly to the stethoscope and her lungs had a perceptible movement. Van Helsing's face almost beamed, and as we lifted her from the bath and rolled her in a hot sheet to dry her he said to me, "The first gain is ours! Check to the King!"

We took Lucy into another room, which had by now

been prepared, and laid her in bed and forced a few drops of brandy down her throat. Van Helsing called in one of the women, and told her to stay with her and not to take her eyes off her till we returned. He then beckoned me out of the room.

"We must consult as to what is to be done," he said as we descended the stairs. In the hall he opened the dining room door, and we passed in. He closed the door carefully behind him. The shutters had been opened, but the blinds were already down, with that obedience to the etiquette of death, which the British woman of the lower classes always rigidly observes. The room was, therefore, dimly dark. It was, however, light enough for our purposes. Van Helsing's sternness was somewhat relieved by a look of perplexity. He was evidently torturing his mind about something, so I waited for an instant, and he spoke.

"What are we to do now? Where are we to turn for help? We must have another blood transfusion, and that soon, or that poor girl's life won't be worth an hour's purchase. You are exhausted. I am exhausted too. I fear to trust those women, even if they would have courage to submit. What are we to do for someone who will open his veins for her?"

"What's the matter with me, anyhow?"

The voice came from the sofa across the room, and its

tones brought relief and joy to my heart, for they were those of Quincey Morris.

Van Helsing started angrily at the first sound, but his face softened and a glad look came into his eyes as I cried out, "Quincey Morris!" and rushed towards him with outstretched hands.

"What brought you here?" I cried as our hands met.

"I guess Art is the cause."

He handed me a telegram – 'Have not heard from Seward for three days, and am terribly anxious. Cannot leave. Father still in same condition. Send me word on how Lucy is. Do not delay. – Holmwood.'

"I think I came just in the nick of time. You know you have only to tell me what to do."

Van Helsing took his hand and said, "A brave man's blood is the best thing on earth when a woman is in trouble. You're a man and no mistake. The devil may work against us, but God sends us men when we want them."

Once again we went through the operation. Lucy had got a terrible shock and it told on her more than before, for though plenty of blood went into her veins, her body did not respond to the treatment as well as on the other occasions. Her struggle back into life was something frightful to see and hear. However, the action of both heart and lungs improved, and her faint became a deep sleep. The Professor watched whilst I went downstairs and sent one of the maids to pay off one of the cabmen who were waiting.

In the hall I met Quincey Morris, with a telegram for Arthur telling him that Mrs Westenra was dead, that Lucy had been ill, but was now going on better, and that Van Helsing and I were with her. I told him where I was going, and he hurried me out, but as I was going said,

"When you come back, Jack, may I have a word with you alone?" I nodded in reply and went out. When I got back Quincey was waiting for me. I told him I would see him as soon as I knew about Lucy, and went up to her room. She was still sleeping, and the Professor had not moved from his seat at her side. From his putting his finger to his lips, I gathered that he expected her to wake before long and was afraid of fore-stalling nature. So I went down to Quincey and took him to the breakfast room.

When we were alone, he said to me, "Jack Seward, I don't want to shove myself in anywhere where I've no right to be, but this is no ordinary case. You know I loved that girl and wanted to marry her, but although that's all past and gone, I can't help feeling anxious about her all the same. What exactly is it that's wrong with her? The Dutchman said, that time you two came into the room, that you must have another transfusion of blood, and that both you and he were exhausted. Now I know that a man must not expect to know what they consult about in private. But this is no common matter, and whatever it is, I have done my part. Is not that so?"

"That's so," I said, and he went on.

"I take it that both you and Van Helsing had done already what I did today. Is not that so?"

"That's so."

"And I guess Art was in it too. When I saw him four days ago down at his own place he looked queer. I have not seen anything pulled down so quick since I was on the Pampas and had a mare that I was fond of go to grass all in a night. One of those big bats that they call vampires had got at her in the night, and what with his gorge and the vein left open, there wasn't enough blood in her to let her stand up, and I had to put a bullet through her as she lay. Jack, if you may tell me without betraying confidence, Arthur was the first, is not that so?"

"That's so."

"And how long has this been going on?"

"About ten days."

"Ten days! Then I guess, Jack Seward, that that poor pretty creature that we all love has had put into her veins within that time the blood of four strong men. Man alive, her whole body wouldn't hold it." Then coming close to me, he spoke in a fierce half-whisper. "What took it out?"

I shook my head. "That," I said, "is the crux. Van Helsing is simply frantic about it and I am at my wits' end. I can't even hazard a guess. There has been a series of little circumstances, which have thrown out all our calculations as to Lucy being properly watched. But these shall not occur again. Here we stay until all be well, or ill."

Quincey held out his hand. "Count me in," he said. "You and the Dutchman will tell me what to do, and I'll do it."

When she woke late in the afternoon, Lucy's eyes then lit on Van Helsing and on me too, and gladdened. Then she looked round the room, and seeing where she was, shuddered. She gave a loud cry, and put her poor thin hands before her pale face.

We both understood what was meant, that she had realized to the full her mother's death. So we tried what we could to comfort her. Doubtless sympathy eased her somewhat, but she was very low in thought and spirit, and wept silently and weakly for a long time. We told her that either or both of us would remain with her all the time, and that gave her comfort. Towards dusk she fell into a doze.

19 September. All last night she slept fitfully, being always afraid to sleep, and something weaker when she woke from it. The Professor and I took it in turns to watch her and we never left her for a moment unattended. Quincey Morris said nothing about his intention, but I knew that all night long he patrolled round and round the house.

When the day came, its searching light showed the ravages in poor Lucy's strength. She was hardly able to turn her head, and the little nourishment which she could take

seemed to do her no good. At times she slept, and both Van
Helsing and I noticed the difference in her, between sleeping
and waking. Whilst asleep she looked stronger, although
more haggard, and her breathing was softer. Her open
mouth showed the pale gums drawn back from the teeth,
which looked positively longer and sharper than usual.
When she woke the softness of her eyes evidently changed
the expression, for she looked herself, although a dying one.
In the afternoon she asked for Arthur, and we telegraphed
for him. Quincey went to meet him at the station.

When he arrived it was nearly six o'clock, and the sun
was setting full and warm, and the red light streamed in
through the window giving more colour to the pale cheeks.
When he saw her, Arthur was simply choking with emotion,
and none of us could speak. In the hours that had passed, the
fits of sleep, or the comatose condition that passed for it,
had grown more frequent, so that the pauses when
conversation was possible were shortened. Arthur's
presence, however, seemed to act as a stimulant. She rallied
a little, and spoke to him more brightly than she had done
since we arrived. He pulled himself together, and spoke as
cheerily as he could, so the best was made of everything.

It is now nearly one o'clock, and he and Van Helsing are
sitting with her. I am to relieve them in a quarter of an hour,

and I am entering this on Lucy's phonograph. Until six o'clock they are to try to rest. I fear that tomorrow will end our watching, for the shock has been too great. The poor child cannot rally. God help us all.

DR SEWARD'S DIARY: 20 September. Only resolution and habit can let me make an entry tonight. I am too miserable, too low spirited, too sick of the world and all in it, including life itself, that I would not care if I heard this moment the flapping of the wings of the angel of death. And he has been flapping those grim wings to some purpose of late, Lucy's mother and Arthur's father, and now . . . Let me get on with my work.

⁂

I DULY RELIEVED Van Helsing in his watch over Lucy. We wanted Arthur to rest also, but he refused at first. It was only when I told him that we should want him to help us during the day, and that we must not all break down for want of rest, lest Lucy should suffer, that he agreed to go.

Van Helsing was very kind to him. "Come, my child," he said. "Come with me. You are sick and weak, and have had much sorrow and much mental pain, as well as that tax on your strength that we know of. You must not be alone, for to be alone is to be full of fears and alarms. Come to the drawing room where there is a big fire and two sofas. You shall lie on one, and I on the other, and our sympathy will be comfort to each other, even though we do not speak, and even if we sleep."

Arthur went off with him, casting back a longing look on Lucy's face, which lay in her pillow, almost whiter than the lawn. She lay quite still and I looked around the room to see that all was as it should be. I could see that the Professor had carried out in this room, as in the other, his purpose of using the garlic. The whole of the window sashes reeked with it, and round Lucy's neck, over the silk handkerchief which Van Helsing made her keep on, was a rough chaplet of the same odorous flowers.

Lucy's breathing was laboured and her face was at its worst, for the open mouth showed the pale gums. Her teeth, in the dim, uncertain light, seemed longer and sharper than they had been in the morning. In particular, by some trick of the light, the canine teeth looked longer and sharper than the rest.

I sat down beside her and she moved uneasily. At the same moment there came a sort of dull flapping or buffeting at the window. I went over to it softly and peeped out by the corner of the blind. There was a full moonlight, and I could

see that the noise was made by a great bat, which wheeled
around, doubtless attracted by the light, although so dim,
and every now and again struck the window with its wings.
When I came back to my seat, I found that Lucy had moved
slightly and had torn the garlic flowers from her throat. I
replaced them as well as I could and sat watching her.

Presently she woke, and I gave her food, as Van Helsing
had prescribed. She took but a little, and that languidly. It
struck me as curious that the moment she became conscious
she pressed the garlic flowers close to her. It was certainly
odd that whenever she got into that lethargic state, with the
stertorous breathing, she put the flowers from her, but that
when she waked she clutched them close. There was no
possibility of making any mistake about this, for in the long
hours that followed, she had many spells of sleeping and
waking and repeated both actions many times.

At six o'clock Van Helsing came to relieve me. Arthur
had then fallen into a doze, and he mercifully let him sleep
on. When he saw Lucy's face I could hear the hissing indraw
of breath, and he said to me in a sharp whisper. "Draw up
the blind. I want light!" Then he bent down, and, with his
face almost touching Lucy's, examined her carefully. He
removed the flowers and lifted the silk handkerchief from
her throat. As he did so he started back and I could hear his

exclamation, "*Mein Gott!*" as it was smothered in his throat. I bent over and looked, too, and as I noticed some queer chill came over me. The wounds on the throat had disappeared.

For a full five minutes Van Helsing stood looking at her, with his face at its sternest. Then he turned to me and said calmly, "She is dying. It will not be long now. It will be much difference, mark me, whether she dies conscious or in her sleep. Wake that poor boy, and let him come and see the last. He trusts us, and we have promised him."

I went to the dining room and waked him. He was dazed for a moment, but when he saw the sunlight streaming in through the edges of the shutters he thought he was late, and expressed his fear. I assured him that Lucy was still asleep, but told him as gently as I could that both Van Helsing and I feared that the end was near. He covered his face with his hands, and slid down on his knees by the sofa, where he remained, perhaps a minute, with his head buried, praying, whilst his shoulders shook with grief. I took him by the hand and raised him up. "Come," I said, "my dear fellow, summon all your fortitude. It will be best for her."

When we came into Lucy's room I could see that Van Helsing had, with his usual forethought, been putting matters straight and making everything look as pleasing as possible. He had even brushed Lucy's hair so that it lay on the pillow in its usual sunny ripples. When we came into the room she opened her eyes, and seeing him, whispered softly, "Arthur! Oh, my love, I am so glad you have come!"

He was stooping to kiss her, when Van Helsing motioned him back. "No," he whispered, "not yet! Hold her hand, it will comfort her more."

So Arthur took her hand and knelt beside her, and she looked her best, with all the soft lines matching the beauty of her eyes. Then gradually her eyes closed and she slept. For a little bit her breast heaved softly, and her breath came and went like a tired child's.

And then insensibly there came the strange change, which I had noticed in the night. Her breathing grew stertorous, the mouth opened, and the pale gums, drawn back, made the teeth look longer and sharper than ever. In a sort of half asleep, vague, unconscious way she opened her eyes, which were now dull and hard at once, and said in a soft, voluptuous voice, such as I had never heard from her, "Arthur! Oh, my love, I am so glad you have come! Kiss me!"

Arthur bent eagerly over to kiss her, but at that instant Van Helsing, who, like me, had been startled by her voice, swooped upon him and pulled him back. "Not on your life!" he said, "not for your living soul and hers!" And he stood between them like a lion at bay.

Arthur was so taken aback that he did not what to do or say, and before any impulse of violence could seize him he realized the place and the occasion, and stood silent, waiting.

I kept my eyes fixed on Lucy, as did Van Helsing, and we saw a spasm as of rage flit like a shadow over her face. The sharp teeth clamped together. Then her eyes closed and she breathed heavily.

Very shortly after she opened her eyes

in all their softness, and putting out her poor, pale, thin hand, took Van Helsing's great brown one, drawing it close to her, she kissed it. "My true friend," she said in a faint voice, but with untellable pathos, "My true friend, and his! Oh, guard him, and give me peace!"

"I swear it!" he said solemnly, kneeling beside her and holding up his hand, as one who registers an oath. Then he turned to Arthur, and said to him, "Come, my child, take her hand in yours, and kiss her on the forehead, and only once."

Their eyes met instead of their lips, and so they parted. Lucy's eyes closed, and Van Helsing, who had been watching closely, took Arthur's arm, and drew him away.

And then Lucy's breathing became stertorous again, and all at once it ceased.

"It is all over," said Van Helsing. "She is dead!"

I took Arthur by the arm, and led him away to the drawing room, where he sat down, and covered his face with his hands, sobbing in a way that nearly broke me to see.

I went back to the room, and found Van Helsing looking at poor Lucy, and his face was sterner than ever. Some change had come over her body. Death had given back part of her beauty, for her brow and cheeks had recovered some of their flowing lines. Even the lips had lost their deadly pallor. It was as if the blood, no longer needed for the working of the heart, had gone to them.

"We thought her dying whilst she slept, and sleeping when she died."

I stood beside Van Helsing and said, "Ah well, poor girl, there is peace for her at last. It is the end!"

He turned to me and said with grave solemnity, "Not so, alas! Not so. It is only the beginning!"

When I asked him what he meant, he only shook his head and answered, "We can do nothing as yet. Wait and see."

The Beast Within

Gabriel-Ernest

Saki

"THERE IS A WILD BEAST in your woods," said the artist Cunningham, as he was being driven to the station. It was the only remark he had made during the drive, but as Van Cheele had talked incessantly his companion's silence had not been noticeable.

"A stray fox or two and some resident weasels. Nothing more formidable," said Van Cheele. The artist said nothing.

"What did you mean about a wild beast?" said Van Cheele later, when they were on the platform.

"Nothing. My imagination. Here is the train," said Cunningham.

That afternoon Van Cheele went for one of his frequent rambles through his woodland property. It was his custom to take mental notes of everything he saw during his walks.

When the bluebells began to show themselves in flower he made a point of informing everyone of the fact – the season of the year might have warned his hearers of the likelihood of such an occurrence, but at least they felt that he was being absolutely frank with them.

However, what Van Cheele saw on this particular afternoon was very out of the ordinary. On a shelf of smooth stone overhanging a deep pool in the hollow of an oak coppice, sprawled a boy of about sixteen, drying his brown limbs luxuriously in the sun. His wet hair, parted by a recent dive, lay close to his head, and his light-brown eyes, so light that there was an almost tigerish gleam in them, were turned towards Van Cheele with a certain lazy watchfulness. It was an unexpected apparition, and Van Cheele found himself engaged in the novel process of thinking before he spoke. Where on earth could this wild-looking boy hail from? The miller's wife had lost a child two months ago, supposed to have been swept away by a stream, but that had been a mere baby, not a half-grown lad.

"What are you doing there?" he demanded.

"Obviously, sunning myself," replied the boy.

"Where do you live?"

"Here, in these woods."

"You can't live in the woods," said Van Cheele.

"They are very nice woods," said the boy.

"But where do you sleep at night?"

"I don't sleep at night – that's my busiest time."

Van Cheele began to have an irritated feeling that he was grappling with a problem that was eluding him.

"What do you feed on?" he asked.

"Flesh," said the boy, and he pronounced the word with slow relish, as though he were tasting it.

"Flesh! What Flesh?"

"Since it interests you, rabbits, wildfowl, hares, poultry, lambs in their season, children when I can get any – their usually too well locked in at night. It's quite two months since I tasted child-flesh."

Ignoring the last remark Van Cheele tried to draw the boy on the subject of possible poaching operations.

"You're talking nonsense when you speak of feeding on hares. Our hillside hares aren't easily caught."

"At night I hunt on four feet," was the cryptic response.

"I suppose you mean that you hunt with a dog?" hazarded Van Cheele.

The boy rolled slowly over on to his back, and laughed a weird low laugh, that was pleasantly like a chuckle and disagreeably like a snarl.

"I don't fancy any dog would be very anxious for my company, especially at night."

Van Cheele began to feel that there was something positively uncanny about the strange-eyed, strange-tongued youngster.

"I can't have you staying in these woods," he declared authoritatively.

"I fancy you'd rather have me here than in your house," said the boy.

The prospect of this wild, nude animal in Van Cheele's

primly ordered house was certainly an alarming one.

"If you don't go, I shall make you," said Van Cheele.

The boy turned like a flash, plunged into the pool, and in a moment had flung his wet and glistening body halfway up the bank where Van Cheele was standing. In an otter the movement would not have been remarkable – in a boy Van Cheele found it startling. His foot slipped as he made an involuntarily backward movement, and he found himself almost prostrate on the slippery weed-grown bank, with those tigerish yellow eyes not very far from his own. Almost instinctively he half raised his hand to his throat. The boy laughed again, a laugh in which the snarl had nearly driven out the chuckle, and then, with another astonishing movement, plunged out of view into a yielding tangle of weed and fern.

"What an extraordinary wild animal!" said Van Cheele as he picked himself up. And then he recalled Cunningham's remark – "There is a wild beast in your woods."

Walking slowly homeward, Van Cheele began to turn over in his mind various local occurrences, which might be traceable to the existence of this astonishing young savage.

Something had been thinning the game in the woods lately, poultry had been missing from the farms, hares were growing unaccountably scarcer, and complaints had reached him of lambs being carried off bodily from the hills. Was it possible that this wild boy was really hunting the countryside in company with some clever poacher dogs? It was certainly puzzling. And then, as Van Cheele ran his mind over the various depredations that had been committed during the last month or two, he came suddenly to a dead stop. The child missing from the mill two months ago – the accepted theory was that it had tumbled into the stream and been swept away. But the mother had always declared she had heard a shriek on the hillside of the house, in the opposite direction from the water. It was unthinkable, of course, but he wished that the boy had not made that uncanny remark about child-flesh eaten two months ago. Such dreadful things should not be said even in jest. At dinner that night he was quite unusually silent.

"Where's your voice gone to?" said his aunt. "One would think you had seen a wolf."

Van Cheele, who was not familiar with the old saying, thought the remark rather foolish – if he HAD seen a wolf on his property his tongue would have been extraordinarily busy with the subject.

At breakfast next morning Van Cheele was conscious that his feeling of uneasiness had not wholly disappeared, and he resolved to go by train to the neighbouring cathedral town, hunt down Cunningham, and learn what had prompted the remark about a wild beast in the woods. With this resolution taken, his usual cheerfulness partially returned, and he hummed a bright little melody as he sauntered to the morning room for his customary cigarette. As he entered the room the melody made way abruptly for a pious invocation. Gracefully asprawl on the ottoman, in an attitude of almost exaggerated repose, was the boy of the woods. He was drier than when Van Cheele had last seen him, but no other alteration was noticeable.

"How dare you come here?" asked Van Cheele furiously.

"You told me that I was not to stay in the woods," said the boy calmly.

"But I did not say to come here. Supposing my aunt should see you!"

And with a view to minimising that catastrophe, Van Cheele hastily obscured as much of his unwelcome guest as possible under the folds of a Morning Post. At that moment his aunt entered the room.

"This is a poor boy who has lost his way – and lost his memory. He doesn't know who he is or where he comes from," explained Van Cheele desperately.

Miss Van Cheele was enormously interested.

"Perhaps his underlinen is marked," she suggested.

"He seems to have lost most of that, too," said Van Cheele, making frantic little grabs at the Morning Post to keep it in its place.

A naked, homeless child appealed to Miss Van Cheele as warmly as a stray kitten or derelict puppy would have done.

"We must do all we can for him," she decided, and in a very short time a messenger, dispatched to the rectory, had returned with a suit of clothes, and the necessary accessories of shirt, shoes, collar, etc. Clothed, clean, and groomed, the boy lost none of his uncanniness in Van Cheele's eyes, but his aunt found him sweet.

"We must call him something until we know who he really is," she said. "I think Gabriel-Ernest are nice, suitable names for him."

Van Cheele agreed, but he doubted they were being grafted on to a nice, suitable child. His misgivings were not diminished by the fact that his staid and elderly spaniel had bolted out of the house at the first incoming of the boy, and remained shivering and yapping at the farther end of the orchard, while the canary had put itself on an allowance of frightened cheeps. More than ever he was resolved to consult Cunningham.

As he drove off to the station his aunt was arranging that Gabriel-Ernest should help her to entertain the infant members of her Sunday-school class at tea that afternoon.

Cunningham was not at first disposed to be communicative.

"My mother died of some brain trouble," he explained, "so you will understand why I am averse to dwelling on anything of an impossibly fantastic nature that I may see or think that I have seen."

"But what DID you see?" persisted Van Cheele.

"What I thought I saw was something so extraordinary that no really sane man could dignify it with the credit of having actually happened. I was standing half-hidden in the hedge growth by the orchard gate, watching the sunset. Suddenly I became aware of a naked boy, a bather from some neighbouring pool, I took him to be, who was standing out on the bare hillside also watching the sunset. His pose was so suggestive of some wild faun of pagan myth that I instantly wanted to engage him as a model, and in another moment I think I should have hailed him. But just then the sun dipped out of view, and all the orange and pink slid out of the landscape, leaving it cold and grey. And at the same moment an astounding thing happened – the boy vanished too!"

"What! Vanished away into nothing?" asked Van Cheele excitedly.

"No – that is the dreadful part of it,"
answered the artist. "On the open hillside
where the boy had been standing a second
ago, stood a large wolf, blackish in
colour, with gleaming fangs and cruel,
yellow eyes. You may think – "
But Van Cheele did not stop for
anything as futile as thought.
Already he was tearing at top
speed towards the station.
He dismissed the idea of

a telegram. *'Gabriel-Ernest is a werewolf'* was a hopelessly inadequate effort at conveying the situation, and his aunt would think it was a code message to which he had omitted to give her the key. His one hope was that he might reach home before sundown. The cab, which he chartered at the other end of the railway journey, bore him with what seemed exasperating slowness along the country roads, which were pink and mauve with the flush of the sinking sun. His aunt was putting away some unfinished jams and cake when he arrived.

"Where is Gabriel-Ernest?" he almost screamed.

"He is taking the little Toop child home," said his aunt. "It was getting so late, I thought it wasn't safe to let him go back alone. What a lovely sunset, isn't it?"

But Van Cheele, although not oblivious of the glow in the western sky, did not stay to discuss its beauties. At a speed for which he was scarcely geared he raced along the narrow lane that led to the home of the Toops. On one side ran the swift current of the mill stream, on the other rose the stretch of bare hillside. A dwindling rim of red sun showed still on the skyline, and the next turning must bring him in view of the ill-assorted couple he was pursuing. Then the colour went suddenly out of things, and a grey light settled itself with a quick shiver over the landscape. Van Cheele heard a shrill wail of fear, and stopped running.

Nothing was ever seen again of the Toop child or Gabriel-Ernest, but the latter's discarded garments were found lying in the road so it was assumed that the child had fallen into the water, and that the boy had stripped and jumped in, in a vain endeavour to save him. Van Cheele and some workmen who were near by at the time testified to having heard a child scream loudly just near the spot where the clothes were found. Mrs Toop, who had eleven other children, was decently resigned to her bereavement, but Miss Van Cheele sincerely mourned her lost foundling. It was on her initiative that a memorial brass was put up in the parish church to "Gabriel-Ernest, an unknown boy, who bravely sacrificed his life for another."

Van Cheele gave way to his aunt in most things, but he flatly refused to subscribe to the Gabriel-Ernest memorial.

A Tragedy
of the Forest

Stanley Waterloo

IT IS CHRISTMAS EVE. A man lies stretched on his blanket in a copse in the depths of a black pine forest of the Saginaw Valley. He has been hunting all day, fruitlessly, and is exhausted. So wearied is he with long hours of walking, that he will not even seek to reach the lumbermen's camp, half a mile distant, without a few moment's rest. He has thrown his blanket down on the snow in the bushes and has thrown himself upon the blanket, where he lies half dreaming. No thought of danger comes to him. He sees nothing, but there is an unusual sensation which alarms him. He recognizes near him a presence – fierce, intense, unnatural. A rustle in the twigs a few feet away falls upon his ears. He raises his head. There, where it has drawn itself closely and stealthily from its covert in the underbrush, is a huge grey wolf.

The man can see the gaunt figure distinctly, though the sombre light is deepening quickly into darkness. He can see the grisly coat, the yellow fangs, the flaming eyes. He can almost feel the hot breath of the beast. But something far more disturbing than that meets his eye and affects him. His own individuality has become obscured and another is taking its place. He struggles against the transformation, but in vain. He can read the wolf's thoughts, or rather its fierce instincts and desires. He is the wolf. He knows the wolf's heart. The man trembles in fear. The perspiration comes in great drops upon his forehead, and his features are distorted. It is a horrible thing. Now a change comes. The wolf moves. He glides off in the darkness. The spell upon the man is weakened, but it is not gone. He staggers to his feet, and half an hour later is in the lumbermen's camp again. But he comes in like one insane – pallid of face and muttering. His comrades, startled by his appearance, ply him with questions, receiving only incoherent answers. They place him in his bunk, where he lies writing and twisting about. His eyes are staring, as if they must see what those about him cannot see, and his breath comes quickly. He pants like a wild beast. His thoughts are with the wolf. He is the wolf. The personalities of the ravening brute and of the man are blended now in one, or rather the personality of the man has been eliminated. The man's body is in the lumbermen's camp, but his mind is in the depths of the forest. He is seeking prey!

⟨⟨◖◗⟩⟩

"I am hungry! I must have warm blood and flesh! The darkness is here and my time has come. There are no deer tonight in the pine forest on the hill, where I have run them down and torn them. The deep snow has driven them into the lower forest, where men have been at work. The deer will be feeding tonight on the buds of the trees the men have cut down. How I hate men and fear them! They are different from the other animals in the wood. I shun them. They are stronger than I in some way. There is death about them. As I crept by the farm beside the river this morning I saw a young one, a child with yellow hair. Ah, how I would like to feed upon her! Her throat was white and soft. But I dare not rush through the field and seize her. The man was there, and he would have killed me. The odour of flesh came to me in the wind across the clearing. It was the same way at this time when the snow was deep last year. It is some day on which they feast. But I will feed better. I will have hot blood. The deer are in the tops of the fallen trees now!"

Across frozen streams, gliding like a shadow through the underbrush, swift, silent, with only its gleaming eyes to betray it, the gaunt figure goes. Miles are past. The figure threads its way between the trunks of massive trees. It passes over fallen logs with long, noiseless leaps. It casts a shifting shadow itself as it sweeps across some lighter spot, where faint moonbeams find their way to the ground through overhanging branches. The figure approaches the spot where the lumbermen have been at work. Among the tops of the fallen trees are other figures – light, graceful, flitting about. The deer are feeding on the buds.

The eyes of the long grey figure grow more flaming still. The yellow fangs are disclosed cruelly. Slowly it creeps forward. It is close upon the flitting figures now. There is a rush, a fierce, hungry yelp, a great leap. There is a crash of twigs and limbs. The flitting figures assume another character – the beautiful deer, wild with fright, bounding away with gigantic springs. The steady stroke of their hoofs echoes away through the forest. In the treetops there is a great struggle, and then the sound comes of another series of great leaps dying off in the distance. The prey has escaped. But not altogether! A grisly figure is following. The pace had changed to one of fierce pursuit. It is steady and relentless.

The man in the bunk in the lumbermen's camp half leaps

to his feet. His eyes are staring more wildly, his breathing is more rapid. He appears a man in a spasm. His comrades force him to his bed again, but find it necessary to restrain him by sheer strength. They think he has gone mad. But only his body is with them. He is in the forest. His prey has escaped him. He is pursuing it.

"It has escaped me! I almost had it by its slender throat when it shook me off and leaped away. But I will have it yet! I will follow swiftly till it tires and falters, and then I will tear and feed upon it. The old wolf never tires! Leap away, you fool, if you will. I am coming, hungry, never resting. You are mine!"

With the speed of light the deer bounds away in the direction its fellows have taken. The snow crackles as its feet strike the frozen earth and flies off in a white shower. The fallen treetops are left behind. Miles are covered. But ever, in the rear, with almost the speed of the flying deer, sweeps along the trailing shadow. It is long past midnight. The moon has risen high and the bright spots in the forest are more frequent. The deer crosses these with a rush. Still they are far apart.

Will they remain so?

Swiftly between the dark pines again, across frozen streams again, through valleys and over hills, the relentless chase continues. The leaps of the fleeing deer become less vaulting, a look of terror in its liquid eyes has deepened. Its tongue projects from its mouth, its wet flanks heave distressfully, but it flies on in desperation. The distance between it and the dark shadow behind has lessened plainly. There is no abatement to the speed of this silent thing. It follows noiselessly, persistently.

'I shall have it! It is mine – the weak thing, with its rich, warm blood! Swift of foot as it is, did it think to escape the old wolf? It falters as it leaps. It is faint and tottering. How I will tear it! The day has nearly come. How I hate the day! But the prey is mine. I will kill it in the grey light.'

The man in the bunk in the lumbermen's camp is seized with another spasm. He struggles to escape from his friends, though he does not see them. He is fiercely intent on something. His teeth are set and his eyes glare fiercely. It requires half a dozen men to restrain him.

The deer struggles on, still swiftly but with effort. Its breath comes in agony, its eyes are staring from its sockets. It is a pitiable spectacle, but the struggle for life continues. With a last desperate effort the deer vaults over a brushwood fence. The scene has changed again. The morning has broken. A farmhouse stands out revealed plainly in the increasing light. With flagging movement the fugitive passes across the field, but there is a sudden, slight noise behind. The deer turns its head. Its pursuer is close upon it. It sees the death which nears it. The monster, sure now of its prey, gives a fierce howl of triumph. Terror lends the victim strength. It turns toward the farmhouse, struggling through the banks of snow and leaps the low palings, where, beside great straw stacks, the cattle of the farm are herded. It disappears among them.

The door of the farmhouse opens, and from it comes a man who strides away toward where the cattle are gathered, lowing for their morning feed. After the man there emerges from the door a little girl with yellow hair. She dances along the footpath in a direction opposite that taken by the man. Not far distant, creeping along a deep furrow, is a lank, skulking figure.

"Can it be? Has it escaped me, when it was mine? I would have torn it at the farmhouse door, but the man appeared. Must I hunger for another day, when I am raging for blood! What is that! It is the child, and alone! It has wandered away from the farmhouse. Where is the great hound that guards the house at night? Oh, the child! I can see its white throat again. I will tear it. I will throttle the weak thing and still its cries in an instant!"

✦

The man in the bunk in the lumbermen's camp is wild again. His comrades struggle to hold him down.

✦

A horrible, hairy thing, with flaming eyes and hot breath, leaps upon and bears down a child with yellow hair. A hoarse growl, the rush of a great hound, a desperate struggle in the snow, and the still air of morning is burdened suddenly with wild clamour. There is an opening of doors, there are shouts and calls and flying footsteps – and then, mingling with the cries of the writhing brutes, rings out sharply the report of the farmer's rifle. There is a howl of rage and agony, and a gaunt grey figure leaps upward and falls quivering across the form of the child. The child is lifted from the ground unhurt. The great hound has by the throat the old wolf – dead!

The man in the lumbermen's camp has leaped from his bunk. His appearance is ghastly. His comrades spring forward to restrain him, but he throws them off. There is a furious struggle with the madman. He has the strength of a dozen men. The sturdy lumbermen at last gain the advantage over him. Suddenly he throws up his hands and falls forward upon the floor – dead.

They could never understand – the simple lumbermen – why the life of the merry, light-hearted hunter of the party came to an end so suddenly on the eve of Christmas Day. He was in in perfect health, they said, but he went mad on the eve of Christmas Day, and in the morning died.

THE GREY WOLF

George Macdonald

AT TWILIGHT, one evening in spring, a young English student had wandered northwards as far as the outlying fragments of Scotland called the Orkney and Shetland Islands. He found himself on a small island of the latter group, caught in a storm of wind and hail, which had come on suddenly. It was in vain to look about for any shelter, for not only did the storm entirely obscure the landscape, but there was nothing around him save a desert of moss.

However, as he walked on for mere walking's sake, he found himself on the verge of a cliff. Over the brow of it he saw a ledge of rock a few feet below him, where he might find some shelter from the blast that blew from behind. Letting himself down by his hands, he alighted upon something that crunched beneath his tread, and found the bones of many small animals scattered about in front of a little cave in the rock, offering the refuge he sought. He went in and sat upon a stone. The storm increased in violence, and as the darkness grew he became uneasy, for he did not relish the thought of spending the night in the cave. He had parted from his companions on the opposite side of the island and it added to his uneasiness that they must be full of apprehension about him. At last there came a lull in the storm, and at the same instant he heard a footfall, stealthy and light as that of a wild beast, upon the bones at the mouth of the cave. He started up in some fear, though the least thought might have satisfied him that there could be no very dangerous animals upon the island. Before he had time to think the face of a woman appeared in the opening. Eagerly the wanderer spoke. She started at the sound of his voice. He could not see her well, because she was turned towards the darkness of the cave.

"Will you tell me how to find my way across the moor to Shielness?" he asked.

"You cannot find it tonight," she answered, in a sweet tone, and with a smile that bewitched him, revealing the whitest of teeth.

"What am I to do, then?"

"My mother will give you shelter, but that is all she has to offer."

"And that is far more than I expected a minute ago," he replied. "I shall be most grateful."

She turned in silence and left the cave. The youth followed.

She was barefooted, and her pretty brown feet went catlike over the sharp stones, as she led the way down a rocky path to the shore. Her garments were scanty and torn, and her hair blew tangled in the wind. She seemed about five and twenty, lithe and small. Her long fingers kept clutching and pulling nervously at her skirts as she went. Her face was very grey in complexion, and very worn, but delicately formed, and smooth-skinned.

At the foot of the cliff, they came upon a little hut leaning against it, and having for its inner apartment a natural hollow within. Smoke was spreading over the face of the rock, and the grateful odour of food gave hope to the hungry student. His guide opened the door of the cottage. He followed her in and saw a woman bending over a fire in the middle of the floor. On the fire lay a large fish broiling. The daughter spoke a few words, and the mother turned and welcomed the stranger. She had an old and very wrinkled, but honest face, and looked troubled. She dusted the only chair in the cottage, and placed it for him by the side of the fire, opposite the one window. He could see a little patch of yellow sand over which the spent waves spread themselves out listlessly. Under this window there was a bench, upon which the daughter threw herself in an unusual posture, resting her chin upon her hand. A moment after, the youth caught the first glimpse of her blue eyes. They were fixed upon him with a strange look of greed, amounting to craving, but, as if aware that they belied or betrayed her, she dropped them instantly.

When the fish was ready, the old woman wiped the table, steadied it upon the uneven floor and covered it with a piece of fine table linen. She then laid the fish on a wooden platter and invited the guest to help himself. Seeing no other provision, he pulled from his pocket a hunting knife, and divided a portion of the fish, offering it to the mother first.

"Come, my lamb," said the old woman, and the daughter approached the table. But her nostrils and mouth quivered with disgust.

The next moment she turned and hurried from the hut.

"She doesn't like fish," said the old woman, "and I haven't anything else to give her."

"She does not seem in good health," he said.

The woman answered only with a sigh and they ate their fish with the help of a little rye bread. As they finished their supper, the youth heard a sound like the pattering of a dog's feet upon the sand close to the door. But before he had time to look out of the window, the door opened, and the young woman entered. She looked better, perhaps from having just washed her face. She drew a stool to the corner of the fire opposite him. But as she sat down, to his bewilderment, and even horror, the student spied a single drop of blood on her white skin within her torn dress. The woman brought out a jar of whisky, put a rusty old kettle on the fire, and took her place in front of it. As soon as the water boiled, she proceeded to make some toddy in a wooden bowl.

The youth could not take his eyes off the young woman, he found himself fascinated, or rather bewitched. She kept her eyes for the most part veiled with the loveliest eyelids fringed with dark lashes, and he gazed entranced, for the red glow of the little oil lamp covered all the strangeness of her complexion. But as soon as he met a stolen glance out of those eyes, his soul shuddered within him. Lovely face and craving eyes alternated fascination and repulsion.

The mother placed the bowl in his hands. He drank sparingly, and passed it to the girl. She lifted it to her lips, and as she tasted – only tasted it – looked at him. He thought the drink must have been drugged and have affected his brain. Her hair smoothed itself back, and drew her forehead backwards with it, while the lower part of her face projected towards the bowl, revealing, before she sipped, her dazzling teeth in strange prominence. But the moment the vision vanished she returned the vessel to her mother, and rising, hurried out of the cottage.

Then the old woman pointed to a bed in one corner with a murmured apology, and the student, wearied both with the fatigues of the day and the strangeness of the night, threw himself upon it, wrapped in his cloak. The moment he lay down, the storm began afresh, and the wind blew so keenly through the crannies of the hut, that it was only by drawing his cloak over his head that he could protect himself from its currents. Unable to sleep, he lay listening to the uproar which grew in violence, till the spray was dashing against the window. The door opened and the young woman came in. She made up the fire, drew the bench before it, and lay down in the same strange posture, with her chin propped on her hand and elbow, and her face turned towards the youth. He moved a little – she dropped her head, and lay on her face, with her arms crossed beneath her forehead. The mother had disappeared.

Drowsiness crept over him. A movement of the bench roused him and he fancied he saw some four-footed creature, as tall as a large dog, trot quietly out of the door. He was sure he felt a rush of cold wind. Gazing fixedly through the darkness, he thought he saw the eyes of the damsel encountering his, but a glow from the falling together of the remnants of the fire revealed clearly enough that the bench was vacant. Wondering what could have made her go out in such a storm, he fell asleep.

In the middle of the night he felt a pain in his shoulder, came wide awake, and saw the gleaming eyes and grinning teeth of some animal close to his face. Its claws were in his shoulder and its mouth seeking his throat. However, before it had fixed its fangs he had its throat in one hand, and sought his knife with the other. A terrible struggle followed, but regardless of the tearing claws, he found and opened his knife. He had made one futile stab, and was drawing it for another, when, with a spring of the whole body and one wildly contorted effort, the creature twisted its neck from his hold, and with something betwixt a scream and a howl, darted from him. Again he heard the door open and again the wind blew in upon him. It continued blowing – a sheet of spray dashed across the floor, and over his face. He sprung from his bed and bounded to the door.

It was a wild night – dark, but for the flash of whiteness from the waves as they broke within a few yards of the cottage. The wind was raving and the rain pouring down. A gruesome sound as of mingled weeping and howling came from somewhere in the dark. He turned again into the hut and closed the door, but could find no way of securing it.

The lamp was nearly out, and he could not be certain whether the form of the young woman was upon the bench or not. Overcoming a strong repugnance, he approached it and put out his hands – there was nothing. He sat down and waited for daylight – he dared not sleep any more.

When the day dawned at length, he went out yet again and looked around. The morning was dim and gusty and grey. The wind had fallen, but the waves were tossing wildly. He wandered up and down the little strand, longing for more light.

At length he heard a movement in the cottage. By and by the voice of the old woman called to him from the door.

"You're up early, sir. I doubt you didn't sleep well."

"Not very well," he said. "But where is your daughter?"

"She's not awake yet," said the mother. "I'm afraid I have but a poor breakfast for you. But you'll take a dram and a bit of fish. It's all I've got."

Unwilling to hurt her, though hardly in good appetite, he sat down at the table. While they were eating, the daughter came in, but turned her face away and went to the far end of the hut. When she came forward after a minute or two, the youth saw that her hair was drenched and her face whiter than before. She looked ill and faint, and when she raised her eyes, all their fierceness had vanished, and sadness had taken its place. Her neck was now covered with a cotton handkerchief. She was modestly attentive to him and no longer shunned his gaze. He was gradually yielding to the temptation of braving another night in the hut, and seeing what would follow, when the old woman spoke.

"The weather will be broken all day, sir," she said. "You had better be going, or your friends will leave without you."

Before he could answer, he saw such a beseeching glance on the face of the girl, that he hesitated, confused. Glancing at the mother, he saw the flash of wrath in her face. She rose and approached her daughter, with her hand lifted to strike her. The young woman stooped her head with a cry. He darted round the table to interpose between them. But the

mother had caught hold of her.
The handkerchief had fallen from
her neck and the youth saw five
blue bruises on her lovely throat –
the marks of the four fingers and
the thumb of a left hand. With a
cry of horror he darted from the
house, but as he reached the
door he turned. His hostess was
lying motionless on the floor,
and a huge grey wolf came
bounding after him.

There was no weapon at hand – and
if there had been, his inborn chivalry
would never have allowed him to harm
a woman even under the guise of a
wolf. Instinctively, he set himself
firm, leaning a little forward, with
half outstretched arms and hands
curved ready to clutch again at the
throat upon which he had left those
pitiful marks. But as the creature
sprung she eluded his grasp, and just
as he expected to feel her fangs, he

150

found a woman weeping on his bosom, with her arms around his neck. The next instant, the grey wolf broke from him, and bounded howling up the cliff. Recovering himself as he best might, the youth followed, for it was the only way to the moor above, across which he must now make his way to find his companions.

All at once he heard the sound of crunching of bones — not as if a creature was eating them, but as if they were ground by the teeth of rage and disappointment. Looking up, he saw close above him the mouth of the little cavern in which he had taken refuge the day before. Summoning all his resolution, he passed it slowly and softly. From within came the sounds of a mingled moaning and growling.

Having reached the top, he ran at full speed for some distance across the moor before venturing to look behind him. When at length he did so, he saw, against the sky, the girl standing on the edge of the cliff, wringing her hands. One solitary wail crossed the space between. She made no attempt to follow him and he reached the opposite shore in safety.

The Mark
of the Beast

Rudyard Kipling

MY FRIEND STRICKLAND of the police, who knows as much of natives of India as is good for any man, can bear witness to the facts of the case.

Dumoise, our doctor, also saw what Strickland and I saw. The conclusions that he drew from the evidence were entirely incorrect.

When Fleete came to India he owned a little money and some land in the Himalayas, near a place called Dharmsala. Both properties had been left to him by an uncle and he came out to finance them. He was a big, heavy, genial and inoffensive man. His knowledge of natives was, of course, limited and he complained of the difficulties of the language.

He rode in from his place in the hills to spend New Year in the station, and he stayed with Strickland. On New Year's

Eve there was a big dinner at the club, and the night was excusably riotous – when men gather from the uttermost ends of the empire, they have a right to be. The frontier had sent down a contingent of pioneers who were used to riding fifteen miles to dinner at the next Fort at the risk of a Khyberee bullet where their drinks should lie. They profited by their new security, for they tried to play pool with a curled-up hedgehog found in the garden, and one of them carried the marker round the room in his teeth.

Half a dozen planters had come in from the south and were talking 'horse' to the Biggest Liar in Asia, who was trying to cap all their stories at once. Everybody was there, and there was a general closing up of ranks and taking stock of our losses in dead or disabled that had fallen during the past year. It was a very wet night, and I remember that we sang 'Auld Lang Syne' with our feet in the polo championship cup, and our heads among the stars, and swore that we were all dear friends.

Fleete began the night with sherry and bitters, drank champagne steadily up to dessert, then raw, rasping Capri with all the strength of whisky, took Benedictine with his coffee, four or five whiskies and sodas to improve his pool strokes, beer and bones at half-past two, winding up with old brandy. Consequently, when he came out, at half-past three in the morning, into fourteen degrees of frost, he was very angry with his horse for coughing and tried to leapfrog into the saddle. The horse broke away and went to his stables, so Strickland and I formed a Guard of Dishonour to take Fleete home.

Our road lay through the bazaar, close to a little temple of Hanuman, the Monkey God, who is a leading divinity worthy of respect. All gods have good points, just as have all priests. Personally, I attach much importance to Hanuman and am kind to his people – the great grey apes of the hills. One never knows when one may want a friend.

There was a light in the temple and as we passed we could hear voices of men chanting hymns. In a native temple, the priests rise at all hours of the night to do honour to their god. Before we could stop him, Fleete dashed up the steps, patted two priests on the back, and was gravely grinding the ashes of his cigar butt into the forehead of the stone image of Hanuman. Strickland tried to drag him out, but he sat down and said solemnly,

"Shee that? Mark of the beasht! I made it. Ishn't it fine?"

In half a minute the temple was alive and noisy, and Strickland, who knew what came of polluting gods, said that things might occur. He, by virtue of his official position, long residence in the country, and going among the natives, was known to the priests and he felt unhappy.

Then, without any warning, a Silver Man came out of a recess behind the image of the god. He was perfectly naked in that bitter, bitter cold, and his body shone like frosted silver, for he was what the Bible calls 'a leper as white as snow.' Also he had no real face, because he was a leper of some years and his disease was heavy upon him. We two stooped to haul Fleete up, and the temple was filling and filling with folk who seemed to spring from the earth. Suddenly, the Silver Man ran in under our arms, making a noise exactly like the mewing of an otter, caught Fleete round the body

155

and dropped his head on Fleete's breast before we could wrench him away. Then he retired to a corner and sat mewing while the crowd blocked all the doors.

The priests were very angry until the Silver Man touched Fleete. That nuzzling seemed to sober them.

At the end of a few minutes silence one of the priests came to Strickland and said, in perfect English, "Take your friend away. He has done with Hanuman, but Hanuman has not done with him." The crowd gave way and we carried Fleete into the road.

Strickland was very angry. He said that all three of us might have been knifed, and that Fleete should thank his stars that he had escaped without injury.

Fleete thanked no one. He said that he wanted to go to bed. He was gorgeously drunk.

We moved on, Strickland silent and wrathful, until Fleete was taken with violent shivering fits and sweating. He said that the smells of the bazaar were overpowering and he wondered why slaughter houses were permitted so near English residences. "Can't you smell the blood?" said Fleete.

We put him to bed at last, just as the dawn was breaking, and Strickland invited me to have another whisky and soda. While we were drinking he talked of the trouble in the temple and admitted that it baffled him completely.

"They should have mauled us," he said, "instead of mewing at us. I wonder what they meant. I don't like it one little bit."

I said that the Managing Committee of the temple would in all probability bring a criminal action against us for insulting their religion. There was a section of the Indian Penal Code, which exactly met Fleete's offence. Strickland said he only hoped and prayed that they would do this. Before I left I looked into Fleete's room, and saw him lying on his right side scratching his left breast. Then at seven o'clock in the morning I went to bed cold and unhappy.

At one o'clock I rode over to Strickland's house to inquire after Fleete's head. I imagined that it would be a sore one. Fleete was breakfasting and seemed unwell. His temper was gone, for he was abusing the cook for not supplying him with an underdone chop. A man who can eat raw meat after a heavy night is a curiosity. I told Fleete this and he laughed.

"You breed queer mosquitoes in these parts," he said. "I've been bitten to pieces, but only in one place."

"Let's have a look at the bite," said Strickland. "It may have gone down since this morning."

While the chops were being cooked, Fleete opened his shirt and showed us, just over his left breast, a mark, the

perfect double of the black rosettes – the five or six
irregular blotches arranged in a circle – on a leopard's hide.
Strickland looked and said, "It was only pink this morning.
It's grown black now."

Fleete ran to a glass.

"By Jove!" he said, "this is nasty. What is it?"

We could not answer. Here the chops came in, all red
and juicy, and Fleete bolted three in a most offensive
manner. He ate on his right grinders only and threw his head
over his right shoulder as he snapped the meat. When he had
finished, it struck him that he had been behaving strangely,
for he said apologetically, "I don't think I ever felt so hungry
in my life. I've bolted like an ostrich."

After breakfast Strickland said to me, "Don't go. Stay
here, and stay for the night."

Seeing that my house was not three miles from
Strickland's, this request was absurd. But Strickland insisted,
and was going to say something when Fleete interrupted by
declaring in a shamefaced way that he felt hungry again.
Strickland sent a man to my house to fetch over my bedding
and a horse, and we three went down to Strickland's stables
to pass the hours until it was time to go out for a ride. The
man who has a weakness for horses never wearies of
inspecting them.

There were five horses in the stables, and I shall never forget the scene as we tried to look them over. They seemed to have gone mad. They reared and screamed and nearly tore up their pickets. They sweated, shivered and lathered, distraught with fear. Strickland's horses used to know him as well as his dogs, which made the matter more curious. We left the stable for fear of the brutes throwing themselves in their panic. Then Strickland turned back and called me. The horses were still frightened, but they let us 'gentle' and make much of them, and put their heads in our bosoms.

"They aren't afraid of us," said Strickland. "D'you know, I'd give three months pay if Outrage here could talk."

But Outrage was dumb, and could only cuddle up to his master and blow out his nostrils, as is the custom of horses when they wish to explain things but can't. Fleete came up when we were in the stalls, and as soon as the horses saw him, their fright broke out afresh. It was all that we could do to escape from the place unkicked. Strickland said, "They don't seem to love you, Fleete."

"Nonsense," said Fleete, "My mare will follow me like a dog." He went to her, but as he slipped the bars she plunged, knocked him down and broke away into the garden. I laughed, but Strickland was not amused. He took his moustache in both fists and pulled at it till it nearly came out. Fleete, instead of going off to chase his property, yawned, saying he was sleepy. He went to the house to lie down, which was a foolish way of spending New Year's Day.

Strickland sat with me in the stables and asked if I had noticed anything peculiar in Fleete's manner. I said that he ate his food like a beast, but that this might have been the result of living alone, in the hills, out of the reach of society as refined and elevating as ours for instance. Strickland was not amused. I do not think that he listened to me, for his next sentence referred to the mark on Fleete's breast. I said that it might have been caused by blister flies, or that it was possibly a birthmark newly born and now visible for the first time. We both agreed that it was unpleasant to look at and Strickland found occasion to say that I was a fool.

"I can't tell you what I think now," said he, "because you would call me a madman, but you must stay with me for the next few days, if you can. I want you to watch Fleete, but don't tell me what you think until I have made up my mind."

"But I am dining out tonight," I said.

"So am I," said Strickland, "and so is Fleete. At least if he doesn't change his mind."

We walked about the garden smoking, but saying nothing – because we were friends, and talking spoils good tobacco – till our pipes were out. Then we went to wake up Fleete. He was wide awake and fidgeting about his room.

"I want some more chops," he said. "Can I get them?"

We laughed and said, "Go and change. The ponies will be round in a minute."

"All right," said Fleete. "I'll go when I get the chops – underdone ones, mind."

He seemed to be quite in earnest. It was four o'clock, and we had had breakfast at one – still, for a long time, he demanded those underdone chops. Then he changed into riding clothes and went out into the verandah. His pony would not let him come near. All three horses were unmanageable – mad with fear – and finally Fleete said that he would stay at home and get something to eat. Strickland and I rode out wondering. As we passed the temple of Hanuman, the Silver Man came out and mewed at us.

"He is not one of the regular priests of the temple," said Strickland. "I think I should peculiarly like to lay my hands on him."

There was no spring in our gallop on the racecourse that evening. The horses were stale and moved as though they had been ridden out.

"The fright after breakfast has been too much for them," said Strickland.

That was the only remark he made through the remainder of the ride. Once or twice I think he swore to himself, but that did not count.

We came back in the dark at seven o'clock and saw that there were no lights in the bungalow. "Careless ruffians my servants are!" said Strickland.

My horse reared at something on the carriage drive and Fleete stood up under its nose.

"Why are you grovelling about the garden?" said Strickland.

But both horses bolted and nearly threw us. We dismounted by the stables and returned to Fleete, who was on his hands and knees under the orange bushes.

"What the devil's wrong with you?" said Strickland.

"Nothing, nothing in the world," said Fleete, speaking very quickly and thickly. "I've been gardening, botanising you know. The smell of the earth is delightful. I think I'm going for a walk – a long walk – all night."

I saw that there was something excessively out of order somewhere, and said to Strickland, "I am not dining out."

"Bless you!" said Strickland. "Here, Fleete, get up. You'll catch fever there. Come in to dinner and let's have the lamps lit. We will all dine at home."

Fleete stood up unwillingly, and said, "No lamps. No lamps. It's much nicer here. Let's dine outside and have some more chops –lots of 'em and underdone – bloody ones with gristle."

Now a December evening in Northern India is bitterly cold and Fleete's suggestion was that of a maniac.

"Come in," said Strickland sternly. "Come in at once."

Fleete came, and when the lamps were brought, we saw that he was literally plastered with dirt from head to foot. He must have been rolling in the garden. He shrank from the light and went to his room. His eyes were horrible to look at. There was a green light behind them, not in them, if you understand, and the man's lower lip hung down.

Strickland said, "There is going to be trouble, big

trouble, tonight. Don't you change your riding-things."

We waited for Fleete's reappearance, ordering dinner in the meantime. We could hear him moving about his own room, but there was no light there. Presently from the room came the long drawn howl of a wolf.

People write and talk lightly of blood running cold and hair standing up, and things of that kind. Both sensations are too horrible to be trifled with. My heart stopped as though a knife had been driven through it, and Strickland turned as white as the tablecloth.

The howl was repeated and was answered by another howl far across the fields.

That set the gilded roof on the horror. Strickland dashed into Fleete's room. I followed and we saw Fleete climbing out of the window. He made beast noises his throat. He could not answer when we shouted at him. He spat.

I don't quite remember what followed, but I think that Strickland must have stunned him with the long boot-jack or else I should never have been able to sit on his chest. Fleete could not speak, he could only snarl, and his snarls were those of a wolf, not of a man. The human spirit must have been giving way all day and have died out with the twilight. We were dealing with a beast that had once been Fleete.

The affair was beyond any human and rational

experience. I tried to say "Hydrophobia," but the word wouldn't come, because I knew that I was lying.

We bound this beast with leather thongs, and tied its thumbs and big toes together. We gagged it with a shoe-horn, which makes a very efficient gag if you know how to arrange it. Then we carried it into the dining-room, and sent a man to Dumoise, the doctor, telling him to come over at once. After we had despatched the messenger and were drawing breath, Strickland said, "It's no good. This isn't any doctor's work." I knew he spoke the truth.

The beast's head was free and it threw it about from side to side. Any one entering the room would have believed that we were curing a wolf's pelt.

Strickland sat with his chin in the heel of his fist, watching the beast as it wriggled on the ground, but saying nothing at all.

In the silence we heard something mewing like a she-otter. We both rose to our feet, and, I answer for myself, not Strickland, felt sick – actually and physically sick.

Dumoise arrived, and I never saw a little man so unprofessionally shocked. He said that it was a heart-rending case of hydrophobia, and that nothing could be done. At least any palliative measures would only prolong the agony. The beast was foaming at the mouth. Fleete, as we told

Dumoise, had been bitten by dogs once or twice. Any man who keeps half a dozen terriers must expect a nip now and again. Dumoise could offer no help. He could only certify that Fleete was dying of hydrophobia. The beast was then howling, for it had managed to spit out the shoe horn. Dumoise said that he would be ready to certify to the cause of death and that the end was certain.

So Dumoise left, deeply agitated. As soon as the noise of the cartwheels had died away, Strickland told me, in a whisper, his suspicions. They were so wildly improbable that he dared not say them aloud, and I – who entertained all Strickland's beliefs – was so ashamed of owning to them that I pretended to disbelieve.

"Even if the Silver Man had bewitched Fleete for polluting the image of Hanuman, the punishment could not have fallen so quickly."

As I was whispering this the cry outside the house rose again. The beast fell into a fresh paroxysm of struggling till we were afraid that the thongs that held it would give way.

"Watch!" said Strickland. "If this happens six times I shall take the law into my own hands. I order you to help me."

He went into his room and came out a few minutes later with the barrels of an old shotgun, a piece of fishing line, some thick cord and his heavy wooden bedstead. I reported that the convulsions had followed the cry by two seconds in each case and the beast seemed perceptibly weaker.

Strickland muttered, "But he can't take away the life! He can't take away the life!"

I said, though I knew that I was arguing against myself, "It may be a cat. It must be a cat. If the Silver Man is responsible, why does he dare to come here?"

Strickland arranged the wood on the hearth, put the gun barrels into the glow of the fire, spread the twine on the table and broke a walking stick in two. There was one yard of fishing line, gut, lapped with wire, such as is used for mahseer-fishing, and he tied the two ends together in a loop.

Then he said, "How can we catch him? He must be taken alive and unhurt."

I said that we must trust in Providence, and go out softly with polo sticks into the shrubbery at the front of the house. The man or animal that made the cry was evidently moving round the house as regularly as a night watchman. We could wait in the bushes till he came by and knock him over.

Strickland accepted this suggestion, and we slipped out from a bathroom window into the front verandah and then across the carriage drive into the bushes.

In the moonlight we could see the leper coming round the corner of the house. He was perfectly naked, and from

time to time he mewed and stopped to dance with his
shadow. I put away all my doubts and resolved to help
Strickland from the heated gun barrels to the loop of
twine – from the loins to the head and back again – with all
tortures that might be needful.

The leper halted in the front porch for a moment and we
jumped out on him with the sticks. He was wonderfully
strong, and we were afraid that he might escape or be fatally
injured before we caught him. We had an idea that lepers
were frail creatures, but this proved to be incorrect.

Strickland knocked his legs from under him and I put my
foot on his neck. He mewed hideously, and even through my
riding-boots I could feel that his flesh was not the flesh of a
clean man.

He struck at us with his hand and feet stumps. We looped
the lash of a dog whip round him, under the armpits, and
dragged him backwards into the hall and so into the dining
room where the beast lay. There we tied him with trunk
straps. He made no attempt to escape, but mewed.

When we confronted him with the beast the scene was
beyond description. The beast doubled backwards into a
bow, as though he had been poisoned with strychnine, and
moaned in the most pitiable fashion. Several other things
happened also, but they cannot be put down here.

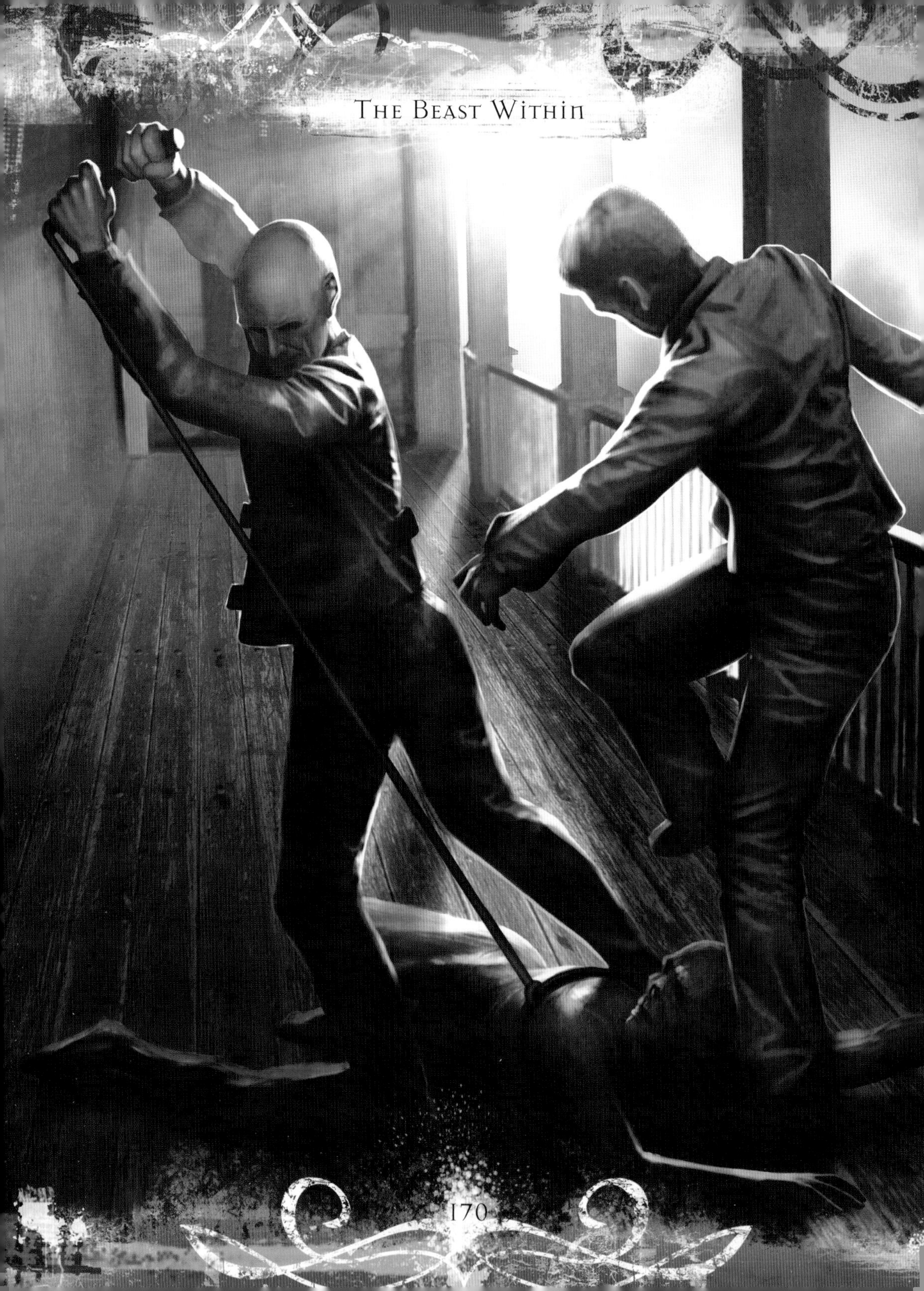

"I think I was right," said Strickland. "Now we will ask him to cure this case."

But the leper only mewed. Strickland wrapped a towel round his hand and took the gun barrels out of the fire. I put the half of the broken walking stick through the loop of fishing line and buckled the leper comfortably to Strickland's bedstead. I understood then how men and women and little children can endure to see a witch burnt alive. The beast was moaning on the floor, and though the Silver Man had no real face, you could see horrible feelings passing through the slab that took its place, exactly as waves of heat play across red-hot iron – gun barrels for instance.

Strickland shaded his eyes with his hands for a moment and we got to work. This part is not to be printed.

The dawn was beginning to break when the leper spoke. His mewings had not been satisfactory up to that point. The beast had fainted from exhaustion and the house was very still. We unstrapped the leper and told him to take away the evil spirit. He crawled to the beast and laid his hand upon the left breast. That was all. Then he fell face down and whined, drawing in his breath as he did so.

We watched the face of the beast and saw the soul of Fleete coming back into the eyes. Then a sweat broke out on the forehead and the eyes – the human eyes – closed. We waited for an hour, but Fleete still slept. We carried him to his room and bade the leper go, giving him the bedstead, and the sheet on the bedstead to cover his nakedness, the gloves and the towels with which we had touched him, and the whip that had been hooked round his body. He put the sheet about him and went out into the early morning without speaking or mewing.

Strickland wiped his face and sat down. A night gong, far away in the city, made seven o'clock.

"Exactly four-and-twenty hours!" said Strickland. "And I've done enough to ensure my dismissal from the service, besides permanent quarters in a lunatic asylum. Do you believe that we are awake?"

The red-hot gun barrel had fallen on the floor and was singeing the carpet. The smell was entirely real.

That morning at eleven we two together went to wake up Fleete. He was very drowsy and tired, but as soon as he saw us, he said, "Oh! Confound you fellows. Happy New Year to you. Never mix your liquors. I'm nearly dead."

"Thanks for your kindness, but you're over time," said Strickland. "Today is the morning of the second. You've slept the clock round with a vengeance."

The door opened and Dumoise put his head in. He had come on foot and fancied that we were laying out Fleete.

"I've brought a nurse," said Dumoise. "I suppose that she can come in for... what is necessary."

"By all means," said Fleete cheerily, sitting up in bed. "Bring on your nurses."

Dumoise was dumb. Strickland led him out and explained that there must have been a mistake in the diagnosis. Dumoise remained dumb and left the house hastily. Strickland went out too. When he came back, he said that he had been to call on the Temple of Hanuman to offer redress for the pollution of the god, and had been solemnly assured that no white man had ever touched the idol and that he was an incarnation of all the virtues labouring under a delusion.

One other curious thing happened which frightened me as much as anything in all the night's work. When Fleete was dressed he came into the dining room and sniffed. He had a quaint trick of moving his nose when he sniffed. "Horrid doggy smell, here," said he. "You should really keep those terriers of yours in better order. Try sulphur, Strick."

But Strickland did not answer. He caught hold of the back of a chair, and, without warning, went into an amazing fit of hysterics. It is terrible to see a strong man overtaken with hysteria. Then it struck me that we had fought for Fleete's soul with the Silver Man in that room, and had disgraced ourselves as Englishmen forever. I laughed and gasped and gurgled just as shamefully as Strickland, while Fleete thought that we had both gone mad. We never told him what we had done.

Some years later, when Strickland had married and was a church-going member of society for his wife's sake, we reviewed the incident dispassionately, and Strickland suggested that I should put it before the public.

I cannot myself see that this step is likely to clear up the mystery. In the first place, no one will believe a rather unpleasant story, and, in the second, it is well-known to every right-minded man that the gods of the heathen are stone and brass, and any attempt to deal with them otherwise is justly condemned.

THE WHITE WOLF OF HARTZ MOUNTAIN

Frederick Marryat

This is an extract from an 1839 novel called The Phantom ship.
*In this passage, a man tells the story of his tragic childhood.
The children use the term 'mother-in-law' for their father's new
wife — this is an old term for a stepmother.*

MY FATHER had been married for about five years.
From his marriage he had three children – my
eldest brother Caesar, myself (Hermann), and my
sister, Marcella. My oldest recollections are knit to a
comfortable cottage, in which I lived with my father,
brother and sister. It was on the confines of one of those vast
forests that cover the northern part of Germany. Around it
were a few acres of ground, which my father cultivated
during the summer months, and which, though they yielded

a doubtful harvest, were sufficient for our support. In the winter we remained much in doors, for, as my father followed the chase, we were left alone, and the wolves, during that season, incessantly prowled about. I can call to mind the whole landscape now – the tall pines, which rose up on the mountain above us, and the wide expanse of forest beneath. We looked down from our cottage on the topmost boughs and heads of trees, as the mountain below us rapidly descended into the distant valley. In summertime the prospect was beautiful, but during the severe winter, a more desolate scene could not well be imagined.

I mentioned that, in the winter, my father occupied himself with the chase. Every day he left us, and often he would lock the door, so that we did not leave the cottage. You may suppose we were sadly neglected – indeed, we suffered much, for my father, fearful that we might come to some harm, would not allow us fuel, when he left the cottage. We were obliged, therefore, to creep under the heaps of bearskins to keep ourselves as warm as we could until he returned in the evening, when a blazing fire was our delight. Such was our peculiar and savage sort of life until my brother Caesar was nine, myself seven, and my sister five, years old, when circumstances occurred on which is based the extraordinary narrative I am about to relate.

One evening my father returned home later than usual. He had been unsuccessful, and as the weather was very severe, and many feet of snow were upon the ground, he was not only very cold, but in a very bad humour. He had brought in wood, and all three of us were gladly assisting each other in blowing on the embers to create the blaze, when he caught poor little Marcella by the arm and threw her aside. The child fell, struck her mouth and bled very much. A cheerful blaze was soon the result of his exertions, but we did not, as usual, crowd round it. Marcella, still bleeding, retired to a corner, and my brother and I took our seats beside her, while my father hung over the fire gloomily and alone.

Such had been our position for about half an hour, when the howl of a wolf, close under the window of the cottage, fell on our ears. My father started up and seized his gun. The howl was repeated. He examined the priming and then hastily left the cottage, shutting the door after him. We all waited (anxiously listening), for we thought that if he succeeded in shooting the wolf, he would return in a better humour – and although he was harsh to all of us, and particularly so to our little sister, still we loved our father, and loved to see him cheerful and happy, for who else had we to look up to? We waited for some time, but the report

of the gun did not reach us
and my elder brother then
said, "Our father has followed
the wolf and will not be back
for some time. Marcella, let us
wash the blood from your
mouth, and then we will go to the
fire and warm ourselves."

"We have had no supper," said I,
for my father usually cooked the meat
as soon as he came home – during
his absence we had nothing but the
fragments of the preceding day.

"And if our father comes
home after his hunt, Caesar," said
Marcella, "he will be pleased to
have some supper – let us cook
it for him and for ourselves."
Caesar climbed upon the stool
and got down some meat – I
forget now whether it was venison
or bear's meat, but we cut off the
usual quantity, and proceeded to
dress it, as we used to do under our

father's supervision.

Perhaps I had better now relate, what was only known to me many years afterwards. When my father had left the cottage, he perceived a large white wolf about thirty yards from him. As soon as the animal saw my father, it retreated slowly, growling and snarling. My father followed – the animal did not run, but always kept at some distance. My father did not like to fire until he was pretty certain that his ball would take effect. They went on for some time, the wolf now leaving my father far behind, and then stopping and snarling defiantly, and then again, on his approach, setting off at speed.

Anxious to shoot the animal (for the white wolf is very rare), my father continued the pursuit for several hours, during which he continually ascended the mountain. You must know that there are peculiar spots on those mountains which are supposed, and, as my story will prove, truly supposed, to be inhabited by the evil influences – they are well-known to the huntsmen, who invariably avoid them. Now, one of these spots, an open space in the pine forests above us, had been pointed out to my father as dangerous on that account. But, whether he disbelieved these wild stories, or whether, in his eager pursuit of the chase, he disregarded them, I know not. However, it is certain that he was decoyed by the white wolf to this open space, when the animal appeared to slacken her speed. My father approached, came close up to her, raised his gun to his shoulder, and was about to fire when the wolf suddenly disappeared. He thought that the snow on the ground must have dazzled his sight and he let down his gun to look for the beast – but she was gone. How she escaped over the clearance without his seeing her, was beyond his comprehension. Mortified at the ill success of his chase, he was about to retrace his steps, when he heard the distant sound of a horn. Astonishment at such a sound – at such an hour – in such a wilderness, made him forget for the moment his disappointment, and he remained riveted to the spot. In a minute the horn was blown a second time and at no great distance. My father stood still and listened. A third time it was blown. I forget the term used to express it, but it was the signal which, my father well knew, implied that the party was lost in the woods. In a few minutes more my father beheld a man on horseback, with a female seated on the crupper, enter the cleared space, and ride up to him. At first, my father called to mind the strange stories which he had heard of the supernatural beings who were said to frequent these mountains, but the nearer approach of the parties satisfied him that they were mortals like himself. As soon as they came up to him, the man who guided the horse accosted him.

"Friend Hunter, you are out late, the better fortune for us. We have ridden far and are in fear of our lives, which are eagerly sought after. These mountains have enabled us to elude our pursuers, but if we do not find shelter and refreshment, that will avail us little, as we must perish from hunger and the inclemency of the night. My daughter, who rides behind me, is now more dead than alive – say, can you assist us in our difficulty?"

"My cottage is some few miles distant," replied my father, "but I have little to offer you besides a shelter from the weather – to the little I have you are welcome."

In about an hour and a half, during which my father walked at a rapid pace, the party arrived at the cottage, and, as I said before, came in.

THE BEAST WITHIN

"We are in good time, apparently," observed the dark hunter, catching the smell of the roasted meat, as he walked to the fire and surveyed my brother and sister, and myself. "You have young cooks here, Sir."

"I am glad that we shall not have to wait," replied my father. "Come, mistress, seat yourself by the fire – you require warmth after your cold ride."

The woman must be particularly described. She was young, and apparently twenty years of age. She was dressed in a travelling dress, deeply bordered with white fur, and wore a cap of white ermine on her head.

Her features were very beautiful, at least I thought so, and so my father has since declared. Her hair was flaxen, glossy, shiny, and as bright as a mirror. Her mouth – although somewhat large when it was open – showed the most brilliant teeth I have ever beheld. But there was something about her eyes, bright as they were, which made us children afraid. They were so restless, so furtive. I could not at that time tell why, but I felt as if there was cruelty in her eye and when she beckoned us to come to her, we approached her with fear and trembling. My father, having put the horse into a close shed, soon returned and supper was placed upon the table. When it was over, my father requested that the young lady would take possession of his bed and he would remain at the fire and sit up with her father. After some hesitation on her part this arrangement was agreed to, and I and my brother crept into the other bed with Marcella, for we had as yet always slept together.

When we awoke the next morning, we found that the hunter's daughter had risen before us. I thought she looked more beautiful than ever. She came up to little Marcella and caressed her – the child burst into tears and sobbed as if her heart would break.

But, not to detain you with too long a story, the huntsman and his daughter were accommodated in the cottage. My father and he went out hunting daily, leaving Christina with us. She performed all the household duties, was very kind to us children, and gradually the dislike even of little Marcella wore away. But a great change took place in my father. He appeared to have conquered his aversion to the opposite sex and was most attentive to Christina. Often, after her father and we were in bed, he would sit up with her, conversing in a low tone by the fire. I ought to have mentioned, that my father and the huntsman Wilfred, slept in another portion of the cottage, and that the bed which he formerly occupied, and which was in the same room as ours, had been given up to the use of Christina. These visitors had been about three weeks at the cottage, when, one night, after we children had been sent to bed, a consultation was held. My father had asked for Christina's hand in marriage, and had obtained both her own consent and that of her father.

Such was the second marriage of my father. The next morning, the hunter Wilfred rode away on his horse.

My father resumed his bed, which was in the same room as ours, and things went on much as before the marriage, except that our new mother-in-law did not show any kindness towards us. Indeed, during my father's absence, she would often beat us, particularly little Marcella, and her eyes would flash fire, as she looked eagerly upon the fair and lovely child.

One night, my sister woke me and my brother.

"What is the matter?" said Caesar.

"She has gone out," whispered Marcella.

"Gone out?"

"Yes, gone out at the door, in her nightclothes," replied the child. "I saw her get out of bed, look at my father to see if he slept, and then she went out at the door."

What could induce her to leave her bed, and all undressed to go out, in such bitter wintry weather, with the snow deep on the ground, was to us incomprehensible. We lay awake, and in about an hour we heard the growl of a wolf, close under the window.

"There is a wolf," said Caesar, "she will be torn to pieces."

"Oh, no!" cried Marcella.

In a few minutes afterwards our mother-in-law appeared – she was in her night-dress, as Marcella had stated. She let down the latch of the door, so as to make no noise, went to a pail of water, and washed her face and hands, and then slipped into the bed where my father lay.

We all three trembled, we hardly knew why, but we resolved to watch the next night. We did so – and not only on the ensuing night, but on many others. And always at about the same hour, would our mother-in-law rise from her bed, and leave the cottage – and after she was gone, we invariably heard the growl of a wolf under our window, and always saw her, on her return, wash herself before she retired to bed. We observed, also, that she seldom sat down to meals, and that when she did, she appeared to eat with dislike, but when the meat was taken down to be prepared for dinner, she would often furtively put a raw piece into her mouth.

My brother Caesar was a courageous boy – he did not like to speak to my father until he knew more. He resolved that he would follow her out and ascertain what she did. Marcella and I endeavoured to dissuade him from this project, but he would not be controlled. The very next night he lay down in his clothes, and as soon as our mother-in-law had left the cottage, he jumped up, took down my father's gun, and followed her.

You may imagine in what a state of suspense Marcella and I remained, during his absence. After a few minutes, we heard the report of a gun. It did not awaken my father and we lay trembling with anxiety. In a minute afterwards we saw our mother-in-law enter the cottage – her dress was bloody. I put my hand to Marcella's mouth to prevent her crying out, although I was myself in great alarm. Our

mother-in-law approached my
father's bed, looked to see if he was
asleep, and then went to the chimney
and blew up the embers into a blaze.

"Who is is?" said my father, waking up.

"Lie still, dearest," replied my mother-in-
law, "it is only me. I have lighted the fire to warm
some water – I am not quite well."

My father turned round and was soon asleep, but we
watched our mother-in-law. She changed her linen, and
threw the garments she had worn into the fire. We then
perceived that her right leg was bleeding profusely, as if
from a gunshot wound. She bandaged it up, and then
dressing herself, remained before the fire until daybreak.

Poor little Marcella, her heart beat quickly as she pressed me to her side – so indeed did mine. Where was our brother, Caesar? How did my mother-in-law receive the wound unless from his gun? At last my father rose, and then, for the first time I spoke, saying, "Father, where is my brother, Caesar?"

"Your brother!" exclaimed he, "Why, where can he be?"

"Merciful Heaven! I thought as I lay very restless last night," observed our mother-in-law, "that I heard somebody open the latch of the door – and, dear me, husband, what has become of your gun?"

My father cast his eyes up above the chimney and perceived that his gun was missing. For a moment he looked perplexed, then seizing a broad axe, he went out of the cottage without saying another word.

He did not remain away from us long. In a few minutes he returned, bearing in his arms the mangled body of my poor brother. He laid it down, and covered up his face.

My mother-in-law rose up, and looked at the body, while Marcella and I threw ourselves by its side wailing and sobbing bitterly.

"Go to bed again, children," said she sharply. "Husband," continued she, "your boy must have taken the gun down to shoot a wolf, and the animal has been too powerful for him.

Poor boy! He has paid dearly for his rashness."

That day my father went out and dug a grave, and when he laid the body in the earth, he piled up stones over it, so that the wolves should not be able to dig it up. The shock of this catastrophe was to my poor father very severe – for several days he never went to the chase, although at times he would utter bitter words of vengeance against the wolves.

But during this time of mourning on his part, my mother-in-law's nocturnal wanderings continued with the same regularity as before.

At last, my father took down his gun and went into the forest, but he soon returned and appeared very annoyed.

"Would you believe it, Christina, that the wolves – perdition to the whole race – have actually contrived to dig up the body of my poor boy, and now there is nothing left of him but his bones?"

"Indeed!" replied my mother-in-law. Marcella looked at me, and I saw in her eye all she would have uttered.

"A wolf growls under our window at night, father," said I.

"Aye, indeed? Why did you not tell me, boy? Wake me the next time you hear it."

I saw my mother-in-law turn away – her eyes flashed fire and she gnashed her teeth.

My father went out again, and covered up with a larger

pile of stones the little remnants of my poor brother which the wolves had spared. Such was the first act of the tragedy.

The spring now came on. The snow disappeared and we were permitted to leave the cottage – but never would I quit, for one moment, my dear little sister, to whom, since the death of my brother, I was more attached than ever. Indeed I was afraid to leave her alone with my mother-in-law, who appeared to have a particular pleasure in ill-treating the child. My father was now employed upon his little farm and I was able to render him some assistance.

Marcella used to sit by us while we were at work, leaving my mother-in-law alone in the cottage. I ought to observe that, as the spring advanced, so did my mother-in-law decrease her nocturnal rambles, and that we never heard the growl of the wolf under the window after I had spoken of it to my father.

One day, when my father and I were in the field, Marcella being with us, my mother-in-law came out, saying that she was going into the forest, to collect some herbs my father wanted, and that Marcella must go to the cottage and watch the dinner. Marcella went, and my mother-in-law soon disappeared in the forest, taking a direction quite contrary to that in which the cottage stood, and leaving my father and I, as it were, between her and Marcella.

About an hour afterwards we were startled by shrieks from the cottage, evidently the shrieks of little Marcella.

"Marcella has burnt herself, father," said I, throwing down my spade. My father threw down his, and we both hastened to the cottage. Before we could gain the door, out darted a large white wolf, which fled swiftly. My father had no weapon. He rushed into the cottage, and there saw poor little Marcella expiring – her body was dreadfully mangled, and the blood pouring from it had formed a large pool on the cottage floor. My father's first intention had been to seize his gun and pursue, but he was checked by this horrid spectacle – he knelt down by his dying child, and burst into tears. Marcella could just look kindly on us for a few seconds, and then her eyes were closed in death.

My father and I were still hanging over my poor sister's body, when my mother-in-law came in. At the dreadful sight she expressed much concern, but she did not appear to recoil from the sight of blood, as most women do.

"Poor child!" said she, "it must have been that great white wolf that passed me just now, and frightened me so – she's quite dead, Krantz."

"I know it – I know it!' cried my father in agony.

I thought my father would never recover from the effects of this second tragedy. He mourned bitterly over the body of his sweet child, and for several days would not consign it to its grave, although frequently requested by my mother-in-law to do so. At last he yielded, and dug a grave for her close by that of my poor brother, and he took every precaution that the wolves should not violate her remains.

I was now really miserable, as I lay alone in the bed that I had formerly shared with my brother and sister. I could not help thinking that my mother-in-law was implicated in both their deaths, although I could not account for the manner, but I no longer felt afraid of her. My little heart was full of hatred and revenge.

The night after my sister had been buried, as I lay awake, I perceived my mother-in-law get up and go out of the cottage. I waited some time, then dressed myself, and dared to look out through the door, which I half opened. The moon shone bright, and I could see the spot where my brother and my sister had been buried. To my horror, I perceived my mother-in-law busily removing the stones from Marcella's grave.

She was in her white nightdress and the moon shone full upon her. She was digging with her hands, and throwing away the

stones behind her with all the ferocity of a wild
beast. It was some time before I could collect my
senses and decide what to do. At last, I saw that
she had arrived at the body, and raised it up
to the side of the grave. I could bear no
more – I ran to wake my father.

"Father! Father" I cried, "Get up
and get your gun."

"What!" cried my father,
"The wolves are there,
are they?"

He jumped out of bed, threw on his clothes, and in his anxiety did not appear to perceive the absence of his wife. As soon as he was ready, I opened the door, he went out, and I followed him.

Imagine his horror, when (unprepared as he was for such a sight) he beheld, as he advanced towards the grave, not a wolf, but his wife, in her nightdress, on her hands and knees, crouching by the body of my sister, and tearing off large pieces of the flesh, devouring them with all the eagerness of a wolf. She was too busy to be aware of our approach. My father dropped his gun his hair stood on end – so did mine. He breathed heavily, and then his breath for a time stopped. I picked up the gun and put it into his hand. Suddenly he appeared as if concentrated rage had restored him to double vigour. He levelled his piece, fired, and with a loud shriek, down fell the wretch whom he had fostered in his bosom.

"God of Heaven!" cried my father, sinking down upon the earth in a swoon, as soon as he had discharged his gun.

I remained some time by his side before he recovered. "Where am I?" said he, "What has happened? – Oh! – Yes, Yes! I recollect now. Heaven forgive me!"

He rose and we walked up to the grave – what again was our astonishment and horror to find that instead of the dead body of my mother-in-law, as we expected, there was lying over the remains of my poor sister, a large, white she-wolf.

"The white wolf!" exclaimed my father, "the white wolf that decoyed me into the forest – I see it all now – I have dealt with the spirits of the Hartz Mountains."

NAMELESS HORROR

CROGLIN GRANGE

From Archdeacon Hare's Autobiography

"FISHER," SAID THE CAPTAIN, "may sound a very plebeian name, but this family is of ancient lineage, and for many hundreds of years they have possessed a very curious old place in Cumberland, which bears the weird name of Croglin Grange. The great characteristic of the house is that never has it been more than one storey high, but it has a terrace from which large grounds sweep away towards the church in the hollow, and a fine distant view.

"When, in lapse of years, the Fishers outgrew Croglin Grange in family and fortune, they were wise enough not to destroy the long-standing characteristic of the place by adding another storey to the house, but they went away to the south, to reside at Thorncombe near Guildford, and they let Croglin Grange.

"They were extremely fortunate in their tenants, two brothers and a sister. They heard their praises from all quarters. On their part the tenants were greatly delighted with their new residence. The arrangement of the house, which would have been a trial to many, was not so to them. In every respect Croglin Grange was exactly suited to them.

"The winter was spent most happily by the new inmates of Croglin Grange, who shared in all the little social pleasures of the district, and became very popular. In the following summer there was one day that was dreadfully, annihilatingly hot. The brothers lay under the trees with their books, for it was too hot for any active occupation. The sister sat in the verandah and worked, or tried to work, for in the heat work was next to impossible. They dined early, and after dinner they still sat on the verandah, enjoying the cool air that came with evening. They watched the sun set, and the moon rise over the belt of trees that separated the grounds from the churchyard, seeing it mount the heavens till the whole lawn was bathed in silver light, across which the long shadows from the shrubbery fell as if embossed, so vivid and distinct were they.

"When they separated for the night, all retiring to their rooms on the ground floor (for there was no upstairs in that house), the sister felt that the heat was still so great that she could not sleep, and having fastened her window, she did not close the shutters – in that very quiet place it was not necessary – and, propped against the pillows, she still watched the wonderful, marvellous beauty of that summer night. Gradually she became aware of two lights, which flickered in and out in the belt of trees that separated the lawn from the churchyard. As her gaze became fixed upon them, she saw them emerge, fixed in a dark substance, a definite ghastly something, which seemed every moment to become nearer, increasing in size and substance as it approached. Every now and then it was lost for a moment in the long shadows that stretched across the lawn from the trees, and then it emerged larger than ever, and still coming closer. As she watched it, the most uncontrollable horror seized her. She longed to get away, but the door was close to the window and the door was locked on the inside, and while she was unlocking it, she must be for an instant nearer to it. She longed to scream, but her voice seemed paralysed, her tongue glued to the roof of her mouth.

"Suddenly, she never could explain why afterwards, the terrible object seemed to turn to one side, seemed to be going round the house, not to be coming to her at all, and immediately she rushed to the door. But as she was unlocking it, she heard scratch, scratch, scratch upon the window, and saw a hideous brown face with flaming eyes glaring in at her. She rushed back to the bed, but the creature continued to scratch upon the window. She felt a sort of mental comfort in the knowledge that the window was securely fastened on the inside. Suddenly the scratching sound ceased and a kind of pecking sound took its place. Then, in her agony, she became aware that the creature was unpicking the lead! The noise continued and a diamond pane of glass fell into the room and shattered. Then a long bony finger of the creature came in and turned the handle of the window. The window opened and the creature came in. It came across the

room and her terror was so great that she could not scream. It came up to the bed, twisted its long, bony fingers into her hair, dragged her head over the side of the bed and bit her violently in the throat.

"As it bit her, her voice was released and she screamed with all her might and main. Her brothers rushed out of their rooms, but the door was locked on the inside. A moment was lost while they got a poker and broke it open. Then the creature had already escaped through the window, and the sister, bleeding violently from a wound in the throat, was lying unconscious over the side of the bed. One brother pursued the creature, which fled before him through the moonlight with gigantic strides, and eventually seemed to disappear over the wall into the churchyard. Then he rejoined his brother by the sister's bedside. She was dreadfully hurt, and her wound was a very definite one; but she was of strong disposition, not either given to romance or superstition, and when she came to herself she said, 'What has happened is most extraordinary and I am very much hurt. It seems inexplicable, but of course there is an explanation, and we must wait for it. It will turn out that a lunatic has escaped from some asylum and found his way here.' The wound healed and she appeared to get better, but the doctor who was sent for would not believe that she could bear so terrible a shock so easily, and insisted that she must have change, mental and physical – so her brothers took her to Switzerland.

"Being a sensible girl, when she went abroad she threw herself at once into the interests of the country she was in. She dried plants, she made sketches, she went up mountains, and, as autumn came on, she was the person who urged that they should return to Croglin Grange. 'We have taken it,' she said, 'for seven years, and we have only been there one. We shall always find it difficult to let a house that is only one storey high, so we had better return there – lunatics do not escape every day.' As she urged it, her brothers wished nothing better, and the family returned to Cumberland. With there being no upstairs to the house it was impossible to make any great change in their arrangements. The sister occupied the same room, but it is unnecessary to say she always closed her shutters, which, however, as in many old houses, always left one top pane of the window uncovered. The brothers moved and occupied a room together, exactly opposite that of their sister, and they always kept loaded pistols in their room.

"The winter passed most peacefully and happily. In the following March the sister was suddenly awakened by a sound she remembered only too well – scratch, scratch,

scratch upon the window. Looking up, she saw quite clearly in the topmost pane of the window the same hideous brown shrivelled face, with glaring eyes, looking in at her. This time she screamed as loud as she could. Her brothers rushed out of their room with pistols and out of the front door. The creature was already scudding away across the lawn. One of the brothers fired and hit it in the leg, but still with the other leg it continued to make way, scrambled over the wall into the churchyard and seemed to disappear into a vault belonging to a family long extinct.

"The next day the brothers summoned all the tenants of Croglin Grange and in their presence the vault was opened. A horrible scene revealed itself. The vault was full of coffins – they had been broken open, and their contents, horribly mangled and distorted, were scattered over the floor. One coffin alone remained intact. Of that the lid had been lifted, but still lay loose upon the coffin. They raised it, and there, brown, withered, shrivelled, mummified, but quite entire, was the same hideous figure that had looked in at the windows of Croglin Grange, with the marks of a recent pistol shot in the leg. They did the only thing that can kill a vampire – they burnt it.

THE OTHER SIDE: A BRETON LEGEND

Eric Stenbock

THERE WAS A FOREST and a village and a brook, the village was on one side of the brook – none had dared to cross to the other side. Where the village was, all was green, glad, fertile and fruitful. On the other side the trees never put forth green leaves, and a dark shadow hung over it even at midday, and at night time one could hear the wolves howling . There were werewolves, wolf-men and men-wolves, and those very wicked men who for nine days in every year are turned into wolves – but on the green side no wolf was ever seen, and only one little running brook like a silver streak flowed between.

It was spring now and the old crones sat no longer by the fire but before their cottages sunning themselves. But Gabriel wandered by the brook as he was accustomed to wander, drawn thither by some strange attraction mingled with intense horror.

His schoolfellows did not like Gabriel. They all laughed and jeered at him, because he was less cruel and more gentle of nature than the rest, and even as a rare and beautiful bird escaped from a cage is hacked to death by the common sparrows, so was Gabriel among his fellows. Everyone wondered how Mère Yvonne, that buxom and worthy matron, could have produced a son like this, with strange dreamy eyes, who was as they said '*pas comme les autres gamins* (not like other kids).' His only friends were the Abbé Félicien whose Mass he served each morning, and one little girl called Carmeille, who loved him – no one could make out why.

The sun had already set. Gabriel still wandered by the brook, filled with vague terror and irresistible fascination. The moon rose. It was a full moon, very large and very clear, and the moonlight flooded the forest both this side and 'the other side.' Just on the 'other side' of the brook, hanging over, Gabriel saw a large deep blue flower, whose strange intoxicating perfume reached him and fascinated him even where he stood.

'If I could only make one step across,' he thought, 'nothing could harm me if I only plucked that one flower. Nobody would know I had been over at all.' The villagers looked with hatred and suspicion on anyone who was said to have crossed to the 'other side,' so summing up courage he leapt lightly to the other side of the brook. Then the moon breaking from a cloud shone with unusual brilliance, and he saw, stretching before him, long reaches of the same strange blue flowers each one lovelier than the last. Unable to make up his mind which one flower to take or whether to take several, he went on and on, and the moon shone very brightly. A strange unseen bird, somewhat like a nightingale, but louder and lovelier, sang, and his heart was filled with longing for he knew not what, and the moon shone and the nightingale sang. But suddenly a black cloud covered the moon entirely and all was black. Through the darkness he heard wolves howling and shrieking, and there passed before him a horrible procession of wolves (black wolves with red fiery eyes). With them were men that had the heads of wolves and wolves that had the heads of men, and above them flew owls (black owls with red fiery eyes), and bats and long serpentine black things. Last of all, seated on an enormous black ram with a hideous human face, the wolf-keeper, on whose face was eternal shadow. They continued their horrific chase and passed him by, and when they had passed the moon shone out more beautifully than ever.

The strange nightingale sang
again, and the strange, intense
blue flowers were in long
reaches in front to the right
and to the left. But one thing
was there which had not been
before, among the deep blue
flowers walked one with long
gleaming golden hair. She
turned once round and her eyes
were of the same colour as the
strange blue flowers, and she walked on and Gabriel could
not choose but follow. But when a cloud passed over the
moon he saw no beautiful woman but a wolf, so in utter
terror he turned and fled, plucking one of the blue flowers
on the way, and leapt again over the brook and ran home.

When he got home Gabriel could not resist showing his
treasure to his mother, though he knew she would not
appreciate it. When she saw the strange blue flower, Mère
Yvonne turned pale and said, "Why child, where have you
been? Sure, it is the witch flower," and so saying she
snatched it from him and cast it into the corner.
Immediately all of its beauty and strange fragrance faded
from it and it appeared charred as though it had been burnt.

So Gabriel sat down silently and rather sulkily, and having eaten no supper went up to bed, but he did not sleep. He waited and waited till all was quiet within the house. Then he crept downstairs in his long white nightshirt and bare feet on the square cold stones and hurriedly picked up the charred and faded flower and put it in his warm bosom next to his heart. Immediately the flower bloomed again lovelier than ever, and he fell into a deep sleep, but through his sleep he seemed to hear a soft, low voice singing underneath his window in a strange language (in which the subtle sounds melted into one another), but he could distinguish no word except his own name.

Carmeille came to see him and begged him to go out with her into the fresh air. So they went out hand in hand, the dark-haired, gazelle-eyed boy, and the fair wavy-haired girl, and something, he knew not what, led his steps (half knowingly and yet not so, for he could not but walk thither) to the brook, and they sat down together on the bank.

Gabriel thought at least he might tell his secret to Carmeille, so he took out the flower from his bosom and said, "Look here, Carmeille, have you seen ever so lovely a flower as this?" Carmeille turned pale and faint and said, "Oh, Gabriel what is this flower? I touched it and I felt something strange come over me. No, no, I don't like its perfume, no there's something not quite right about it, oh, dear Gabriel, do let me throw it away." Before he had time to answer she cast it from her, and again all its beauty and fragrance went from it and it looked charred as though it had been burnt. But suddenly, where the flower had been thrown on this side of the brook, there appeared a wolf, which stood and looked at the children.

Carmeille said, "What shall we do," and clung to Gabriel, but the wolf looked at them very steadfastly and Gabriel recognized in the eyes of the wolf the strange deep intense blue eyes of the wolf-woman he had seen on the 'other side,' so he said, "Stay here, dear Carmeille, see she is looking gently at us and will not hurt us."

"But it is a wolf," said Carmeille, and quivered all over with fear, but again Gabriel said languidly, "She will not hurt us." Then Carmeille seized Gabriel's hand in an agony of terror and dragged him along with her till they reached the village, where she gave the alarm and all the lads of the village gathered together. They had never seen a wolf on this side of the brook, so they excited themselves greatly and arranged a grand wolf hunt for the morning, but Gabriel sat silently apart and said nothing.

That night Gabriel could not sleep at all nor could he bring himself to say his prayers. He sat in his little room by the window with his shirt open at the throat and the strange blue flower at his heart, and again this night he heard a voice singing beneath his window in the same soft, subtle, liquid language as before –

Ma zála liral va jé Cwamûlo zhajéla je Cárma urádi el javé Jàrma, symai, – carmé – Zhála javály thra je al vú al vlaûle va azré Safralje vairálje va já? Cárma seràja Lâja lâja Luzhà!

And as he looked he could see the silver shadows slide on the glimmering light of golden hair, and the strange eyes gleaming dark blue through the night. It seemed to him that he could not but follow, so he walked half clad and barefoot as he was, with eyes fixed as in a dream, silently down the stairs and out into the night.

And again she turned to look on him with her strange blue eyes full of tenderness, passion and sadness beyond the sadness of things human – and as he foreknew his steps led him to the brink of the brook. Then she, taking his hand, said, "Won't you help me over Gabriel?"

Then it seemed to him as though he had known her all his life – so he went with her to the 'other side' but he saw no one next to him. Looking again beside him there were two wolves. In a frenzy of terror, he (who had never thought to kill any living thing before) seized a log of wood lying by and smote one of the wolves on the head.

Immediately he saw the wolf-woman again at his side with blood streaming from her forehead, staining her wonderful golden hair, and with eyes looking at him with infinite reproach, she said, "Who did this?"

Then she whispered a few words to the other wolf, which leapt over the brook and made its way towards the village, and turning again towards him she said, "Oh Gabriel, how could you strike me, who would have loved you for so long and so well." Then it seemed to him again as though he had known her forever, but he felt dazed and said nothing.

She gathered a dark green, strangely shaped leaf and holding it to her forehead, she said, "Gabriel, kiss the place, all will be well again." So he kissed as she told him. He felt the salt taste of blood in his mouth and then he knew no more.

Again he saw the wolf-keeper with his horrible troupe around him, but this time not engaged in the chase but sitting in a circle and the black owls sat in the trees and the black bats hung downwards from the branches. Gabriel stood alone in the middle with a hundred wicked eyes fixed on him. They seemed to deliberate about what should be done with him, speaking in that same strange tongue that he had heard in the songs beneath his window. Suddenly he felt a hand pressing in his and saw the mysterious wolf-woman by his side. Then began what seemed a kind of incantation where human or half-human creatures seemed to howl, and beasts to speak with human speech but in the unknown tongue. The wolf-keeper, whose face was ever veiled in shadow, spoke some words in a voice that seemed to come from far away, but all he could distinguish was his own name Gabriel, and her name, Lilith. Then suddenly he felt arms surrounding him.

Gabriel awoke – in his own room – so it was a dream after all – but what a dreadful dream. Yes, but was it really his own room?

And surely this was not the light of dawn – it was like sunset! He leapt from his small white bed, and a vague terror came over him, he trembled and had to hold on to the chair before he reached the window. No, the solemn spires of the grey church were not to be seen – he was in the depths of the forest, but in a part he had never seen before. Surely he had explored every part, it must be the 'other side'. He dressed himself almost mechanically and walked downstairs, the same stairs it seemed to him down which he would normally run and spring. The broad square stones seemed singularly beautiful, with many strange colours – how was it he had never noticed this before? He was gradually losing the power of wondering – he entered the room below – where the coffee and bread rolls were on the table.

"Why Gabriel, how late you are today" The voice was very sweet but the intonation strange – and there sat Lilith, the mysterious wolf-woman, her glittering gold hair tied in a loose knot. An embroidery whereon she was tracing strange serpentine patterns, lay over the lap of her maize coloured garment. She looked at Gabriel steadfastly with her wonderful dark blue eyes and said, "Why, Gabriel, you are late today" and Gabriel answered, "I was tired yesterday, give me some coffee."

A dream within a dream — yes, he had known her all his life, and they dwelt together — had they not always done so? And she would take him through the glades of the forest and gather flowers for him, such as he had never seen before, and tell him stories, which seemed to be accompanied by the faint vibration of strings, looking at him fixedly with her marvellous blue eyes.

One day in their wanderings he saw a strange, dark blue flower like the eyes of Lilith, and a sudden half remembrance flashed through his mind.

"What is this blue flower?" he said, and Lilith shuddered and said nothing, but as they went a little further there was a brook — the brook he thought, and he prepared to spring over it.

Lilith seized him by the arm and held him back with all her strength, and trembling all over she said, "Promise me Gabriel that you will not cross over."

But he said, "Tell me what is this blue flower and why you will not tell me?"

And she said, "Look at the brook Gabriel." And he looked and saw that though it was just like the brook of separation it was not the same, the waters did not flow.

As Gabriel looked steadfastly into the still waters it seemed to him as though he saw voices — some impression

of the Vespers for the Dead. Yes they were praying for him –
but who were they? He heard again the voice of Lilith in
whispered anguish, "Come away!"

Then he said, this time in monotone, "What is this blue
flower, and what is its use?"

And the low thrilling voice answered, "It is called *lûli
uzhûri*, two drops pressed upon the face of the sleeper and
he will sleep."

He was like a child in her hand and allowed himself to be
led away. He listlessly plucked one of the blue flowers,
holding it downwards in his hand. What did she mean?
Would the sleeper wake? Would the blue flower leave any
stain? Could that stain be wiped off?

But as he lay asleep at early dawn he heard voices from
afar off praying for him – the Abbé Félicien, Carmeille, his
mother too, then some familiar words struck his ear – mass
was being said for the repose of his soul, he knew this. No,
he could not stay, he would leap over the brook, he knew
the way – he had forgotten that the brook did not flow. Ah,
but Lilith would know – what should he do? The blue flower
– there it lay close by his bedside. He crept silently to where
Lilith lay asleep, her hair glistening gold, shining like round
about her. He pressed two drops on her forehead, she sighed
once, and a shade of anguish passed over her beautiful face.

He fled – terror, remorse, and hope tearing his soul and making fleet his feet. He came to the brook – he did not see that the water did not flow – of course, it was the brook for separation. One bound and he would be with humans again. He leapt over but a change had come over him – what was it? He could not tell – did he walk on all fours? Yes, surely. He looked into the brook, whose still waters were fixed as a mirror, and there, in horror, he beheld himself – or was it himself? His head and face, yes, but his body transformed to that of a wolf. Even as he looked he heard a sound of

hideous mocking laughter behind him. He turned round —
there, in a gleam of red lurid light, he saw one whose body
was human, but whose head was that of a wolf, with eyes of
infinite malice. While this hideous being laughed with a loud
human laugh, he could only utter the howl of a wolf.

But we will transfer our thoughts from the alien things
on the 'other side' to the village where Gabriel used to live.
Mère Yvonne was not surprised when Gabriel did not turn
up to breakfast — he often did not, so absent-minded was he.
This time she said, "I suppose he has gone with the others to
the wolf hunt." Not that Gabriel was given to hunting, but,
as she said, "there was no knowing what he might do next."

The wolf hunt was so far a success in that they did
actually see a wolf, but not a success, as they did not kill it
before it leapt over the brook to the 'other side', where of
course they were afraid to pursue it. No emotion is more
inrooted and intense in the minds of common people than
hatred and fear of anything 'strange'.

Days passed by but Gabriel was nowhere to be seen —
and Mère Yvonne began to realize how deeply she loved her
only son, who was so unlike her that she had thought herself
an object of pity to other mothers — the goose and the
swan's egg. People searched and pretended to search, they
even went to the length of dragging the pond, which the

boys thought very amusing, as it enabled them to kill a great number of water rats, and Carmeille sat in a corner and cried all day. At last, as Gabriel was not there, they supposed he must be dead. So it was agreed that an empty bier should be put up in the church with candles round it. Carmeille sat in the corner of the little side chapel and cried and cried. The Abbé Félicien made the boys sing the Vespers for the Dead (this did not amuse them so much as dragging the pond), and the following morning, in the silence of dawn, said the Dirge and the Requiem – and this Gabriel heard.

Then the Abbé Félicien received a message to bring the Holy Viaticum to a sick villager. So they set forth in solemn procession with torches along the brook of separation.

Trying to speak, Gabriel could only utter the howl of a wolf – the most fearful of all bestial sounds. He howled and howled again – perhaps Lilith would hear him? Perhaps she could rescue him? Then he remembered the blue flower – the beginning and end of all his woe. His cries aroused all the denizens of the forest – the wolves, the wolf-men, and the men-wolves. He fled in terror – behind him, seated on the black ram with human face, was the wolf-keeper, whose face was veiled in eternal shadow. Only once he turned to look behind – for among the shrieks and howls of bestial chase he heard a voice moan with pain. And there he saw

Lilith. Her body too was that of a wolf, almost hidden by her golden hair. On her forehead was a stain of blue, alike in colour to her eyes, now veiled with tears she could not cry.

The way of the Most Holy Viaticum lay along the brook of separation. They heard the fearful howlings afar off, the torch bearers turned pale and trembled – but the Abbé Félicien said, "They cannot harm us."

Suddenly the whole chase came in sight. Gabriel sprang over the brook, the Abbé Félicien held the most Blessed Sacrament before him, and his shape was restored to him. Then the wolf-keeper held up in his hands the shape of something horrible and inconceivable – a monstrance to the Sacrament of Hell, and three times he raised it, in mockery of the blessed rite of Benediction. On the third time, streams of fire came from his fingers, and all the 'other side' of the forest began to burn, and great darkness was over all.

The 'other side' is harmless now, just charred ashes, but none dares to cross but Gabriel alone – for once a year for nine days a strange madness comes over him.

THE ROOM IN THE TOWER

E F Benson

IT IS PROBABLE that everybody who is at all a constant dreamer has had at least one experience of an event or a sequence of circumstances, which have come to his mind in sleep, being subsequently realized in the material world. But, in my opinion, so far from this being a strange thing, it would be far odder if this fulfilment did not occasionally happen, since our dreams are, as a rule, concerned with people whom we know and places with which we are familiar, such as might very naturally occur in the awake and daylit world. True, these dreams are often broken into by some absurd and fantastic incident, which puts them out of court in regard to their subsequent fulfilment, but on the mere calculation of chances, it does not appear in the least unlikely that a dream imagined by anyone who dreams constantly should occasionally come true. Not long ago, for instance, I experienced such a fulfilment of a dream that seems to me in no way remarkable and to have no kind of psychic significance. The manner of it was as follows.

A certain friend of mine, living abroad, is amiable enough to write to me about once in a fortnight. Thus, when fourteen days or thereabouts have elapsed since I last heard from him, my mind, probably, either consciously or subconsciously, is expectant of a letter from him. One night last week I dreamt that as I was going upstairs to dress for dinner I heard, as I often heard, the sound of the postman's knock on my front door, and diverted my direction downstairs instead. There, among other correspondence, was a letter from him. Thereafter the fantastic entered, for on opening it I found inside the ace of diamonds, and scribbled across it in his well-known handwriting, 'I am sending you this for safe custody, as you know it is running an unreasonable risk to keep aces in Italy.' The next evening I was just preparing to go upstairs to dress when I heard the postman's knock, and did precisely as I had done in my dream. There, among other letters, was one from my friend. Only it did not contain the ace of diamonds. Had it done so, I should have attached more weight to the matter, which, as it stands, seems to me a perfectly ordinary coincidence. No doubt I consciously or subconsciously expected a letter from him, and this suggested to me my dream. Similarly, the fact that my friend had not written to me for a fortnight suggested to him that he should do so. But occasionally it is not so easy to find such an explanation, and for the following story I can find no explanation at all.

All my life I have been a habitual dreamer. It is rare when I do not find on awaking in the morning that some mental experience has been mine, and sometimes a series of the most dazzling adventures befall me. Almost without exception these adventures are pleasant, though often merely trivial. It is of an exception that I am going to speak.

It was when I was about sixteen that a certain dream first came to me, and this is how it befell. It opened with my being set down at the door of a big red-brick house, where, I understood, I was going to stay. The servant who opened the door told me that tea was being served in the garden, and led me through a low dark-panelled hall, with a large open fireplace, on to a cheerful green lawn set round with flowerbeds. There were grouped about the tea table a small party of people, but they were all strangers to me except one, who was a schoolfellow called Jack Stone. He was clearly the son of the house, and he introduced me to his

mother and father and a couple of
sisters. I was, I remember, somewhat
astonished to find myself here, for
the boy in question was scarcely
known to me, and I rather disliked
what I knew of him; moreover, he
had left school nearly a year before.
The afternoon was very hot, and
an intolerable oppression reigned.
On the far side of the lawn ran a
red-brick wall, with an iron gate
in its centre, outside which stood
a walnut tree. We sat in the
shadow of the house opposite a
row of long windows, inside
which I could see a table with
cloth laid, glimmering with
glass and silver. This garden
front of the house was very
long, and at one end of it
stood a tower of three stories,
which looked to me much
older than the rest of the
building.

Before long, Mrs Stone, who, like the rest of the party, had sat in absolute silence, said to me, "Jack will show you your room. I have given you the room in the tower."

Quite inexplicably my heart sank at her words. I felt as if I had known that I should have the room in the tower, and that it contained something dreadful and significant. Jack instantly got up and I understood that I had to follow him. In silence we passed through the hall, and mounted a great oak staircase with many corners. We arrived at a small landing with two doors set in it. He pushed one of these open for me to enter, and without coming in himself, closed it after me. Then I knew that my conjecture had been right – there was something awful in the room, and with the terror of nightmare growing and enveloping me, I awoke in a spasm of terror.

Now that dream or variations on it occurred to me intermittently for fifteen years. Most often it came in exactly this form, the arrival, the tea laid out on the lawn, the deadly silence succeeded by that one deadly sentence, the mounting with Jack Stone up to the room in the tower where horror dwelt, and it always came to a close in the nightmare of terror at that which was in the room, though I never saw what it was. At other times I experienced variations on this same theme. Occasionally, for instance, we

would be sitting at dinner in the dining room, into the
windows of which I had looked on the first night when the
dream of this house visited me, but wherever we were, there
was the same silence, the same sense of dreadful oppression
and foreboding. And the silence I knew would always be
broken by Mrs Stone saying to me, "Jack will show you your
room. I have given you the room in the tower." Upon which
(this was invariable) I had to follow him up the oak staircase
with many corners, and enter the place that I dreaded more
and more each time that I visited it in sleep. Or, again, I
would find myself playing cards still in silence in a drawing
room lit with immense chandeliers, that gave a blinding
illumination. What the game was I have no idea. What I
remember, with a sense of miserable anticipation, was that
soon Mrs Stone would get up and say to me, "Jack will show
you your room. I have given you the room in the tower."
This drawing room where we played cards was next to the
dining room, and, as I have said, was always brilliantly
illuminated, whereas the rest of the house was full of dusk
and shadows. And yet, how often, in spite of those bouquets
of lights, have I not pored over the cards that were dealt me,
scarcely able for some reason to see them. Their designs,
too, were strange. There were no red suits, but all were
black, and among them there were certain cards that were

black all over. I hated and dreaded those.

As this dream continued to recur, I got to know the greater part of the house. There was a smoking room beyond the drawing room, at the end of a passage with a green baize door. It was always very dark there, and as often as I went there I passed somebody whom I could not see in the doorway coming out. Curious developments, too, took place in the characters that peopled the dream, as might happen to living persons. Mrs Stone, for instance, who, when I first saw her, had been black-haired, became grey, and instead of rising briskly, as she had done at first, she got up very feebly, as if the strength was leaving her limbs. Jack also grew up, and became a rather ill-looking young man, with a brown moustache, while one of the sisters ceased to appear, and I understood she was married.

Then it so happened that I was not visited by this dream for six months or more, and I began to hope, in such inexplicable dread did I hold it, that it had passed away for good. But one night after this interval I again found myself being shown out onto the lawn for tea, and Mrs Stone was not there, while the others were all dressed in black. At once I guessed the reason, and my heart leaped at the thought that perhaps this time I should not have to sleep in the room in the tower, and though we usually all sat in silence, on this occasion the sense of relief made me talk and laugh as I had never yet done. But even then matters were not altogether comfortable, for no one else spoke, but they all looked secretly at each other. And soon the foolish stream of my talk ran dry, and gradually an apprehension worse than anything I had previously known gained on me as the light slowly faded.

Suddenly a voice that I knew well broke the stillness, the voice of Mrs Stone, saying, "Jack will show you your room: I have given you the room in the tower." It seemed to come from near the gate in the red-brick wall that bounded the lawn, and looking up, I saw that the

grass outside was sown thick with gravestones. A curious greyish light shone from them, and I could read the lettering on the grave nearest me, and it was, 'In evil memory of Julia Stone'. And as usual Jack got up, and again I followed him through the hall and up the staircase with many corners. On this occasion it was darker than usual, and when I passed into the room in the tower I could only just see the furniture, the position of which was already familiar to me. Also there was a dreadful odour of decay in the room, and I woke screaming.

The dream, with such variations and developments as I have mentioned, went on at intervals for fifteen years. Sometimes I would dream it two or three nights in succession. Once, as I have said, there was an intermission of about six months, but taking a reasonable average, I should say that I dreamt it quite as often as once in a month. It had, as is plain, something of nightmare about it, since it always ended in the same appalling terror, which, seemed to gather fresh fear every time that I experienced it. There was, too, a strange and dreadful consistency about it. The characters in it, as I have mentioned, got regularly older, death and marriage visited this silent family, and I never in the dream, after Mrs Stone had died, set eyes on her again. But it was always her voice that told me that the room in the tower was prepared for me, and whether we had tea out on the lawn, or the scene was laid in one of the rooms overlooking it, I could always see her gravestone standing just outside the iron gate. It was the same, too, with the married daughter – usually she was not present, but once or twice she returned again, in company with a man, whom I took to be her husband. He, too, like the rest of them, was always silent. But, owing to the constant repetition of the

IN EVIL MEMORY OF JULIA STONE

dream, I had ceased to attach, in my waking hours, any significance to it. I never met Jack Stone again during all those years, nor did I ever see a house that resembled this dark house of my dream. And then something happened.

I had been in London in this year, up till the end of the July, and during the first week in August went down to stay with a friend in a house he had taken for the summer months, in the Ashdown Forest district of Sussex. I left London early, for John Clinton was to meet me at Forest Row Station. We were going to spend the day golfing and go to his house in the evening. He had his motor with him, and we set off, about five of the afternoon, after a thoroughly delightful day, for the drive, the distance being some ten miles. As it was still so early we did not have tea at the club house, but waited till we should get home. As we drove, the weather, which up till then had been, though hot, deliciously fresh, seemed to me to alter in quality, and become very stagnant and oppressive, and I felt that indefinable sense of ominous apprehension that I am accustomed to before thunder. John, however, did not share my views, attributing my loss of lightness to the fact that I had lost both my matches. Events proved, however, that I was right, though I do not think that the thunderstorm that broke that night was the sole cause of my depression.

Our way lay through deep high-banked lanes, and before we had gone very far I fell asleep, and was only awakened by the stopping of the motor. And with a sudden thrill, partly of fear but chiefly of curiosity, I found myself standing in the doorway of the house in my dream. We went, I half wondering whether or not I was dreaming still, through a low oak-panelled hall, and out onto the lawn, where tea was laid in the shadow of the house. It was set in flower beds, a red-brick wall, with a gate in it, bounded one side, and out beyond that was a space of rough grass with a walnut tree. The facade of the house was very long, and at one end stood a three-storied tower, markedly older than the rest.

Here, for the moment, all resemblance to the repeated dream ceased. There was no silent and somehow terrible family, but a large assembly of cheerful persons, all of whom were known to me. And in spite of the horror with which the dream itself had always filled me, I felt nothing of it now that the scene of it was thus reproduced before me. But I felt intense curiosity as to what was going to happen.

Tea pursued its cheerful course and before long Mrs Clinton got up. And at that moment I think I knew what she was going to say. She spoke to me, and what she said was,

"Jack will show you your room. I have given you the room in the tower."

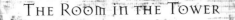
At that, for half a second, the horror of the dream took
hold of me again. But it quickly passed, and again I felt
nothing more than the most intense curiosity. It was not
very long before it was amply satisfied.

John turned to me.

"Right up at the top of the house," he said, "but I think
you'll be comfortable. We're absolutely full up. Would you
like to go and see it now? By Jove, I believe that you are
right, and that we are going to have a thunderstorm. How
dark it has become."

I got up and followed him. We passed through the hall
and up the perfectly familiar staircase. Then he opened the
door and I went in. At that moment unreasoning terror
again possessed me. I did not know what I feared – I simply
feared. Then like a sudden recollection, when one
remembers a name that has long escaped the memory, I
knew what I feared. I feared Mrs Stone, whose grave with
the sinister inscription 'In evil memory' I had so often seen
in my dream, just beyond the lawn that lay below my
window. And then once more the fear passed so completely
that I wondered what there was to fear, and I found myself,
sober and quiet and sane, in the room in the tower, the
name of which I had so often heard in my dream, and the
scene of which was so familiar.

I looked around it with a certain sense of proprietorship, and found that nothing had been changed from the dream I knew so well. Just to the left of the door was the bed, lengthways along the wall, with the head of it in the angle. In line with it was the fireplace and a small bookcase. Opposite the door the outer wall was pierced by two lattice-paned windows, between which stood the dressing table, while ranged along the fourth wall was the washing-stand and a big cupboard.

My luggage had already been unpacked, for the furniture of dressing and undressing lay orderly on the wash stand and toilet table, while my dinner clothes were spread out on the coverlet of the bed. And then, with a sudden start of unexplained dismay, I saw that there were two rather conspicuous objects that I had not seen before in my dreams – one a life-sized oil painting of Mrs Stone, the other a black-and-white sketch of Jack Stone, representing him as he had appeared to me only a week before in the last of the series of these repeated dreams, a rather secret and evil-looking man of about thirty. His picture hung between the windows, looking straight across the room to the other portrait, which hung beside the bed. As I looked at the portrait of Mrs Stone I felt the stifling horror of nightmare seize me.

It represented Mrs Stone as I had seen her last in my dreams – old, withered and white-haired. But in spite of the evident feebleness of body, a dreadful exuberance and vitality shone through the envelope of flesh, an exuberance wholly malign, a vitality that foamed and frothed with unimaginable evil. Evil beamed from the narrow, leering eyes – it laughed in the demon-like mouth. The whole face was instinct with some secret and appalling mirth – the hands, clasped together on the knee, seemed to be shaking with suppressed and nameless glee. Then I saw also that it was signed in the left-hand bottom corner, and wondering who the artist could be, I looked more closely, and read the inscription, 'Julia Stone by Julia Stone.'

There came a tap at the door and John Clinton entered.

"Got everything you want?" he asked.

"Rather more than I want," said I, pointing to the picture. He laughed.

"Hard-featured old lady," he said. "By herself, too, I remember. Anyhow she can't have flattered herself much."

"But don't you see?" said I. "It's scarcely a human face at all. It's the face of some witch, of some devil."

He looked at it more closely.

"Yes – it isn't very pleasant," he said. "Scarcely a bedside manner, eh? Yes – I can imagine getting a nightmare if I went to sleep with that close by my bed. I'll have it taken down if you like."

"I really wish you would," I said. He rang the bell, and with the help of a servant we detached the picture and carried it out onto the landing, and put it with its face to the wall.

"By Jove, the old lady is a weight," said John, mopping his forehead. "I wonder if she had something on her mind."

The extraordinary weight of the picture had struck me too. I was about to reply, when I caught sight of my own hand. There was blood on it, in considerable quantities, covering the whole palm.

"I've cut myself somehow," said I.

John gave a little startled exclamation.

"Why, I have too," he said.

Simultaneously the footman took out his handkerchief and wiped his hand with it. I saw that there was blood also on his handkerchief.

John and I went back into the tower room and washed the blood off, but neither on his hand nor on mine was there the slightest trace of a scratch or cut. It seemed to me that, having ascertained this, we both, by a sort of tacit consent, did not allude to it again. Something in my case had dimly occurred to me that I did not wish to think about. It was but a conjecture, but I fancied that I knew the same thing had occurred to him.

The heat and oppression of the air, for the storm we had expected was still undischarged, increased very much after dinner, and for some time most of the party, among whom were John Clinton and myself, sat outside on the path bounding the lawn, where we had had tea. The night was absolutely dark, and no twinkle of star or moon ray could penetrate the pall of cloud that overset the sky. By degrees our assembly thinned, the women went up to bed, men dispersed to the smoking or billiard room, and by eleven o'clock my host and I were the only two left. All the evening I thought that he had something on his mind and as soon as we were alone he spoke.

"The man who helped us with the picture had blood on his hand, too, did you notice?" he said.

"I asked him just now if he had cut himself, and he said he supposed he had, but that he could find no mark of it. Now where did that blood come from?"

I had succeeded in not thinking about it and I did not want, especially at bedtime, to be reminded of it.

"I don't know," I said, "and I don't really care so long as the picture of Mrs Stone is not by my bed."

He got up. "But it's odd," he said. "Ha! Now you'll see another odd thing."

A dog of his, an Irish terrier by breed, had come out of the house as we talked. The door behind us into the hall was open, and a bright oblong of light shone across the lawn to the iron gate which led on to the rough grass outside, where the walnut tree stood. I saw that the dog had all his hackles up, bristling with rage and fright; his lips were curled back from his teeth, as if he was ready to spring at something, and he was growling to himself. He took not the slightest notice of his master or me, but stiffly and tensely walked across the grass to the iron gate. There he stood, looking through the bars and still growling. Then all of a sudden his courage seemed to desert him. He gave a howl, and scuttled back to the house with a curious crouching sort of movement.

"He does that half-a-dozen times a day." said John. "He sees something that he both hates and fears."

I walked to the gate and looked over it. Something was moving on the grass outside, and soon a sound that I could not instantly identify came to my ears. Then I remembered what it was — the purring of a cat. I lit a match, and saw a big blue Persian, walking round in a little circle just outside the gate, stepping high and ecstatically, with tail carried aloft like a banner. Its eyes were bright and shining, and every now and then it put its head down and sniffed at the grass.

I laughed.

"The end of that mystery, I am afraid." I said. "Here's a large cat having Walpurgis Night all alone."

"Yes, that's Darius," said John. "He spends half the day and all night there. But that's not the end of the dog mystery, for Toby and he are the best of friends, but the beginning of the cat mystery. What's the cat doing there? And why is Darius pleased, while Toby is terror-stricken?"

At that moment I remembered the horrible detail of my dreams when I saw through the gate, just where the cat was now, the tombstone with the sinister inscription. But before I could answer the rain began, as suddenly and heavily as if a tap had been turned on. The big cat squeezed through the bars of the gate, and came leaping across the lawn to the house for shelter. Then it sat in the doorway, looking out eagerly into the dark. It spat and struck at John with its paw, as he pushed it in, in order to close the door.

Somehow, with the portrait of Julia Stone in the passage outside, the room in the tower had absolutely no alarm for me, and as I went to bed I had nothing more than interest for the curious incident about our bleeding hands, and the conduct of the cat and dog. The last thing I looked at before I put out my light was the square empty space by my bed where the portrait had been. Here the paper was of its original full tint – over the rest of the walls it had faded. Then I blew out my candle and instantly fell asleep.

My awaking was equally instantaneous. I sat bolt upright in bed under the impression that some bright light had been flashed in my face, though it was now absolutely pitch black. I knew exactly where I was, in the room which I had dreaded in dreams, but no horror that I ever felt when asleep approached the fear that now invaded and froze my brain. Immediately after a peal of thunder crackled just above the house, but the probability that it was only a flash of lightning that awoke me gave no reassurance to my galloping heart. Something I knew was in the room with me, and instinctively I put out my right hand, which was nearest the wall, to keep it away. And my hand touched the

edge of a picture frame hanging close to me.

I sprang out of bed, upsetting the small table that stood by it, and I heard my watch, candle and matches clatter onto the floor. But for the moment there was no need of light, for a blinding flash leaped out of the clouds, and showed me that by my bed again hung the picture of Mrs Stone. And instantly the room went into darkness again. But in that flash I saw another thing also, namely a figure that leaned over the end of my bed, watching me. It was dressed in some close-clinging white garment, spotted and stained with mould, and the face was that of the portrait.

Overhead the thunder cracked and roared, and when it ceased and the deathly stillness succeeded, I heard the rustle of movement coming nearer me, and perceived an odour of corruption and decay. And then a hand was laid on the side of my neck, and close beside my ear I heard quick-taken, eager breathing. Yet I knew that this thing, though it could be perceived by touch, by smell, by eye and by ear, was still not of this earth, but something that had passed out of the body and had power to make itself manifest. Then a voice, already familiar to me, spoke.

"I knew you would come to the room in the tower," it said. "I have long been waiting for you. At last you have come. Tonight I shall feast – soon we will feast together."

And the quick breathing came closer to me; I could feel it on my neck.

At that the terror, which I think had paralyzed me for the moment, gave way to the wild instinct of self-preservation. I hit wildly with both arms, kicking out at the same moment, and heard a little animal-squeal, and something soft dropped with a thud beside me. I took a couple of steps forward, nearly tripping up over whatever it was that lay there, and by the merest good luck found the handle of the door. In another second I ran out on the landing and had banged the door behind me. Almost at the same moment I heard a door open somewhere below, and John Clinton, candle in hand, came running upstairs.

"What is it?" he said. "I sleep just below you and heard a noise as if – Good heavens, there's blood on your shoulder."

I stood there, so he told me afterwards, swaying from side to side, white as a sheet, with the mark on my shoulder as if a hand covered with blood had been laid there.

"It's in there," I said, pointing. "She, you know. The portrait is in there, too, hanging in the same place we removed it from."

At that he laughed.

"My dear fellow, this is mere nightmare," he said.

He pushed by me, and opened the door, I standing there inert with terror, unable to stop him, unable to move.

"Phew! What an awful smell," he said.

Then there was silence – he had passed out of my sight behind the open door. Next moment he came out again, as white as myself, and instantly shut it.

"Yes, the portrait's there," he said, "and on the floor is a thing – a thing spotted with earth, like what they bury people in. Come away, quick, come away."

How I got downstairs I hardly know. An awful shuddering and nausea of the spirit rather than of the flesh had seized me, and more than once he had to place my feet upon the steps, while every now and then he cast glances of terror and apprehension up the stairs. But in time we came to his dressing room on the floor below, and there I told him what I have here described.

The sequel can be made short. Indeed, some of my readers have perhaps already guessed what it was, if they remember that inexplicable affair of the churchyard at West Fawley, some eight years ago, where an attempt was made three times to bury the body of a certain woman who had committed suicide. On each occasion the coffin was found in the course of a few days, protruding from the ground. After the third attempt, in order that the thing should not be talked about, the body was buried elsewhere in unconsecrated ground. It was buried just outside the iron gate of the garden belonging to the house where this woman had lived. She had committed suicide in a room at the top of the tower in that house. Her name was Julia Stone.

Subsequently the body was again secretly dug up and the coffin was found to be full of blood.

THE HOUND

H P Lovecraft

IN MY TORTURED ears there sounds unceasingly a
nightmare whirring and flapping, and a faint distant
baying as of some gigantic hound. It is not dream – it is
not, I fear, even madness – for too much has already
happened to give me these merciful doubts.

St John is a mangled corpse – I alone know why. Such is
my knowledge that I am about to blow out my brains for
fear I shall be mangled in the same way. May heaven forgive
the folly that led us both to such a monstrous fate! Wearied
with a world where even the joys of romance and adventure
soon grow stale, St John and I had followed every
intellectual movement, but each new mood was drained too
soon of its diverting novelty and appeal.

Only the sombre philosophy of the decadents could help

us. It was this frightful emotional need which led us to that detestable course that even in my present fear I mention with shame and timidity – that hideous extremity of human outrage, the practice of grave-robbing.

I cannot reveal the details of our shocking expeditions, or catalogue even partly the worst of the trophies adorning the nameless museum we prepared in the great stone house where we jointly dwelt. Our museum was a blasphemous, unthinkable place, where we had assembled a universe of terror and decay. It was a secret room far underground, where winged demons carved from basalt and onyx vomited weird green and orange light from grinning mouths.

Around the walls of this repellent chamber were cases of antique mummies alternating with lifelike bodies perfectly stuffed and cured by the taxidermist's art, and with headstones snatched from the oldest churchyards of the world. Niches here and there contained skulls of all shapes, and heads preserved in various stages of dissolution. There one might find the rotting, bald pates of famous noblemen, and the fresh and golden heads of new-buried children.

There were statues and paintings, all of fiendish subjects – some executed by St John and myself. A locked portfolio, bound in tanned human skin, held certain unknown and unnameable drawings, whilst in a multitude of inlaid ebony cabinets reposed the most incredible and unimaginable variety of tomb-loot ever assembled by human madness and perversity. It is of this loot in particular that I must not speak – thank God I had the courage to destroy it long before I thought of destroying myself!

By what malign fatality were we lured to that terrible Holland churchyard? I think it was the dark rumour of one buried for five centuries, who had himself been a ghoul in his time and had stolen a potent thing from a mighty sepulchre. I can recall the scene in these final moments – the pale autumnal moon over the graves, casting long horrible shadows, the grotesque trees, the vast legions of strangely colossal bats that flew against the moon, the antique ivied church pointing a huge spectral finger at the sky – and, worst of all, the faint deep-toned baying of some gigantic hound which we could neither see nor definitely place. As we heard this suggestion of baying we shuddered as he whom we sought had centuries before been found in this self same spot, torn and mangled by the claws and teeth of some unspeakable beast.

I remember how we delved in the ghoul's grave with our spades, and how we thrilled at the picture of ourselves, the grave, the pale watching moon, the horrible shadows and the strange, half-heard directionless baying of whose objective existence we could scarcely be sure.

Then we struck a substance harder than the damp mould, and beheld a rotting oblong box crusted with mineral deposits from the long undisturbed ground. It was incredibly tough and thick. We finally pried it open and feasted our eyes on what it held.

Amazingly, much was left of the object despite the lapse of five hundred years. The skeleton, though crushed in places by the jaws of the thing that had killed it, held together with surprising firmness, and we gloated over the clean white skull, its long, firm teeth and its eyeless sockets. In the coffin lay an amulet of curious and exotic design, which had been worn around the sleeper's neck. It was the figure of a crouching winged hound, or sphinx with a semi-canine face, and was exquisitely carved in antique Oriental fashion from a small piece of green jade.

Immediately upon beholding this amulet we knew that we must possess it. Even had its outlines been unfamiliar we would have desired it, but as we looked more closely we saw that it was not wholly unfamiliar. Alien it indeed was to all art and literature that sane and balanced readers know, but we recognized it as the thing hinted of in the forbidden Necronomicon of the mad Arab Abdul Alhazred – the ghastly soul-symbol of the corpse-eating cult of inaccessible Leng, in Central Asia. Seizing the green jade object, we gave a last glance at the bleached and cavern-eyed face of its owner and closed up the grave as we found it. As we hastened from the spot, the stolen amulet in

St John's pocket, we thought we saw the bats descend in a body to the earth we had so lately rifled, as if seeking for some cursed and unholy nourishment. But the autumn moon shone weak and pale, and we could not be sure.

So, too, as we sailed the next day away from Holland to our home, we thought we heard the faint distant baying of some gigantic hound in the background. But the autumn wind moaned sad and wan, and we could not be sure.

Less than a week after our return to England, strange things began to happen. We lived as recluses, devoid of friends, alone and without servants in a few rooms of an old manor house on a bleak and unfrequented moor. Our doors were seldom disturbed by the knock of the visitor.

Now, however, we were troubled by what seemed to be a frequent fumbling in the night, not only around the doors but around the windows also, upper as well as lower. Once we fancied that a large, opaque body darkened the library window when the moon was shining against it, and another time we thought we heard a whirring or flapping sound not far off. The jade amulet now reposed in a niche in our museum and sometimes we burned a scented candle before it. We read much in Alhazred's Necronomicon about its properties, and about the relation of ghosts' souls to the objects it symbolized, and were disturbed by what we read.

Then terror came.

On the night of September 24, 19 – , I heard a knock at my chamber door. Fancying it St John's, I bade the knocker enter, but was answered only by a shrill laugh. There was no one in the corridor. When I aroused St John from his sleep, he professed entire ignorance of the event and became as worried as I. It was the night that the faint, distant baying over the moor became to us a certain and dreaded reality.

Four days later, whilst we were both in the hidden museum, there came a low, cautious scratching at the single door which led to the secret library staircase. Our alarm was now divided, for, besides our fear of the unknown, we had always entertained a dread that our grisly collection might be discovered. Extinguishing all lights, we proceeded to the door and threw it suddenly open. We felt an unaccountable rush of air and heard, as if receding far away, a queer combination of rustling, tittering and articulate chatter. Whether we were mad, dreaming or in our senses, we did not try to determine. We only realized, with the blackest of apprehensions, that the apparently disembodied chatter was in the Dutch language.

After that we lived in growing horror and fascination. Mostly we believed we were going mad from our life of unnatural excitements, but sometimes it pleased us more to dramatize ourselves as the victims of some creeping and appalling doom. Every night that demoniac baying rolled over the windswept moor, always louder and louder. On October 29 we found in the soft earth underneath the library window a series of footprints utterly impossible to describe. They were as baffling as the hordes of great bats that haunted the old manor house in unprecedented and increasing numbers.

The horror reached a culmination on November 18, when St John, walking home after dark, was seized by some frightful carnivorous thing and torn to ribbons. His screams had reached the house, and I had hastened to the terrible scene in time to hear a whir of wings and see a vague black cloud silhouetted against the rising moon.

My friend was dying when I spoke to him and could not answer coherently. All he could do was to whisper, "The amulet – that damned thing –"

Then he collapsed, an inert mass of mangled flesh.

I buried him the next midnight in one of our neglected gardens and mumbled over his body one of the devilish rituals he had loved in life. And as I pronounced the last daemoniac sentence I heard afar on the moor the faint baying of some gigantic hound. The moon was up, but I dared not look at it. Being now afraid to live alone in the

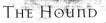
ancient house on the moor, I departed on the following day for London, taking with me the amulet after destroying by fire and burial the rest of the impious collection in the museum. But after three nights I heard the baying again, and before a week was over felt strange eyes upon me whenever it was dark. One evening as I strolled on Victoria Embankment for some needed air, I saw a black shape obscure one of the reflections of the lamps in the water. A strong wind rushed past and I knew that what had befallen St John must soon befall me.

The next day I wrapped the green jade amulet and sailed for Holland. What mercy I might gain by returning the thing to its silent, sleeping owner I knew not, but I felt that I must try any step conceivably logical. What the hound was, and why it had pursued me, were questions still vague, but I had first heard the baying in that ancient churchyard. Every subsequent event including St John's dying whisper, connected the curse with the stealing of the amulet. Accordingly I sank into the nethermost abysses of despair when, at an inn in Rotterdam, I discovered that thieves had robbed me of this sole means of salvation.

So at last I stood again in the churchyard. The baying was very faint now, and it ceased altogether as I approached the ancient grave and frightened away an abnormally large horde of bats which hovered curiously around it.

I know not why I went thither unless to pray, or gibber out insane pleas and apologies to the calm white thing that lay within – but, whatever my reason, I attacked the half frozen earth with a desperation partly mine and partly that of a dominating will outside myself. Excavation was much easier than I expected, though at one point I encountered a queer interruption. A lean vulture darted down out of the cold sky and pecked frantically at the grave-earth until I killed him with a blow of my spade. Finally, I reached the rotting oblong box and removed the damp nitrous cover. This is the last rational act I ever performed.

For crouched within that coffin, embraced by a close packed nightmare retinue of sleeping bats, was the bony thing my friend and I had robbed. It was no longer clean and placid, but covered with caked blood and shreds of alien flesh and hair. It leered at me with phosphorescent sockets and its sharp ensanguined fangs yawned twistedly in mockery of my inevitable doom. And when it gave a deep, sardonic bay as of some gigantic hound, and I saw the lost and fateful amulet of green jade in its gory, filthy claw, I merely screamed and ran away idiotically, my screams soon dissolving into hysterical laughter.

Now, as the baying of that dead fleshless monstrosity

grows louder, and the stealthy whirring and flapping of those accursed web-wings draw closer, I shall seek with my revolver the oblivion which is my only refuge from the unnamed and unnameable.

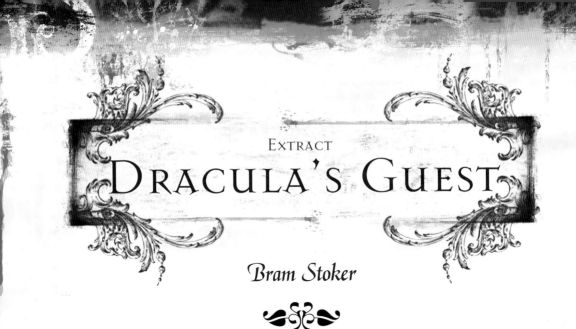

DRACULA'S GUEST

Bram Stoker

*This dramatic episode is said to be the original first chapter of
Dracula, which Bram Stoker decided not to use in the finished
novel. It was eventually published as a separate story.*

WHEN WE STARTED for our drive the sun was
shining brightly on Munich and the air was full
of the joyousness of early summer. As we were
about to depart, Herr Delbruck (the maitre d'hotel of the
Quatre Saisons, where I was staying) came down bareheaded
to the carriage and, after wishing me a pleasant drive, said
to the coachman, still holding his hand on the handle of the
carriage door, "Remember to be back by nightfall. The sky
looks bright, but there is a shiver in the north wind that says
there may be a storm. But I am sure you will not be late."

places, where the living lived and the dead were dead and not – not something. He was evidently afraid to speak the last words. As he proceeded with his narration, he grew more and more excited. It seemed as if his imagination had got hold of him, and he ended in a perfect paroxysm of fear – white-faced, perspiring, trembling and looking round him as if expecting that some dreadful presence would manifest itself there in the bright sunshine on the open plain.

Finally, in an agony of desperation, he cried, "*Walpurgis Nacht!*" and pointed to the carriage for me to get in.

All my English blood rose at this and standing back I said, "You are afraid, Johann – you are afraid. Go home, I shall return alone, the walk will do me good." The carriage door was open. I took from the seat my oak walking stick – which I always carry on my holiday excursions – and closed the door, pointing back to Munich, and said, "Go home, Johann – *Walpurgis Nacht* doesn't concern Englishmen."

The horses were now more restless than ever, and Johann was trying to hold them in, while excitedly imploring me not to do anything so foolish. I pitied the poor fellow, he was so deeply in earnest, but all the same I could not help laughing. His English was quite gone now. In his anxiety he had forgotten that his only means of making me understand was to talk my language, so he jabbered away in his native

German. It began to be a little tedious. After giving the direction, "Home!" I turned to go down the cross road into the valley.

With a despairing gesture, Johann turned his horses towards Munich. I leaned on my stick and looked after him. He went slowly along the road for a while, then there came over the crest of the hill a man tall and thin. I could see so much in the distance. When he drew near the horses, they began to jump and kick about, then to scream with terror. Johann could not hold them in; they bolted down the road, running away madly. I watched them out of sight, then looked for the stranger, but he, too, was gone.

With a light heart I turned

264

down the side road through the deepening valley to which
Johann had objected. There was not the slightest reason, that
I could see, for his objection. I daresay I tramped for a
couple of hours without thinking of time or distance and
certainly without seeing a person or a house. So far as the
place was concerned, it was desolation itself. But I did not
notice this particularly till, on turning a bend in the road, I
came upon a scattered fringe of wood. Then I recognized
that I had been impressed unconsciously by the desolation of
the region through which I had passed.

I sat down to rest myself and began to look around. It
struck me that it was considerably colder than it had been at
the commencement of my walk. A sort of sighing sound
seemed to be around me with, now and then, high
overhead, a sort of muffled roar. Looking upwards I noticed
that great thick clouds were drafting rapidly across the sky
from north to south at a great height. There were signs of a
coming storm in some lofty stratum of the air. I was a little
chilly, and, thinking that it was the sitting still after the
exercise of walking, I resumed my journey.

The ground I passed over was now much more
picturesque. There were no striking objects that the eye
might single out, but in all there was a charm of beauty. I
took little heed of time, and it was only when the deepening

twilight forced itself upon me that I began to think about how I should find my way home. The air was cold and the drifting of clouds high overhead was more marked. They were accompanied by a sort of far away rushing sound, through which seemed to come at intervals that mysterious cry which the driver had said came from a wolf. For a while I hesitated. I had said I would see the deserted village, so on I went and presently came on a wide stretch of open country, shut in by hills all around. Their sides were covered with trees which spread down to the plain, dotting in clumps the gentler slopes and hollows which showed here and there. I followed with my eye the winding of the road and saw that it curved close to one of the densest of these clumps and was lost behind it.

As I looked there came a cold shiver in the air, and the snow began to fall. I thought of the miles and miles of bleak country I had passed, and then hurried on to seek shelter of the wood in front. Darker and darker grew the sky, and faster and heavier fell the snow, till the earth before and around me was a glistening white carpet, the further edge of which was lost in misty vagueness. The road was here but crude, and in a little while I found that I must have strayed from it, for I missed underfoot the hard surface, and my feet sank deeper in the grass and moss. Then the wind grew stronger and blew with ever increasing force, till I was fain to run before it. The air became icy cold and in spite of my exercise I began to suffer. The snow was now falling so thickly and whirling around me in such rapid eddies that I could hardly keep my eyes open. Every now and then the heavens were torn asunder by vivid lightning, and in the flashes I could see ahead of me a great mass of trees, chiefly yew and cypress all heavily coated with snow.

I was soon amongst the shelter of the trees, and there in comparative silence I could hear the rush of the wind high overhead. Presently the blackness of the storm had become merged in the darkness of the night. By-and-by the storm seemed to be passing away, it now only came in fierce puffs or blasts. At such moments the weird sound of the wolf appeared to be echoed by many similar sounds around me.

Now and again, through the black mass of drifting cloud, came a straggling ray of moonlight which lit up the expanse and showed me that I was at the edge of a dense mass of cypress and yew trees. As the snow had ceased to fall, I walked out from the shelter and began to investigate more closely. It appeared to me that, amongst so many old foundations as I had passed, there might be still standing a house in which, though in ruins, I could find some sort of shelter for a while. As I skirted the edge of the copse, I found that a low wall encircled it, and following this I presently found an opening. Here the cypresses formed an alley leading up to a square mass of some kind of building. Just as I caught sight of this, however, the drifting clouds obscured the moon, and I passed up the path in darkness. The wind must have grown colder, for I felt myself shiver as I walked – but there was hope of shelter, and I groped my way blindly on.

I stopped, for there was a sudden stillness. The storm had passed, and perhaps in sympathy with nature's silence, my heart seemed to cease to beat. But this was only momentarily. Suddenly the moonlight broke through the clouds showing me that I was in a graveyard and that the square object before me was a great massive tomb of marble, as white as the snow that lay on and all around it. With the moonlight there came a fierce sigh of the storm, which appeared to resume its course with a long, low howl, as of many dogs or wolves. I was awed and shocked, and I felt the cold perceptibly grow upon me till it seemed to grip

Dracula's Guest

me by the heart. Then while the flood of moonlight still fell on the marble tomb, the storm gave further evidence of renewing, as though it were returning on its track. Impelled by some sort of fascination, I approached the sepulchre to see what it was and why such a thing stood alone in such a place. I walked around it and read, over the Doric door, in German:

COUNTESS DOLINGEN OF GRATZ IN STYRIA

SOUGHT AND FOUND DEATH
1801

On top of the tomb, seemingly driven through the marble – for the structure was composed of a few vast blocks of stone – was an iron spike or stake. On going to the back I saw, graven in Russian letters: 'The dead travel fast.'

There was something so weird and uncanny about the whole thing that it gave me a turn and made me feel quite faint. I began to wish, for the first time, that I had taken Johann's advice. Here a thought struck me, which came under almost mysterious circumstances and with a terrible shock. This was Walpurgis Night!

Walpurgis Night was when, according to the belief of millions of people, the devil was abroad – when the graves were opened and the dead came forth and walked. When all evil things of earth, air and water held revel. This very place the driver had specially shunned. This was the depopulated village of centuries ago. This was where the suicide lay; and this was the place where I was alone – unmanned, shivering with cold in a shroud of snow with a wild storm gathering again upon me! It took all my philosophy, all the religion I had been taught, all my courage, not to collapse in a paroxysm of fright.

And now a perfect tornado burst upon me. The ground shook as though thousands of horses thundered across it. This time the storm bore on its icy wings, not snow, but great hailstones which drove with such violence that they might have come from the thongs of Balearic slingers – hailstones that beat down leaf and branch and made the shelter of the cypresses of no more avail than if their stems were standing corn. At first I had rushed to the nearest tree, but I was soon fain to leave it and seek the only spot that seemed to afford refuge – the deep Doric doorway of the marble tomb. There, crouching against the bronze door, I gained a certain amount of protection from the beating of the hailstones, for now they only drove against me as they ricocheted from the ground and the side of the marble.

As I leaned against the door, it moved slightly and opened inwards. The shelter of even a tomb was welcome in that pitiless tempest and I was about to enter it when there came a flash of forked lightning that lit up the whole expanse of the heavens. In the instant, as I am a living man, I saw, as my eyes turned into the darkness of the tomb, a beautiful woman with rounded cheeks and red lips, seemingly sleeping on a bier. As the thunder broke overhead, I was grasped as by the hand of a giant and hurled out into the storm. The whole thing was so sudden that, before I could realize the shock, moral as well as physical, I found the hailstones beating me down. At the same time I had a strange, dominating feeling that I was not alone. I looked towards the tomb. Just then there came another blinding

flash which seemed to strike the iron stake that surmounted
the tomb and to pour through to the earth, blasting and
crumbling the marble, as in a burst of flame. The dead
woman rose for a moment of agony while she was lapped in
the flame, and her bitter scream of pain was drowned in the
thundercrash. The last thing I heard was this mingling of
dreadful sound, as again I was seized in the giant grasp and
dragged away, while the hailstones beat on me and the air
around seemed reverberant with the howling of wolves. The
last sight that I remembered was a vague, white, moving
mass, as if all the graves around me had sent out the
phantoms of their sheeted dead, and that they were closing
in on me through the white cloudiness of the driving hail.

Gradually there came a sort of vague beginning of
consciousness, then a sense of weariness that was dreadful.
For a time I remembered nothing, but slowly my senses
returned. My feet were racked with pain, yet I could not
move them. They seemed to be numbed. There was an icy
feeling at the back of my neck and all down my spine. My
ears, like my feet, were dead yet in torment, but there was
in my chest a sense of warmth, which by comparison, was
delicious. It was as a nightmare – a physical nightmare, if
one may use such an expression, for some heavy weight
upon my chest was making it difficult for me to breathe.

This period of semi-lethargy seemed to remain a long time, and as it faded away I must have slept or swooned. Then came a sort of loathing, like the first stage of seasickness, and a wild desire to be free of something – I knew not what. A vast stillness enveloped me, as though all the world were asleep or dead – only broken by the low panting as of some animal close to me. I felt a warm rasping at my throat, then came a consciousness of the awful truth which chilled me to the heart and sent the blood surging up through my brain. Some great animal was lying on me and now licking my throat. I feared to stir, for some instinct of prudence bade me lie still, but the brute seemed to realize that there was now some change in me for it raised its head. Through my eyelashes I saw above me the two flaming eyes of a huge wolf. Its white teeth gleamed in the gaping red mouth, and I could feel its breath fierce and acrid upon me.

For another spell of time I remembered no more. Then I became conscious of a low growl, followed by a yelp, renewed again and again. Then seemingly very far away, I heard a "Holloa! holloa!" of many voices calling in unison. Cautiously I raised my head and looked in the direction whence the sound came, but the cemetery blocked my view. The wolf still continued to yelp in a strange way, and a red glare began to move round the grove of cypresses, as though following the sound. As the voices drew closer, the wolf yelped faster and louder. I feared to make either sound or motion. Nearer came the red glow over the white pall which stretched into the darkness around me. Then all at once from beyond the trees there came a troop of horsemen bearing torches. The wolf rose from my breast and made for the cemetery. I saw one of the horsemen (soldiers by their caps and their long military cloaks) raise his carbine and take aim. A companion knocked up his arm and I heard the ball whiz over my head. He had evidently taken my body for that of the wolf. Another sighted the animal as it slunk away and a shot followed. Then, at a gallop, the troop rode forward –

some towards me, others following the wolf as it quickly disappeared amongst the snow-clad cypresses.

As they drew nearer I tried to move but was powerless, although I could see and hear all that went on around me. Two or three of the soldiers jumped from their horses and knelt beside me. One of them raised my head and placed his hand over my heart.

"Good news, comrades!" he cried. "His heart still beats!"

Then some brandy was poured down my throat. It put vigour into me, and I was able to open my eyes fully and look around. Lights and shadows were moving among the trees, and I heard men call to one another. They drew together, uttering frightened exclamations, and the lights flashed as the others came pouring out of the cemetery pell-mell, like men possessed. When the further ones came close to us, those who were around me asked them eagerly, "Well, have you found him?"

The reply rang out , "No! no! Come away quick-quick! This is no place to stay, and on this of all nights!"

"What was it?" was the question, asked in all manner of keys. The answer came variously and all indefinitely as though the men were moved by some common impulse to speak yet were restrained by some common fear from giving their thoughts.

"It – it – indeed!" gibbered one, whose wits had plainly given out for the moment.

"A wolf – and yet not a wolf!" another put in shudderingly.

"No use trying for him without the sacred bullet," a third remarked in a more ordinary manner.

"Serve us right for coming out on this night! We have earned our thousand marks!" were the words of a fourth.

"There was blood on the broken marble," another said after a pause, "the lightning never brought that there. And for him – is he safe? Look at his throat! See comrades, the wolf has been lying on him and keeping his blood warm."

The officer looked at my throat and replied, "He is all right, the skin is not pierced. What does it mean? We should never have found him but for the yelping of the wolf."

"What became of it?" asked the man who was holding up my head and who seemed the least panic-stricken of the party, for his hands were steady and without tremor. On his sleeve was the chevron of a petty officer.

"It went home," answered the man, whose long face was pallid and who actually shook with terror as he glanced around him fearfully. "There are graves enough there in which it may lie. Come, comrades – come quickly! Let us leave this cursed spot."

The officer raised me to a sitting posture, as he uttered a word of command, then several men placed me upon a horse. He sprang to the saddle behind me, took me in his arms, gave the word to advance, and turning our faces away from the cypresses, we rode away in swift military order.

As yet my tongue refused its office, and I was perforce silent. I must have fallen asleep for the next thing I remembered was finding myself standing up, supported by a soldier on each side of me. It was almost broad daylight, and to the north a red streak of sunlight was reflected like a path of blood over the waste of snow. The officer was telling the men to say nothing of what they had seen, except that they found an English stranger, guarded by a large dog.

"Dog! That was no dog," cut in the man who had exhibited such fear. "I think I know a wolf when I see one."

The young officer answered calmly, "I said a dog."

"Dog!" reiterated the other ironically. It was evident that his courage was rising with the sun. Pointing to me, he said, "Look at his throat. Is that the work of a dog, master?"

Instinctively I raised my hand to my throat and as I touched it I cried out in pain. The men crowded round to look, some stooping down from their saddles, and again there came the calm voice of the young officer, "A dog, as I said. If aught else were said we should only be laughed at."

I was then mounted behind a trooper and we rode on into the suburbs of Munich. Here we came across a stray carriage into which I was lifted and it was driven off to the Quatre Saisons – the young officer accompanying me, whilst a trooper followed with his horse, and the others rode off to their barracks.

When we arrived, Herr Delbruck rushed so quickly down the steps to meet me, that it was apparent he had been watching within. Taking me by both hands he solicitously led me in. The officer saluted me and was turning to withdraw, when I recognized his purpose and insisted that he should come to my rooms. Over a glass of wine I warmly thanked him and his brave comrades for saving me. He replied simply that he was more than glad, and that Herr Delbruck had at the first taken steps to make all the searching party pleased. With this ambiguous utterance the maitre d'hotel smiled, while the officer pleaded duty and withdrew.

"But Herr Delbruck," I enquired, "how and why was it that the soldiers searched for me?"

He shrugged his shoulders, as if in depreciation of his own deed, as he replied, "I was so fortunate as to obtain leave from the commander of the regiment in which I serve, to ask for volunteers."

"But how did you know I was lost?" I asked.

"The driver came hither with the remains of his carriage, which had been upset when the horses ran away."

"But surely you would not send a search party of soldiers merely on this account?"

"Oh, no!" he answered, "but even before the coachman arrived, I had this telegram from the Boyar whose guest you are," and he took from his pocket a telegram which he handed to me, and I read:

Bistritz. Be careful of my guest – his safety is most precious to me. Should aught happen to him, or if he be missed, spare nothing to find him and ensure his safety. He is English and therefore adventurous. There are often dangers from snow and wolves and night. Lose not a moment if you suspect harm to him. I answer your zeal with my fortune. – Dracula.

As I held the telegram, the room seemed to spin, and if the maitre d'hotel had not caught me, I should have fallen.

There was something so strange in all this, so impossible to imagine, that there grew in me a sense of my being in some way the sport of opposite forces – the mere idea of which seemed in a way to paralyze me. I was under some form of protection. From a distant country had come, in the very nick of time, a message that took me out of the danger of the snow sleep and the jaws of the wolf.

FATAL WOMEN

The Vampire Cat of Nabéshima

Anon

THERE IS A TRADITION in the Nabéshima family that, many years ago, the Prince of Hizen was bewitched and cursed by a cat that had been kept by one of his retainers. This prince had in his house a lady of rare beauty, called O Toyo. Amongst all his ladies she was the favourite, and there was none who could rival her charms and accomplishments.

One day the Prince went into the garden with O Toyo, enjoying the fragrance of the flowers until sunset, when they returned to the palace, never noticing that they were being followed by a large cat. Having parted with her lord, O Toyo retired to her own room and went to bed. At midnight she awoke with a start and became aware of a huge cat that crouched watching her. When she cried out, the beast

sprang on her, and fixing its cruel teeth in her
delicate throat, throttled her to death. What a
piteous end for so fair a dame, the darling of her
prince's heart, to die suddenly, bitten to death by
a vampire cat! Then the cat, having scratched out
a grave under the verandah, buried the corpse of
O Toyo, and assuming her form, began to
bewitch the Prince.

But my lord the Prince knew nothing of all
this, and little thought that the beautiful creature
was an impish and foul beast that had slain his
mistress and assumed her shape in
order to drain out
his life's blood. Day
by day, as time went
on, the Prince's

strength dwindled away. The colour of his face was changed, and became pale and livid – he was as a man suffering from a deadly sickness. Seeing this, his councillors and his wife became greatly alarmed. They summoned the physicians, who prescribed various remedies for him, but the more medicine he took, the more serious did his illness appear, and no treatment was of any avail. But most of all he suffered at night when his sleep would be troubled and disturbed by hideous dreams. His councillors appointed every night a hundred of his retainers to sit up and watch over him. However, strange to say, towards ten o'clock on the very first night that the watch was set, the guard were seized with a sudden and unaccountable drowsiness, which they could not resist, until one by one every man had fallen asleep. The following night the same thing occurred, and the Prince was subjected to the false O Toyo's tyranny, while his guards slept helplessly around him. Night after night this was repeated, until at last three of the Prince's councillors determined to sit up themselves on guard, and see whether they could overcome this mysterious drowsiness. They fared no better than the others and by ten o'clock were fast asleep. The next day the three councillors held a solemn conclave, and their chief, one Isahaya Buzen, said, "This is a marvellous thing, that a guard of a hundred men should thus be overcome by sleep. For certain, the spell that is upon my lord and upon his guard must be the work of witchcraft. Now, as all our efforts are of no avail, let us seek out Ruiten, the chief priest of the temple and beseech him to put up prayers for the recovery of my lord."

And the other councillors approving what Isahaya Buzen had said, went to the priest Ruiten and engaged him to recite litanies that the Prince might be restored to health.

So it came to pass that Ruiten, the chief priest offered up prayers nightly for the Prince. One night, at midnight, when he had finished his religious exercises and was preparing to lie down to sleep, he fancied that he heard a noise outside in the garden, as if some one were washing himself at the well. Thinking this strange, he looked down from the window. There in the moonlight he saw a young soldier, some twenty-four years of age, washing himself. When he had finished, and had put on his clothes, he stood before the figure of Buddha and prayed fervently for the recovery of my lord the Prince. Ruiten looked on with admiration and when the young man finished his prayer and was going away, the priest stopped him, calling out, "Sir, I cannot conceal my admiration that you, being so young a man, should have so loyal a spirit. I am Ruiten, the chief priest of this temple, who is engaged in praying for the recovery of my lord. Pray what is your name?"

"My name, sir, is Itô Sôda, and I am serving in the infantry of Nabéshima. Since my lord has been sick, my one desire has been to assist in helping him — but, being only a simple soldier, I am not of sufficient rank to come into his presence, so I have no choice but to pray to the gods of the country and to Buddha that my lord may regain his health."

"Your purpose is, indeed, a good one, but what a strange sickness this is that my lord is afflicted with! Every night he suffers from horrible dreams and the retainers who sit up with him are all seized with a mysterious sleep, so that not one can keep awake. It is very odd."

"Yes," replied Sôda, after a moment's reflection, "this certainly must be witchcraft. If I could obtain leave to sit up one night with the Prince, I would see whether I could not resist this drowsiness."

At last the priest said, "I am friends with Isahaya Buzen, the chief councillor of the Prince. I will speak to him about you and of your loyalty, in the hope that you may attain your wish."

"Thank you, sir, and farewell." And so they parted.

On the following evening Itô Sôda returned to the temple Miyô In, and having found Ruiten, accompanied him to the house of Isahaya Buzen. The priest then left Sôda outside, went in to talk with the councillor, and inquire after the Prince's health.

"And pray, sir, how is my lord? Is he in any better condition since I have been offering up prayers for him?"

"Indeed, no — his illness is very severe. We are certain that he must be the victim of some foul sorcery, but as there are no means of keeping a guard awake after ten o'clock, we cannot catch a sight of the goblin. We are in the greatest trouble."

"I feel deeply for you. It must be most distressing. However, I have something to tell you. I think that I have found a man who will detect the goblin and I have brought him with me."

The priest presented Itô Sôda to the councillor, who looked at him attentively, and being pleased with his entle appearance, said, "So I hear that you are anxious to be permitted to guard in my lord's room at night. Well, I must consult with the other councillors, and we will see what can be done for you."

The next day the councillors held a meeting and sent for Itô Sôda. They told him that he might keep watch with the other retainers that very night. So he went his way in high spirits, and at nightfall, having made all his preparations, took his place among the hundred gentlemen who were on duty in the prince's bedroom.

Now the Prince slept in the centre of the room, and the hundred guards around him sat keeping themselves awake with entertaining conversation and pleasant conceits. But, as ten o'clock approached, they began to doze off. In spite of all their endeavours to keep one another awake, by degrees they all fell asleep. Itô Sôda all this while felt an irresistible desire to sleep creeping over him, and, though he tried by

all sorts of ways to rouse himself, he saw that there was no help for it, but by resorting to an extreme measure, for which he had already made his preparations. Drawing out a piece of oil paper which he had brought with him, and spreading it over the mats, he sat down upon it. He then took the small knife which he carried in the sheath of his dirk and stuck it into his own thigh. For a while the pain of the wound kept him awake, but as the slumber by which he was assailed was the work of sorcery, little by little he became drowsy again. Then he twisted the knife round and round in his thigh, so that the pain became unbearable. He fought against the feeling of sleepiness and kept a faithful watch. Now the oil paper that he had spread under his legs was in order to prevent the blood, which might spurt from his wound, from spoiling the mats.

So Itô Sôda remained awake, but the rest of the guard slept. As he watched, suddenly the sliding doors of the Prince's room were drawn open, and he saw a figure coming in stealthily. As it drew nearer, the form was that of a beautiful woman some twenty-three years of age. Cautiously she looked around her and when she saw that all the guard were asleep, she smiled an ominous smile, and was going up to the Prince's bedside, when she perceived that in one corner of the room there was a man still awake. This seemed to startle her, but she went up to Sôda and said, "I am not used to seeing you here. Who are you?"

"My name is Itô Sôda, and this is the first night that I have been on guard."

"A troublesome office, truly! Why, here are all the rest of the guard asleep. How is it that you alone are awake? You are a trusty watchman."

"There is nothing to boast about. I'm asleep myself, fast and sound."

"What is that wound on your knee? It is red with blood."

"Oh! I felt very sleepy, so I stuck my knife into my thigh and the pain of it has kept me awake."

"What wondrous loyalty!" said the lady.

"Is it not the duty of a retainer to lay down his life for his master? Is such a scratch as this worth thinking about?"

Then the lady went up to the sleeping prince and said, "How fares it with my lord tonight?" But the Prince, worn out with sickness, made no reply.

But Sôda was watching her, and guessed that it was O Toyo, and made up his mind that if she attempted to attack the Prince he would kill her on the spot. The goblin, however, which in the form of O Toyo had been tormenting the Prince every night, and had come again that night for no other purpose, was defeated by the watchfulness of Itô Sôda. Whenever she drew near to the sick man, thinking to put her spells upon him, she would turn and look behind her, and there she saw Itô Sôda glaring at her. So she had no choice but to go away and leave the Prince undisturbed.

At last the day broke. The other officers awoke and saw that Itô Sôda had kept awake by stabbing himself in the thigh. They felt greatly ashamed and went home crestfallen.

That morning Itô Sôda went to the house of Isahaya Buzen and told him all that had occurred the previous night. The councillors were loud in their praises of Itô Sôda's behaviour and ordered him to keep watch again that night. At the same hour, the false O Toyo came and looked all round the room, and all the guard were asleep, excepting Itô Sôda, who was wide awake. Frustrated, she returned to her own apartments.

Since Sôda had been on guard the Prince had passed quiet nights and his sickness began to get better. There was great joy in the palace, and Sôda was promoted and rewarded with an estate. Meanwhile O Toyo, seeing that her nightly visits bore no fruits, kept away, and from that time forth the night-guard were no longer subject to fits of drowsiness. This coincidence struck Sôda as very strange, so he went to Isahaya Buzen and told him that almost certainly this O Toyo was no other than a goblin. Isahaya Buzen reflected for a while, and said, "Well, then, how shall we kill the foul thing?"

"I will go to the creature's room and try to kill her. But, in case she should try to escape, I will beg you to order eight men to stop outside and lie in wait for her."

Having agreed upon this plan, Sôda went at nightfall to O Toyo's apartment, pretending to have been sent with a message from the Prince. When she saw him arrive she said, "What message have you brought me from my lord?"

"Oh, nothing in particular. Be so kind as to look at this letter." As he spoke, he drew near to her, and suddenly drawing his dirk cut at her — but the goblin, springing back, seized a halberd, and glaring fiercely at Sôda, said,

"How dare you behave like this to one of your lord's ladies? I will have you dismissed," and she tried to strike Sôda with the halberd. But Sôda fought desperately with his dirk, and the goblin, seeing that she was no match for him, threw away the halberd, and from a beautiful woman became suddenly transformed into a cat, which, springing up the sides of the room, jumped onto the roof. Isahaya Buzen and his eight men who were watching outside shot at the cat, but missed it, and the beast escaped.

So the cat fled to the mountains, and did much mischief among the surrounding people, until at last the Prince of Hizen ordered a great hunt, and the beast was killed.

But the Prince recovered from his sickness — and Itô Sôda was richly rewarded.

Mrs Amworth

E F Benson

THE VILLAGE OF MAXLEY, where, last summer and autumn, these strange events took place, lies on a heathery and pine-clad upland of Sussex. In all England you could not find a sweeter and saner place. Should the wind blow from the south, it comes laden with the spices of the sea, to the east, high downs protect it from the inclemencies of March, and from the west and north, the breezes that reach it travel over miles of aromatic forest and heather. Halfway down the single street, with its broad road and spacious areas of grass on each side, stands the little Norman Church and the antique graveyard long disused. For the rest there are a dozen small, sedate Georgian houses, red-bricked and long-windowed, each with a square of flower garden in front, and an ampler strip behind. A score of shops, and a couple of score of thatched cottages belonging to labourers on neighbouring estates, complete the entire cluster of its peaceful habitations.

I am the fortunate possessor of one of these small Georgian houses, and consider myself no less fortunate in having so interesting and stimulating a neighbour as Francis Urcombe, who devoted himself to the study of the occult and curious phenomena that seem equally to concern the physical and the psychical sides of human nature.

Here, then, in Francis Urcombe, was a delightful neighbour to one who, like myself, has an uneasy and burning curiosity about what he called the 'misty and perilous places'. This last spring we had a further and most welcome addition to our pleasant little community, in the form of Mrs Amworth, widow of an Indian civil servant. Big and energetic, her vigorous and genial personality speedily woke Maxley up to a higher degree of sociality than it had ever known.

She was always cheery and jolly. She was interested in everything, including music and gardening, and was a competent performer in games of all sorts . Everybody (with one exception) liked her, everybody felt her to bring with her the tonic of a sunny day. That one exception was Francis Urcombe – though he confessed he did not like her, he acknowledged that he was vastly interested in her.

Often as our quite unsentimental friendship ripened, Mrs Amworth would ring me up and propose her arrival. If I was busy writing, I was to give her, so we definitely bargained, a frank negative, and in answer I could hear her jolly laugh and her wishes for a successful evening of work. Sometimes, before her proposal arrived, Urcombe would already have stepped across from his house opposite for a smoke and a chat, and he, hearing who my intending visitor was, always urged me to beg her to come. She and I should play our piquet, said he, and he would look on, if we did not object, and learn something of the game.

But I doubt whether he paid much attention to it, for nothing could be clearer than that, under that penthouse of forehead and thick eyebrows, his attention was fixed not on the cards, but on one of the players. But he seemed to enjoy an hour spent thus, and often, until one particular evening in July, he would watch her with the air of a man who has some deep problem in front of him. Then came that evening, when, as I see in the light of subsequent events, began the first twitching of the veil that hid the secret horror from my eyes. I did not know it then, though I noticed that thereafter, if she rang up to propose coming round, she always asked not only if I was at leisure, but whether Mr Urcombe was with me. If so, she said, she would not spoil the chat of two old bachelors, and laughingly wished me goodnight.

Urcombe, on this occasion, had been with me for some half-hour before Mrs Amworth's appearance. He had been talking to me about the medieval beliefs concerning vampirism, one of those borderland subjects that he declared had not been sufficiently studied before it had been consigned by the medical profession to the dust heap of superstitions. There he sat, grim and eager, tracing, with that clearness that had made him in his Cambridge days so admirable a lecturer, the history of those mysterious visitations. In them all there were the same general features – one of those ghoulish spirits took up its abode in a living man or woman, conferring supernatural powers of bat-like flight and glutting itself with nocturnal blood feasts.

When its host died it continued to dwell in the corpse, which remained undecayed. By day it rested, by night it left the grave and went on its awful errands. No European country in the Middle Ages seemed to have escaped them. Earlier yet, parallels were to be found in Roman, Greek and Jewish history.

"It's a large order to set all that evidence aside as being moonshine," he said. "Hundreds of totally independent witnesses in many ages have testified to the occurrence of these phenomena and there's no explanation known to me that covers all the facts. And if you feel inclined to say 'Why, then, if these are facts, do we not come across them now?' there are two answers I can make you. One is that there were diseases known in the Middle Ages, such as the black death, which were certainly existent then and which have become extinct since, but for that reason we do not assert that such diseases never existed. Just as the black death visited England and decimated the population of Norfolk, so here in this very district about three hundred years ago there was certainly an outbreak of vampirism, and Maxley was the centre of it. My second answer is even more convincing, for I tell you that vampirism is by no means extinct now. An outbreak of it certainly occurred in India a year or two ago."

At that moment I heard a knock at the door in the cheerful and peremptory manner in which Mrs Amworth is accustomed to announce her arrival, and I went to the door to open it.

"Come in at once," I said, "and save me from having my blood curdled. Mr Urcombe has been trying to alarm me."

Instantly her vital, voluminous presence seemed to fill the room.

"Ah, but how lovely!" she said. "I delight in having my

blood curdled. Please carry on with the story Mr Urcombe.
I adore ghost stories."

I saw that, as his habit was, he was intently observing her.

"It wasn't a ghost story exactly," said he. "I was only
telling our host how vampirism was not extinct yet. I was
saying that there was an outbreak of it in India only a few
years ago."

There was a more than perceptible pause, and I saw that,
if Urcombe was observing her, she on her side was
observing him with fixed eye and parted mouth. Then her
jolly laugh invaded that rather tense silence.

"Oh, what a shame!" she said. "You're not going to curdle my blood at all. Where did you pick up such a tale, Mr Urcombe? I have lived for years in India and never heard a rumour of such a thing. Some storyteller in the bazaars must have invented it – they are famous at that."

I could see that Urcombe was on the point of saying something further, but checked himself.

"Ah! Very likely that was it," he said.

But something had disturbed our usual peaceful sociability that night, and something had dampened Mrs Amworth's usual high spirits. She had no gusto for her piquet and left after a couple of games. Urcombe had been silent too, indeed he hardly spoke again till she departed.

"That was unfortunate," he said, "for the outbreak of – of a very mysterious disease, let us call it, took place at Peshawar, where she and her husband were. And – "

"Well?" I asked.

"He was one of the victims of it," said he. "Naturally I had quite forgotten that when I spoke."

The summer was unreasonably hot and rainless, and Maxley suffered much from drought, and also from a plague of big black night-flying gnats, the bite of which was very irritating and virulent. They came sailing in of an evening, settling on one's skin so quietly that one perceived nothing till the sharp stab announced that one had been bitten. They did not bite the hands or face, but chose always the neck and throat for their feeding ground. Then about the middle of August appeared the first of those mysterious cases of illness, which our local doctor attributed to the long-continued heat coupled with the bite of these venomous insects. The patient was a boy of sixteen or seventeen, the son of Mrs Amworth's gardener, and the symptoms were an anaemic pallor and a languid prostration, accompanied by great drowsiness and an abnormal appetite. He had, too, on his throat two small punctures where, so Dr Ross conjectured, one of these great gnats had bitten him. But the odd thing was that there was no swelling or inflammation round the place where he had been bitten.

The heat at this time had begun to abate, but the cooler weather failed to restore him, and the boy, in spite of the quantity of good food that he so ravenously swallowed, wasted away to a skin-clad skeleton.

I met Dr Ross in the street one afternoon about this time, and in answer to my inquiries about his patient he said that he was afraid the boy was dying. The case, he confessed, completely puzzled him. Some obscure form of pernicious anaemia was all he could suggest. But he wondered whether Mr Urcombe would consent to see the boy, on the chance of

his being able to throw some new light on the case, and
since Urcombe was dining with me that night, I proposed to
Dr Ross to join us. He could not do this, but said he would
look in later. When he came, Urcombe at once consented to
put his skill at the other's disposal, and together they went
off at once. Being thus shorn of my sociable evening, I
telephoned to Mrs Amworth to know if I might inflict
myself on her for an hour. Her answer was a welcoming
affirmative, and between piquet and music the hour
lengthened itself into two. She spoke of the boy who was
lying so desperately and mysteriously ill, and told me that
she had often been to see him, taking him nourishing and
delicate food. But today – and her kind eyes moistened as
she spoke – she was afraid she had paid her last visit.
Knowing the animosity between her and Urcombe, I did not
tell her that he had been called into consultation. When I
returned home she accompanied me to my door, for the
sake of a breath of night air, and in order to borrow a
magazine that contained an article on gardening that she
wished to read.

"Ah, this delicious night air," she said, luxuriously sniffing
in the coolness. "Night air and gardening are the great
tonics. There is nothing so stimulating as bare contact with
rich mother earth. You are never so fresh as when you have

been grubbing in the soil – black hands, black nails and boots covered with mud." She gave her great jovial laugh. "I'm a glutton for air and earth," she said. "Positively I look forward to death, for then I shall be buried and have the earth all round me. No leaden caskets for me – I have given explicit instructions. But what shall I do about air? I suppose one can't have everything. The magazine? A thousand thanks, I will return it. Good night – garden and keep your windows open, and you won't have anaemia."

"I always sleep with my windows open," I said.

I went straight up to my room, of which one of the windows looks over the street, and as I undressed I thought I heard voices talking outside not far away. But I paid no particular attention, put out my lights, and falling asleep plunged into the depths of a most horrible dream, distortedly suggested no doubt, by my last words with Mrs Amworth. I dreamt that I woke, and found that both my bedroom windows were shut. Half-suffocating I dreamt I sprang out of bed and went across to open them. The blind over the first was drawn down, and pulling it up I saw, with the indescribable horror, Mrs Amworth's face suspended close to the pane in the darkness outside, nodding and smiling at me. Pulling down the blind again to keep that terror out, I rushed to the second window on the other side

of the room, and there again was Mrs Amworth's face. Then the panic came upon me in full blast – here was I suffocating in the airless room, and whichever window I opened Mrs Amworth's face would float in, like those noiseless black gnats that bit before one was aware. The nightmare rose to screaming point, and with strangled yells I awoke to find my room cool and quiet with both windows open and blinds up and a half-moon high in its course, casting an oblong of tranquil light on the floor. But even when I was awake the horror persisted, and I lay tossing and turning.

I must have slept long before the nightmare seized me, for now it was nearly day, and soon in the east the drowsy eyelids of morning began to lift.

I was scarcely downstairs next morning – for after the

305

dawn I slept late – when Urcombe rang up to know if he might see me immediately. He came in, grim and preoccupied, and I noticed that he was pulling on a pipe that was not even filled.

"I want your help," he said, "and so I must tell you first of all what happened last night. I went round with the little doctor to see his patient, and found him just alive, but scarcely more. I instantly diagnosed in my own mind what this anaemia, unaccountable by any other explanation, meant. The boy is the prey of a vampire."

He put his empty pipe on the breakfast table, by which I had just sat down, and folded his arms, looking at me steadily from under his overhanging brows.

"Now about last night," he said. "I insisted that he should be moved from his father's cottage into my house. As we were carrying him on a stretcher, whom should we meet but Mrs Amworth? She expressed shocked surprise that we were moving him. Now why do you think she did that?"

With a start of horror, as I remembered my dream that night before, I felt an idea come into my mind so preposterous that I instantly turned it out again.

"I haven't the smallest idea," I said.

"Then listen, while I tell you what happened later. I put out all light in the room where the boy lay, and watched.

One window was a little open, for I had forgotten to close it, and about midnight I heard something outside, trying apparently to push it farther open. I guessed who it was – yes, it was a full twenty feet from the ground – and I peeped round the corner of the blind."

"Just outside was the face of Mrs Amworth and her hand was on the frame of the window. Very softly I crept close, and then banged the window down, and I think I just caught the tip of one of her fingers."

"But it's impossible," I cried. "How could she be floating in the air like that? And what had she come for? Don't tell me such – "

Once more, with closer grip, the remembrance of my nightmare seized me.

"I am telling you what I saw," said he. "And all night long, until it was nearly day, she was fluttering outside, like some terrible bat, trying to gain admittance. Now put together various things I have told you."

He began checking them off on his fingers.

"Number one," he said: "there was an outbreak of disease similar to that which this boy is suffering from at Peshawar, and her husband died of it. Number two: Mrs Amworth protested against my moving the boy to my house. Number three: she, or the demon that inhabits her body, a creature powerful and deadly, tries to gain admittance. And add this, too: in medieval times there was an epidemic of vampirism here at Maxley. The vampire, so the accounts run, was found to be Elizabeth Chaston … I see you remember Mrs Amworth's maiden name. Finally, the boy is stronger this morning. He would certainly not have been alive if he had been visited again."

"And what do you make of it?"

There was a long silence, during which I found this incredible horror assuming the hues of reality.

"I have something to add," I said, "which may or may not bear on it. You say that the – the spectre went away shortly before dawn."

"Yes."

I told him of my dream, and he smiled grimly.

"Yes, you did well to awake," he said. "That warning came from your subconscious self, which never wholly slumbers, and cried out to you of deadly danger. For two reasons, then, you must help me: one to save others, the second to save yourself."

"What do you want me to do?" I asked.

"I want you first of all to help me in watching this boy and ensuring that she does not come near him. Eventually I want you to help me in tracking the thing down, in exposing

and destroying it. It is not human – it is an incarnate fiend.
What steps we shall have to take I don't yet know."

It was now eleven of the forenoon, and presently I went
across to his house for a twelve-hour vigil while he slept, to
come on duty again that night, so that for the next twenty-
four hours either Urcombe or myself was always in the
room where the boy, now getting stronger every hour, was
lying. The following day was Saturday and a morning of
brilliant, pellucid weather, and already when I went across
to his house to resume my duty the stream of motors down
to Brighton had begun. Simultaneously I saw Urcombe with
a cheerful face, which boded good news of his patient,
coming out of his house, and Mrs Amworth, with a gesture
of salutation to me and a basket in her hand, walking up the
broad strip of grass that bordered the road. There we all
three met. I noticed (and saw that Urcombe noticed it too)
that one finger of her left hand was bandaged.

"Good morning to you both," said she. "And I hear your
patient is doing well, Mr Urcombe. I have come to bring
him a bowl of jelly and to sit with him for an hour. He and I
are great friends. I am overjoyed at his recovery."

Urcombe paused a moment, as if making up his mind,
and then shot out a pointing finger at her.

"I forbid that," he said. "You shall not sit with him or see him. And you know the reason as well as I do."

I have never seen so horrible a change pass over a human face as that which now blanched hers to the colour of a grey mist. She put up her hand as if to shield herself from that pointing finger, which drew the sign of the cross in the air, and shrank back cowering on to the road.

There was a wild hoot from a horn, a grinding of brakes, a shout – too late – from a passing car, and one long scream suddenly cut short. Her body rebounded from the roadway after the first wheel had gone over it, and the second followed. It lay there, quivering and twitching, and was still.

She was buried three days afterwards in the cemetery outside Maxley, in accordance with the instructions that she had told me.

The shock that her sudden and awful death had caused to the little community began by degrees to pass off. To two people only, Urcombe and myself, the horror of it was mitigated from the first by the nature of the relief that her death brought. But, naturally enough, we kept our own counsel, and no hint of what greater horror had been thus averted was ever let slip.

However, oddly enough, so it seemed to me, he was still not completely satisfied about something in connection with her, and would give no answer to my questions on the subject. Then as the days of a tranquil mellow September and the October that followed began to drop away like the leaves of the yellowing trees, his uneasiness relaxed. But before the entry of November the seeming tranquillity broke into a hurricane.

I had been dining one night at the far end of the village and about eleven o'clock was walking home again. The moon was of an unusual brilliance, rendering everything that it shone on as distinct as in some etching. I had just come opposite the house which Mrs Amworth had occupied, where there was a board up telling that it was to let, when I heard the click of her front gate, and next moment I saw, with a sudden chill and quaking of my very spirit, that she stood there. Her profile, vividly illuminated, was turned to me, and I could not be mistaken in my identification of her. She appeared not to see me (indeed the shadow of the yew hedge in front of her garden enveloped me in its blackness) and she went swiftly across the road, and entered the gate of the house directly opposite. There I lost sight of her completely.

My breath was coming in short pants as if I had been running – and now indeed I ran, with fearful backward glances, along the hundred yards that separated me from my house and Urcombe's. It was to his that my flying steps took me, and the next minute I was within.

"What have you come to tell me?" he asked. "Or shall I hazard a guess?"

"You can't guess," said I.

"No – it's no guess. She has come returned and you have

seen her. Tell me about it."

I gave him my story.

"That's Major Pearsall's house," he said. "Come back with me there at once."

"But what can we do?" I asked.

"I've no idea. That's what we have got to find out."

A minute later, we were opposite the house. When I had passed it before, it was completely dark – now lights wer gleaming from a couple of the windows upstairs. Even as we faced it, the front door opened, and the next moment Major Pearsall emerged from the gate. He saw us and stopped, looking flustered.

"I'm on my way to Dr Ross," he said quickly, "My wife has been taken suddenly ill. She had been in bed an hour when I came upstairs, and I found her white as a ghost and utterly exhausted. She had been to sleep, it seemed – but you will excuse me."

"One moment, Major," said Urcombe. "Was there any mark on her throat?"

"How did you guess that?" said he. "There was. One of those beastly gnats must have bitten her twice there. She was streaming with blood."

"And there's someone with her?" asked Urcombe.

"Yes, I roused her maid."

He went off, and Urcombe turned to me. "I know now what we have to do," he said. "Change your clothes and I'll join you at your house."

"What is it?" I asked.

"I'll tell you on our way. We're going to the cemetery."

He carried a pick, a shovel and a screwdriver when he rejoined me, and wore round his shoulders a long coil of rope. As we walked, he gave me the outlines of the ghastly hour that lay before us.

"What I have to tell you," he said, "will seem to you now too fantastic for credence, but before dawn we shall see whether it outstrips reality. If I am right, we shall find her body undecayed and untouched by corruption."

"But she has been dead nearly two months," said I.

"If she had been dead two years it would still be so, if the vampire has possession of her. So remember, whatever you see happening, it will be happening not to her, who in the natural course of events would now be feeding the grasses far above her grave, but to a spirit of unimagineable evil and malignancy, which gives a phantom life to her body."

"But what shall I see happen?" said I.

"I will tell you. We know that now, at this very moment, the vampire clad in her mortal semblance is out – dining out. But it must get back before dawn and it will pass into the material form that lies in her grave. We must wait for that, and then with your help I shall dig up her body. And then, when dawn has arrived, and the vampire cannot leave the lair of her body, I shall strike her with this —" and he pointed to his pick "—through the heart, and she will be dead indeed. Then we must bury her again, delivered at last of the vampire curse."

We had come to the cemetery, and in the silvery brightness of the moonlight there was no difficulty in identifying Mrs Amworth's grave. It lay some twenty yards from the small chapel, in the porch of which, obscured by shadow, we concealed ourselves. From there we had a very clear view of the grave, and now we must wait till its infernal visitor returned home.

The moon had long set, but a twilight of stars shone in a clear sky, when five o'clock in the morning sounded from the turret. A few minutes more passed, and then I felt Urcombe's hand softly nudging me.

Looking out in the direction of his pointing finger, I saw that the form of a woman, tall and large in build, was approaching from the right. Noiselessly, with a motion more of gliding and floating than of walking, she moved across the cemetery to the grave which was the centre of our observation. In the greyness to which now my eyes had grown accustomed, I could easily see her face, and recognize its features. She had a trickle of blood inching down her chin, and as we watched and listened she broke into a chuckle of such laughter as made my hair stir on my head.

Then she leapt on to the grave, holding her hands high above her head, and inch by inch disappeared into the earth. Urcombe's hand was laid on my arm, in an injunction to keep still, but now he removed it.

Mrs Amworth

"Follow me," he said.

With pick and shovel and rope we went
to the grave. The earth was light and
sandy, and soon after six struck, we
had delved down to the coffin lid.
With his pick he loosened the
earth round it, and

adjusting the rope through the handles by which it had been lowered, we tried to raise it.

This was a laborious business, and light had begun to herald day before we had it out by the side of the grave. With his screwdriver he loosed the fastenings of the lid, and slid it aside, and we looked on the face of Mrs Amworth. The eyes were open, the cheeks were flushed with colour, the red, full-lipped mouth seemed to smile.

"One blow and it's all over," he said. "You need not look."

As he spoke he took up the pick, and laying the point of it on her left breast, measured his distance.

He took the pick in both hands, raised it an inch or two to take aim, and then with brought it down on her breast. Blood spouted, falling with the thud of a heavy splash over the shroud. Simultaneously came one appalling cry. With that came the touch of corruption on her face, the colour of it faded to ash, the cheeks fell in, the mouth dropped.

"Thank God, that's over," said he, and without pause slipped the coffin lid back into its place.

Day was coming fast now, and we lowered the coffin into its place, and shovelled earth over it. The birds were busy with their earliest pipings as we went back to Maxley.

Carmilla

Sheridan Le Fanu

Laura and her father live in a remote part of Austria in a magnificent castle – or schloss as it is called in Austria. Laura has two women who care for her, whom she calls Madame and Mademoiselle, but no other companions. Until, that is, her father takes care of Carmilla, whose mother is away on business.

NEXT DAY CAME and we met again. I was delighted with my companion – that is to say, in many respects. She was slender and wonderfully graceful. Except that her movements were languid – very languid – indeed, there was nothing in her appearance to indicate an invalid. Her complexion was rich and brilliant, and her features were small and beautifully formed. Her eyes were large, dark and lustrous and her hair was quite wonderful. I never saw hair so magnificently thick and long when it was down about her shoulders. I loved to let it down, tumbling with its own weight, as she lay back in her chair talking in her sweet low voice, I used to fold and braid it, and spread it out and play with it. Heavens! If I had but known all!

I now write, after an interval of more than ten years, with a trembling hand, with a confused and horrible recollection of certain occurrences and situations, in the ordeal through which I was unconsciously passing – though with a vivid and very sharp remembrance of the main current of my story.

Sometimes after an hour of apathy, my strange and beautiful companion would take my hand and hold it fondly. She would whisper, almost in sobs, "You are mine, you shall be mine, you and I are one forever." Then she would throw herself back in her chair, with her small hands over her eyes, leaving me trembling.

"Are we related," I used to ask, "what can you mean by all this? I remind you perhaps of someone whom you know – but you must not, I hate it. I don't know you – I don't know myself when you look so and talk so."

She used to sigh at my vehemence, then turn away and drop my hand.

Between these moments there were long intervals of

gaiety, of brooding melancholy, during which, I detected her eyes so full of fire, following me, at times I might have been as nothing to her. Except in these brief periods of mysterious excitement, her ways were girlish and there was always a languor about her.

In some respects her habits were odd. Perhaps not so singular in the opinion of a town lady like you, as they appeared to us rustic people. She used to come down very late, generally not till one o'clock, she would then take a cup of chocolate, but eat nothing. We then went out for a walk, which was a mere saunter, and she seemed almost immediately exhausted, and either returned to the *schloss* or sat on one of the benches that were placed among the trees. She was always an animated talker, and very intelligent.

As we sat under the trees one afternoon a funeral passed us by. It was that of a pretty young girl, whom I had often seen, the daughter of one of the rangers of the forest. The poor man was walking behind the coffin of his daughter – she was his only child, and he looked quite heartbroken.

Peasants walking in twos came behind the coffin singing a funeral hymn.

I rose to mark my respect as they passed and joined in the hymn they were very sweetly singing.

My companion shook me a little roughly and I turned to

look at her in surprise.

"You pierce my ears," said Carmilla, almost angrily, and stopping her ears with her tiny fingers. "What a fuss! Why you must die – everyone must die, and all are happier when they do. Come home."

"My father has gone on with the clergyman to the churchyard. I thought you knew she was to be buried today."

"She? I don't trouble my head about peasants. I don't know who she is," answered Carmilla, with a flash from her fine eyes.

"She is a poor girl who fancied she saw a ghost a fortnight ago, and has been dying ever since, till yesterday, when she expired."

"Tell me nothing about ghosts. I won't sleep tonight if you do."

"I hope there is no plague or fever coming, all this looks very like it," I continued. "The swineherd's young wife died only a week ago, and she thought something seized her by the throat as she lay in her bed and nearly strangled her. Papa says such horrible fancies do accompany some forms of fever. She was quite well the day before. She sank afterwards and died before a week."

"Well, her funeral is over, I hope, and her hymn sung. Our ears shan't be tortured with that discord and jargon. It has made me feel nervous. Please sit down close beside me and hold my hand."

We had moved a little further back and had come to another seat.

She sat down. Her face underwent a change that alarmed and even terrified me for a moment. It darkened and became horribly livid. Her teeth and hands were clenched, and she frowned and compressed her lips, while she stared down upon the ground at her feet, and trembled all over with a continued shudder as irrepressible as fever. This was the first time I had seen her exhibit any delicacy of health. It was also the first time I had seen her exhibit anything close to temper.

Both passed away like a summer cloud, and never but once afterwards did I witness on her part a momentary sign of anger. I will tell you how it happened.

She and I were looking out of one of the long drawing room windows, when there entered the courtyard, over the drawbridge, a figure of a wanderer whom I knew very well. He used to visit the *schloss* generally twice a year.

It was the figure of a hunchback, with the sharp lean features that generally accompany deformity. He wore a pointed black beard, and he was smiling from ear to ear, showing his white fangs. He was dressed in buff, black and scarlet, and crossed with more straps and belts than I could count, from which hung all manner of things. His companion was a rough spare dog, that followed at his heels, but stopped short, suspiciously at the drawbridge, and in a little while began to howl dismally.

Then he advanced to the window with many smiles and salutations, and his hat in his left hand.

"Will your ladyships be pleased to buy an amulet against the *oupire*, which is going like the wolf, I hear, through these woods," he said dropping his hat on the pavement. "They are dying of it right and left and here is a charm that never fails – pin it to your pillow, and you may laugh in his face."

These charms consisted of oblong slips of

vellum, with ciphers and diagrams upon them.

Carmilla instantly purchased one, and so did I.

He was looking up, and we were smiling down upon him, amused – at least, I can answer for myself. His piercing black eye, as he looked up in our faces, seemed to detect something that fixed for a moment his curiosity.

In an instant he unrolled a leather case full of all manner of odd little steel instruments.

"See here, my lady," he said, displaying it and addressing me, "I profess, among other things less useful, the art of dentistry. Plague take the dog!" he remarked. "Silence, beast! He howls so that your ladyships can scarcely hear a word. Your noble friend, the young lady at your right, has the sharpest tooth, – long, thin, pointed like a needle. Now if it happens to hurt the young lady, and I think it must, here am I with my file, my punch and my nippers. I will make it round and blunt, if her ladyship pleases – no longer the tooth of a fish, but of a beautiful young lady as she is. Hey? Is the young lady displeased? Have I been too bold? Have I offended her?"

The young lady, indeed, looked very angry as she drew back from the window.

"How dare you insult us so? My father would have you tied up to the pump and flogged with a cart whip, and burnt to the bones with the cattle brand!"

My father was out of spirits that evening. On coming in he told us that there had been another case very similar to the two fatal ones which had lately occurred. The sister of a young peasant on his estate was very ill. She had been attacked very nearly in the same way, and was now slowly but steadily sinking.

"The doctor said he would come here today," said my father, after a silence. "I want to know what he thinks about it and what he thinks we had better do."

"Doctors never did me any good," said Carmilla.

"Then you have been ill?" I asked.

"More ill than ever you were," she answered.

"Long ago?"

"Yes, a long time. I suffered from this very illness. I forget all but my pain and weakness, and they were not so bad as are suffered in other diseases."

"You were very young then?"

"I dare say, let us talk no more of it. You would not wound a friend?"

She looked languidly in my eyes, and passed her arm round my waist lovingly, and led me out of the room. My father was busy over some papers near the window.

"Why does your papa like to frighten us?" she said with a

sigh and a little shudder.

"He doesn't, dear Carmilla, it is the very furthest thing from his mind."

"Are you afraid, dearest?"

"I should be very much if I fancied there was any real danger of my being attacked as those poor people were."

"You are afraid to die?"

"Yes, everyone is."

"But to die as lovers may – to die together, so that they may live together."

Later in the day the doctor came, and was closeted with papa for some time.

He was a skilful man, of sixty and upwards, he wore powder, and shaved his pale face as smooth as a pumpkin. He and papa emerged from the room together, and I heard papa laugh, and say as they came out, "I do wonder at a wise man like you. What do you say to hippogriffs and dragons?"

The doctor was smiling, and made answer, shaking his head, "Nevertheless life and death are mysterious states, and we know little of the resources of either."

And so they walked on and I heard no more. I did not then know what the doctor had been broaching, but I think I guess it now.

This evening there arrived from Gratz the grave, dark-faced son of the picture cleaner, with a horse and cart laden with two large packing cases, having many pictures in each. It was a journey of ten leagues, and whenever a messenger arrived at the schloss from our little capital of Gratz, we used to crowd about him in the hall, to hear the news.

This arrival created in our secluded quarters quite a sensation. With assistants, and armed with hammer, ripping chisel and turnscrew, he met us in the hall, where we had assembled to witness the unpacking of the cases.

Carmilla sat looking listlessly on, while one after the other the old pictures, nearly all portraits, which had undergone the process of renovation, were brought to light. My mother was of an old Hungarian family, and most of these pictures, which were about to be restored to their places, had come to us through her.

"There is a picture that I have not seen yet," said my father. "In one corner, at the top of it, is the name, as well as I could read, 'Marcia Karnstein,' and the date '1698'. I am curious to see how it has turned out."

I remembered it. It was a small picture, about a foot and a half high, and nearly square, without a frame, but it was so blackened by age that I could not make it out.

The artist now produced it, with evident pride. It was

quite beautiful. It was
startling – it seemed to
live. It was the effigy of
Carmilla!

"Carmilla, dear, here is
an absolute miracle. Here
you are, living, smiling,
ready to speak, in this
picture. Isn't it beautiful,
Papa? And see, even the
little mole on her throat."

My father laughed, and
said, "Certainly it is a
wonderful likeness of her,"
but he looked away, and to my surprise seemed but little
struck by it, and went on talking to the picture cleaner
while I was more and more lost in wonder the more I
looked upon the picture.

"Will you let me hang this picture in my bedroom, papa?"
I asked.

"Certainly, dear," said he, smiling, "I'm very glad you
think it so like. And now you can read the name that is
written in the corner. It is not Marcia – it looks as if it was
done in gold. The name is Mircalla, Countess Karnstein, and

this is a little coronet over and underneath AD."

"How interesting," Carmilla said, languidly. "But see what beautiful moonlight!" She glanced through the hall door, which stood a little open. "Suppose you take a little ramble round the court, and look down at the road and river."

"It is so like the night you came to us," I said.

She sighed, smiling.

She rose, and each with her arm about the other's waist, we walked out upon the pavement.

In silence, slowly we walked down to the drawbridge, where the beautiful landscape opened before us.

"And so you were thinking of the night I came here?" she almost whispered.

"Are you glad I came?"

"Delighted, dear Carmilla," I answered. "I am sure you have been in love – that there is, at this moment, an affair of the heart going on."

"I have been in love with no one, and never shall," she whispered.

How beautiful she looked in the moonlight!

Shy and strange was the look with which she quickly hid her face in my neck and hair, and seemed almost to sob, and pressed in mine a hand that trembled.

I started from her.

She was gazing at me with eyes from which all fire, all meaning had flown.

"Is there a chill in the air, dear?" she said drowsily. "I almost shiver – have I been dreaming? Let us go in. Come, come, come in."

"You look ill, Carmilla, a little faint. You certainly must take some wine," I said.

"Yes. I will. I'm better now. I shall be quite well in a few minutes. Yes, do give me a little wine," answered Carmilla, as we approached the door.

"Let us look again for a moment. It is the last time, perhaps, I shall see the moonlight with you."

When we got into the drawing room, and had sat down to our coffee and chocolate, although Carmilla did not take any, she seemed quite herself again. When the game was over he sat down beside Carmilla on the sofa, and asked her, a little anxiously, whether she had heard from her mother since her arrival.

She answered "No."

He then asked whether she knew where a letter would reach her at present.

"I cannot tell," she answered ambiguously, "but I have been thinking of leaving you – you have been already too hospitable and too kind to me. I have given you an infinity of trouble. I should wish to take a carriage tomorrow and post in pursuit of her – I know where I shall ultimately find her, although I dare not yet tell you."

"But you must not dream of any such thing," exclaimed my father, to my great relief. "We can't afford to lose you so, and I won't consent to your leaving us, except under the care of your mother, who was so good as to consent to your remaining with us till she should herself return."

"Thank you, sir, a thousand times for your hospitality," she answered, smiling bashfully. "You have all been too kind to me. I have seldom been so happy in all my life before, as in your beautiful chateau, under your care, and in the society of your dear daughter."

So he gallantly, in his old-fashioned way, kissed her hand, smiling and pleased at her little speech.

I accompanied Carmilla as usual to her room and sat and chatted with her while she was preparing for bed.

"Do you think," I said at length, "that you will ever confide fully in me?"

She turned round smiling, but made no answer, only continued to smile on me.

"You won't answer that?" I said. "You can't answer pleasantly – I ought not to have asked you."

"You were quite right to ask me that, or anything. You do

not know how dear you are to me, or you could not think any confidence too great to look for.

But I am under vows, and I dare not tell my story yet, even to you. The time is very near when you shall know everything. You will think me cruel, very selfish, but love is always selfish. How jealous I am you cannot know. You must come with me, loving me, to death, or else hate me and still come with me – hating me through death and after. "

"Now, Carmilla, you are going to talk your wild nonsense again," I said hastily.

"Not I, silly little fool as I am, and full of whims and fancies. For your sake I'll talk like a sage. Have you ever been to a ball?"

"No. How you do run on. What is it like? How charming it must be."

"I almost forget, it is years ago."

I laughed.

"You are not so old. Your first ball can hardly be forgotten yet."

"I remember everything about it – with an effort. There occurred that night what has confused the picture and made its colours faint. I was all but assassinated in my bed, wounded here," she touched her breast, "and never was the same since."

"Were you near dying?"

"Yes, very – a cruel love – strange love, that would have taken my life. Love will have its sacrifices. No sacrifice without blood. Let us go to sleep now. I feel so tired. How can I get up just now and lock my door?"

She was lying with her tiny hands buried in her rich wavy hair, under her cheek, her little head upon the pillow, and her glittering eyes followed me wherever I moved, with a kind of shy smile.

I bid her goodnight and crept from the room with an uncomfortable sensation.

I often wondered whether our pretty guest ever said her prayers. I certainly had never seen her do so. In the morning she never came down until long after our family prayers were over, and at night she never left the drawing room to attend our brief evening prayers in the hall.

The precautions of nervous people are infectious, and persons of a like temperament are pretty sure, after a time, to imitate them. I had adopted Carmilla's habit of locking her bedroom door, having taken into my head all her whimsical alarms about midnight invaders and prowling assassins. These wise measures taken, I got into my bed and fell asleep. A light was burning in my room. This was an old habit, of very early date, and which nothing could have tempted me to dispense with.

Thus fortifed I might take my rest in peace. But dreams come through stone walls, light up dark rooms, or darken light ones, and their persons make their exits and their entrances as they please, and laugh at locksmiths.

I had a dream that night that was the beginning of a very strange agony.

I cannot call it a nightmare, for I was quite conscious of being asleep.

But I was equally conscious of being in my room, and lying in bed, precisely as I actually was. I saw, or fancied I saw, the room and its furniture just as I had seen it last, except that it was very dark, and I saw something moving round the foot of the bed, which at first I could not accurately distinguish. But I soon saw that it was a sooty-black animal that resembled a monstrous cat. It appeared to me about four or five feet long for it measured fully the length of the hearth rug as it passed over it. It continued to-ing and fro-ing with the lithe, sinister restlessness of a beast in a cage. I could not cry out, although as you may suppose, I was terrified. Its pace was growing faster, and the room rapidly darker and darker, and at length so dark that I could no longer see anything of it but its eyes. I felt it spring lightly on the bed. The two broad eyes approached my face, and suddenly I felt a stinging pain as if two large needles darted, an inch or two apart, deep into my breast. I waked with a scream. The room was lighted by the candle that burnt there all through the night, and I saw a female figure standing at the foot of the bed, a little at the right side. It was in a dark loose dress, and its hair was down and covered its shoulders. A block of stone could not have been more still. As I stared at it, the figure appeared to have changed its place and was now nearer the door. Then the door opened and it passed out.

I was now relieved, and able to breathe and move. My first thought was that Carmilla had been playing a trick on me, and that I had forgotten to secure my door. I hastened to it and found it locked as usual on the inside. I was afraid to open it – I was horrified. I sprang into my bed and covered my head up in the bedclothes, and lay there more dead than alive till morning.

I could not bear next day to be alone for a moment. I should have told papa, but for two opposite reasons. At one time I thought he would laugh at my story, and I could not bear its being treated as a jest, and at another I thought he might fancy that I had been attacked by the mysterious complaint which had invaded our neighbourhood.

At this distance of time I cannot tell you, or even understand, how I overcame my horror so effectually as to lie alone in my bedroom that night. I remember distinctly that I pinned the charm to my pillow. I fell asleep almost immediately and slept even more soundly than usual all through the night.

Next night I passed as well. My sleep was delightfully deep and dreamless.

But I wakened with a strange sense of lassitude and melancholy, which, however, did not exceed a degree that was almost luxurious.

"Well, I told you so," said Carmilla, when I described my quiet sleep, "I had such delightful sleep myself last night – I pinned the charm to the breast of my nightdress. It was too far away the night before. I am quite sure it was all fancy, except the dreams. I used to think that evil spirits made dreams, but our doctor told me it is no such thing. Only a fever passing by, or some other malady, as they often do, he said, knocks at the door, and not being able to get in, passes on, with that alarm."

"And what do you think the charm is?" said I.

"It has been fumigated or immersed in some drug, and is an antidote against the malaria," she answered.

"Then it acts only on the body?"

"Certainly. You don't suppose that evil spirits are frightened by bits of ribbon or the perfumes of a druggist's shop? It is nothing magical, it is simply natural.

I should have been happier if I could have quite agreed with Carmilla, but I did my best, and the impression was a little losing its force.

For some nights I slept profoundly, but still every morning I felt the same lassitude, and a languor weighed upon me all day. I felt myself a changed girl. A strange melancholy was stealing over me, a melancholy that I would not have interrupted. Dim thoughts of death began to open, and an idea that I was slowly sinking took gentle, and, somehow, not unwelcome, possession of me. If it was sad, the tone of mind which this induced was also sweet.

I would not admit that I was ill, I would not consent to

tell my papa, or to have the doctor sent for.

Carmilla became more devoted to me than ever, and her strange adoration more frequent. She used to gloat over me the more my strength and spirits waned. This always shocked me like a momentary glare of insanity.

Without knowing it, I was now in a pretty advanced stage of the strangest illness under which mortals ever suffered. Certain vague and strange sensations visited me in my sleep. The prevailing one was of that pleasant, peculiar cold thrill which we feel in bathing, when we move against the current of a river. This was soon accompanied by dreams that seemed so vague that I could never recollect their scenery and persons, or anyone connected portion of their action. But they left an awful impression, and a sense of exhaustion, as if I had passed through a long period of great mental exertion and danger.

After all these dreams there remained on waking a remembrance of having been in a place very nearly dark. Sometimes there came a sensation as if a hand was drawn softly along my cheek and neck. Sometimes it was as if warm lips kissed me, and longer and longer and more lovingly as they reached my throat, but there the caress fixed itself. My heart beat faster, my breathing rose and fell rapidly and full drawn.

It was now three weeks since the commencement of this unaccountable state.

My sufferings had, during the last week, told upon my appearance. I had grown pale, my eyes were dilated and darkened underneath, and the languor that I had long felt began to display itself in my countenance.

My father asked me often whether I was ill, but with an obstinacy that now seems to me unaccountable, I persisted in assuring him that I was quite well.

In a sense this was true. I had no pain. My complaint seemed to be one of the imagination, or the nerves, and, horrible as my sufferings were, I kept them, with a morbid reserve, very nearly to myself.

It could not be that terrible complaint which the peasants called the *oupire*, for I had now been suffering for three weeks, and they were seldom ill for much more than three days, when death put an end to their miseries.

I am going to tell you now of a dream that led immediately to an odd discovery.

One night, instead of the voice I was accustomed to hear in the dark, I heard one, sweet and tender, and at the same time terrible, which said, "Your mother warns you to beware of the assassin." At the same time a light unexpectedly sprang up, and I saw Carmilla, standing, near

the foot of my bed, in her white
nightdress, bathed, from her
chin to her feet, in one
great stain of blood.
I wakened with a
shriek, possessed with
the one idea that
Carmilla was being
murdered. I remember
springing from my
bed, and my next
recollection is that of
standing on the lobby,
crying for help.
Madame and
Mademoiselle came
scurrying in alarm. A
lamp burned always on
the lobby, and seeing me,
they soon learned the
cause of my terror.
I insisted on our knocking
at Carmilla's door. Our knocking
was unanswered.

It soon became a pounding and an uproar. We shrieked her name, but all was vain.

We all grew frightened, for the door was locked. We hurried back, in panic, to my room. There we rang the bell long and furiously. If my father's room had been at that side of the house, we would have called him up at once to our aid. But, alas! He was quite out of hearing, and to reach him involved an excursion for which none of us had courage.

Servants, however, soon came running up the stairs. I had got on my dressing gown and slippers meanwhile. Recognizing the voices of the servants on the lobby, we sallied out together. Having renewed, as fruitlessly, our summons at Carmilla's door, I ordered the men to force the lock. They did so, and we stood, holding our lights aloft, in the doorway, and so stared into the room.

We called her by name, but there was still no reply. We looked round the room. Everything was undisturbed. It was exactly in the state in which I had left it on bidding her good night. But Carmilla was gone.

At sight of the room, perfectly undisturbed except for our violent entrance, we began to cool a little, and soon recovered our senses sufficiently to dismiss the men. It had struck Mademoiselle that possibly Carmilla had been wakened by the uproar at her door, and in her first panic had jumped from her bed, and hid herself in a press, or behind a curtain. We now recommenced our search and began to call her name again.

It was all to no purpose. We examined the windows, but they were secured. I was utterly puzzled. Had Carmilla discovered one of those secret passages which the old housekeeper said were known to exist in the schloss, although the tradition of their exact situation had been lost? A little time would, no doubt, explain all – utterly perplexed as, for the present, we were.

It was past four o'clock and I preferred passing the remaining hours of darkness in Madame's room. Daylight brought no solution of the difficulty.

The whole household, with my father at its head, was in a state of agitation next morning. Every part of the chateau was searched. The grounds were explored. No trace of the missing lady could be discovered. It was now one o'clock and still no tidings.

I ran up to Carmilla's room and found her standing at her dressing table. I was astounded. I could not believe my eyes. She beckoned me to her with her pretty finger, in silence. Her face expressed extreme fear.

"Dear Carmilla, what has become of you all this time? We have been in agonies of anxiety about you," I exclaimed.

"Where have you been? How did you come back?"

"Last night has been a night of wonders," she said.

"For mercy's sake, explain all you can."

"It was past two last night," she said, "when I went to sleep as usual in my bed, with my doors locked, that of the dressing room, and that opening upon the gallery. My sleep was uninterrupted, and, so far as I know, dreamless. But I woke just now on the sofa in the dressing room there, and I found the door between the rooms open, and the other door forced.

"How could all this have happened without my being wakened? It must have been accompanied with a great deal of noise, and I am particularly easily wakened – and how could I have been carried out of my bed without my sleep having been interrupted, I whom the slightest stir startles?"

By this time, Madame, Mademoiselle, my father and a number of the servants were in the room. Carmilla was, of course, overwhelmed with inquiries, congratulations and welcomes. She had but one story to tell, and seemed the least able of all the party to suggest any way of accounting for what had happened.

My father took a turn up and down the room, thinking. I saw Carmilla's eye follow him for a moment with a cruel sly, dark glance.

When my father had sent the servants away, Mademoiselle having gone in search of a little bottle of valerian and salvolatile, and there being no one now in the room with Carmilla, except my father, Madame and myself, he came to her thoughtfully, took her hand very kindly, led her to the sofa, and sat down beside her.

"Will you forgive me, my dear, if I risk a conjecture and ask a question?"

"Who can have a better right?" she said.

"My question is this. Have you ever been suspected of walking in your sleep?"

"Never, since I was very young indeed."

"But you did walk in your sleep when you were young?"

"Yes — I know I did. I have been told so often by my old nurse."

My father smiled and nodded.

"Well, what has happened is this. You got up in your sleep, unlocked the door, not leaving the key, as usual, in the lock, but taking it out and locking it on the outside. You again took the key out, and carried it away with you to some one of the five-and-twenty rooms on this floor, or perhaps upstairs or downstairs.

"There are so many rooms and closets, so much heavy furniture, and such accumulations of lumber, that it would require a week to search this old house thoroughly. Do you see, now, what I mean?"

"I do, but not all," she answered.

"And how, papa, do you account for her finding herself on the sofa in the dressing room, which we had searched so carefully?"

"She came there after you had searched it, still in her sleep, and at last awoke spontaneously, and was as much surprised to find herself where she was as any one else. I wish all mysteries were as easily and innocently explained as yours, Carmilla," he said, laughing.

Carmilla was looking charmingly. Her beauty was, I think, enhanced by that graceful languor that was peculiar to her. I think my father was silently contrasting her looks with mine, for he said, "I wish my poor Laura was looking more like herself" and sighed.

So our alarms were happily ended and Carmilla restored to her friends.

⦂⊰○⊱⦂

As Carmilla would not hear of an attendant sleeping in her room with her, my father arranged that a servant should sleep right outside her door, so that she would not attempt to make another similar excursion without being arrested at her own bedroom door.

That night passed quietly and early next morning, the doctor, whom my father had sent for without telling me a word about it, arrived to see me.

Madame accompanied me to the library and there the grave little doctor, with white hair and spectacles, whom I mentioned before, was waiting to receive me.

I told him my story, and as I proceeded he grew graver and graver.

We were standing, he and I, in the recess of one of the windows, facing one another. When my statement was over, he leaned with his shoulders against the wall, and with his eyes fixed on me earnestly, with an interest in which was a dash of horror.

After a minute's reflection, he asked Madame if he could see my father.

He was sent for accordingly, and as he entered, smiling, he said, "I dare say, doctor, you are going to tell me that I am an old fool for having brought you here – I hope I am."

But his smile faded into shadow as the doctor, with a very grave face, beckoned him to him.

He and the doctor talked for some time in the same recess where I had just conferred with the physician. It seemed an earnest conversation. The room is very large, and

I and Madame stood together, burning with curiosity, at the farther end. Not a word could we hear, however, for they spoke in a very low tone, and the deep recess of the window quite concealed the doctor from view.

After a time my father's face looked into the room – it was pale, thoughtful, and, I fancied, agitated.

"Laura, dear, come here for a moment. Madame, we shan't trouble you, the doctor says, at present."

Accordingly I approached, for the first time a little alarmed, for although I felt very weak I did not feel ill, and strength, one always fancies, is a thing that may be picked up when we please.

My father held out his hand to me, as I drew near, but he was looking at the doctor, and he said:

"It certainly is very odd. I don't understand it quite. Laura, come here, dear. Now attend to Doctor Spielsberg and recollect yourself."

"You mentioned a sensation like that of two needles piercing the skin, somewhere about your neck, on the night when you experienced your first horrible dream. Is there still any soreness?"

"None at all," I answered.

"Can you indicate with your finger about the point at which you think this occurred?"

"Very little below my throat – about here," I replied to the doctor.

I was wearing a morning dress, which covered the area that I pointed to.

"Now you can satisfy yourself," said the doctor. "You won't mind your papa's lowering your dress just a very little. It is necessary, to detect a symptom of the complaint under which you have been suffering."

I acquiesced. It was only an inch or two below the edge of my collar.

"God bless me! So it is," said my father, growing pale.

"You see it now with your own eyes," said the doctor, with a gloomy triumph.

"What is it?" I exclaimed, beginning to be frightened.

"Nothing, my dear young lady, but a small blue spot, about the size of the tip of your little finger. Now," he continued, turning to papa, "the question is what is best to be done?"

"Is there any kind of danger?" I urged, in great trepidation.

"I trust not, my dear," answered the doctor. "I don't see why you should not recover. I don't see why you should not begin immediately to get better. That is the point at which the sense of strangulation begins?"

"Yes," I answered.

"And – recollect as well as you can – the same point was a kind of centre of that thrill which you described just now, like the current of a cold stream running against you?"

"It may have been – I think it was."

"Ay, you see?" he added, turning to my father. "Shall I say a word to Madame?"

"Certainly," said my father.

He called Madame to him, and said:

"I find my young friend here far from well. It won't be of any great consequence, I hope, but it will be necessary that some steps be taken, which I will explain by-and-by. In the meantime, Madame, you will be so good as not to let Miss Laura be alone for one moment. That is the only direction I need give for the present. It is indispensable."

"We may rely upon you, Madame," added my father.

Madame satisfied him eagerly.

"And you, dear Laura, I know you will observe the doctor's direction."

"I shall have to ask your opinion upon another patient, whose symptoms slightly resemble those of my daughter. She is a young lady – our guest, but as you say you will be passing this way again this evening, you can't do better than take your supper here, and you can then see her. She does not come down till the afternoon."

"I thank you," said the doctor. "I shall be with you, then, at about seven this evening."

"Papa, darling, will you tell me this?" said I, laying my hand on his arm, and looking imploringly in his face.

"Perhaps," he answered, smoothing my hair.

"Does the doctor think me very ill?"

"No, dear. He thinks if right steps are taken, you will be quite well again, on the road to recovery, in a day or two," he answered, a little dryly "But do tell me, papa," I insisted, "what does he think is the matter with me?"

"Nothing – you must not plague me with questions," he answered, with more irritation than I ever remember him to have displayed before. Seeing that I looked wounded, I suppose, he kissed me, and added, "You shall know all about it in a day or two — that is, all that I know. In the meantime you are not to trouble your head about it."

❖◦❖

A friend of Laura and her father visits them and tells them a terrible story of how his daughter was killed by a beautiful vampire. He then is shocked to see Carmilla entering the family chapel and reveals to them to them that Carmilla is that same vampire, who has been alive for centuries under a different name: Mircalla. Countess Karnstein. Carmilla disappears and Laura's father prepares to try and save her from the curse of the vampire.

❖◦❖

My father came to me, kissed me again and again, and leading me from the chapel said:

"It is time to return, but before we go home, we must add to our party the good priest, who lives but a little way from this, and persuade him to accompany us to the *schloss*."

In this quest we were successful and I was glad, being unspeakably fatigued when we reached home. But my satisfaction was changed to dismay, on discovering that there were no tidings of Carmilla.

The arrangements for the night were singular. Two servants, and Madame were to sit up in my room that night, and the ecclesiastic with my father kept watch in the adjoining dressing room.

The priest had performed certain solemn rites that night, the purport of which I did not understand any more than I comprehended the reason of this extraordinary precaution taken for my safety during sleep.

I saw all clearly a few days later.

The disappearance of Carmilla was followed by the discontinuance of my nightly sufferings.

You have heard, no doubt, of the appalling superstition that prevails in Upper and Lower Styria, in Moravia, Silesia, in Turkish Serbia, in Poland, even in Russia – the superstition, so we must call it, of the Vampire.

If human testimony is worth anything, it is difficult to deny, or even to doubt the existence of such a phenomenon as the Vampire.

For my part I have heard no theory by which to explain what I myself have witnessed and experienced, other than that supplied by the ancient and well-attested belief of the country.

The next day the formal proceedings took place in the Chapel of Karnstein.

The grave of the Countess Mircalla was opened, and the General and my father each recognized his perfidious and beautiful guest, in the face now disclosed to view.

The features, although one hundred and fifty years had passed since her funeral, were tinted with the warmth of life. Her eyes were open – no cadaverous smell exhaled from the coffin.

The two medical men, one officially present, the other on the part of the promoter of the inquiry, attested the marvellous fact that there was a faint but appreciable respiration, and a corresponding action of the heart. The limbs were perfectly flexible, the flesh elastic, and the leaden coffin floated with blood, in which to a depth of seven inches, the body lay immersed.

Here then, were all the admitted signs and proofs of vampirism. The body, therefore, in accordance with the ancient practice, was raised, and a sharp stake driven through the heart of the vampire, who uttered a piercing shriek that might escape from a living person in the last agony. Then the head was struck off and a torrent of blood flowed from the severed neck.

The body and head was next placed on a pile of wood, and reduced to ashes, which were thrown upon the river and borne away, and that territory has never since been plagued by the visits of a vampire.

My father has a copy of the report of the Imperial

Commission, with the signatures of all who were present at these proceedings, attached in verification of the statement. It is from this official paper that I have summarized my account of this last shocking scene.

CARMILLA

THE VAMPIRE MAID

Hume Nisbet

IT WAS THE EXACT KIND of abode that I had been looking after for weeks, for I was in that condition of mind when absolute renunciation of society was a necessity. I had become diffident of myself and wearied of my kind. Familiar objects and faces had grown distasteful to me. I wanted to be alone.

I hastily packed up my knapsack, and taking the train to Westmorland, I began my tramp in search of solitude, bracing air and romantic surroundings.

Many places I came upon during that early summer wandering appeared to have almost the required conditions, yet some petty drawback prevented me from deciding. Sometimes it was the scenery that I did not take kindly to. At other places I took sudden antipathies to the landlady or landlord. Fate was driving me to this Cottage on the Moor and no one can resist destiny.

One day I found myself on a wide and pathless moor near the sea. I had slept the night before at a small hamlet, but that was already eight miles behind me, and since I had turned my back upon it I had not seen any signs of humanity. How far the moor stretched I had no knowledge. I only knew that by keeping in a straight line I would come to the ocean cliffs, then perhaps after a time arrive at some fishing village.

I had provisions in my knapsack and being young did not fear a night under the stars. I was inhaling the delicious summer air and once more getting back the vigour and happiness I had lost – my city-dried brains were again becoming juicy.

Thus hour after hour slid past me, with the paces, until I had covered about fifteen miles since morning, when I saw before me in the distance a solitary stone-built cottage with roughly slated roof. "I'll camp there if possible," I said to myself as I quickened my steps towards it.

To one in search of a quiet, free life, nothing could have possibly been more suitable than this cottage. It stood on the edge of lofty cliffs, with its front door facing the moor and the backyard wall overlooking the ocean.

As I approached, taking notice of the orderly cleanness of the windows, the front door opened. A woman appeared who impressed me at once as she walked along the pathway to the gate, and drew it back as if to welcome me.

She was of middle age, and when young must have been remarkably good-looking. She was tall and still shapely, with smooth, clear skin, regular features and a calm expression that at once gave me a sensation of rest.

To my inquiries she said that she could give me both a sitting and bedroom, and invited me in to see them. As I looked at her smooth black hair and cool brown eyes, I felt I would not be too particular about the accommodation. With such a landlady, I was sure to find what I was after here.

The rooms surpassed my expectation, dainty white curtains and bedding with the perfume of lavender about them. The sitting room was homely yet cosy without being crowded. With a sigh of infinite relief I flung down my knapsack and clinched the bargain.

She was a widow with one daughter, whom I did not see the first day, as she was unwell and confined to her room, but the next day she was somewhat better, and we met.

The fare was simple, yet it suited me exactly for the time, delicious milk and butter with homemade scones, fresh eggs and bacon. After a hearty tea I went to bed early in a condition of perfect content with my quarters.

Yet happy and tired out as I was I had by no means a comfortable night. I put this down to the strange bed. I slept certainly, but my sleep was filled with dreams, and I woke late and unrefreshed. However, a walk on the moor restored me, and I returned with a fine appetite for breakfast.

Certain conditions of mind, with aggravating circumstances, are required before even a young man can fall in love at first sight. In the city, where many fair faces passed me every hour, I had remained like a stoic, yet no sooner did I enter the cottage after that morning walk than I succumbed instantly before the strange charms of my landlady's daughter, Ariadne Brunnell.

She was somewhat better this morning and able to meet me at breakfast, for we had our meals together while I was their lodger. Ariadne was not beautiful in the strictly classical sense, her complexion being too white and her expression too set to be quite pleasant at first

361

sight – yet, as her mother had informed me, she had been ill for some time, which accounted for that defect.

She rose from her chair as her mother introduced her and smiled while she held out her hand. I clasped that soft snowflake, and as I did so a faint thrill tingled over me and rested on my heart, stopping for the moment its beating.

This contact seemed also to have affected her as it did me. A clear flush, like a white flame, lit up her face, so that it glowed as if an alabaster lamp had been lit. Her black eyes became softer and more humid as our glances crossed, and her scarlet lips grew moist. She was a living woman now, while before she had seemed half a corpse.

She permitted her white slender hand to remain in mine longer than most people do at an introduction, and then she slowly withdrew it, still regarding me with steadfast eyes for a second or two afterwards.

Fathomless velvety eyes these were, yet before they were shifted from mine they appeared to have absorbed all my willpower and made me her abject slave. They looked like deep dark pools of clear water, yet they filled me with fire and deprived me of strength. I sank into my chair almost as languidly as I had risen from my bed that morning.

I had come here seeking solitude, but since I had seen Ariadne it seemed as if I had come for her only. She was not

very lively – indeed, thinking back, I cannot recall any
spontaneous remark of hers. She answered my questions by
monosyllables and left me to lead in words. I cannot
describe her minutely, I only know that from the first glance
and touch she gave me I was bewitched and could think of
nothing else.

It was a rapid, distracting and devouring infatuation that
possessed me. All day long I followed her about like a dog,
every night I dreamt of that white, glowing face, those
steadfast black eyes, those moist scarlet lips, and each
morning I rose more languid than I had been the day before.
Sometimes I dreamt that she was kissing me with those red
lips, while I shivered at the contact of her silky black tresses
as they covered my throat. Sometimes we were floating in
the air, her arms about me and her long hair enveloping us
both like an inky cloud, while I lay supine and helpless.

She went with me after breakfast on that first day to the
moor, and before we came back I had spoken my love and
received her assent. I held her in my arms and had taken her
kisses in answer to mine, nor did I think it strange that all
this had happened so quickly. She was mine, or rather I was
hers, without a pause. I told her it was fate that had sent me
to her, for I had no doubts about my love and she replied
that I had restored her to life.

Acting upon Ariadne's advice, and also from a natural shyness, I did not inform her mother how quickly matters had progressed between us, yet although we both acted as circumspectly as possible, I had no doubt Mrs Brunnell could see how engrossed we were in each other. Lovers are not unlike ostriches in their modes of concealment. I was not afraid of asking Mrs Brunnell for her daughter, for she already showed her partiality towards me, and had bestowed upon me some confidences regarding her own position in life, and I therefore knew that, so far as social position was concerned, there could be no real objection to our marriage. They lived in this lonely spot for the sake of their health and kept no servant because they could not get any to take service so far away from other humanity. My coming had been opportune and welcome to both mother and daughter.

However, for the sake of decorum I resolved to delay my confession for a week or two, and trust to some favourable opportunity of doing it discreetly.

Meantime, Ariadne and I passed our time in a thoroughly idle and lotus-eating style. Each night I retired to bed meditating starting work next day, each morning I rose languid from those disturbing dreams with no thought for anything outside my love. She grew stronger every day, while I appeared to be taking her place as the invalid, yet I was more frantically in love than ever, and only happy when with her. She was my lodestar, my only joy – my life.

We did not go great distances, for I liked best to lie on the dry heath and watch her glowing face and intense eyes while I listened to the surging of the distant waves. It was love that made me lazy, I thought, for unless a man has all he longs for beside him, he is apt to copy the domestic cat and bask in the sunshine.

I had been enchanted quickly. My disenchantment came just as rapidly, although it was a long time before the poison left my blood.

One night, about a couple of weeks after my coming to the cottage, I had returned after a delicious moonlight walk with Ariadne. The night was warm and the moon at the full, therefore I left my bedroom window open to let in what little air there was.

I was more than usually tired out, so that I had only strength enough to remove my boots and coat before I flung myself wearily on the coverlet. I fell almost instantly asleep without tasting the nightcap draught that was constantly placed on the table, and which I had always drained thirstily.

I had a ghastly dream this night. I thought I saw a monster bat, with the face and tresses of Ariadne, fly into the open window and fasten its white teeth on my arm. I tried to beat the horror away, but could not, for I seemed chained down and enthralled with drowsy delight as the beast sucked my blood with a gruesome rapture.

I looked out dreamily and saw a line of dead bodies of young men lying on the floor, each with a red mark on their arms, on the same part where the vampire was then sucking me, and I remembered having seen and wondered at such a mark on my own arm for the past fortnight. In a flash I understood the reason for my strange weakness, and at the same moment a sudden prick of pain roused me from my dreamy pleasure.

The vampire in her eagerness had bitten me a little too deeply that night, unaware that I had not tasted the drugged draught. As I awoke I saw her fully revealed by the midnight moon, with her black tresses flowing loosely, and with her red lips glued to my arm. With a shriek of horror I dashed her backwards, getting one last glimpse of her savage eyes, glowing white face and bloodstained red lips. I rushed out into the night, moved on by my fear and hatred, and I did not pause in my mad flight until I had left many miles between me and that accursed cottage on the Moor.

CLARIMONDE

Théophile Gautier

❦

Romuald, a young French Catholic priest (called a curé *in France)
has become utterly infatuated with a mysterious beauty called
Clarimonde, who lives in his home town. He strives to lead a simple
and pure life in his presbytery (priest's house) helped by his fellow
priest, the Abbé Sérapion but his love for Clarimonde consumes him.
At this point in the story, he has just been informed she has died,
and he has been fetched to her castle to pray alone at night in the
room where her body lies.*

I COULD NO LONGER maintain my constrained attitude of
prayer. The air of the alcove intoxicated me, that
perfume of half-faded roses penetrated my very brain,
and I commenced to pace restlessly up and down the
chamber, pausing at each turn before the bier to

contemplate the graceful corpse lying beneath the transparency of its shroud. Wild fancies came thronging to my brain. I thought to myself that she might not, perhaps, be really dead – that she might only have feigned death for the purpose of bringing me to her castle, and then declaring her love. At one time I even thought I saw her foot move under the whiteness of the coverings and slightly disarrange the long straight folds of the winding sheet.

I approached the bed again and fixed my eyes with redoubled attention upon the object of my incertitude. Ah, must I confess it? That exquisite perfection of bodily form, although purified and made sacred by the shadow of death, affected me more voluptuously than it should have done. That repose so closely resembled slumber that one might well have mistaken it for such. I forgot that I had come there to perform a funeral ceremony. I fancied myself a young bridegroom entering the chamber of the bride, who all modestly hides her fair face, and through coyness seeks to keep herself wholly veiled. Heartbroken with grief, yet wild with hope, shuddering at once with fear and pleasure, I bent over her and grasped the corner of the sheet. I lifted it back, holding my breath all the while through fear of waking her. My arteries throbbed with such violence that I felt them hiss through my temples, and the sweat poured from my forehead in streams, as though I had lifted a mighty slab of marble. There, indeed, lay Clarimonde, even as I had seen her at the church on the day of my ordination. She was not less charming than then. The pallor of her cheeks, the less brilliant carnation of her lips, her long eyelashes lowered and relieving their dark fringe against that white skin, lent her an unspeakably seductive aspect of melancholy chastity and mental suffering. Her long loose hair, still intertwined with some little blue flowers, made a shining pillow for her head and veiled the nudity of her shoulders with its thick ringlets. Her beautiful hands were crossed on her bosom in an attitude of pious rest and silent prayer. I remained long in mute contemplation, and the more I gazed, the less could I persuade myself that life had really abandoned that beautiful body forever.

I do not know whether it was an illusion or a reflection of the lamplight, but it seemed to me that the blood was again commencing to circulate under that lifeless pallor, although she remained motionless. I resumed my position, bending my face above her, bathing her cheek with the warm dew of my tears. Ah, what bitter feelings of despair and helplessness, what agonies unutterable did I endure in that long watch! Vainly did I wish that I could have gathered all my life into one mass that I might give it all to her and breathe into her chill remains the flame that devoured me. The night advanced, and feeling the moment of eternal separation approach, I could not deny myself the last sad sweet pleasure of imprinting a kiss upon the dead lips of her who had been my only love.... Oh, miracle! A faint breath mingled itself with my breath and the mouth of Clarimonde responded to the passionate pressure of mine. Her eyes opened and lit up with something of their former brilliancy. She uttered a long sigh, and uncrossing her arms, passed them around my neck with a look of ineffable delight.

"Ah, it is thou, Romuald!" she murmured in a voice languishingly sweet as the last vibrations of a harp. "What ailed thee, dearest? I waited so long for thee that I am dead, but we are now betrothed. I can see thee and visit thee. Adieu, Romuald, adieu! I love thee. That is all I wished to tell thee, and I give thee back the life which thy kiss for a moment recalled. We shall soon meet again."

Her head fell back, but her arms yet encircled me, as though to retain me still. A furious whirlwind suddenly burst in the window and entered the chamber. The last remaining leaf of the white rose for a moment palpitated at the extremity of the stalk like a butterfly's wing, then it detached itself and flew forth through the open casement, bearing with it the soul of Clarimonde. The lamp was extinguished and I fell insensible upon the bosom of the beautiful dead.

When I came to myself again I was lying on the bed in my little room, and the old dog of the former *curé* was licking my hand, which had been hanging down outside of the covers. Afterward I learned that I had lain thus for three days, giving no evidence of life beyond the faintest respiration. Those three days do not reckon in my life, nor could I ever imagine whither my spirit had departed during those three days. I have no recollection of aught relating to them.

One morning I found the Abbé Sérapion in my room. Barbara had advised him that I was ill, and he had come with all speed to see me. Although this haste on his part testified to an affectionate interest in me, his visit did not cause me the pleasure which it should have done. The Abbé Sérapion had something penetrating and inquisitorial in his gaze which made me feel very ill at ease. His presence filled me with embarrassment and a sense of guilt. At the first glance he divined my interior trouble and I hated him for his clairvoyance.

While he inquired after my health in hypocritically honeyed accents, he constantly kept his two great yellow lion eyes fixed upon me, and plunged his look into my soul like a lead weight. Then he asked me how I directed my parish, if I was happy in it, how I passed the leisure hours allowed me in the intervals of pastoral duty, whether I had become acquainted with many of the inhabitants of the place, what was my favourite reading, and a thousand other such questions. I answered these inquiries as briefly as possible, and he, without ever waiting for my answers, passed rapidly from one subject of query to another.

That conversation had evidently no connection with what he actually wished to say. At last, without any premonition, but as though repeating a piece of news that he had recalled on the instant, and feared might otherwise be forgotten subsequently, he suddenly said, in a clear vibrant voice, which rang in my ears like the trumpets of the Last Judgment, "The great courtesan Clarimonde died a few days ago. There have always been very strange stories told of this Clarimonde, and all her lovers came to a violent or miserable end. They used to say that she was a ghoul, a female vampire – but I believe she was none other than Beelzebub himself."

He ceased to speak, and commenced to regard me more attentively than ever, as though to observe the effect of his words on me. I could not refrain from starting when I heard him utter the name of Clarimonde, and this news of her death filled me with an agony and terror which my face betrayed, despite my utmost endeavours to appear composed. Sérapion fixed an anxious and severe look upon me, and then observed, "My son, I must warn you that you are standing with a foot raised upon the brink of an abyss – take heed lest you fall therein. Satan's claws are long and tombs are not always true to their trust. The tombstone of Clarimonde should be sealed down with a triple seal, for if report be true, it is not the first time she has died. May God watch over you, Romuald!"

And with these words the Abbé walked slowly towards the door.

I became completely restored to health and resumed my accustomed duties. The memory of Clarimonde and the words of the old Abbé were constantly in my mind. Nevertheless, no extraordinary event had occurred to verify the predictions of Sérapion, and I had commenced to believe that his fears and my own terrors were over-exaggerated, when one night I had a strange dream. I had hardly fallen asleep when I heard my bed curtains drawn apart, as their rings slid back upon the curtain rod with a sharp sound. I rose up quickly upon my elbow and beheld the shadow of a woman standing before me. I recognized Clarimonde immediately. She bore in her hand a little lamp, shaped like

those which are placed in tombs, and its light lent her
fingers a rosy transparency, which extended itself by
lessening degrees even to the opaque and milky whiteness of
her bare arm. Her only garment was the linen winding sheet
that had shrouded her when lying upon the bed of death.
She sought to gather its folds over her bosom as though
ashamed of being so scantily clad, but her little hand was not
equal to the task. She was so white that the colour of the

drapery blended with that of her flesh under the pallid rays of the lamp. Enveloped with this subtle tissue. She seemed more like the marble statue of some fair antique bather than a woman endowed with life. But dead or living, statue or woman, shadow or body, her beauty was still the same, only that the green light of her eyes was less brilliant, and her mouth, once so warmly crimson, was only tinted with a faint tender rosiness, like that of her cheeks. She was so charming that, notwithstanding the strange character of the adventure, and the unexplainable manner in which she had entered my room, I felt not the least fear.

She placed the lamp on the table and seated herself at the foot of my bed. Then bending toward me, she said, in that voice at once silvery clear and yet velvety in its sweet softness, such as I never heard from any lips save hers, "I have kept thee long in waiting, dear Romuald, and it must have seemed to thee that I had forgotten thee. But I come from afar off, very far off, and from a land whence no other has ever yet returned. There is neither sun nor moon in that land whence I come. All is but space and shadow. There is neither road nor pathway, no earth for the foot, no air for the wing and nevertheless behold me here, for Love is stronger than Death and must conquer him in the end. Oh what sad faces and fearful things I have seen on my way hither! What difficulty my soul, returned to earth through the power of will alone, has had in finding its body and reinstating itself therein! What terrible efforts I had to make ere I could lift the ponderous slab with which they had covered me! See, the palms of my poor hands are all bruised! Kiss them, sweet love, that they may be healed!"

She laid the cold palms of her hands upon my mouth, one after the other. I kissed them, indeed, many times, and she the while watched me with a smile of ineffable affection.

I confess to my shame that I had entirely forgotten the advice of the Abbé Sérapion and the sacred office wherewith I had been invested. I had fallen without resistance at the first assault. I had not even made the least effort to repel the tempter. The fresh coolness of Clarimonde's skin penetrated my own. Poor child! In spite of all I saw afterward, I can hardly yet believe she was a demon – at least she had no appearance of being such, and never did Satan so skilfully conceal his claws and horns. She had drawn her feet up beneath her and sat down on the edge of the couch. From time to time she passed her little hand through my hair and twisted it into curls, as though trying how a new style of wearing it would become my face. The most remarkable fact was that I felt no astonishment whatsoever at so extraordinary an adventure, and as in dreams one finds no difficulty in accepting the most fantastic of events as simple facts, so all of these circumstances seemed to me perfectly natural in themselves.

"I loved thee long ere I saw thee, dear Romuald, and sought thee everywhere. Thou wast my dream, and I first saw thee in the church I said at once, 'It is he!' I gave thee a look into which I threw all the love I ever had, all the love I now have, all the love I shall ever have for thee – a look that would have damned a cardinal or brought a king to his knees at my feet in view of all his court. Thou remainedst unmoved, preferring thy God to me!

"Ah, how jealous I am of that God whom thou didst love and still lovest more than me!

"Woe is me, unhappy one that I am! I can never have thy heart all to myself, I whom thou didst recall to life with a kiss – dead Clarimonde, who for thy sake bursts asunder the gates of the tomb, and comes to consecrate to thee a life which she has resumed only to make thee happy!"

All her words were accompanied with the most impassioned caresses, which bewildered my sense and my reason to such an extent, that I did not fear to utter a frightful blasphemy for the sake of consoling her, and to declare that I loved her as much as God.

Her eyes rekindled and shone. "In truth? – in very truth?

– as much as God!' she cried, flinging her beautiful arms around me. 'Since it is so, thou wilt come with me, thou wilt follow me wheresoever I desire.. Thou shalt be the proudest and most envied – thou shalt be my lover! To be the acknowledged lover of Clarimonde, who has refused even a Pope! That will be something to feel proud of. Ah, the fair, unspeakably happy existence, the beautiful golden life we shall live together! And when shall we depart, my fair sir?"

"Tomorrow! Tomorrow!" I cried in my delirium.

"Tomorrow, then, so let it be!" she answered. "Meanwhile I must notify all my friends who believe me dead, and mourn for me as deeply as they are capable of doing. The money, the dresses, the carriages – all will be ready. I shall call for thee at this same hour. Adieu, dear heart!" And she lightly touched my forehead with her lips. The lamp went out, the curtains closed again and all became dark. A leaden, dreamless sleep fell on me and held me unconscious until the morning following.

I awoke later than usual and the recollection of this singular adventure troubled me during the whole day. I finally persuaded myself that it was a mere vapour of my heated imagination. Nevertheless its sensations had been so vivid that it was difficult to persuade myself that they were not real. It was not without some presentiment of what was going to happen that I got into bed at last, after having prayed to God to drive far from me all thoughts of evil, and to protect the chastity of my slumber.

I soon fell into a deep sleep and my dream was continued. The curtains again parted, and I beheld Clarimonde, not as on the former occasion, pale in her pale winding sheet, with the violets of death upon her cheeks, but gay, sprightly, jaunty, in a superb travelling dress of green velvet, trimmed with gold lace and looped up on either side to allow a glimpse of satin petticoat. Her hair escaped in thick ringlets from beneath a broad black felt hat, decorated with white feathers whimsically twisted into various shapes. In one hand she held a little riding whip terminated by a golden whistle. She tapped me lightly with it, and exclaimed, "Well, my fine sleeper, is this the way you make your preparations? I thought I would find you up and dressed. Arise quickly, we have no time to lose."

I leaped out of bed at once.

"Come, dress yourself, and let us go," she continued, pointing to a little package she had brought with her. "The horses are becoming impatient of delay and champing their bits at the door. We ought to have been by this time at least ten leagues distant from here."

I dressed myself hurriedly, and she handed me the articles of apparel herself one by one, bursting into laughter from time to time at my awkwardness, as she explained to me the use of a garment when I had made a mistake. She hurriedly arranged my hair, and this done, held up before me a little pocket mirror of Venetian crystal, rimmed with silver filigree work, and playfully asked, 'How dost find thyself now?'

I was no longer the same person, and I could not even recognize myself. I resembled my former self no more than a finished statue resembles a block of stone. My old face seemed but a coarse daub of the one reflected in the mirror. I was handsome, and my vanity was sensibly tickled by the metamorphosis.

That elegant apparel, that richly embroidered vest had made of me a totally different personage, and I marvelled at the power of transformation owned by a few yards of cloth cut after a certain pattern.

I had one arm around Clarimonde's waist and one of her hands clasped in mine. Her head leaned upon my shoulder. I had never known such intense happiness. In that hour I had forgotten everything, and I no more remembered having ever been a priest than I remembered what I had been doing in my mother's womb, so great was the fascination that the evil spirit exerted upon me. From that night my nature seemed in some sort to have become halved, and there were two men within me, neither of whom knew the other. At one moment I believed myself a priest who dreamed nightly that he was a gentleman, at another that I was a gentleman who dreamt he was a priest. I could no longer distinguish the dream from the reality, nor could I discover where the reality began or where the dream ended. Despite the strange character of my condition, I do not believe that I ever inclined, even for a moment, to madness. I always retained with extreme vividness all the perceptions of my two lives.

Be that as it may, I lived, at least I believed that I lived, in Venice. I have never been able to discover rightly how much of illusion and how much of reality there was in this fantastic adventure. We dwelt in a great palace on the Canaleio, filled with frescoes and statues, and containing two Titians in the noblest style of the great master, which were hung in Clarimonde's chamber. It was a palace well worthy of a king. We each had our gondola, our music hall and our special poet. Clarimonde always lived upon a magnificent scale – there was something of Cleopatra in her nature. I always remained faithful to Clarimonde. I loved her wildly. Of gold she had enough. She wished no longer for anything but love – a love youthful, pure, evoked by herself, and which should

be a first and last passion. I would have been perfectly happy
but for a cursed nightmare that recurred every night, and in
which I believed myself to be a poor village *curé*, practising
mortification and penance for my excesses during the day.
Reassured by my constant association with her, I never
thought further of the strange manner in which I had
become acquainted with Clarimonde. But the words of the
Abbé Sérapion concerning her recurred often to my
memory and never ceased to cause me uneasiness.

For some time the health of Clarimonde had not been so
good as usual – her complexion grew paler day by day. The
physicians who were summoned could not comprehend the
nature of her malady and knew not how to treat it. They all
prescribed some insignificant remedies and never called a
second time. Her paleness, nevertheless, visibly increased,
and she became colder and colder, until she seemed almost
as white and dead as upon that memorable night in the
unknown castle. I grieved with anguish unspeakable to
behold her thus slowly perishing. She, touched by my agony,
smiled upon me sweetly and sadly with the fateful smile of
those who feel that they must die.

One morning I was seated at her bedside, breakfasting
from a little table placed close at hand, so that I might not
be obliged to leave her for a single instant. In the act of

cutting some fruit I accidentally inflicted rather a deep gash on my finger. The blood immediately gushed forth in a little purple jet, and a few drops spurted upon Clarimonde. Her eyes flashed, her face suddenly assumed an expression of savage and ferocious joy such as I had never before observed in her. She leaped out of her bed with animal agility – the agility, as it were, of an ape or a cat – and sprang upon my wound, which she commenced to suck with an air of unutterable pleasure. She swallowed the blood in little mouthfuls, slowly and carefully, like a connoisseur tasting a wine from Xeres or Syracuse. Gradually her eyelids half closed, and the pupils of her green eyes became oblong instead of round. From time to time she paused in order to kiss my hand, then she would recommence to press her lips to the wound in order to coax forth a few more ruddy drops. When she found that the blood would no longer come, she arose with eyes liquid and brilliant, rosier than a May dawn. Her face was full and fresh, her hand warm and moist – she was more beautiful than ever, and in perfect health.

"I shall not die! I shall not die!" she cried, clinging to my

neck, half mad with joy. "I can love thee yet for a long time. My life is thine and all that is of me comes from thee. Just a few drops of thy rich and noble blood, more precious and more potent than all the elixirs in the world, have given me back my life."

This scene long haunted my memory and inspired me with strange doubts in regard to Clarimonde. The same evening, when slumber had transported me to my presbytery, I beheld the Abbé Sérapion, graver and more anxious of aspect than ever. He gazed attentively at me, and sorrowfully exclaimed, "Not content with losing your soul, you now desire also to lose your body. Wretched young man, into how terrible a plight have you fallen!" The tone in which he uttered these words powerfully affected me, but in spite of its vividness even that impression was soon dissipated, and a thousand other cares erased it from my mind. At last one evening, while looking into a mirror whose traitorous position she had not taken into account, I saw Clarimonde in the act of emptying a powder into the cup of spiced wine that she had long been in the habit of preparing after our repasts. I took the cup, feigned to carry it to my lips, and then placed it on the nearest article of furniture as though intending to finish it at my leisure.

Taking advantage of a moment when the fair one's back

was turned, I threw the contents under the table, after which I retired to my chamber and went to bed, fully resolved not to sleep, but to watch and discover what should come of all this mystery. I did not have to wait long, Clarimonde entered in her nightdress, and having removed her apparel, crept into bed and lay down beside me. When she felt assured that I was asleep, she bared my arm, and drawing a gold pin from her hair, commenced to murmur in a low voice, "One drop, only one drop! One ruby at the end of my needle…. Since thou lovest me yet, I must not die!… Ah, poor love! His blood, so brightly purple, I must drink it. Sleep, my only treasure! Sleep, my god, my child! I will do thee no harm. I will only take of thy life what I must to keep my own from being forever extinguished. But that I love thee so much, I could well resolve to have other lovers whose veins I could drain – but since I have known thee all other men have become hateful to me…. Ah, the beautiful arm! How round it is! How white it is! How shall I ever dare to prick this pretty blue vein!" And while thus murmuring to herself she wept and I felt her tears raining on my arm as she clasped it with her hands. At last she took the resolve, slightly punctured me with her pin, and commenced to suck up the blood which oozed from the place. Although she swallowed only a few drops, the fear of weakening me soon seized her, and she carefully tied a little band around my arm, afterward rubbing the wound with an ointment that immediately healed it. Further doubts were impossible. The Abbé Sérapion was right.

Notwithstanding this positive knowledge, however, I could not cease to love Clarimonde, and I would gladly of my own accord have given her all the blood she required to sustain her factitious life. Moreover, I felt but little fear of her. The woman seemed to plead with me for the vampire, and what I had already heard and seen sufficed to reassure me completely. In those days I had plenteous veins, which would not have been so easily exhausted as at present and I would not have thought of bargaining for my blood, drop by drop. I would rather have opened myself the veins of my arm and said to her, "Drink, and may my love infiltrate itself throughout thy body together with my blood!" I carefully avoided ever making the least reference to the narcotic drink she had prepared for me, or to the incident of the pin, and we lived in the most perfect harmony.

Yet my priestly scruples commenced to torment me more than ever. In the effort to avoid falling under the influence of these wearisome hallucinations, I strove to prevent myself from being overcome by sleep. I held my eyelids open with my fingers, and stood for hours together leaning upright against the wall, fighting sleep with all my might; but the dust of drowsiness invariably gathered upon my eyes at last, and finding all resistance useless, I would have to let my arms fall in the extremity of despairing weariness, and the current of slumber would again bear me away to the perfidious shores. Sérapion addressed me with the most vehement exhortations, severely reproaching me for my softness and want of fervour.

Finally, one day when I was more wretched than usual, he said to me, "There is but one way by which you can obtain relief from this continual torment, and though it is an extreme measure it must be made use of – violent diseases require violent remedies. I know where Clarimonde is buried. It is necessary that we shall disinter her remains, and that you shall behold in how pitiable a state the object of your love is. Then you will no longer be tempted to lose your soul for the sake of an unclean corpse devoured by worms, and ready to crumble into dust. That will assuredly restore you to yourself." For my part, I was so tired of this double life that I at once consented, desiring to ascertain beyond a doubt whether a priest or a gentleman had been the victim of delusion. I had become fully resolved either to kill one of the two men within me for the benefit of the other, or else to kill both, for so terrible an existence could not last long and be endured. The Abbé Sérapion provided himself with a mattock, a lever and a lantern, and at midnight we made our way to the cemetery. After having directed the rays of the dark lantern upon the inscriptions of several tombs, we came at last upon a great slab, half concealed by huge weeds and devoured by mosses and parasitic plants, whereupon we deciphered the opening lines of the epitaph:

HERE LIES CLARIMONDE WHO WAS FAMED IN HER LIFE TIME AS THE FAIREST OF WOMEN.

"It is here without a doubt,' muttered Sérapion, and placing his lantern on the ground, he

forced the point of the lever under the edge of the stone and
commenced to raise it. The stone yielded and he proceeded
to work with the mattock. Darker and more silent than the
night itself, I stood by and watched him do it, while he,
bending over his dismal toil, streamed with sweat, panted,
and his hard-coming breath seemed to have the harsh tone
of a death rattle. It was a weird scene, and had any persons
from without beheld us, they would assuredly have taken us
rather for profane wretches and shroud-stealers than for
priests of God. There was something grim and fierce in
Sérapion's zeal which lent him the air of a demon rather
than of an apostle or an angel, and his great aquiline face,
with all its stern features, brought out in strong relief by the
lantern light, had something fearsome in it which enhanced
the unpleasant fancy. I felt an icy sweat come out upon my
forehead in huge beads and my hair stood up with a hideous
fear. The owls which had been nestling in the cypress trees,
startled by the gleam of the lantern, flew against it from
time to time, striking their dusty wings against its panes,
and uttering plaintive cries of lamentation. Wild foxes
yelped in the far darkness and a thousand sinister noises
detached themselves from the silence.

At last Sérapion's mattock struck the coffin itself, making
its planks re-echo with a deep sonorous sound, with that

terrible sound nothingness utters when stricken. He wrenched apart and tore up the lid, and I beheld Clarimonde, pallid as a figure of marble, with hands joined – her white winding sheet made but one fold from her head to her feet. A little crimson drop sparkled like a speck of dew at one corner of her colourless mouth. Sérapion, at this spectacle, burst into fury, "Ah, thou art here, demon! Drinker of blood and gold!" And he flung holy water upon the corpse and the coffin, over which he traced the sign of the cross with his sprinkler. Poor Clarimonde had no sooner been touched by the blessed spray than her beautiful body crumbled into dust, and became only a shapeless and frightful mass of cinders and half-burnt bones.

"Behold your mistress, my Lord Romuald!" cried the priest, as he pointed to these sad remains. I covered my face with my hands. I returned to my presbytery, and the noble Lord Romuald, the lover of Clarimonde, separated himself from the poor priest with whom he had kept such strange company so long. But once only, the following night, I saw Clarimonde. She said to me, as she had said the first time at the portals of the church, "Unhappy man! Unhappy man! What hast thou done? Wherefore have hearkened to that imbecile priest? Wert thou not happy? And what harm had I ever done thee that thou shouldst violate my poor tomb, and lay bare the miseries of my nothingness? All communication between our souls and our bodies is henceforth forever broken. Adieu! Thou wilt yet regret me!" She vanished like smoke and I never saw her again.

Alas! She spoke truly indeed. I have regretted her more than once, and I regret her still. My soul's peace has been very dearly bought. The love of God was not too much to replace such a love as hers. And this, brother, is the story of my youth. Never gaze upon a woman and walk abroad only with eyes ever fixed upon the ground. For however chaste and watchful one may be, the error of a single moment is enough to make one lose eternity.

THE CAPTURED
SOUL

THE HORLA

Guy de Maupassant

MAY 8. What a lovely day! I have spent all the morning lying on the grass in front of my house, under the enormous plantain tree which shades and shelters the whole of it. I like this part of the country. I am fond of living here because I am attached to it by the roots which attach a man to the soil on which his ancestors were born and died, to their traditions, their usages, their food and to the atmosphere itself.

I love the house in which I grew up. From my windows I can see the Seine, which flows by the side of my garden, the great and wide Seine, which goes to Rouen and Havre, and which is covered with boats passing to and fro.

What a delicious morning it was! About eleven o'clock, a long line of boats drawn by a steam tug, as big a fly, and emitting thick smoke, passed my gate.

After two English schooners, whose red flags fluttered towards the sky, there came a magnificent Brazilian three-master. It was perfectly white, and wonderfully clean and shining. I saluted it, I hardly know why, except that the sight of the vessel gave me great pleasure.

MAY 12. I have had a slight feverish attack for the last few days, and I feel ill, or rather I feel low-spirited.

Whence come those mysterious influences that change our happiness into discouragement, and our self confidence into diffidence? One might almost say that the air, the invisible air, is full of unknowable forces, whose mysterious presence we have to endure. I wake up in the best of spirits, with an inclination to sing in my heart. Why? I go down by the side of the water, and suddenly, after walking a short distance, I return home wretched, as if some misfortune were awaiting me there. Why? Is it a cold shiver which, passing over my skin, has upset my nerves and given me a fit of low spirits?

MAY 16. I am ill, decidedly! I was so well last month! I am feverish, which makes my mind suffer as much as my body. I have without ceasing the horrible sensation of some danger threatening me, the apprehension of some coming misfortune or of approaching death, a presentiment which is no doubt, an attack of some illness still unnamed, which germinates in the flesh and in the blood.

MAY 18. I have just come from consulting my doctor, for I can no longer get any sleep. He found that my pulse was high, my eyes dilated, but no alarming symptoms.

MAY 25. No change! My state is really very peculiar. As the evening comes on, an incomprehensible feeling of dread seizes me, just as if night concealed some terrible menace towards me. I dine quickly and then try to read, but I do not understand the words and can scarcely distinguish the letters. Then I walk up and down my drawing-room, oppressed by a feeling of confused and irresistible fear, a fear of sleep and a fear of my bed.

About ten o'clock I go up to my room. As soon as I have entered I lock and bolt the door. I am frightened – of what? Up till the present time I have been frightened of nothing. I open my cupboards, and look under my bed. I listen – I listen – to what? Then I go to bed and wait for sleep as a man might wait for the executioner. My heart beats and my legs tremble, while my whole body shivers beneath the warmth of the bedclothes, until the moment

THE HORLA

I suddenly fall asleep, as a man throws himself into a pool of water in order to drown.

I sleep – two or three hours perhaps – then a dream – no – a nightmare lays hold on me. I feel that I am in bed and asleep – I feel it and I know it – and I feel also that somebody is coming close to me, looking at me, touching me, is getting onto my bed, kneeling on my chest, is taking my neck between his hands and squeezing it – squeezing it with all his might in order to strangle me.

I struggle, bound by that terrible powerlessness that paralyzes us in our dreams. I try to cry out – but I cannot. I want to move – I cannot. I try, with the most violent efforts and out of breath, to turn over and throw off this being that is crushing and suffocating me – I cannot!

And then suddenly I wake up, shaken and bathed in perspiration. I light a candle and find that I am alone, and after that crisis, which occurs every night, I at length fall asleep and slumber tranquilly till morning.

JUNE 2. My state has grown worse. What is the matter with me? Sometimes, in order to tire myself out, though I am fatigued enough already, I go for a walk in the forest of Roumare. I used to think at first that the fresh light and soft air, impregnated with the odour of herbs and leaves, would instill new life into my veins and impart fresh energy to my heart. One day I turned into a broad ride in the wood, and then I diverged toward La Bouille, through a narrow path, between two rows of exceedingly tall trees, which placed a thick, green, almost black roof between the sky and me.

A sudden shiver ran through me, not a cold shiver, but a shiver of agony, and so I hastened my steps, uneasy at being alone in the wood, frightened stupidly and without reason at the profound solitude. Suddenly it seemed as if I were being followed, that somebody was walking at my heels, close, quite close to me, near enough to touch me.

I turned round suddenly, but I was alone. I saw nothing behind me except the straight, broad ride, empty and bordered by high trees, horribly empty. On the other side it extended until it was lost in the distance and looked just the same – terrible.

JUNE 3. I have had a terrible night. I shall go away for a few weeks, for no doubt a journey will set me up again.

July 2. I have come back, quite cured, and have had a most delightful trip into the bargain. I have been to Mont Saint-Michel, which I had not seen before.

JULY 3. I have slept badly – certainly there is some feverish influence here, for my coachman is suffering in the same way as I am. When I went back home yesterday, I noticed his singular paleness, and I asked him, "What is the matter with you, Jean?"

"The matter is that I never get any rest and my nights devour my days. Since your departure, Monsieur, there has been a spell over me."

However, the other servants are all well, but I am very frightened of having another attack, myself.

JULY 4. I am decidedly taken again. My old nightmares have returned. Last night I felt somebody leaning on me who was sucking my life from between my lips with his mouth. Yes, he was sucking it out of my neck like a leech would have done. Then he got up and I woke, so beaten, crushed and annihilated that I could not move. If this continues for a few days, I shall certainly go away again.

JULY 5. Have I lost my reason? What has happened? What I saw last night is so strange that my head wanders when I think of it!

As I do now every evening, I had locked my door, then being thirsty, I drank half a glass of water, and I accidentally noticed that the water bottle was full up to the cut-glass stopper.

Then I went to bed and fell into one of my terrible sleeps, from which I was aroused in about two hours by a still more terrible shock.

Picture to yourself a sleeping man who is being murdered, who wakes up with a knife in his chest, a gurgling in his throat, is covered with blood, can no longer breathe, is going to die and does not understand anything at all about it – there you have it.

Having recovered my senses, I was thirsty again, so I lit a candle and went to the table on which my water-bottle was. I lifted it up and tilted it over my glass, but nothing came out. It was empty! It was completely empty! At first I could not understand it at all – then suddenly I was seized by such a terrible feeling that I had to sit down, or rather fall into a chair! Then I sprang up with a bound to look about me. I sat down again, overcome by astonishment and fear, in front of the transparent crystal bottle! I looked at it with fixed eyes, trying to solve the puzzle, and my hands trembled! Somebody had drunk the water, but who? I? I without any doubt. It could surely only be I? Oh! Who will understand my horrible agony? Who will understand the emotion of a man sound in mind, wide awake, full of sense, who looks in horror at the disappearance of a little water while he was asleep, through the glass of a water bottle! And I remained sitting until it was daylight, without venturing to go to bed again.

JULY 6. I am going mad. Again all the contents of my water bottle have been drunk in the night – or rather I have drunk it!

But is it I? Who could it be? Who? Oh! God! Am I going mad? Who will save me?

JULY 10. I have just been through some surprising ordeals. Undoubtedly I must be mad! And yet!

On July 6, before going to bed, I put some wine, milk, water, bread and strawberries on my table. Somebody drank – I drank – all the water and a little of the milk, but neither the wine, nor the bread, nor the strawberries were touched.

On July 7 I renewed the same experiment, with the same results, and on July 8 I left out the water and the milk and nothing was touched.

Lastly, on July 9 I put only water and milk on my table, taking care to wrap up the bottles in white muslin and to tie down the stoppers. Then I rubbed my lips, my beard and my hands with pencil lead, and went to bed.

Deep slumber seized me, soon followed by a terrible awakening. I had not moved and my sheets were not marked. I rushed to the table. The muslin round the bottles remained intact. I undid the string, trembling with fear. All the water had been drunk and so had the milk! Ah! Great God! I must start for Paris immediately.

JULY 12. Paris. I must have lost my head during the last few days!

Yesterday after doing some business and paying some visits, which instilled fresh and invigorating mental air into me, I wound up my evening at the Theatre Francais. A drama by Alexander Dumas the Younger was being acted, and his brilliant and powerful play completed my cure. I returned along the boulevards to my hotel in excellent spirits. Amid the jostling of the crowd I thought of my terrors and surmises of the previous week, because I believed, yes, I believed, that an invisible being lived beneath my roof. How weak our mind is. How quickly it is terrified and unbalanced as soon as we are confronted with a small, incomprehensible fact. Instead of dismissing the problem with, 'We do not understand because we cannot find the cause,' we immediately begin to imagine terrible mysteries and supernatural powers.

AUGUST 2. Nothing new – it is good weather and I spend my days in watching the Seine flow past.

AUGUST 4. Quarrels among my servants. They declare that the glasses are broken in the cupboards at night. The footman accuses the cook, she accuses the needlewoman, and the latter accuses the other two. Who is the culprit? It would take a clever person to tell.

AUGUST 6. This time, I am not mad. I have seen – I have seen – I have seen! – I can doubt no longer – I have seen it!

I was walking at two o'clock among my rose trees, in the full sunlight – in the walk bordered by autumn roses which are beginning to fall. As I stopped to look at a *Geant de Bataille*, which had three splendid blooms, I distinctly saw the stalk of one of the roses bend close to me, as if an invisible hand had bent it, and then break, as if that hand had picked it! Then the flower raised itself, following the curve which a hand would have described in carrying it towards a

mouth, and remained suspended in the transparent air, alone and motionless, a terrible red spot, three yards from my eyes. In desperation I rushed at it to take it! I found nothing; it had disappeared. Then I was seized with furious rage against myself, for it is not wholesome for a reasonable and serious man to have such hallucinations.

But was it a hallucination? I turned to look for the stalk and found it immediately under the bush, freshly broken, between the two other roses which remained on the branch. I returned home with a much disturbed mind. I am certain now, certain as I am of the alternation of day and night, that there exists close to me an invisible being who lives on milk and on water, who can touch objects, take them and change their places – who lives as I do, under my roof.

AUGUST 7. I slept tranquilly. He drank the water out of my decanter, but did not disturb my sleep.

I walked by the side of the water. The sun was shining brightly on the river and made earth delightful, while it filled me with love for life, for the swallows, whose swift agility is always delightful in my eyes, for the plants by the riverside, whose rustling is a pleasure to my ears.

By degrees, however, an inexplicable feeling of discomfort seized me. It seemed to me as if some unknown force was numbing and stopping me, was preventing me from going further and was calling me back. I felt that painful wish to return which comes on you when you have left a beloved invalid at home and are seized by a feeling that he is worse.

I therefore returned, despite feeling certain that I should find some bad news awaiting me, a letter or a telegram. However, there was nothing and I was surprised and uneasy, more so than if I had had another fantastic vision.

AUGUST 8. I spent a terrible evening yesterday. He does not show himself any more, but I feel that he is near me, watching me, looking at me, penetrating me, dominating me, and more terrible to me when he hides himself thus than if he were to manifest his constant and invisible presence by supernatural phenomena. However, I slept.

AUGUST 9. Nothing, but I am afraid.

AUGUST 10. Nothing, but what will happen tomorrow?

AUGUST 11. Still nothing. I cannot remain at home with this constant fear hanging over me and these thoughts in my mind – I shall go away.

AUGUST 12. Ten o'clock at night. All day long I have been trying to get away and have not been able. I contemplated a simple and easy act of liberty, a carriage ride to Rouen – and I have not been able to do it. What is the reason for this?

AUGUST 13. When one is attacked by certain maladies, the springs of our physical being seem broken, our energies destroyed, our muscles relaxed, our bones to be as soft as our flesh, and our blood as liquid as water. I am experiencing the same in my moral being, in a strange and distressing manner. I have no longer any strength, any courage, any self control, nor even any power to set my own will in motion. I have no power left to will anything, but someone does it for me and I obey.

AUGUST 14. I am lost! Somebody possesses my soul and governs it! Somebody orders all my acts, all my movements, all my thoughts. I am no longer master of myself, nothing except an enslaved and terrified spectator of the things which I do. I wish to go out – I cannot. HE does not wish to – and so I remain, trembling and distracted in the armchair in which he keeps me sitting. I merely wish to get up and to rouse myself, so as to think that I am still master of myself. I cannot! I am riveted to my chair, and my chair adheres to the floor in such a manner that no force of mine can move us.

Then suddenly, I must, I MUST go to the foot of my garden to pick some strawberries and eat them – and I go there. I pick the strawberries and I eat them! Oh! My God! My God! Is there a God? If there be one, deliver me! Save me! Succour me! Pardon! Pity! Mercy! Save me! Oh! What sufferings! What torture! What horror!

AUGUST 16. I managed to escape today for two hours, like a prisoner who finds the door of his dungeon accidentally open. I suddenly felt that I was free and that he was far away. I gave orders to put the horses in as quickly as possible and I drove to Rouen. Oh! How delightful to be able to say to my coachman, "Go to Rouen!"

I made him pull up before the library, and I begged them to lend me Dr Herrmann Herestauss's treatise on the unknown inhabitants of the ancient and modern world.

Then, as I was getting into my carriage, I intended to say, "To the railway station!" but instead of this I shouted – I did not speak, but I shouted – in such a loud voice that all the passersby turned round, "Home!" and I fell back on to the cushion of my carriage, overcome by mental agony. He had found me out and regained possession of me.

AUGUST 17. Oh! What a night! What a night! And yet it seems to me that I ought to rejoice. I read until one o'clock in the morning! Herestauss, Doctor of Philosophy and Theogony, wrote the history and the manifestation of all those invisible beings that hover around man, or of whom he dreams. He describes their origin, their domains, their power, but none resembles the one that haunts me. Having, therefore, read until one o'clock in the morning, I went and sat down at the open window, in order to cool my forehead and my thoughts in the calm night air. It was very pleasant and warm! How I should have enjoyed such a night!

There was no moon, but the stars darted out their rays in the dark. Who inhabits those worlds? What forms, what living beings, what animals are there out there? Will not one of them, some day or other, traversing space, appear on our earth to conquer it, just as the Norsemen once crossed the sea in order to subjugate nations feebler than themselves?

We are so weak, so powerless, so ignorant, so small – we who live on this particle of mud that revolves in liquid air.

I fell asleep, dreaming thus in the cool night air, and then, having slept for about three-quarters of an hour, I opened my eyes without moving, awakened by an indescribably confused and strange sensation. At first I saw nothing, and then suddenly it appeared to me as if a page of the book, which had remained open on my table, turned over of its own accord. Not a breath of air had come in at my window, and I was surprised and waited. In about four minutes, I saw, I saw – yes I saw with my own eyes – another page lift itself up and fall down on the others, as if a finger had turned it over. My armchair was empty, appeared empty, but I knew that he was there, he, and sitting in my place, and that he was reading. With a furious bound, the bound of an enraged wild beast that wishes to disembowel its tamer, I crossed my room to seize him, to strangle him, to kill him! But before I could reach it, my chair fell over as if somebody had run away from me. My table rocked, my lamp fell and went out, and my window closed as if some thief had been surprised and had fled out into the night, shutting it behind him.

So he had run away; he had been afraid; he, afraid of me!

So tomorrow, or later – some day, I should be able to hold him in my clutches and crush him against the ground! Do not dogs occasionally bite and strangle their masters?

AUGUST 18. I have been thinking the whole day long. Oh! yes, I will obey him, follow his impulses, fulfill all his wishes, show myself humble, submissive, a coward. He is the stronger – but an hour will come.

AUGUST 19. I know, I know, I know all! I have just read the following: *A curious piece of news comes to us from Rio de Janeiro. Madness, an epidemic of madness, which may be compared to that contagious madness that attacked the people of Europe in the Middle Ages, is at this moment raging in the Province of San-Paulo. The frightened inhabitants are leaving their houses, deserting their villages, abandoning their land, saying that they are pursued, possessed, governed like human cattle by invisible, though tangible beings, by a species of vampire, which feeds on their life while they are asleep, and which, besides, drinks water and milk without appearing to touch any other nourishment.*

Ah! Ah! I remember now that fine Brazilian three-master that passed in front of my windows as it was going up the Seine, on the eighth of last May! I thought it looked so pretty, so white and bright! That being was on board of her, coming from there, where its race sprang from. And it saw me! It saw my house, which was also white, and He sprang from the ship onto the land. Oh! Good heavens!

The reign of man is over and he has come. He whom disquieted priests exorcised, whom sorcerers evoked on dark nights without seeing him appear, he to whom the imaginations of the transient masters of the world lent all the monstrous or graceful forms of gnomes, spirits, genii, fairies and familiar spirits. Woe to us! Woe to man! He has come, the – the – what does he call himself – the – I fancy that he is shouting out his name to me and I do not hear him – the – yes – he is shouting it out – I am listening – I cannot – repeat – it – Horla – I have heard – the Horla – it is he – the Horla – he has come!

Ah! The vulture has eaten the pigeon, the wolf has eaten the lamb, the lion has devoured the sharp-horned buffalo, man has killed the lion with an arrow, with a spear, with gunpowder – but the Horla will make of man what man has made of the horse and of the ox – his chattel, his slave, and his food, by the mere power of his will. Woe to us!

But, nevertheless, sometimes the animal rebels and kills the man who has subjugated it. I should also like – I shall be able to – but I must know him, touch him, see him! Learned men say that eyes of animals, as they differ from ours, do not distinguish as ours do. And my eye cannot distinguish this newcomer who is oppressing me.

A new being! Why not? It was assuredly bound to come! Why should we be the last?

Why not one more? Why not, also, other trees with immense, splendid flowers, perfuming whole regions? Why not other elements beside fire, air, earth and water?

What is the matter with me? It is he, the Horla who haunts me and makes me think of these foolish things! He is within me, he is becoming my soul – I shall kill him!

AUGUST 20. I shall kill him. I have seen him! Yesterday I sat down at my table and pretended to write very assiduously. I knew quite well that he would come prowling round me, quite close to me, so close that I might perhaps be able to touch him, to seize him. And then – then I should have the strength of desperation. I should have my hands, my knees, my chest, my forehead, my teeth to strangle him, to crush him, to bite him, to tear him to pieces. And I watched for him with all my overexcited nerves.

I had lit my two lamps and the eight wax candles on my mantelpiece, as if, by this light I should discover him.

My bed, my old oak bed with its columns, was opposite to me. On my right was the fireplace, on my left the door, which was carefully closed, after I had left it open for some time, in order to attract him. Behind me was a very high wardrobe with a looking glass in it, which served me to dress by every day, and in which I was in the habit of inspecting myself from head to foot every time I passed it.

So I pretended to be writing in order to deceive him, for he also was watching me, and suddenly I felt, I was certain, that he was reading over my shoulder, that he was there, almost touching my ear.

I got up so quickly, with my hands extended, that I almost fell. Horror! It was as bright as at midday, but I did not see myself in the mirror! It was empty, clear, profound, full of light! But my figure was not reflected – and I was stood opposite to it! I saw the large, clear glass from top to bottom and I looked at it with unsteady eyes. I did not dare advance. I did not venture to make a movement, feeling certain nevertheless, that he was there, but that he would escape me again, he whose body had absorbed my reflection.

How frightened I was! And then suddenly I began to see myself through a mist in the depths of the looking-glass, in a mist as it were, or through a veil of water. It seemed to me as if this water were flowing slowly from left to right, and making my figure clearer every moment. It was like the end of an eclipse. Whatever hid me did not appear to possess clearly defined outlines, but was a sort of opaque transparency, which gradually grew clearer.

At last I was able to distinguish myself completely, as I do every day when I look at myself.

I had seen him! And the horror of it remained with me and makes me shudder even now.

AUGUST 21. How could I kill him, since I could not get hold of him? Poison? But he would see me mix it with the water. Even so, would our poisons have any effect on his impalpable body? No – no – no doubt about the matter. Then what?

AUGUST 22. I sent for a blacksmith from Rouen and ordered iron shutters for my room, such as some private hotels in Paris have on the ground floor, for fear of thieves, and he is going to make me a similar door as well. I have made myself out a coward, but I do not care about that!

SEPTEMBER 10. Rouen, Hotel Continental. It is done, it is done – but is he dead? My mind is thoroughly upset by what I have seen.

Well then, yesterday, the locksmith having put on the iron shutters and door, I left everything open until midnight, although it was getting cold.

Suddenly I felt that he was there, and mad joy took hold of me. I got up softly, and I walked to the right and left for some time, so that he might not guess anything. Then I took off my boots and put on my slippers. I fastened the iron shutters and going back to the door quickly I double-locked it with a padlock, putting the key into my pocket.

Suddenly I noticed that he was moving restlessly round me, that in his turn he was frightened and was ordering me to let him out. I nearly yielded, though I did not quite, but putting my back to the door, I half opened it, just enough to allow me to go out backward, and as I am very tall, my head touched the lintel. I was sure that he had not been able to escape, and I shut him up quite alone. What happiness! I had Him fast. Then I ran downstairs into the drawing room which was under my bedroom. I took the two lamps and poured all the oil onto the carpet, the furniture, everywhere. Then I set fire to it and made my escape, after having carefully double-locked the door.

I went and hid myself at the bottom of the garden, in a clump of laurel bushes. How long it was! How long it was! Everything was dark, silent, motionless, not a breath of air and not a star, but heavy banks of clouds that one could not see, but which weighed oh so heavily on my soul.

I looked at my house and waited. How long it was! I already began to think that the fire had gone out of its own accord, or that He had extinguished it, when one of the lower windows gave way under the violence of the flames, and a long, soft, caressing sheet of red flame mounted up the white wall and kissed it as high as the roof. The light fell onto the trees, the branches and the leaves, and a shiver of fear pervaded them also! The birds awoke, a dog began to howl and it seemed to me as if the day were breaking! Almost immediately two other windows flew into fragments and I saw that the whole of the lower part of my house was nothing but a terrible furnace. But a cry, a horrible, shrill, heartrending cry, a woman's cry, sounded through the night and two garret windows were opened! I had forgotten the servants! I saw the terror-struck faces and the frantic waving of their arms!

Then, overwhelmed with horror, I ran off to the village, shouting, "Help! Help! Fire! Fire!" Meeting some people who were already coming to the scene, I went back with them to see!

By this time the house was nothing but a horrible and magnificent funeral pile, a monstrous pyre which lit up the whole country, a pyre where men were burning – where he was burning also, he, he, my prisoner, that new being, the new master, the Horla!

Suddenly the whole roof fell in between the walls, and a volcano of flames darted up to the sky. Through all the windows that opened onto that furnace, I saw the flames darting and I reflected that he was there, in that kiln, dead.

Dead? Perhaps? His body? Was not his body, which was transparent, indestructible by such means as would kill ours?

If he were not dead? Perhaps time alone has power over that invisible and redoubtable being. Why this transparent, unrecognisable body, this body belonging to a spirit, if it also had to fear ills, infirmities and premature destruction?

Premature destruction? All human terror springs from

420

that! After man the Horla. After him who can die every day, at any hour, at any moment, by any accident, he came, he who was only to die at his own proper hour and minute, because he had touched the limits of his existence!

No – no – there is no doubt about it – he is not dead. Then – then – I suppose I must kill myself!

THE WEREWOLF

Eugene Field

IN THE REIGN of Egbert the Saxon there dwelt in Britain a maiden named Yseult, who was loved by all, both for her goodness and for her beauty. But, though many a youth came wooing her, she loved Harold only, and she promised to marry him.

Yseult was also loved by Alfred, and he was angered that she showed favour to Harold, so one day Alfred said to Harold, "Is it right that old Siegfried should come from his grave and have Yseult for his wife?" Then added he, "Good sir, why do you turn so white when I speak your grandfather's name?"

Then Harold asked, "What know you of Siegfried that you taunt me? What memory of him should vex me now?"

"We know and we know," retorted Alfred. "There are

some tales told to us by our grandmas we have not forgot."

So ever after that, Alfred's words and Alfred's bitter smile haunted Harold by day and night.

Harold's grandfather, Siegfried the Teuton, had been a man of cruel violence. The legend said that a curse rested upon him and that at certain times he was possessed of an evil spirit that wreaked its fury on mankind. But Siegfried had been dead for many years, and there was nothing to remind the world of him save the legend and a cunning-wrought spear that he had from Brunehilde, the witch. This spear was such a weapon that it never lost its brightness, nor had its point been blunted. It hung in Harold's chamber and it was the marvel among weapons of that time.

Yseult knew that Alfred loved her, but she did not know of the bitter words that Alfred had spoken to Harold. Her love for Harold was perfect in its trust and gentleness. But Alfred had hit the truth. The curse of old Siegfried was upon Harold – slumbering a century, it had awakened in the blood of the grandson. Harold knew the curse that was upon him, and it was this that seemed to stand between him and Yseult. But love is stronger than all else, and Harold loved.

Harold did not tell Yseult of the curse that was upon him for he feared that she would not love him if she knew. Whenever he felt the fire of the curse burning in his veins he would say to her, "Tomorrow I hunt the wild boar in the uttermost forest," or, "Next week I go stag-stalking among the distant northern hills." So it was that he made good excuse for his absence, and Yseult thought no evil things, for she was trustful. Though he went away many times and was long gone, Yseult suspected no wrong. So none beheld Harold when the curse was upon him in its violence.

Alfred alone thought of evil things. "It is strange," said he, "that this gallant lover should quit our company and take himself where none know. "

Harold knew that Alfred watched him zealously and he was tormented by a constant fear that Alfred would discover the curse that was on him. But what gave him greater anguish was the fear that at some moment when he was in Yseult's presence, the curse would seize upon him and cause him to do great evil to her, whereby she would be destroyed or her love for him would be undone forever. So Harold lived in terror, feeling that his love was hopeless, yet knowing not how to combat it.

Now, it befell in those times that the country round about was ravaged by a werewolf, a creature that was feared by all men. This werewolf was by day a man, but by night a wolf given to ravage and to slaughter, and having a charmed life. Wherever he went he attacked and devoured mankind, spreading terror and desolation round about, and the dream-readers said that the earth would not be freed from the werewolf until some man offered himself a voluntary sacrifice to the monster's rage.

Now, although Harold was known far and wide as a mighty huntsman, he had never set forth to hunt the werewolf, and strange enough, the werewolf never ravaged the domain while Harold was there.

It happened that Yseult said to Harold, "Wilt thou go with me tomorrow to the feast in the sacred grove?"

"That I cannot do," answered Harold. "I am summoned hence to Normandy upon a mission of which I shall some time tell thee. And I pray thee, on thy love for me, go not to the feast in the sacred grove without me."

"What say'st thou?" cried Yseult. "Shall I not go to the feast of Saint Aelfreda? My father would be displeased if I were not there with the other maidens. "

"But do not, I beseech thee," Harold implored. "Go not to the feast in the sacred grove – see, thou my life, on my two knees I ask it!"

"How pale thou art," said Yseult, "and trembling."

"Go not to the sacred grove," he begged.

Yseult marvelled at his acts and at his speech. Then, for the first time, she thought him to be jealous – whereat she secretly rejoiced (being a woman).

"Ah," said she, "thou dost doubt my love," but when she saw a look of pain come on his face she added — as if she repented of the words she had spoken — "or dost thou fear the werewolf?"

Then Harold answered, fixing his eyes on hers, "Thou hast said it — it is the werewolf that I fear."

"Why dost thou look at me so strangely, Harold?" cried Yseult. "By the cruel light in thine eyes one might almost take thee to be the werewolf!"

"Come hither, sit beside me," said Harold tremblingly, "and I will tell thee why I fear to have thee go to the feast tomorrow evening. Hear what I dreamt last night. I dreamt that I was the werewolf — do not shudder, dear love, for it was only a dream.

"A grizzled old man stood at my bedside and strove to pluck my soul from my bosom.

'What would'st thou?' I cried.

'Thy soul is mine,' he said, 'thou shalt live out my curse. Give me thy soul — give me thy soul, I say.'

'Thy curse shall not be upon me,' I cried. 'What have I done that thy curse should rest upon me? Thou shalt not have my soul.'

'For my offence shalt thou suffer, and in my curse thou

shalt endure hell – it is so decreed.'

"So spoke the old man, and he strove with me, and he prevailed against me, and he plucked my soul from my bosom, and he said, 'Go, search and kill' – and lo, I was a wolf upon the moor.

"The dry grass crackled beneath my tread. The darkness of the night was heavy and it oppressed me. Strange horrors tortured my soul, and it groaned and groaned, gaoled in that wolfish body. The wind whispered to me. With its myriad of voices it spoke to me and said, 'Go, search and kill.' And above these voices sounded the hideous laughter of an old man. I fled the moor – whither I knew not, nor knew I what motive lashed me on.

"I came to a river and I plunged in. A burning thirst consumed me and I lapped the waters of the river – they were waves of flame. They flashed around me and hissed, and what they said was, 'Go, search and kill,' and I heard the old man's laughter again.

"A forest lay before me with its gloomy thickets and its sombre shadows – with its ravens, its vampires, its serpents, its reptiles and all its hideous brood of night. I darted among its thorns and crouched amid the leaves, the nettles and the brambles. The owls hooted at me and the thorns pierced my flesh. 'Go, search and kill,' said everything. The hares sprang from my pathway, the other beasts ran bellowing away, every form of life shrieked in my ears – the curse had taken hold of me – I was the werewolf.

"On, on I went with the fleetness of the wind, and my soul groaned in its wolfish prison, and the winds and the waters and the trees bade me, 'Go, search and kill, thou accursed brute – go, search and kill.'

"Nowhere was there pity for the wolf. What mercy, thus, should I, the werewolf, show? The curse was on me and it filled me with a hunger and a thirst for blood. Skulking on my way within myself I cried, 'Let me have blood, oh, let me have human blood, that this wrath may be appeased, that this curse may be removed.'

"At last I came to the sacred grove. Sombre loomed the poplars, the oaks frowned upon me. Before me stood an old man – 'twas he, grizzled and taunting, whose curse I bore. He feared me not. All other living things fled before me, but the old man feared me not. A maiden stood beside him. She did not see me, for she was blind.

'Kill, kill,' cried the old man, and he pointed at the girl beside him.

"Hell raged within me – the curse impelled me – I sprang at her throat. I heard the old man's laughter once more, and then – then I awoke, trembling, cold, horrified."

Scarce had Harold told this dream when Alfred
strode that way. Yseult told him of Harold's going
away and how Harold had besought her not to venture to
the feast in the sacred grove.

"These fears are childish," cried Alfred boastfully. "Sweet
lady, I will bear thee company to the feast, and a score of my

yeomen with their good yew bows and honest spears, they shall attend me. There be no werewolf will chance about with us."

Whereat Yseult laughed merrily, and Harold said, "It is well – thou shalt go to the sacred grove, and may my love and Heaven's grace forefend all evil."

Then Harold went to his abode, and he fetched old Siegfried's spear back unto Yseult, and he gave it into her two hands, saying, "Take this spear with thee to the feast. It is old Siegfried's spear, possessing mighty virtue."

And Harold took Yseult to his heart and blessed her, and he kissed her upon her brow and upon her lips, saying, "Farewell, oh, my beloved. How wilt thou love me when thou know'st my sacrifice. Farewell, farewell forever."

So Harold went on his way and Yseult was lost in wonderment.

On the morrow night Yseult came to the sacred grove wherein the feast was spread and she bore old Siegfried's spear with her in her girdle. Alfred attended her and a score of yeomen were with him. In the grove there was great merriment, and with singing and dancing and games did the honest folk celebrate the feast of the fair Saint Aelfreda.

But suddenly a mighty tumult arose and there were cries of "The werewolf! The werewolf!" Terror seized upon all –

stout hearts were frozen with fear. Out from the further
forest rushed the werewolf bellowing hoarsely, gnashing his
fangs and tossing hither and thither the yellow foam from his
snapping jaws. He sought Yseult straight, as if an evil power
drew him to the spot where she stood. But Yseult was not
feared – like a marble statue she stood and saw the
werewolf's coming. The yeomen, dropping their torches and
casting aside their bows, had fled. Alfred alone abided there
to do the monster battle.

At the approaching wolf he hurled his heavy lance, but as
it struck the werewolf's bristling back the weapon was
broken in pieces.

Then the werewolf, fixing his eyes upon Yseult, skulked
for a moment in the shadow of the yews and thinking then
of Harold's words, Yseult plucked old Siegfried's spear from
her girdle, raised it on high, and with the strength of despair
sent it hurtling through the air.

The werewolf saw the shining weapon and a cry burst
from his gaping throat – a cry of human agony. And Yseult
saw in the werewolf's eyes the eyes of someone she had seen
and known, but it was for an instant only, and then the eyes
were no longer human, but wolfish in their ferocity. A
supernatural force seemed to speed the spear in its flight.
With fearful precision the weapon smote home and buried

itself by half its length in the werewolf's shaggy breast just above the heart, and then, with a monstrous sigh – as if he yielded up his life without regret – the werewolf fell dead in the shadow of the yews.

Then, ah, then in very truth there was great joy and loud were the acclaims, while, beautiful in her trembling pallor, Yseult was led home, where the people set about to give a great feast to do her homage, for the werewolf was dead, and it was she that had slain him.

But Yseult cried out, "Go, search for Harold – go, bring him to me. I will not eat, nor sleep till he be found."

"Good my lady," quoth Alfred, "how can that be, since he hath betaken himself to Normandy?"

"I care not where he be," she cried. "My heart stands still until I look into his eyes again."

"Surely he hath not gone to Normandy," spoke Hubert. "This very eventide I saw him enter his abode."

They hastened thither – a vast company. His chamber door was barred.

"Harold, Harold, come forth!" they cried, as they beat upon the door, but no answer came to their calls and knockings. Afeared, they battered down the door and when it fell they saw that Harold lay upon his bed.

"He sleeps," said one. "See how he holds a portrait in his

hand – and it is her portrait. How fair he is and how tranquilly he sleeps."

But no, Harold was not asleep. His face was calm and beautiful, as if he dreamt of his beloved, but his clothing was red with the blood that streamed from a wound in his breast – a gaping, ghastly spear wound just above his heart.

Aylmer Vance and the Vampire

Alice and Claude Askew

Aylmer Vance is a clairvoyant detective — that is, someone who has power to communicate with spirits and see ghosts and other supernatural beings. He is sometimes described as the ghost-seer. The stories are told by his friend Dexter.

AYLMER VANCE had rooms in Dover Street, Piccadilly, and I found it convenient to lodge in the same house. Aylmer and I quickly became close friends, and he showed me how to develop that faculty of clairvoyance which I had possessed without being aware of it. At the same time I made myself useful to Vance in other ways, not least of which was that of acting as recorder of his many strange adventures. For himself, he never cared much about publicity, and it was some time before I could persuade him, in the interests of science, to allow me to give any detailed account of his experiences to the world.

The incidents that I will now narrate occurred very soon after we had taken up our residence together, and while I was still, so to speak, a novice.

It was about ten o'clock in the morning when a visitor was announced. He sent up a card that bore upon it the name of Paul Davenant.

The name was familiar to me, and I wondered if this could be the same Mr Davenant who was so well-known for his polo playing and for his success as an amateur rider, especially over the hurdles? He was a young man of wealth and position, and I recollected that he had married, about a year ago, a girl who was reckoned the greatest beauty of the season. Mr Davenant was ushered in, and at first I was uncertain as to whether this could be the individual whom I had in mind, so wan and pale and ill did he appear. A finely built, upstanding man at the time of his marriage, he had now acquired a languid droop of the shoulders and a shuffling gait, while his face, especially about the lips, was bloodless to an alarming degree.

And yet it was the same man, for behind all this I could recognize the shadow of the good looks that had once distinguished Paul Davenant.

He took the chair which Aylmer offered him — after the usual preliminary civilities had been exchanged — and then glanced doubtfully in my direction. "I wish to consult you privately, Mr Vance," he said. "The matter is of considerable importance to myself and of a somewhat delicate nature."

Of course I rose immediately to withdraw from the room, but Vance laid his hand upon my arm.

"If the matter is connected with research in my particular line, Mr Davenant," he said, "if there is any investigation you wish me to take up on your behalf, I shall be glad if you will include Mr Dexter in your confidence. Mr Dexter assists me in my work. But, of course — ."

"Oh, no," interrupted the other, "if that is the case, pray let Mr Dexter remain."

He began by calling attention to his personal appearance. "You would hardly recognize me for the same man I was a year ago," he said. "I've been losing flesh steadily for the last six months. I came up from Scotland about a week ago, to consult a London doctor. I've seen two — in fact, they've held a sort of consultation over me — but the result, I may say, is far from satisfactory. They don't seem to know what is really the matter with me."

"Anaemia — heart," suggested Vance. He was scrutinizing his visitor keenly and yet without any appearance of doing so. "I believe it not infrequently happens that you athletes overdo yourselves – put too much strain upon the heart."

"My heart is quite sound," responded Davenant. "Physically it is in perfect condition. The trouble seems to be that it hasn't enough blood to pump into my veins. The doctors wanted to know if I had met with an accident involving a great loss of blood – but I haven't. I've had no accident at all, and as for anaemia, well, I don't seem to show the ordinary symptoms of it. The inexplicable thing is that I've lost blood without knowing it, and apparently this has been going on for some time, for I've been getting steadily worse. It was almost imperceptible at first – not a sudden collapse, you understand, but a gradual failure of health."

"I wonder," remarked Vance slowly, "what induced you to consult me? For you know, of course, the direction in which I pursue my investigations. May I ask if you have reason to consider that your state of health is due to some cause which we may describe as super-physical?"

A slight colour came to Davenant's white cheeks.

"There are curious circumstances," he said in a low and earnest voice. "I've been turning them over in my mind, trying to see light through them. I daresay it's all the sheerest folly – and I must tell you that I'm not a superstitious sort of man. But, as I have said, there are curious circumstances about my case, and that is why I decided upon consulting you."

"Will you tell me everything without reserve?" said Vance. I could see that he was interested.

He was sitting up in his chair, his feet supported on a stool, his elbows on his knees, his chin in his hands – a favourite attitude of his. "Have you," he suggested, slowly, "any mark upon your body, anything that you might associate, however remotely, with your present weakness and ill-health?"

"It's a curious thing that you should ask me that question," returned Davenant, "because I have got a curious mark, a sort of scar, that I can't account for. But I showed it to the doctors and they assured me that it could have nothing whatever to do with my condition. I think they imagined it to be nothing more than a birthmark, a sort of mole, for they asked me if I'd had it all my life. But that I can swear I haven't. I only noticed it for the first time about six months ago, when my health began to fail. But you can see for yourself."

He loosened his collar and bared his throat. Vance rose and made a careful scrutiny of the suspicious mark. It was situated a very little to the left of the central line, just above the clavicle, and, as Vance pointed out, directly over the big vessels of the throat. My friend called to me so that I might examine it, too. Whatever the opinion of the doctors may have been, Aylmer was obviously deeply interested. And yet there was very little to show. The skin was quite intact and there was no sign of inflammation. There were two red marks, about an inch apart, each of which was inclined to be crescent in shape. They were more visible than they might otherwise have been owing to the peculiar whiteness of Davenant's skin.

"It can't be anything of importance," said Davenant, with a slightly uneasy laugh. "I'm inclined to think the marks are dying away."

"Have you ever noticed them more inflamed than they are at present?" inquired Vance. "If so, was it at any special time?"

Davenant reflected. "Yes," he replied slowly, "there have been times, usually, I think perhaps invariably, when I wake up in the morning, that I've noticed them larger and more angry looking. And I've felt a slight sensation of pain – a tingling – oh, very slight, and I've never worried about it. Only now you suggest it , I believe that those same mornings I have felt particularly tired. And once, Mr Vance, I remember quite distinctly that there was a stain of blood close to the mark. I didn't think anything of it at the time and just wiped it away."

"I see." Aylmer Vance resumed his seat and invited his visitor to do the same. "And now," he resumed, "you said, Mr Davenant, that there are certain peculiar circumstances you wish to acquaint me with. Will you do so?"

And so Davenant readjusted his collar and proceeded to tell his story. I will tell it as far as I can, without any reference to the few interruptions of Vance and myself.

Paul Davenant, as I have said, was a man of wealth and position, and so, in every sense of the word, he was a suitable husband for Miss Jessica MacThane, the young lady who eventually became his wife. Before coming to the incidents attending his loss of health, he had a great deal to recount about Miss MacThane and her family history.

She was of Scottish descent, and although she had certain characteristic features of her race, she was not really Scotch in appearance. Hers was the beauty of the far South rather than that of the Highlands from which she had her origin. Miss MacThane was especially remarkable for her wonderful long red hair. It had an extraordinary gloss upon it so that it seemed almost to have individual life of its own.

Then she had just the complexion that one would expect with such hair, the purest ivory white. Her beauty was derived from an ancestress who had been brought to Scotland from some foreign shore – no one knew exactly where from.

Davenant fell in love with her almost at once and he had every reason to believe, in spite of her many admirers, that his love was returned. At this time he knew very little about her personal history. He was aware only that she was very wealthy in her own right, an orphan, and the last representative of a race that had once been famous in the annals of history – or rather infamous, for the MacThanes had distinguished themselves more by cruelty than by deeds of chivalry. A clan of turbulent robbers in the past, they had helped to add many a bloodstained page to the history of their country.

Jessica had lived with her father, who owned a house in London, until his death when she was about fifteen years of age. Her mother had died in Scotland when Jessica was still a tiny child. Mr MacThane had been so affected by his wife's death that, with his little daughter, he had abandoned his Scotch estate altogether – or so it was believed – leaving it to the management of a bailiff – though, indeed, there was but little work for the bailiff to do, since there were practically no tenants left. Blackwick Castle had borne for many years a most unenviable reputation.

After the death of her father, Miss MacThane had gone to live with a certain Mrs Meredith, who was a connection of her mother's – on her father's side she had not a single relation left.

Jessica was absolutely the last of a clan once so extensive that intermarriage had been a tradition of the family, but for which the last two hundred years had been gradually dwindling to extinction.

Well, I have said that Paul Davenant quickly fell in love with Jessica, and it was not long before he proposed. To his great surprise, for he had good reason to believe that she cared for him, he met with a refusal. She would not give any explanation, though she burst into a flood of pitiful tears.

Bewildered and bitterly disappointed, he consulted Mrs Meredith, with whom he happened to be on friendly terms, and from her he learnt that Jessica had already had several proposals, all from quite desirable men, but that one after another had been rejected.

Paul consoled himself with the reflection that perhaps Jessica did not love them, whereas he was quite sure that she cared for himself. Under these circumstances he determined to try again.

He did so and with better result. Jessica admitted her love, but at the same time repeated that she would not marry him. Love and marriage were not for her. Then, to his utter amazement, she declared that she had been born under a curse – a curse which, sooner or later was bound to show itself in her, and which, moreover, must react cruelly, perhaps fatally, upon anyone with whom she linked her life. How could she allow a man she loved to take such a risk? Above all, since the evil was hereditary, she had made up her mind – no child should ever call her mother. She must be the last of her race.

Of course, Davenant was amazed and inclined to think that Jessica had got some absurd idea into her head which a little reasoning on his part would dispel. There was only one other possible explanation. Was it lunacy she was afraid of? But Jessica shook her head. She did not know of any lunacy in her family. The ill was deeper, more subtle than that. And then she told him all that she knew.

The curse – she made use of that word for want of a better – was attached to the ancient race from which she had her origin. Her father had suffered from it, and his father and grandfather before him. All three had taken to themselves young wives who had died mysteriously, of some wasting disease, within a few years. 'Do you know what my father said we have it in us to become?' said Jessica with a shudder. 'He used the word vampires. Paul, think of it – vampires – preying upon the life blood of others.' And then, when Davenant was inclined to laugh, she checked him. 'No,' she cried out, 'it is not impossible. Think. We are a decadent race. From the earliest times our history has been marked by bloodshed and cruelty. The walls of Blackwick Castle are impregnated with evil. Every stone could tell its tale of violence, pain, lust and murder. What can one expect of those who have spent their lifetime between its walls?'

'But you have not done so,' exclaimed Paul. 'You have been spared that, Jessica. You were taken away after your mother died, and you have no recollection of Blackwick Castle, none at all. And you need never set foot in it again.'

'I'm afraid the evil is in my blood,' she replied sadly, 'although I am unconscious of it now. And as for not returning to Blackwick – I'm not sure I can help myself. At least, that is what my father warned me of. He said there is something there, some compelling force, that will call me to it in spite of myself. But, oh, I don't know – I don't know, and that is what makes it so difficult. If I could only believe that all this is nothing but an idle superstition, I might be happy again, for I have it in me to enjoy life, and I'm young, very young, but my father told me these things when he was on his deathbed.' She added the last words in a low, awe-stricken tone.

Paul pressed her to tell him all that she knew and eventually she revealed another fragment of family history which seemed to have some bearing upon the case. It dealt with her own astonishing likeness to an ancestress of a couple of hundred years ago.

A certain Robert MacThane, departing from the traditions of his family, which demanded that he should not marry outside his clan, brought home a wife from foreign shores, a woman of wonderful beauty, who was possessed of glowing masses of red hair and a complexion of ivory whiteness – such as had more or less distinguished since then every female of the race.

It was not long before this woman came to be regarded in the neighbourhood as a witch. Stories were circulated abroad as to her doings and the reputation of Blackwick Castle became worse than ever before.

And then one day she disappeared. Robert MacThane had been absent on business and it was upon his return that he found her gone. The neighbourhood was searched, but without avail, and then Robert, who was a violent man but

adored his wife, called together his
tenants whom he suspected of foul
play, and had them murdered in cold
blood. Murder was easy in those
days, yet such an outcry was raised
that Robert had to take flight,
leaving his two children in the
care of their nurse, and for a
long while Blackwick Castle
was without a master.

But its evil reputation
persisted. It was said that
Zaida, the witch, though
dead, still made her presence
felt. Many children and
young people of the
neighbourhood sickened and
died – possibly of natural
causes, but this did not prevent a
terror settling upon the
countryside. It was said that
Zaida had been seen – a pale
woman clad in white –
flitting about the cottages at

night, and where she passed sickness and death were sure.

And from that time the fortune of the family gradually declined. Heir succeeded heir, but no sooner was he installed at Blackwick Castle than his nature, whatever it may previously have been, seemed to undergo a change. It was as if he absorbed into himself all the weight of evil that had stained his family name – as if he did, indeed, become a vampire, bringing blight upon any not directly connected with his own house. And yet it seemed that the last representatives of the MacThanes could not desert their ancestral home. Riches they had, sufficient to live happily upon elsewhere, but, drawn by some power they could not contend against, they had preferred to spend their lives in the solitude of the now half-ruined castle, shunned by their neighbours, feared and execrated by the few tenants that still clung to their soil.

So it had been with Jessica's grandfather and great-grandfather. Each of them had married a young wife, and in each case their love story had been all too brief. The vampire spirit was still abroad, expressing itself – or so it seemed – through the living representatives of bygone generations of evil and young blood had been demanded as the sacrifice.

And to them had succeeded Jessica's father. He had not

profited by their example, but had followed directly in their footsteps. And the same fate had befallen the wife whom he passionately adored. She had died of anaemia – so the doctors said – but he had regarded himself as her murderer.

But, unlike his predecessors, he had torn himself away from Blackwick – and this for the sake of his child. Unknown to her, however, he had returned year after year, for there were times when the passionate longing for the gloomy, mysterious halls and corridors of the old castle, for the wild stretches of moorland, and the dark pinewoods, would come upon him too strongly to be resisted. And so he knew that for his daughter, as for himself, there was no escape. When the relief of death was at last granted to him, he warned her of what her fate must be.

This was the tale that Jessica told the man who wished to make her his wife, and he made light of it, as such a man would, regarding it all as foolish superstition, the delusion of a mind overwrought. And at last – perhaps it was not very difficult, for she loved him with all her heart and soul – he succeeded in inducing Jessica to think as he did and to consent to marry him at an early date.

"I'll take any risk you like," he declared. "I'll even go and live at Blackwick if you should desire it. To think of you a vampire! Why, I never heard such nonsense in my life."

"Father said I'm very like Zaida, the witch," she protested, but he silenced her with a kiss.

And so they were married and spent their honeymoon abroad, and in the autumn Paul accepted an invitation to a house party in Scotland for the grouse shooting, a sport to which he was absolutely devoted, and Jessica agreed with him that there was absolutely no reason why he should forgo his pleasure, and they journeyed there together.

Perhaps it was an unwise thing to do, to venture to Scotland, but by this time the young couple, more deeply in love with each other than ever, had got quite over their fears. Jessica was redolent with health and spirits, and more than once she declared that if they should be anywhere in the neighbourhood of Blackwick Castle she would like to see the place out of sheer curiosity, and just to show how absolutely she had recovered from the foolish terrors that used to assail her.

This seemed to Paul to be quite a wise plan, and so one day, since they were actually staying at no great distance, they motored over to Blackwick, and finding the bailiff, got him to show them over the castle.

It was a great castellated pile, grey with age and in places falling into ruin. It stood on a steep hillside, with the rock of which it seemed to form part, and on one side of it there was a precipitous drop to a mountain stream a hundred feet below. At the back, climbing up the mountainside were dark pinewoods, from which rugged crags protruded. These were fantastically shaped, some like gigantic and misshapen human forms, which stood up as if they mounted guard over the castle and the narrow gorge, by which alone it could be approached.

Well, Mr and Mrs Davenant visited as much as the bailiff could show them of this ill-omened edifice, and Paul, for his part, thought pleasantly of his own Derbyshire home, replete with every modern comfort, where he proposed to settle with his wife. And so he received something of a shock when, as they drove away, she slipped her hand into his and whispered, 'Paul, you promised, didn't you, that you would refuse me nothing?'

She had been strangely silent till she spoke those words. Paul, slightly apprehensive, assured her that she only had to ask – but the speech did not come from his heart, for he guessed vaguely what she desired.

She wanted to go and live at the castle – oh, only for a little while, for she was sure she would soon tire of it. But the bailiff had told her that there were papers, documents, which she ought to examine, since the property was now hers – and, besides, she was interested in this home of her ancestors and wanted to explore it more thoroughly. Oh, no, she wasn't in the least influenced by the old superstition – that wasn't the attraction – she had quite got over those silly ideas. Paul had cured her, and since he himself was so convinced that they were without foundation he ought not to mind granting her her whim.

And so, a week later, when their stay with their friends was concluded, they went to Blackwick, the bailiff having engaged a few servants and generally made things as comfortable for them as possible. Paul was worried and apprehensive, but he could not admit this to his wife after having so loudly proclaimed his theories on the subject of superstition.

They had been married for three months at this time – nine had passed since then, and they had never left Blackwick for more than a few hours – till now Paul had come to London – alone.

"Over and over again," he declared, "my wife has begged me to go. With tears in her eyes, almost upon her knees, she has begged me to leave her, but I have steadily refused unless she will accompany me. But that is the trouble, Mr Vance, she cannot leave. There is something, some mysterious horror, that holds her there as surely as if she were bound with fetters."

"Did you never attempt to take your wife away from the castle?" asked Vance.

"Yes, several times – but it was hopeless. She would become so ill as soon as we were beyond the limit of the estate that I invariably had to take her back. Once we got as far as Dorekirk – that is the nearest town, you know – and I thought I should be successful if only I could get through the night. But she escaped me. She climbed out of a window – she meant to go back on foot, at night, all those long miles.

Then I have had doctors down, but it is I who wanted the doctors, not she. They have ordered me away, but I have refused to obey them till now."

"Has your wife changed physically?" interrupted Vance.

Davenant reflected. "Changed," he said, "yes, but so subtly that I hardly know how to describe it. She is more beautiful than ever – and yet it isn't the same beauty, if you can understand me. I have spoken of her white complexion, well, one is more than ever conscious of it now, because her lips have become so red – they are almost like a splash of blood upon her face. And the upper one has a peculiar curve that I don't think it had before, and when she laughs she doesn't smile –

"Do you know what I mean? Then her hair – it has lost its wonderful gloss. Of course, I know she is fretting about me, but that is so peculiar, too, for at times, as I have told you, she will implore me to go and leave her, and then perhaps only a few minutes later, she will wreathe her arms round my neck and say she cannot live without me. And I feel that there is a struggle going on within her, that she is only yielding slowly to the horrible influence – whatever it is – that she is herself when she begs me to go, but when she entreats me to stay – and it is then that her fascination is most intense – oh, I can't help remembering what she told me before we were married, and that word" – he lowered his voice – "the word 'vampire' –"

He passed his hand over his brow that was wet with perspiration. 'But that's absurd, ridiculous,' he muttered. "These fantastic beliefs have been exploded years ago. We live in the twentieth century."

A pause ensued, then Vance said quietly, "Mr Davenant, since you have taken me into your confidence, since you have found doctors of no avail, will you let me try to help you? I think I may be of some use – if it is not already too late. Should you agree, Mr Dexter and I will accompany you, as you have suggested, to Blackwick Castle as early as possible – by tonight's mail North. Under ordinary circumstances I should tell you as you value your life, not to return –". Davenant shook his head.

"That is advice which I should never take," he declared.

"I had already decided, under any circumstances, to travel North tonight. I am glad that you both will accompany me."

And so it was decided. We settled to meet at the station and presently Paul Davenant took his departure. Any other details that remained to be told he would put us in possession of during the course of the journey.

Of our long journey to Scotland I need say nothing. We did not reach Blackwick Castle till late in the afternoon of the following day. The place was just as I have already described it. And a sense of gloom settled upon me as our car jolted us over the rough road that led through the Gorge of the Winds – a gloom that deepened when we penetrated into the vast cold hall of the castle.

Mrs Davenant, who had been informed by telegram of our arrival, received us cordially. She knew nothing of our actual mission, regarding us merely as friends of her husband's. She was most solicitous on his behalf, but there was something strained about her tone, and it made me feel vaguely uneasy. In every other aspect she was charming, and she had an extraordinary fascination of appearance and manner that made me readily understand the force of a remark made by Davenant during our journey.

"I want to live for Jessica's sake. Get her away from Blackwick, Vance, and I feel that all will be well. I'd go through hell to have her restored to me – as she was."

And now that I had seen Mrs Davenant I realized what he meant by those last words. Her fascination was stronger than ever, but it was not a natural fascination – not that of a normal woman, such as she had been. We had a strong proof of the evil within her soon after our arrival. It was a test that Vance had quietly prepared. Davenant had mentioned that no flowers grew at Blackwick and Vance declared that we

must take some with us as a present
for the lady of the house. He
purchased a bouquet of roses
at the little town where
we left the train, for
the motor car has
been sent to meet us.
Soon after our arrival he
presented these to
Mrs Davenant. She took
them it seemed to me
nervously, and hardly had her
hand touched them before they
fell to pieces, in a shower of
crumpled petals, to the floor.

"We must act at once," said
Vance to me when we were
descending to dinner that night.
"There must be no delay."

"What are you afraid of?"
I whispered.

"Davenant has been
absent a week," he
replied grimly. "He is

stronger than when he went away, but not strong enough to survive the loss of more blood. He must be protected. There is danger tonight."

"You mean from his wife?" I shuddered at the ghastliness of the suggestion.

"That is what time will show." Vance turned to me and added a few words with intense earnestness. "Mrs Davenant, Dexter, is at present hovering between two conditions. The evil thing has not yet completely mastered her – you remember what Davenant said, how she would beg him to go away and the next moment entreat him to stay? She has made a struggle, but she is gradually succumbing, and this last week, spent here alone, has strengthened the evil. And that is what I have got to fight – it is to be a contest of will, a contest that will go on silently till one or the other obtains the mastery. If you watch, you may see. Should a change show itself in Mrs Davenant you will know that I have won."

Thus I knew the direction in which my friend proposed to act. It was to be a war of his will against the mysterious power that had laid its curse upon the house of MacThane. Mrs Davenant must be released from the fatal charm that held her.

Later, as we sat in the drawing room, I could feel the clash of wills. The air in the room felt electric and heavy, charged with tremendous but invisible forces. And outside, round the castle, the wind whistled and shrieked and moaned – it was as if all the dead and gone MacThanes, a grim army, had collected to fight the battle of their race.

And all this while we four in the drawing room were sitting and talking the ordinary commonplaces of after dinner conversation! That was the extraordinary part of it – Paul Davenant suspected nothing, and I, who knew, had to play my part. But I hardly took my eyes from Jessica's face. When would the change come, or was it, indeed, too late!

At last Davenant rose and remarked that he was tired and would go to bed. There was no need for Jessica to hurry. He would sleep that night in his dressing room and did not want to be disturbed.

And it was at that moment, as his lips met hers in a goodnight kiss, as she wreathed her enchantress arms about him, careless of our presence, her eyes gleaming hungrily, that the change came.

It came with a fierce and threatening shriek of wind, and a rattling of the casement, as if the horde of ghosts was about to break in upon us. A long, quivering sigh escaped from Jessica's lips, her arms fell from her husband's shoulders, and she drew back, swaying from side to side.

"Paul," she cried, and somehow the whole timbre of her

voice was changed, "what a wretch I've been to bring you back to Blackwick, ill as you are! But we'll go away, dear. Yes, I'll go, too. Oh, will you take me away – take me away tomorrow?" She spoke with an intense earnestness – unconscious all the time of what had been happening to her. Long shudders were convulsing her frame. "I don't know why I've wanted to stay here," she kept repeating. "I hate the place, really – it's evil – evil."

Having heard these words I exulted, for surely Vance's success was assured. But I was to learn that the danger was not yet past.

Husband and wife separated, each going to their own room. I noticed the grateful, if mystified glance that Davenant threw at Vance, vaguely aware, as he must have been, that my friend was somehow responsible for what had happened. It was settled that plans for departure were to be discussed the next day.

"I have succeeded," Vance said hurriedly, when we were alone, "but the change may be a transitory. I must keep watch tonight. Go you to bed, Dexter, there is nothing that you can do."

I obeyed – though I would sooner have kept watch against a danger of which I had no understanding. I went to my room, a gloomy and sparsely furnished apartment, but I knew that it was quite impossible for me to think of sleeping. And so, dressed as I was, I went and sat by the open window, for now the wind that had raged round the castle had died down to a low moaning in the pine trees – a whimpering of time-worn agony.

And it was as I sat thus that I became aware of a white figure that stole out from the castle by a door that I could not see, and, with hands clasped, ran swiftly across the terrace to the wood. I had but a momentary glance, but I felt convinced that the figure was that of Jessica Davenant.

And instinctively I knew that some great danger was imminent. It was, I think, the suggestion of despair conveyed by those clasped hands. At any rate, I did not hesitate.

My window was some height from the ground, but the wall below was ivy-clad and afforded good foothold. The descent was quite easy. I achieved it, and was just in time to take up the pursuit in the right direction, which was into the thickness of the wood that clung to the slope of the hill.

I shall never forget that wild chase. There was just sufficient room to enable me to follow the rough path, which, luckily, since I had now lost sight of my quarry, was the only possible way that she could have taken – there were no intersecting tracks, and the wood was too thick on either side to permit of deviation.

And the wood seemed full of dreadful sounds – moaning, wailing and hideous laughter.

The wind, of course, and the screaming of night birds – once I felt the fluttering of wings in close proximity to my face. But I could not rid myself of the thought that I, in my turn, was being pursued, that the forces of hell were combined against me.

The path came to an abrupt end on the border of the sombre lake that I have already mentioned. And now I realized that I was indeed only just in time, for in front of me, plunging knee deep in the freezing water, I recognized the white-clad figure of the woman I had been pursuing.

Hearing my footsteps, she turned her head, and then threw up her arms and screamed. Her red hair fell in heavy masses about her shoulders, and her face, as I saw it in that moment, was hardly human for the agony of remorse that it depicted.

"Go!" she screamed. "Please leave me! For God's sake please let me die!"

But I was by her side almost as she spoke. She struggled with me – sought vainly to tear herself from my clasp – implored me, with panting breath, to let her drown.

"It's the only way to save him!" she gasped. "Don't you understand that I am a thing accursed? For it is I – I – who have sapped his life blood! I know it now, the truth has been revealed to me tonight! I am a vampire, without hope in this world or the next, so for his sake – for the sake of his unborn child – let me die – let me die!".Was ever so terrible an appeal made? Yet I — what could I do? Gently I overcame her resistance and drew her back to shore. By the time I reached it she was lying a dead weight upon my arm. I laid her down upon a mossy bank, and kneeling by her side, gazed intently into her face.

And then I knew that I had done well. For the face I looked upon was not that of Jessica the vampire, as I had seen it that afternoon, it was the face of Jessica, the woman whom Paul Davenant had loved.

And later Aylmer Vance had his tale to tell.

"I waited", he said, "until I knew that Davenant was asleep, and then I stole into his room to watch by his bedside. And presently she came, as I guessed she would, the vampire, the accursed thing that has preyed upon the souls of her kin, making them like to herself when they too have passed into Shadowland, and gathering sustenance for her horrid task from the blood of those who are alien to her race. Paul's body and Jessica's soul — it is for one and the other, Dexter, that we have fought."

"You mean," I hesitated, "Zaida the witch?"

"Even so," he agreed. "Hers is the evil spirit that has fallen like a blight upon the house of MacThane. But now I think she may be exorcized forever."

"Tell me."

"She came to Paul Davenant last night, as she must have done before, in the guise of his wife. You know that Jessica bears a strong resemblance to her ancestress. He opened his arms, but she was foiled of her prey, for I had taken my precautions. I had placed garlic upon Davenant's breast while he slept which robbed the vampire of her power of ill. She sped wailing from the room – a shadow – she who a minute before had looked at him with Jessica's eyes and spoken to him with Jessica's voice. Her red lips were Jessica's lips, and they were close to his when his eyes were opened and he saw her as she was – a hideous phantom of the corruption of the ages. And so the spell was removed, and she fled away to the place whence she had come –"

He paused. "And now?" I inquired.

"Blackwick Castle must be razed to the ground," he replied. "That is the only way. Every stone of it, every brick, must be ground to powder and burnt with fire, for therein is the cause of all the evil. Davenant has consented."

"And Mrs Davenant?"

"I think," Vance answered cautiously, "that all may be well with her. The curse will be removed with the destruction of the castle. She has not – thanks to you – perished under its influence. She was less guilty than she imagined – herself preyed upon rather than preying. But can't you understand her remorse when she realized, as she was bound to realize, the part she had played? And the knowledge of the child to come – its fatal inheritance –"

"I understand." I muttered with a shudder. And then, under my breath, I whispered, "Thank God!"

Vampire

Jan Neruda

THE EXCURSION steamer brought us from Constantinople to the shore of the island of Prinkipo and we disembarked. The number of passengers was not large. There was one Polish family, a father, a mother, a daughter and her bridegroom, and then we two. Oh, yes, I must not forget that when we were already on the wooden bridge that crosses the Golden Horn to Constantinople, a Greek, a rather youthful man, joined us. He was probably an artist, judging by the portfolio he carried under his arm. Long black locks floated to his shoulders, his face was pale and his black eyes were deeply set in their sockets. From the first moment he interested me, especially for his obligingness and for his knowledge of local conditions. But he talked too much and I then turned away from him.

All the more agreeable was the Polish family. The father
and mother were good-natured, fine people, the lover a
handsome young fellow of direct and refined manners. They
had come to Prinkipo to spend the summer months for the
sake of the daughter, who was slightly ailing. The beautiful
pale girl was either just recovering from a severe illness or
else a serious disease was just fastening its hold upon her.
She leaned upon her lover when she walked and very often
sat down to rest, while a frequent dry little cough
interrupted her whispers. Whenever she coughed, her
escort would considerately pause in their walk. He always
cast upon her a glance of sympathetic suffering and she
would look back at him as if she would say, 'It is nothing. I
am happy!' They believed in health and happiness.

On the recommendation of the Greek, who departed
from us immediately at the pier, the family secured quarters
in the hotel on the hill. The hotel keeper was a Frenchman
and his entire building was equipped comfortably and
artistically, according to the French style.

We breakfasted together and when the noon heat had
abated somewhat we all betook ourselves to the heights,
where in the grove of Siberian stone-pines we could refresh
ourselves with the view. Hardly had we found a suitable spot
and settled ourselves when the Greek appeared again. He

greeted us lightly, looked about and seated himself only a few steps from us. He opened his portfolio and began to sketch.

"I think he purposely sits with his back to the rocks so that we can't look at his sketch," I said.

"We don't have to," said the young Pole. "We have enough before us to look at." After a while he added, "It seems to me he's sketching us in as a sort of background. Well – let him!"

We truly did have enough to gaze at. There is not a more beautiful or more happy corner in the world than that very Prinkipo! If I could live a month of my life there I would be happy with the memory of it for the rest of my days! I shall never forget even that one day spent at Prinkipo.

The air was as clear as a diamond, so soft, so caressing, that one's whole soul swung out upon it into the distance. At the right beyond the sea projected the brown Asiatic summits, to the left in the distance purpled the steep coasts of Europe. In the distance the sea was as white as milk, then rosy, between the two islands a glowing orange and below us it was beautifully greenish-blue, like a transparent sapphire. It was resplendent in its own beauty. Nowhere were there any large ships – only two small crafts flying the English flag sped along the shore. One was a steamboat as big as a watchman's booth, the second had about twelve oarsmen, and when their oars rose simultaneously molten silver dripped from them. Trustful dolphins darted in and out among them and dove with long, arching flights above the surface of the water. Through the blue heavens now and then calm eagles winged their way, measuring the space between two continents.

The entire slope below us was covered with blossoming roses whose fragrance filled the air. Music was carried up to us from the coffee house near the sea through the clear air, hushed somewhat by the distance.

The effect was enchanting. We all sat silent and steeped our souls completely in the picture of paradise. The young Polish girl lay on the grass with her head supported on the bosom of her lover. The pale oval of her delicate face was slightly tinged with soft colour and from her blue eyes tears suddenly gushed forth. The lover understood, bent down and kissed tear after tear. Her mother also was moved to tears, and I – even I – felt a strange twinge.

"Here mind and body both must get well," whispered the girl. "How happy a land this is!"

"God knows I haven't any enemies, but if I had I would forgive them here!" said the father in a trembling voice.

And again we became silent. We were all in such a

wonderful mood – so unspeakably sweet it all was! Each felt for himself a whole world of happiness and each one would have shared his happiness with the whole world. All felt the same – and so no one disturbed another. We had scarcely even noticed the Greek, who after an hour or so, had arisen, folded his portfolio and with a slight nod had taken his departure. We remained.

Finally after several hours, when the distance was becoming overspread with a darker violet, so magically beautiful in the south, the mother reminded us it was time to depart. We arose and walked down towards the hotel with the easy, elastic steps of carefree children. We sat down in the hotel under the handsome veranda.

Hardly had we been seated when we heard below the sounds of quarrelling and oaths. Our Greek was wrangling the hotel keeper, and for the entertainment of it we listened.

The amusement did not last long. "If I didn't have other guests," growled the hotel keeper, and ascended the steps towards us.

"I beg you to tell me, sir," asked the young Pole of the approaching hotel keeper, "who is that gentleman?"

"Eh – who knows what the fellow's name is?" grumbled the hotel keeper, and he gazed venomously downwards. "We call him the Vampire."

"An artist?"

"Fine trade! He sketches only corpses. Just as soon as someone in Constantinople or here in the neighbourhood dies, that very day he has a picture of the dead one completed. That fellow paints them beforehand – and he never makes a mistake – just like a vulture!"

The old Polish woman shrieked affrightedly. In her arms lay her daughter pale as chalk. She had fainted.

In one bound the lover had leaped down the steps. With one hand he seized the Greek and with the other reached for the portfolio.

We ran down after him. Both men were rolling in the sand. The contents of the portfolio were scattered all about. On one sheet, sketched with a crayon, was the head of the young Polish girl, her eyes closed and a wreath of myrtle on her brow.

THE FREEING OF LUCY

Bram Stoker

Lucy has been buried for some time, but Van Helsing fears she is walking as a vampire. He brings John Seward to see her tomb, and they find her body in the coffin looking fresh and undecayed. Van Helsing is now returning with Seward, their friend Quincy Morris and Lucy's fiancé, Arthur, to show them what Lucy has become. 'The Host' referred to in the story is the consecrated bread served at Holy Communion, and believed by Roman Catholics, of which Van Helsing is one, to be the actual body of Jesus Christ.

IT WAS JUST A QUARTER before twelve o'clock when we got into the churchyard over the low wall. The night was dark with occasional gleams of moonlight between the dents of the heavy clouds that scudded across the sky. We all kept somehow close together, with Van Helsing slightly in

front as he led the way. When we had come close to the
tomb I looked hard at Arthur, for I feared a place laden with
so sorrowful a memory would upset him, but he bore
himself well. The Professor unlocked the door, and seeing a
natural hesitation amongst us for various reasons, solved the
difficulty by entering first himself. The rest of us followed
and he closed the door. He lit a dark lantern and pointed to
a coffin. Arthur stepped forwards hesitatingly. Van Helsing
said to me, "You were with me here yesterday. Was the body
of Miss Lucy in that coffin?"

"It was."

The Professor turned to the rest saying, "You hear, and
yet there is one who does not believe with me."

He took his screwdriver and again took off the lid of the
coffin. Arthur looked on, very pale but silent. When the lid
was removed he stepped forwards. When he saw the rent in
the lead, the blood rushed to his face for an instant, but as
quickly fell away again, so that he remained of a ghastly
whiteness. He was still silent. Van Helsing forced back the
leaden rim, and we all looked in and recoiled.

The coffin was empty!

For several minutes no one spoke a word. The silence
was broken by Quincey Morris. "Professor, I answered for
you. Your word is all I want. I wouldn't ask such a thing

ordinarily, I wouldn't so dishonour you as to imply a doubt, but this is a mystery that goes beyond any honour or dishonour. Is this your doing?"

"I swear to you by all that I hold sacred that I have not removed or touched her. What happened was this. Two nights ago my friend Seward and I came here, with good purpose, believe me. I opened that coffin, which was then sealed up, and we found it as now, empty. We then waited and saw something white come through the trees. The next day we came here in daytime and she lay there. Did she not, friend John?"

"Yes."

"That night we were just in time. One more small child was missing, and we found it, thank God, unharmed amongst the graves. Yesterday I came here before sundown, for at sundown the Undead can move. I waited here all night till the sun rose, but I saw nothing. It was most probable that it was because I had laid over the clamps of those doors garlic, which the Undead cannot bear, and other things which they shun. Last night there was no exodus, so tonight before sundown I took away my garlic and other things. And so it is we find this coffin empty. But bear with me. So far there is much that is strange. Wait with me outside, unseen and unheard, and things much stranger are yet to be. So," here he shut the dark slide of his lantern, "now to the outside." He opened the door, and we filed out, he coming last and locking the door behind him.

Oh! But it seemed fresh and pure in the night air after the terror of that vault. How sweet it was to see the clouds race by, and the passing gleams of the moonlight between the scudding clouds crossing and passing, like the gladness and sorrow of a man's life. Arthur was silent, and was, I could see, striving to grasp the purpose and the inner meaning of the mystery. I was myself tolerably patient, and half inclined again to throw aside doubt and to accept Van Helsing's conclusions. As to Van Helsing, he was employed in a definite way. First he took from his bag a mass of what looked like thin, wafer-like biscuit, which was carefully rolled up in a white napkin. Next he took out a double handful of some whitish stuff, like dough. He crumbled the wafer up fine and worked it into the mass between his hands. This he then took, and rolling it into thin strips, began to lay them into the crevices between the door and its setting in the tomb. I was somewhat puzzled at this, and being close, asked him what it was that he was doing. Arthur and Quincey drew near also, as they too were curious.

He answered, "I am closing the tomb so that the Undead may not enter."

"And is that stuff you have there going to do it?"

"It is."

"What is it that you are using?" This time the question was from Arthur. Van Helsing reverently lifted his hat as he answered.

"The Host. I brought it from Amsterdam."

It was an answer that appalled the most sceptical of us, and we felt individually that in the presence of such earnest purpose as the Professor's, a purpose which could thus use the host, to him, most sacred of things, it was impossible to distrust. In respectful silence we took the places assigned to us close round the tomb, but hidden from the sight of any one approaching. There was a long spell of silence, big, aching, void, and then from the Professor a keen "S-s-s-s!" He pointed, and far down the avenue of yews we saw a white figure advance, a dim white figure, which held something dark at its breast. The figure stopped, and at the moment a ray of moonlight fell upon the masses of driving clouds, and showed in startling prominence a woman. We could not see the face, for it was bent down over what we saw to be a fair-haired child. There was a pause and a sharp little cry, such as a child gives in sleep, or a dog as it lies before the fire and dreams. We were starting forward, but the Professor's warning hand, seen by us as he stood behind a yew tree, kept us back. And then as we looked the white figure moved forwards again. It was now near enough for us to see clearly and the moonlight still held. My own heart grew cold as ice and I could hear the gasp of Arthur as we recognized the features of Lucy Westenra. Lucy Westenra, but yet how changed. The sweetness was turned to adamantine, heartless cruelty and the purity to voluptuous wantonness.

Van Helsing stepped out and obedient to his gesture, we all advanced too. The four of us ranged in a line before the door of the tomb. Van Helsing raised his lantern. By the concentrated light that fell on Lucy's face we could see that the lips were crimson with fresh blood, and that the stream had trickled over her chin and stained the purity of her lawn death robe.

We shuddered with horror. I could see by the tremulous light that even Van Helsing's iron nerve had failed. Arthur was next to me, and if I had not seized his arm and held him up, he would have fallen.

When Lucy, I call the thing that was before us Lucy because it bore her shape, saw us she drew back with an angry snarl, such as a cat gives when taken unawares, then her eyes ranged over us. Lucy's eyes in form and colour, but Lucy's eyes unclean and full of hell fire, instead of the pure,

gentle orbs we knew. At that moment the remnant of my
love passed into hate and loathing. Had she then to be killed,
I could have done it with savage delight. As she looked, her
eyes blazed with unholy light and the face became wreathed
with a voluptuous smile. Oh, God, how it made me shudder
to see it! With a careless motion, she flung to the ground,
callous as a devil, the child that up to now she had clutched
strenuously to her breast, growling over it as a dog growls
over a bone. The child gave a sharp cry and lay there
moaning. There was a cold-bloodedness in the act which
wrung a groan from Arthur. When she advanced to him with
outstretched arms and a wanton smile he fell back and hid
his face in his hands.

She still advanced, however, and with a languorous grace,
said, "Come to me, Arthur. Leave these others and come to
me. My arms are hungry for you. Come, and we can rest
together. Come, my husband, come!"

There was something diabolically sweet in her tones,
something of the tinkling of glass when struck, which rang
through the brains even of us who heard the words
addressed to another.

As for Arthur, he seemed under a spell, moving his hands
from his face, he opened wide his arms. She was leaping for
them, when Van Helsing sprang forward and held between

them his little golden crucifix. She recoiled from it, and, with a suddenly distorted face, full of rage, dashed past him as if to enter the tomb.

When within a foot or two of the door, however, she stopped, as if arrested by some irresistible force. Then she turned, and her face was shown in the clear burst of moonlight and by the lamp, which had now no quiver from Van Helsing's nerves. Never did I see such baffled malice on a face, and never, I trust, shall such ever be seen again by mortal eyes. If ever a face meant death, if looks could kill, we saw it at that moment.

And so for a full half a minute, which seemed an eternity, she remained between the lifted crucifix and the sacred closing of her means of entry.

Van Helsing broke the silence by asking Arthur, "Answer me, oh my friend! Am I to proceed in my work?"

"Do as you will, friend. Do as you will. There can be no horror like this ever anymore." And he groaned in spirit.

Coming close to the tomb, he began to remove from the chinks some of the sacred emblem which he had placed there. We all looked on with horrified amazement as we saw, when he stood back, the woman, with a corporeal body as real at that moment as our own, pass through where scarce a knife blade could have gone. We all felt a glad sense of relief when we saw the Professor calmly restoring the strings of putty to the edges of the door.

When this was done, he lifted the child and said, "Come now, my friends. We can do no more till tomorrow. There is a funeral at noon, so here we shall all come before long after that. The friends of the dead will all be gone by two and when the sexton locks the gate we shall remain. Then there is more to do, but not like this of tonight. As for this little one, he is not much harmed and by tomorrow night he shall be well. We shall leave him where the police will find him and then go home."

Coming close to Arthur, he said, "My friend Arthur, you have had a sore trial, but after, when you look back, you will see it was necessary. You are now in the bitter waters. By this time tomorrow you will, please God, have passed them and have drunk of the sweet waters. So do not mourn too much. Till then I shall not ask you to forgive me."

Arthur and Quincey came home with me and we tried to cheer each other on the way. We had left behind the child in safety and were tired. So we all slept with more or less reality of sleep.

29 September, night. — A little before twelve o'clock we three, Arthur, Quincey Morris and myself, called for the Professor. It was odd to notice that by common consent we

had all put on black clothes. Of course, Arthur wore black, for he was in deep mourning, but the rest of us wore it by instinct. We got to the graveyard by half-past one, and strolled about, keeping out of official observation, so that when the gravediggers had completed their task and the sexton under the belief that everyone had gone, had locked the gate, we had the place all to ourselves. Van Helsing, instead of his little black bag, had with him a long leather one, something like a cricketing bag.

When we were alone and had heard the last of the footsteps die out up the road, we silently, and as if by ordered intention, followed the Professor to the tomb. He unlocked the door and we entered, closing it behind us. When he again lifted the lid off Lucy's coffin we all looked, Arthur trembling like an aspen, and saw that the corpse lay there in all its death beauty. But there was no love in my own heart, nothing but loathing for the foul Thing that had taken Lucy's shape without her soul. I could see even Arthur's face grow hard as he looked. Presently he said to Van Helsing, "Is this really Lucy's body, or only a demon in her shape?"

"It is her body, and yet not it. But wait a while and you shall see her as she was, and is."

She seemed like a nightmare of Lucy as she lay there, the

pointed teeth, the bloodstained, voluptuous mouth, which
made one shudder to see. Van Helsing, with his usual
methodicalness, began taking the various contents from his
bag and placing them ready for use. First he took out a
soldering iron and some plumbing solder, and then a small
oil lamp, which gave out, when lit in a corner of the tomb,
gas which burned at a fierce heat with a blue flame. Then he
took out his operating knives, which he placed to hand, and
last a round wooden stake, some two and a half or three
inches thick and about three feet long. One end of it was
hardened by charring in the fire and was sharpened to a fine
point. With this stake came a heavy hammer, such as in
households is used in the coal cellar for breaking the lumps.
To me, a doctor's preparations for work of any kind are
stimulating and bracing, but the effect of these things on
both Arthur and Quincey was to cause them a sort of
consternation. They both, however, kept their courage, and
remained silent and quiet.

When all was ready, Van Helsing said, "Before we do
anything, let me tell you this. It is out of the lore and
experience of the ancients and of all those who have studied
the powers of the Undead. When they become such, there
comes with the change the curse of immortality. They
cannot die, but must go on age after age adding new victims

and multiplying the evils of the world. For all that die from the preying of the Undead become themselves Undead and prey on their kind. And so the circle goes on ever widening, like the ripples from a stone thrown in the water. Friend Arthur, if you had met that kiss which you know of before poor Lucy died, or again, last night when you open your arms to her, you would in time, when you had died, have become *nosferatu*, as they call it in Eastern Europe, and would for all time make more of those Undeads that so have filled us with horror.

The career of this so unhappy dear lady is but just begun. Those children whose blood she sucked are not as yet so much the worse, but if she lives on, Undead, more and more they lose their blood and by her power over them they come to her, and so she draws their blood with that so wicked mouth. But if she die in truth, then all cease. The tiny wounds of the throats disappear and they go back to their play unknowing ever of what has been. But of the most blessed of all, when this now Undead be made to rest as true dead, then the soul of the poor lady whom we love shall again be free. Instead of working wickedness by night and growing more debased in the assimilating of it by day, she shall take her place with the other Angels. So that, my friend, it will be a blessed hand for her that shall strike the blow that sets her free. To this I am willing, but is there none amongst us who has a better right? Will it be no joy to think of hereafter in the silence of the night when sleep is not, 'It was my hand that sent her to the stars. It was the hand of him that loved her best, the hand that of all she would herself have chosen, had it been to her to choose?' Tell me if there be such a one amongst us?"

We all looked at Arthur. He saw too, what we all did, the infinite kindness which suggested that his should be the hand that would restore Lucy to us as a holy, and not an unholy, memory. He stepped forwards and said bravely, though his hand trembled and his face was as pale as snow, "My true friend, from the bottom of my broken heart I thank you. Tell me what I am to do and I shall not falter!"

Van Helsing laid a hand on his shoulder, and said, "Brave lad! A moment's courage and it is done. This stake must be driven through her. It will be a fearful ordeal, be not deceived in that, but it will be only a short time and you will then rejoice more than your pain was great. From this grim tomb you will emerge as though you tread on air. But you must not falter when once you have begun. Only think that we, your true friends, are round you, and that we pray for you all the time."

"Go on," said Arthur hoarsely. "Tell me what I am to do."

"Take this stake in your left hand, ready to place to the point over the heart, and the hammer in your right. Then when we begin our prayer for the dead, I shall read him, I have here the book, and the others shall follow, strike in God's name, that so all may be well with the dead that we love and that the Undead pass away." Arthur took the stake and the hammer, and once his mind was set on action his hands never trembled nor even quivered. Van Helsing opened his missal and began to read, and Quincey and I followed as well as we could.

Arthur placed the point over the heart and as I looked I could see its dint in the white flesh. Then he struck with all his might.

The thing in the coffin writhed and a hideous, bloodcurdling screech came from the opened red lips. The body shook and quivered and twisted in wild contortions. The sharp white teeth champed together till the lips were cut, and the mouth was smeared with a crimson foam. But Arthur never faltered. He looked like a figure of Thor as his untrembling arm rose and fell, driving deeper and deeper the mercy-bearing stake, whilst the blood from the pierced heart welled and spurted up.

His face was set and high duty seemed to shine through it. The sight of it gave us courage so that our voices seemed to ring through the little vault.

And then the writhing and quivering of the body became less, and the teeth ceased to champ and the face to quiver. Finally it lay still. The terrible task was over.

The hammer fell from Arthur's hand. He reeled and would have fallen had we not caught him. The great drops of sweat sprang from his forehead and his breath came in broken gasps. It had indeed been an awful strain on him, and had he not been forced to his task by more than human considerations he could never have gone through with it.

For a few minutes we were so taken up with him that we did not look towards the coffin. When we did, however, a murmur of startled surprise ran from one to the other of us. We gazed so eagerly that Arthur rose, for he had been seated on the ground, and came and looked too, and then a glad strange light broke over his face and dispelled altogether the gloom of horror that lay upon it.

There, in the coffin lay no longer the foul Thing that we had so dreaded and grown to hate that the work of her destruction was yielded as a privilege to the one best entitled to it. But it was Lucy as we had seen her in life, with her face of unequalled sweetness and purity. True that there were there, as we had seen them in life, the traces of care and pain and waste. But these were all dear to us, for

they marked her truth to what we knew. One and all we felt
that the holy calm that lay like sunshine over her wasted face
and form was only an earthly token and
symbol of the calm that was to
reign forever.

Van Helsing came and laid his hand on Arthur's shoulder, and said to him, "And now, Arthur my friend, dear lad, am I not forgiven?"

The reaction of the terrible strain came as he took the old man's hand in his, and raising it to his lips, pressed it, and said, "Forgiven! God bless you that you have given my dear one her soul again, and me peace." He put his hands on the Professor's shoulder, and laying his head on his breast, cried for a while silently, whilst we stood unmoving.

When he raised his head Van Helsing said to him, "And now, my child, you may kiss her. Kiss her dead lips if you will, as she would have you to, if for her to choose. For she is not a grinning devil now, no longer a foul Thing for all eternity. No longer she is the devil's Undead. She is God's true dead, whose soul is with Him!"

Arthur bent and kissed her, and then we sent him and Quincey out of the tomb. The Professor and I sawed the top off the stake leaving the point of it in the body. Then we cut off the head and filled the mouth with garlic. We soldered up the coffin, screwed on the lid, and gathering up our belongings, came away. When the Professor locked the door he gave the key to Arthur.

Outside the air was sweet, the sun shone, and the birds sang, and it seemed as if all nature were tuned to a different pitch. There was gladness and mirth and peace everywhere, for we were at rest ourselves on one account, and we were glad, though it was with a tempered joy.

THE COLD EMBRACE

Mary E Braddon

HE WAS AN ARTIST – such things as happened to him happen sometimes to artists. He was a German – such things as happened to him happen sometimes to Germans. He was young, handsome, studious, enthusiastic, reckless, unbelieving, heartless. And being young, handsome and eloquent, he was beloved.

He was an orphan, under the guardianship of his dead father's brother, his Uncle Wilhelm, in whose house he had been brought up from a little child. She who loved him was his cousin – his cousin Gertrude, whom he swore he loved in return.

Did he love her? Yes, when he first swore it. It soon wore out, this passionate love. How threadbare and wretched a sentiment it became at last in the selfish heart of the student! But in its first golden dawn, when he was only nineteen, and had just returned from his apprenticeship to a great painter at Antwerp, and they wandered together in the most romantic outskirts of the city at rosy sunset, by holy moonlight, or bright and joyous morning, how beautiful a dream!

They keep it a secret from Wilhelm, as he has the father's ambition of a wealthy suitor for his only child – a cold and dreary vision beside the lover's dream.

So they are betrothed, and standing side by side when the dying sun and the pale rising moon divide the heavens, he puts the betrothal ring upon her finger, the white finger whose slender shape he knows so well. This ring is a peculiar one, a massive golden serpent, its tail in its mouth, the symbol of eternity – it had been his mother's, and he would know it amongst a thousand. If he were to become blind tomorrow, he could select it from amongst a thousand by the touch alone.

He places it on her finger, and they swear to be true to each other forever and ever – through trouble and danger – sorrow and change – in wealth or poverty. Her father must be won to consent to their union by-and-by, for they were now betrothed and death alone could part them.

But the young student asks, "Can death part us? I would

return to you from the grave, Gertrude. My soul would come back to be near my love. And you – you, if you died before me – the cold earth would not hold you from me. If you loved me, you would return, and again these fair arms would be clasped round my neck as they are now."

But she told him, with a holier light in her deep-blue eyes than had ever shone in his – she told him that the dead who die at peace with God are happy in heaven and cannot return to the troubled earth. And that it is only the suicide – the lost wretch on whom sorrowful angels shut the door of Paradise – whose unholy spirit haunts the living.

The first year of their betrothal is passed, and she is alone, for he has gone to Italy, on a commission for some rich man, to copy Raphaels, Titians, Guidos, in a gallery at Florence. He has gone to win fame, perhaps, but it is not the less bitter – he is gone!

Of course her father misses his young nephew, who has been as a son to him, and he thinks his daughter's sadness no more than a cousin should feel for a cousin's absence.

In the meantime, the weeks and months pass. The lover writes – often at first, then seldom – at last, not at all.

How many excuses she invents for him! How many times she goes to the little post office, to which he is to address his letters! How many times she hopes, only to be disappointed!

How many times she despairs, only to hope again!

But real despair comes at last and will not be put off any more. The rich suitor appears on the scene and her father is determined. She is to marry at once. The wedding day is fixed – the fifteenth of June.

The date seems burnt into her brain.

The date, written in fire, dances forever before her eyes.

The date, shrieked by the Furies, sounds continually in her ears.

But there is time yet – it is the middle of May – there is time for a letter to reach him at Florence. There is time for him to come to Brunswick, to take her away and marry her, in spite of her father – in spite of the whole world.

But the days and weeks fly by and he does not write – he does not come. This is indeed despair which usurps her heart and will not be put away.

It is the fourteenth of June. For the last time she goes to the little post office. For the last time she asks the old question, and they give her for the last time the dreary answer, "No – no letter."

For the last time – for tomorrow is the wedding day. Her father will hear no pleas. Her suitor will not listen to her prayers. They will not be put off a day – an hour. Tonight is hers – this night, which she may employ as she will.

She takes another path than that which leads home. She hurries through some by-streets of the city, out on to a lonely bridge, where he and she had stood so often in the sunset, watching the rose-coloured light glow, fade and die upon the river.

He returns from Florence. He had received her letter. That letter, blotted with tears, entreating, despairing – he had received it, but he loved her no longer. A young Florentine, who has sat to him as a model, had bewitched his fancy – that fancy which with him stood in place of a heart – and Gertrude had been half-forgotten. If she had a rich suitor, good – let her marry him. Better for her, better far for himself. He had no wish to fetter himself with a wife. Had he not his art always? – his eternal bride, his unchanging mistress.

Thus he thought it wiser to delay his journey to Brunswick, so that he should arrive when the wedding was over – arrive in time to salute the bride.

And the vows – the mystical fancies – the belief in his return, even after death, to the embrace of his beloved? O, gone out of his life – melted away forever, those foolish dreams of his boyhood.

So on the fifteenth of June he enters Brunswick, by that very bridge on which she stood, the stars looking down on

her, the night before. He strolls across the bridge and down
by the water's edge, a great rough dog at his heels, and the
smoke from his short pipe curling in blue wreaths
fantastically in the pure morning air. He has his sketch book
under his arm, and attracted now and then by some object
that catches his artist's eye, stops to draw. A few weeds and
pebbles on the river's brink – a crag on the opposite shore –
a group of pollard willows in the distance. When he has
done, he admires his drawing, shuts his sketch book, empties
the ashes from his pipe, refills from his tobacco pouch, sings
the refrain of a gay drinking song, calls to his dog, smokes
again and walks on. Suddenly he opens his sketch-book
again. This time he is attracted a group of figures – but what
is it? It is not a funeral, for there are no mourners.

It is not a funeral, but a corpse lying on a rough bier,
covered with an old sail, carried between two bearers.

It is not a funeral, for the bearers are fishermen –
fishermen in their everyday garb.

About a hundred yards from him they rest their burden
on a bank – one stands at the head of the bier, the other
throws himself down at the foot of it.

And thus they form a perfect group. He walks back two
or three paces, selects his point of sight, and begins to
sketch a hurried outline. He has finished it before they

move. He hears their voices, though he cannot hear their words, and wonders what they can be talking of. Presently he walks on and joins them.

"You have a corpse there, my friends?" he says.

"Yes – a corpse washed ashore an hour ago."

"Drowned?"

"Yes, drowned. A young girl, very handsome."

"Suicides are always handsome," says the painter. And then he stands for a little while idly smoking and meditating, looking at the sharp outline of the corpse and the stiff folds of the rough canvas covering.

Life is such a golden holiday for him – young, ambitious, clever – that it seems as though sorrow and death could have no part in his destiny.

At last he says that, as this poor suicide is so handsome, he should like to make a sketch of her.

He gives the fishermen some money and they offer to remove the sailcloth that covers her features.

No – he will do it himself. He lifts the rough, coarse, wet canvas from her face. What face?

The face that shone on the dreams of his foolish boyhood, the face which once was the light of his uncle's home. His cousin Gertrude – his betrothed!

He sees, in one glance, while he draws one breath, the

rigid features – the marble arms – the hands crossed on the cold bosom, and on the third finger of the left hand, the ring which had been his mother's – the golden serpent. The ring which, if he were to become blind, he could select from a thousand others by the touch alone.

But he is a genius – grief, true grief, is not for such as he. His first thought is flight – flight anywhere out of that accursed city – anywhere far from the brink of that hideous river – anywhere away from remorse – anywhere to forget.

He is miles on the road that leads away from Brunswick before he knows that he has walked a step. It is only when his dog lies panting at his feet that he feels how exhausted he is himself and sits down upon a bank to rest. How the landscape spins round and round before his dazzled eyes, while his morning's sketch of the two fishermen and the canvas-covered bier glares redly at him out of the twilight!

At last, after sitting a long time by the roadside, idly playing with his dog, idly smoking, idly lounging, looking as any idle, light-hearted travelling student might look, yet all the while acting over that morning's scene in his burning brain a hundred times a minute. At last he grows a little more composed and tries presently to think of himself as he is, apart from his cousin's suicide.

Apart from that, he was no worse off than he was yesterday. His genius was not gone. The money he had earned at Florence still lined his pocket – he was his own master, free to go whither he would.

And while he sits on the roadside, trying to separate himself from the scene of that morning – trying to put away the image of the corpse covered with the damp canvas sail – trying to think of what he should do next, where he should go, to be farthest away from Brunswick and remorse, the old diligence comes rumbling and jingling along. He remembers it – it goes from Brunswick to Aix-la-Chapelle.

He whistles to his dog, shouts to the post boy to stop,

and springs into the carriage.

During the whole evening, through the long night, though he does not once close his eyes, he never speaks a word. But when morning dawns, and the other passengers awake and begin to talk to each other, he joins in the conversation. He tells them that he is an artist, that he is going to Cologne and to Antwerp to copy Rubenses, and the great picture by Quentin Matsys, in the museum. He remembered afterwards that he talked and laughed boisterously, and that when he was talking and laughing loudest, a passenger, older and graver than the rest, opened the window near him, and told him to put his head out. He remembered the fresh air blowing in his face, the singing of the birds in his ears, and the flat fields and roadside reeling before his eyes. He remembered this, and then falling in a lifeless heap on the floor.

It is a fever that keeps him for six long weeks on a bed at a hotel in Aix-la-Chapelle.

He grows well and, accompanied by his dog, starts on foot for Cologne. By this time he is his former self once more. Again the blue smoke from his pipe curls upwards in the morning air – again he sings some old university drinking song – again he stops here and there, meditating and sketching.

He is happy and has forgotten his cousin – and so onwards to Cologne.

It is by the great cathedral he is standing, with his dog at his side. It is night, the bells have just chimed the hour and the clocks are striking eleven. The moonlight shines full upon the magnificent pile, over which the artist's eye wanders, absorbed in the beauty of form.

He is not thinking of his drowned cousin, for he has forgotten her and is happy.

Suddenly someone, something from behind, puts two cold arms round his neck clasping its hands on his breast.

And yet there is no one behind him, for on the flags bathed in the broad moonlight there are only two shadows, his own and his dog's. He turns quickly round – there is no one – nothing to be seen in the broad square but himself and his dog. Though he feels, he cannot see the cold arms clasped round his neck.

It is not ghostly, this embrace, for it is palpable to the touch – it cannot be real, for it is invisible.

He tries to throw off the cold caress. He clasps the hands in his own to tear them asunder and to cast them off his neck. He can feel the long delicate fingers cold and wet beneath his touch, and on the third finger of the left hand he can feel the ring which was his mother's – the golden serpent – the ring which he has always said he would know among a thousand by the touch alone. He knows it now!

His dead cousin's cold arms are round his neck – his dead cousin's wet hands are clasped upon his breast. He asks himself if he is mad. "Up, Leo!" he shouts. "Up, up, boy!" and the Newfoundland leaps to his shoulders – the dog's paws are on the dead hands, and the animal utters a howl and springs away from his master.

The student stands in the moonlight, the dead arms around his neck and the dog at a little distance moaning piteously. Presently a watchman, alarmed by the howling of the dog, comes into the square to see what is wrong.

In a breath the cold arms are gone.

He takes the watchman home to the hotel and gives him money. In his gratitude he could have given that man half his little fortune.

Will it ever come to him again, this embrace of the dead?

He tries never to be alone. He makes a hundred acquaintances and shares the chamber of another student. He starts up if he is left by himself in the public room at the inn where he is staying, and runs into the street. People notice his strange actions and begin to think that he is mad.

But, in spite of all, he is alone once more. For one night the public room being empty for a moment, when on some idle pretence he strolls into the street, the street is empty too, and for the second time he feels the cold arms round his neck, and for the second time, when he calls his dog, the animal slinks away from him with a piteous howl.

After this he leaves Cologne, still travelling on foot – of necessity now, for his money is getting low. He joins travelling hawkers, he walks side by side with labourers, he talks to every foot passenger he falls in with and tries from morning till night to get company on the road.

At night he sleeps by the fire in the kitchen of the inn at which he stops, but do what he will, he is often alone, and it is now a common thing for him to feel the cold arms around his neck.

Many months have passed since his cousin's death – autumn, winter, early spring. His money is nearly gone, his health is utterly broken, he is the shadow of his former self and he is getting near to Paris. He will reach that city at the time of the Carnival. To this he looks forward. In Paris, in Carnival time, he need never, surely, be alone, never feel that deadly caress; he may even recover his lost gaiety, his lost health, once more resume his profession, once more earn fame and money by his art.

How hard he tries to get over the distance that divides him from Paris, while day by day he grows weaker, and his step slower and more heavy!

But there is an end at last – the long dreary roads are passed. This is Paris, which he enters for the first time – Paris, of which he has dreamed so much – Paris, whose million voices are to exorcise his phantom.

To him tonight Paris seems one vast chaos of lights, music and confusion – lights which dance before his eyes and will not be still – music that rings in his ears and deafens him – confusion which makes his head whirl round and round.

But, in spite of all, he finds the opera house, where there is a masked ball. He has enough money left to buy a ticket of admission and to hire a domino to throw over his shabby dress. It seems only a moment after his entering the gates of Paris that he is in the very midst of all the wild gaiety of the opera house ball.

No more darkness, no more loneliness, but a mad crowd, shouting and dancing, and a lovely girl hanging on his arm.

The boisterous gaiety he feels surely is his old light-heartedness come back. He hears the people round him talking of the outrageous conduct of some drunken student, and it is to him they point when they say this to him, who has not moistened his lips since yesterday at noon. For even now he will not drink – though his lips are parched and his throat burning, he cannot drink.

His voice is thick and hoarse, and his utterance indistinct, but still this must be his old light-heartedness come back that makes him so wildly gay.

The girl is wearied out – her arm rests on his shoulder heavier than lead – the other dancers one by one drop off.

The lights in the chandeliers one by one die out.

The decorations look pale and shadowy in that dim light which is neither night nor day.

A faint glimmer from the dying lamps, a pale streak of cold grey light from the newborn day, creeping in through half-opened shutters.

And by this light the bright-eyed girl fades sadly. He looks her in the face. How the brightness of her eyes dies out! Again he looks at her. How white she has grown!

Again – and now it is the shadow of a face alone that looks in his.

Again – and they are gone – the bright eyes, the face, the shadow of the face. He is alone – alone in that vast saloon.

Alone, and, in the terrible silence, he hears the echoes of his own footsteps in that dismal dance which has no music.

No music but the beating of his breast. For the cold arms are round his neck – they whirl him round, they will not be flung off, or cast away. He can no more escape from their icy grasp than he can escape from death. He looks behind him – there is nothing but himself in the great empty room, but he can feel – cold, deathlike, but O, how palpable – the long slender fingers and the ring which was his mother's.

He tries to shout, but he has no power in his burning throat. The silence of the place is only broken by the echoes of his own footsteps in the dance from which he cannot extricate himself.

Who says he has no partner? The cold hands are clasped on his breast and now he does not shun their caress. No! One more polka, if he drops down dead.

The lights are all out. Half an hour after, the gendarmes come in with a lantern to see that the house is empty. They are followed by a great dog that they have found seated howling on the steps of the theatre. Near the principal entrance they stumble over a body — the body of a student, who has died from want of food, exhaustion and the breaking of a blood vessel.

The Authors

Alice and Claude Askew (1874–1917),
(1866–1917) were a prolific husband-and-wife writing team,
who produced ninety books in twelve years. They were
drowned when the boat they were travelling on was
torpedoed by an enemy submarine in the First World War.

E F Benson (1867–1940) came from a brilliant and
literary family, and his father was Archbishop of Canterbury.
He was a prolific writer and is best remembered for his
comic novels and chilling ghost stories.

Mary E Braddon (1837–1915) was a writer of
sensation novels – Victorian stories featuring shocking
subject matter such as murder, theft, seduction and adultery.
She supported herself by her writing, which included the
famous *Lady Audley's Secret*.

Guy de Maupassant (1850–1893) is often called the
Father of the Short Story. De Maupassant's full first name
was Henri-René-Albert-Guy. He had a particular hatred for
the Eiffel Tower and often ate lunch in the restaurant at its
foot because he said it was the only place in Paris where he
didn't have to look at it.

EUGENE FIELD (1850–1895) was an American newspaper editor. He wrote articles, novels and stories but was particularly known for his children's poetry. He married his wife when she was sixteen and greatly relied on her judgment. Throughout his life, he insisted that his salary be paid to her, as he had no head for money.

THÉOPHILE GAUTIER (1811–1872) was a French novelist, journalist, poet, playwright, artist and critic who had immense success in his lifetime. He was very fond of cats, and when the love of his life, a beautiful ballerina, refused to marry him, he married her sister.

ARCHDEACON HARE (1834–1903) although born into an aristocratic English family, had an unhappy childhood. He turned to writing, from which he made a comfortable living.

ROBERT ERVIN HOWARD (1906–1936) was born and brought up in Texas. He wrote short stories in a wide range of different fields and is best known for creating the character of Conan the Barbarian. He is often credited with creating the Swords and Sorcery genre.

M R JAMES (1862–1936) was a scholar and Cambridge professor who wrote some of the finest – and scariest – ghost stories in the English language. When asked if he himself believed in ghosts he replied, "I am prepared to consider evidence and accept it if it satisfies me."

Rudyard Kipling (1865–1936) was born in India to English parents. Kipling wrote short stories, poems, novels, and wonderful children's books including *The Jungle Book*, which was made into a film by Walt Disney in 1967.

Sheridan Le Fanu (1814–1873) was born in Dublin to a distinguished Irish family. He is one of the most famous and influential of early horror writers.

H P Lovecraft (1890–1937) is one of the best known writers of horror stories. He once said, "The oldest and strongest emotion of mankind is fear, and the oldest and strongest kind of fear is fear of the unknown."

George Macdonald (1824–1905) was a great writer of fantasies and fairy tales including *The Princess and the Goblin*. He was a mentor to Lewis Carroll and inspired many other writers, including C S Lewis, J R R Tolkien and Madeleine L'Engle.

Frederick Marryat (1792–1848) went to sea aged thirteen. He spent his working life in the Royal Navy, having many dramatic encounters with enemy ships.

Jan Neruda (1834–1891) was a journalist and writer, who lived and died in Prague, the capital of Czechoslovakia.

Hume Nesbit (1849–1923) was born in Scotland but spent much of his adult life in Australia. He always hoped to be an artist but had more success with his writing.

James Malcolm Ryder (1814–1884) wrote one of the earliest vampire stories, *Varney the Vampire*, which he published in a series of pamphlets called 'penny dreadfuls' (so called because they cost a penny and told of dreadful things). He also created the demon barber Sweeny Todd.

Saki (Hector Hugh Monro) (1870–1916) was master of the short story. He volunteered to fight in the First World War, despite being over age. He was shot and killed by a sniper, his last words being, "Put that cigarette out!"

Eric Stenbock (1860–1895) was a German count who wrote strange, fantastic fiction. He lived much of his life in England and went to Oxford University, although he didn't complete his studies. He is buried in Brighton.

Bram Stoker (1847–1912) an Irishman, whose full first name was Abraham, wrote the most famous vampire story of all, *Dracula*, which he originally planned to call *The Un-Dead*.

Stanley Waterloo (1846–1913) was a journalist and short story writer from Chicago. He died, aged 67, of pneumonia.

THE ARTISTS

MALCOM DAVIS has been a freelance illustrator for over 25 years. Working for many clients including Disney, Hasbro, Simon & Schuster and more recently Blizzard's *World of Warcraft* Malcolm has developed a varying collection of illustrative styles in a quest to create the ultimate visual experience.

Varney the Vampyre ❖ The Grey Wolf ❖ Dracula's Guest ❖ The Horla ❖ The Cold Embrace

JASON JUTA was a games industry concept artist and graphic designer. He is now a freelance illustrator specializing in fantasy illustration and photographic fantasy art.

The Death of Lucy ❖ The White Wolf of Hartz Mountain ❖ The Hound ❖ The Vampire Maid Vampire

FABIO LEONE was born in Latina, Italy, and studied oil painting at the Department for Painting of the Academy of Fine Arts in Rome, where he graduated in 2004. Since then he has been studying and practising the traditional iconography technique (egg tempera). In 2007 he started to produce digital art.

The Horror from the Mound ❖ The Mark of the Beast ❖ The Room in the Tower ❖ The Vampire Cat of Nabéshima ❖ The Freeing of Lucy

PATRICIA MOFFETT worked as a designer and art buyer for 15 years before rekindling her desire to be an illustrator. She found the developments in image-making software exciting and liberating, and loves the fact that she can paint in virtual watercolour and then send her work off across the world over the Internet.

Count Magnus ❖ A Tragedy of the Forest The Other Side: A Breton Legend ❖ Carmilla The Werewolf

DAVE SHEPHARD is not at all good at talking before the first coffee of the day, buying sensible shoes, saying 'no' to apple crumble, or working in offices. However, he's rather handy at drawing, painting, playing the G chord on guitar, pretending to look interested and laughing at himself...no sorry, others. Presently, David is living in Sussex with his family and working in children's publishing.

Gabriel-Ernest ❖ Croglin Grange Mrs Amworth ❖ Clarimonde ❖ Aylmer Vance and the Vampire